BOOK ONE *of* THE ARKHNUET SERIES

TAMING FLAME

A Sci-fi Romance

THERISA PEIMER

One Printers Way
Altona, MB R0G 0B0
Canada

www.friesenpress.com

Copyright © 2022 by Therisa Peimer
First Edition — 2022

All rights reserved.

Cover Design by Brady Sato

No part of this publication may be reproduced in any form, or by any means, electronic or mechanical, including photocopying, recording, or any information browsing, storage, or retrieval system, without permission in writing from FriesenPress.

ISBN
978-1-03-912562-9 (Hardcover)
978-1-03-912561-2 (Paperback)
978-1-03-912563-6 (eBook)

1. FICTION, EROTICA, SCIENCE FICTION, FANTASY & HORROR

Distributed to the trade by The Ingram Book Company

Dedication

This book is dedicated to my husband, Jeff. You are my Flame. You taught me the meaning of the words, courage under fire. To the moon, baby, to the moon.

Also, to my boys, Dani and Ilan, and to my future daughter-in-law, Alyjah, for their candid feedback and advice. I love you guys.

Table of Contents

Dedication   iii
Prologue - The Extraction   vii

Part One   **1**
Chapter One - Perfecta Nobis   1
Chapter Two - Political Games   7
Chapter Three - The Introduction Ceremony   15
Chapter Four - The Reading   19
Chapter Five - Informing Aurelia   27
Chapter Six - Hell, No, I Won't Go!   37
Chapter Seven - May the Best Woman Win!   41
Chapter Eight - The Consummation   45
Chapter Nine - The Beginning   51
Chapter Ten - Stay Calm and Follow Protocol   59
Chapter Eleven - Things You Wished You'd Never Done   65
Chapter Twelve - The Game's Afoot!   73
Chapter Thirteen - Here Comes The Bride—Wink!   81
Chapter Fourteen - Here Comes The Bride. For Real   93
Chapter Fifteen - Honeymoon, Rifting, and Attempted Murder   109
Chapter Sixteen - Let the Interrogations Begin   127
Chapter Seventeen - Official Coronation   133
Chapter Eighteen - To Catch a Killer   137
Chapter Nineteen - Getting Away with Murder   153

Part Two   **163**
Chapter One - A Murder of Keys   163
Chapter Two - Lady Killer vs. Lady Guardian   165
Chapter Three - Common Goal   175
Chapter Four - Extraction Revisited   183

Chapter Five - Time to Spy	189
Chapter Six - Matilda	201
Chapter Seven - Stupid Clothes	211
Chapter Eight - Arkhnuet-Proofing Earth	215
Chapter Nine - The Manor House with Secrets	225
Chapter Ten - First Wave	233
Chapter Eleven - And So it Begins	239
Chapter Twelve - The Beginning of the End	245
Chapter Thirteen - The Bitter Taste of Betrayal	251
Chapter Fourteen - The Aftermath	269
Chapter Fifteen - Not All it's Cracked Up to Be	273
Chapter Sixteen - The End	285
Acknowledgments	297

Prologue - The Extraction

Earth Year 415

"Let go! I don't care what the king says. I won't leave Nana behind!" the scrawny boy screamed desperately, red-faced from the strain of battling the soldier trying to rip him from an old woman's arms.

A second soldier joined the fight, and the boy lost his grip, tearing the yellow band from his Nana's arm. The old woman lunged for her grandson, but the soldier pushed her hard into the cold, rushing surf. Blinded by fury, the boy bit his captor, who threw him into the foaming water; he sunk below the surface, flailing, noise muffled, breath but a thought.

Flaminius and Marcus walked down the steep path of the jagged outcrop overlooking the beach. Flaminius despaired as he watched the humans, defined by their yellow armbands, wailing as they said a last goodbye to their loved ones.

The boy's frantic cries drew their attention to a group of soldiers nearby. Despite their exhaustion from the day's torment, they rushed to the growing crowd and pushed through to the center to see the small boy gripped in a man's arms, both soaked to the skin.

Flaminius barked at the nearest soldier, "What's going on here?"

"My lord, your father left strict instructions for extraction deadlines; we're falling behind."

"I'll deal with this." When the man hesitated, Flaminius added, "I'll tell the king I dismissed you."

"But General—"

"That's an order, Lieutenant." The soldier saluted and left.

Flaminius spoke to the man holding the child. "Who is this boy to you?"

"He is my son, Sire." The man replied in a quivering voice. "He and his grandmother are very close, and he cannot understand why she must stay."

Flaminius noticed a petite woman standing behind the man, her arms wrapped around his waist, barely containing her sobs. He pointed to the older woman. "Is that your mother, my lady?"

The young woman lifted her face and nodded.

Staring at the yellow armband still clutched in the boy's hand, Flaminius asked the father, "What generation Arkhnuetian-Earther are you?"

"My grandfather was an original," the man said proudly. "Earth is the only home we know."

Turning to Marcus, Flaminius ordered, "Move the onlookers away." Once they were out of earshot, he stepped closer and stroked the boy's back, asking, "What's your name, little one?"

Hiccupping through his tears, he replied, "Barret."

"Barret, I know it's tough to say goodbye, but your mama and papa need you to go with them now."

The little boy shook his head, his disheveled blonde hair spraying water everywhere. "I won't leave Nana alone. She has no one to take care of her."

Swallowing the lump in his throat, Flaminius said, "What if I promise your Nana will never want for anything? Will you go with your mama then?"

Barret wiped his nose on his sleeve, eyeing Flaminius suspiciously. "How will I know if you keep your promise? Papa says we can never come back because Nana is human, and we're not."

The boy's mother gave a loud sob; Flaminius did his best to ignore it. "Your papa is right, but I can bring you proof your Nana is well. She can write to you, and I will make sure you receive those letters."

The boy's grandmother gasped. "Sire, we cannot disobey the law. We are to have no contact."

Smiling deviously, Flaminius said, "This is true, but I have it on good authority that I am heir to the throne; if I wish to make an exception, I can, so you and your family have my permission."

Stunned, the four family members stared at him. Finally, Barret asked, "Can my Nana write every week?"

"If that's what you wish."

His little brown eyes lit up. "Truly? Every week?"

Laughing, Flaminius replied, "Absolutely."

Squeezing the boy's shoulder gently, Flaminius addressed the father. "I will rift here every week to retrieve the letter and bring it to you. All I ask is that you keep our arrangement secret."

Bowing repeatedly, the boy's parents thanked him profusely. Flaminius took the family's name and called for Marcus to join him.

Mussing the child's hair, he turned to leave, only to see Marcus trying to hide his smile. "How many letters have you agreed to retrieve from these shores every week, Sire?"

Raising his eyebrows, Flaminius said, "Officially, none. But between you and me, my last count was . . ." Flaminius removed a notebook from inside his jacket, opened it, and wrote the name of the boy's family down before continuing, ". . . five hundred and seventeen."

"If you need help with that, let me know."

"I can't ask you to do that, Marcus. If my father finds out, the old curmudgeon will charge you with treason."

"I won't fucking tell him."

Flaminius smiled at his friend's comment, but the seriousness of the day took hold quickly. "My father's Extraction Decree is going to come back and bite us in the ass." He spat out bitterly. "We should've never allowed Arkhnuetians to remain on Earth. They should've claimed their mates and brought them back to Arkhnuet. Instead, we're forcing them from the homes they've known for thousands of years, ripping them away from their human families."

"Unfortunately," Marcus replied, "it's three thousand years too late."

Part One

Chapter One -
Perfecta Nobis

585 Years Later
Earth Year 1000

Flaminius Theodore Alexander Esca, heir to the Arkhnuetian throne and general of the Royal Protection Unit, was monumentally pissed off.

The usually serene Mother Guardian tried to calm the prince once more. "Your Highness, as I've explained, it is imperative that you marry if you wish to take the throne."

Even though her voice betrayed none of her unease, Flaminius noticed the hem of her virginal white robes vibrating.

He stopped pacing. "And as I've explained to you, Mother Guardian, I have no desire to consummate Perfecta Nobis and even less to take the throne! As for children, I'm not ready to be a father."

"Flaminius, it's not a matter of want. It's a matter of duty, and you needn't produce an heir immediately."

Flaminius ran his fingers through his too-long chestnut-colored hair. "Don't think me a fool, Mother Guardian. You know royal protocol dictates that the king produce an heir within the first ten years of marriage."

"Pfft, we may be strong, resilient creatures compared to other races, but with our fragile reproductive system, no one would hold you to that ridiculous timeline."

"Another Source-made design flaw," Flaminius muttered.

"It is not a mistake! Source energy made reproduction difficult to protect us from overpopulation."

Flaminius glared at her. "The way you defend Source makes me think you believe it a god as the Oradagra did."

"Don't you dare insult me, Flaminius," she hissed. "You're not the only one who suffered when that purist cult started the civil war. I don't believe in gods or religion, but Source energy is the creator of all life, and it understands balance."

"Balance?" Flaminius roared. "How can you say that? Where's the balance in making it not only difficult to reproduce but also making us genetically compatible with only one other person in the entire universe? It's overkill, not balance."

"Source made it easy to locate a match anywhere in the universe by providing the Keys." Mother Guardian countered. "That doesn't sound stupid to me."

Yes, the Keys. How could Flaminius forget? Those esteemed women whose psychic gift enabled Arkhnuetians to find their Perfecta Nobis, or a perfect match in layman's terms. "Don't you think you're prejudiced because you hold the honorable position as protector and leader of the Keys?"

"No."

Flaminius closed his eyes and sighed. Fighting with Mother Guardian solved nothing. It wasn't her fault Flaminius's parents were putting pressure on him to take the throne. "I won't let anyone bully me into accepting a reading from a Key."

Abandoning all pretense, Mother Guardian closed the short distance between them. In a barely audible whisper, she pleaded, "Flaminius, consider the wrath of the queen if you should refuse the appointment again."

Flaminius intimately knew his mother's ability to inflict pain with her sharp tongue and short temper, and he pitied Mother Guardian.

Deliberately softening his tone, he answered, "I'm truly sorry for the trouble my decision will cause you, but I cannot continue in good conscience."

Mother Guardian's shoulders sank in defeat. Retreating to her dainty desk, she sat, drew a piece of paper toward her, and began scribbling. Without looking up, she said, "You're correct. As disappointing as it is, you have every right to refuse the Key's reading. However, I would like to remind you," she put down her pen and looked at the prince, "there is no guarantee that your match will accept your request of Perfecta Nobis."

Flaminius snorted. "I can't imagine any of the spoiled aristocratic ladies at court refusing the future king as their match."

Mother Guardian motioned for him to sit in the only other chair in the small room. Noticing the skinny legs of the seat, he declined. She pierced the prince with her brilliant blue eyes. "I will admit that I don't know you as well as I would like. The war took up much of your time, and I know the killing left scars, both emotional and physical. However, I do read and watch enough entertainment news to know about your reputation as a playboy."

Flaminius crossed his arms over his barrel chest. "Yes, I'm sure you do," he replied sarcastically. "What's your point?"

Mother Guardian rolled her eyes. "My point is that just because you date, and I use that word loosely, women from aristocratic families, that does not mean your match will come from among them."

Flaminius frowned; he had never considered the possibility. Noticing his confusion, Mother Guardian invited him to sit again. Flaminius raised his eyebrows and looked down at the flimsy chair.

"It will hold your weight." When he still hesitated, she leaned forward. "Do you think you are the only six-foot-four, two-hundred-and-sixty-pound muscle-bound soldier to meet with me in this room?"

Sighing, he gingerly lowered himself onto the powder-blue satin-striped concoction. Once he ascertained he was in no danger, he relaxed but remained vigilant, just in case the overstuffed piece of furniture was lulling him into a false sense of security.

Mother Guardian smiled. "Would it be permissible to speak frankly?"

"Yes."

"Good. I don't believe that your intended will bear any resemblance to your mother."

Unexpectedly, Flaminius felt the need to defend the queen. "Perhaps that is too bold of you, Mother Guardian?"

Waving her tiny hand at him, she continued. "Pish posh. You're afraid that your match will be just as impossible as your mother, and I don't blame you, but my dear boy, you forget one essential fact: you are nothing like your father. Source knows this and would never choose such a person for you."

Carefully shifting his weight, Flaminius shook his head. "Mother Guardian, I appreciate what you are trying to do—"

She banged her fist on her cherrywood desk. "Enough with the excuses!" Her uncharacteristic outburst startled him. "When your father tried to convince you to take your match after the war, you insisted you had demons you needed to exorcise before you could consider it, and I supported you. When he tried again years later, you said you wanted to sow some wild oats. Again, I supported your decision. Now we are decades out of the war. Despite that, you're not ready. The Oradagra is defeated. Peace has returned to Arkhnuet. There is no good reason to delay. Your father has ruled for nine hundred years. Is he not entitled to retirement?"

Flaminius took a deep, calming breath. "Of course he is, but I don't want to get married!"

Muttering something that sounded suspiciously like 'men,' she continued, "We may not be at war any longer, but morale is at an all-time low. Yes, the Oradagra is gone, but the damage it did is tangible, and some remain convinced that it offered a better way."

"Do you honestly think I'm not acutely aware of the situation? We know that people secretly continue to preach its purist, racist garbage, but that's the nature of a cult. If we remain vigilant, it will never rise again."

Mother Guardian shook her head. "Flaminius, you're treating the symptom, not the cause. If you truly wish to eradicate their influence, you must understand the reasons it convinced so many to follow its ideology."

"What difference does it make? As you said, the Oradagra is defeated."

"It matters because we are doomed to repeat our mistakes if we do not learn and change," she replied.

"Change what?"

"Everything."

"Could you be more specific, please?"

She sighed in exasperation. "The reason for the civil war was the monarchy's refusal to recognize that antiquated laws and protocols fostered resentment among our people, creating fertile soil for the Oradagra to plant its poisonous seeds. You need to change these laws."

"Which laws?"

"Where should I begin?" Ticking her points off on her fingers, she said, "Only royals and Keys may wear red, civilians cannot name their children after a royal, a human matched to an Arkhnuetian may never return to Earth—"

"Okay, I get your point," Flaminius said, cutting her off. "But I don't see why I must make my match to effect the required changes."

"Because the changes can only happen once you're the king, and, for you to do that, the law states you must marry. Yet another law you must change so that your children will not have to make the same sacrifices."

Rubbing his fingers over his chin, he replied, "I've never been particularly pleased to be heir to the throne. I honestly believe that my brother would make a far better king. If my father hadn't threatened to produce another heir rather than allow me to abdicate in favor of Tiberius, he would already be king."

Flaminius's father, Romulus, had a stern, unbending nature, but Mother Guardian would never have expected him to threaten with something so cruel. "Surely, you misunderstood. Not that I think your brother should rule, but to threaten that?"

Flaminius shrugged his shoulders. "He knew I would capitulate to his demands to spare Tiberius the hurt our father's decision would cause him."

Mother Guardian sighed. "I am truly sorry that you find yourself in such an untenable situation, Flaminius. But the people need the security of a king with a mate."

Mother Guardian watched Flaminius's face morph from defiance to acceptance. "Very well, Mother Guardian, I will honor the appointment."

Leaping to her feet, she said, "I will inform my secretary to begin preparations at once." She picked up the piece of paper on which she had presumptively written the order for the ceremony to proceed and held it up triumphantly.

"Afraid I will change my mind?" Flaminius snorted.

"Absolutely!" She chuckled.

Flaminius was in no laughing mood, but he cracked a smile. "What do we do now?"

"I'll inform your parents of the good news and prepare my Keys for the introduction ceremony so that you can choose which Key will be your reader."

Flaminius stood. "When?" he asked dejectedly.

Mother Guardian shuffled her feet excitedly. "Tomorrow afternoon at the latest."

Mother Guardian noticed Flaminius wasted no time fleeing her small office. She could hardly blame the young man, but she hoped he wouldn't change his mind. The queen would have her head if he did.

Chapter Two -
Political Games

"What are you doing here, Lily?"

Lily scrambled to her feet and plastered her back to the solid wooden door. Heart pounding, she tried to think of a good excuse for ditching her post-grad orientation. "I . . . I . . ."

Usually, Mother Guardian wouldn't let the young Key off the hook, but she didn't have time to rebuke her today. "Never mind. Get back to class," she barked and walked away.

"Yes, Mother Guardian." Lily started walking in the opposite direction, then thought better of it. Mother Guardian seemed to be in a forgiving mood today, and Lily didn't want to go back to class and listen to Sister Gladys ramble on about Source knew what. Rushing to catch up with her mentor, Lily asked, "Where are you going, Mother Guardian?"

"I thought I told you to go back to class?"

From the moment Lily started her studies as a Key, she felt they shared a special bond. "Are you going to see the king?" Lily asked, bouncing along next to MG, as she liked to call Mother Guardian. Not to her face, of course.

"I am." Mother Guardian replied, recognizing the futility of dismissing Lily.

"It's a long walk from the unmarried Keys' quarters to the throne room. I'll keep you company."

Smiling to herself, Mother Guardian nodded, and for several minutes they walked in silence.

"I've spent eight years roaming the corridors of this castle, and I swear I'll never see it all."

"While you should've been minding your business and studying," Mother Guardian rebuked.

Lily looked guilty. "I never went anywhere I wasn't supposed to."

Mother Guardian laughed. "Oh, that is a blatant lie! Just last week, I caught you trying to sneak a peek at the introduction room, a room you're well aware only graduate Keys may see."

Lily shrugged. "I only wanted to peek. Besides, it was two days to graduation."

"Yes, it was, and the only reason I didn't punish you for your transgression."

Feeling it would be prudent to change the subject, Lily asked, "How big is the castle, actually?"

"Don't let the queen hear you call it a castle."

Lily frowned. "Why?"

Sighing, Mother Guardian said, "If you paid attention in history class, you would know." Lily huffed, but Mother Guardian ignored her insolence and continued. "When King Romulus and Queen Octavia took the throne nine hundred years ago, the queen decided the castle needed modernizing. The council found it cheaper to rebuild, and she favored the square, multi-storied structure with many windows over the turrets and spiral staircases typical of a castle. Therefore, she prefers to call it a palace."

Lily snorted. "You mean, she threw a juvenile tantrum until she got what she wanted."

"Lily! Hush before someone hears you," Mother Guardian admonished, glancing around nervously.

"It's true! This palace has miles of cream marble corridors and ridiculous adornments." Pointing to one of the many doors they passed along the hallway, "Take these doors, for example. Why do they need to be fifteen feet tall and six feet wide? And why must they have gold-leaf beading?" Lily barely stopped to take a breath. "And what's with all the wrought-iron balconies and soaring marble pillars? And who needs twelve kitchens? And don't even get me started on the throne room!"

Mother Guardian laughed. "Calm yourself, child. I swear that temper of yours will get you in real trouble one day." Lily's cheeks puffed as she blew out a frustrated breath. MG patted Lily's hand, "You must understand; the queen was born into an intensely traditional, wealthy, aristocratic family, and her parents groomed her to cling to her pedigree from birth."

"Yeah, and mercilessly impose stupid rules on the citizens of Arkhnuet. Of course, being the only daughter of an overly indulgent father didn't help her any either."

"No, I suppose it didn't."

Smiling mischievously, Lily whispered, "I hear we won't need to worry about the queen much longer. I've heard that the prince is thinking of invoking Perfecta Nobis!"

Mother Guardian was astonished. "Where did you hear that, Lily? Not to say that it's accurate, and even if it were, I wouldn't tell you."

"Oh, please, Mother Guardian," Lily whined, "don't be a spoil-sport."

Just then, Mother Guardian saw Tiberius and his personal royal guard, Andreus, step out of a room at the corridor's end. The young prince didn't see Mother Guardian and Lily, but Andreus did. He cast a desperate look of obsessive desire at Lily before turning in the opposite direction and disappearing around the corner. Of course, Lily didn't notice because she was still whining, but Mother Guardian felt a sense of unease pass through her.

"Well?"

Returning her attention to Lily, Mother Guardian said, "No comment. I have indulged you long enough, child. Time to go back to your orientation."

Lily groaned but did as she was told.

Once Mother Guardian was sure the girl had left and wouldn't be listening at keyholes again, she refocused on the matter at hand.

It took Romulus almost five years to convince his wife, Octavia, to agree to his retirement. When she did, she pursued a favorable result with her usual enthusiasm, which meant Octavia enormously pressured Mother Guardian to coerce Flaminius to accept his birthright.

Finally, the gilded doors of the throne room came into view. Mother Guardian noticed the king's private secretary pacing the marble corridor. He imbued his stiff-backed, protocol-driven personality into every echoing thud of his immaculately polished leather shoes. When he caught sight of her, she saw both relief and anxiety reflected on his face.

"Good gracious, Bartholomew. You look positively conflicted." The man was not known for his sense of humor, so, of course, she liked to tease him.

"Mother Guardian, I'm so pleased to see you at last!" he said in his irritating nasal voice. "The queen is quite beside herself."

"In that case, let's not keep her waiting any longer."

Scurrying forward, he led her through the doors into the reception area of the throne room. "Please sit while I announce you."

"Is that necessary? It's not as if they don't know I'm coming."

Placing his hands behind his back, he pulled himself up to his full lanky height, stared down his large, arrow-straight nose at her, and replied, "We always adhere to protocol, no matter the situation," before he marched through the second set of doors and snapped them shut while glaring at her.

"Nincompoop."

Mother Guardian whipped her head toward the curved reception desk and saw a pretty brunette sitting behind her computer, busily typing away. "Pardon?" Mother Guardian asked.

The brunette looked up and motioned with her head toward Bartholomew without stopping her typing. "Nincompoop," she repeated, "as in, he is one."

The word suited him so well, and the girl's dry wit made it impossible not to laugh.

Fortunately, Mother Guardian had calmed down by the time Bartholomew led her into the throne room. As expected, he announced her with all the pomp and ceremony his billowing black robes suggested he would, and it took all her willpower not to think of the brunette's insult and laugh again. The ostentatious throne room helped subdue her humor.

They designed it to intimidate and showcase the crown's great wealth. A plush scarlet carpet covered the expansive floor to the dais at the far end of the rectangular chamber, which looked larger than it was because of the high-vaulted ceiling. The only furniture that the queen allowed in the room was the ornately carved wooden thrones sending a message to those granted an audience with the king and queen of Arkhnuet that she expected them to stand in the presence of royalty. The alabaster marble walls and six gigantic crystal chandeliers gave the space its grandiose veneer. However, as was the queen's intention, the room made you feel inconsequential.

As protocol demanded, Mother Guardian bowed low. "It is an honor to be permitted into the royal sanctum." She remained in her curtsy, eyes cast down, waiting for the king to speak.

"Please rise, Mother Guardian, and if it is all the same to you, let's dispense with the niceties; we're far too anxious for further delays."

Mother Guardian nodded. "As you wish, Sire."

"What news have you?"

Mother Guardian's eyes slid to the queen. Octavia's long, blonde hair was elaborately styled and must have taken her lady's maid hours to create. As always, she dressed in layers of embroidered silk fabric that enfolded her tall, thin frame and often made Mother Guardian wonder how such a wisp of a woman could manage the weight of it. Today's creation was peacock-blue with emerald-green embroidered flowers along the bodice and skirts' edges. The gown's color accentuated both her blue and the king's green eyes.

The rustling of the queen's clothing brought Mother Guardian back to the question. "The prince has agreed to take the reading and invoke Perfecta Nobis."

The king closed his eyes and sighed with palpable relief. "I do not know what you said to change his mind, Minerva, but I am eternally grateful."

Mother Guardian jerked in surprise when the king addressed her by name. It wasn't unusual. She had known him since he was a boy, and they had many informal meetings where they both used their given names to address one another, but today she was here on official business.

Before she could respond, the queen spoke. "We must arrange the reading immediately before he has time to change his mind. I've already instructed Lady Gladys to prepare herself."

Mother Guardian had to tread carefully. "I agree, Your Majesty. Gladys would conduct a professional reading, but I must remind you that the choice is that of the prince."

Octavia looked surprised at Minerva's statement. "Don't be ridiculous, Mother Guardian. The boy's hardly shown righteous judgment when it comes to women."

"No, but he won't be choosing his genetic match. Source preordains it, as you know."

The queen's nostrils flared. "Of course, I know, and I don't doubt that whoever Source has chosen will be suitable. However, he is likely to choose the most becoming Key in your sanctuary as his reader and seduce the girl with two flicks of a tiger's tail to spite us."

Mother Guardian attempted to intervene, but the queen rushed on. "There is no need to guess how such an assignation will end. The girl will be heartbroken and unable to read for months since the Keys' ability to read depends on their emotions."

The queen's lack of understanding regarding the Keys irritated Minerva. Yes, using their gift was both emotionally and physically draining, but a Key's emotional state had no bearing on her ability to read. However, arguing with the queen would accomplish nothing, so Mother Guardian remained on point.

"Be that as it may, the law dictates that the client choose the reader, and as Mother Guardian, I must enforce the law."

Octavia's cheeks flushed. "Gladys will do the reading according to royal protocol, and I will hear no more of it."

The Keys played an indispensable role in ensuring their species' continued existence, and Arkhnuetians revered them. As such, not even the king had the right to interfere, and today would not be the day a queen started either.

"I understand the necessity for the royal protocol and, therefore, will support the law that insists the heir to the throne's reading be public, but Flaminius will choose his reader."

Romulus tried to intervene before his wife went too far, but as usual, she was quicker.

"How dare you speak to me that way?" she bellowed. "You will do as your queen instructs, and you will do it now!"

Minerva remained calm. "Your Majesty, if you insist on usurping my authority, I will not hesitate to resign as Mother Guardian."

"You cannot do such a thing until Source has designated your successor!" Bartholomew's uncharacteristic break from decorum showed the seriousness of her statement. "The Keys cannot read without a Mother Guardian. They would struggle to connect to Source!"

"That is the point, Bartholomew," Mother Guardian replied sardonically.

The position of Mother Guardian required more than protecting the Keys and the laws governing them. Although a Key's ability to read without a Mother Guardian was significantly more problematic, it wasn't impossible.

The king could barely speak. "Minerva, you would place our nation in an even more precarious position than it already is by following through with your threat?"

"Sire, as you know, there are many laws that govern the House of Keys to ensure that we remain impartial and professional. But there are only three that will guarantee the banishment of a Key."

"We don't need a history lesson, Mother Guardian," the queen rudely interrupted.

She had no intention of elaborating but now couldn't resist irritating the queen. Pretending the woman hadn't interrupted, she continued. "The first is if a Key divulges the identity of a match without the permission of the client. Second, the client must choose the reader, and last, the client must enter the reading willingly. I will place none of my Keys in a position where they would have to refuse a future king's reading because they fear banishment. So, answering your question, Sire, yes, I would follow through with my threat."

No one spoke. Finally, the king broke the silence. "Far be it from me to place anyone in such an untenable position. Flaminius will choose his reader."

Before Octavia could object, Romulus took her hand. "I cannot spare Flaminius the embarrassment of a public reading. The least I can do is grant him the free will to choose his reader."

Octavia pulled her hand from his. "Blame for that can only be laid at the door of your ancestor. If the last king hadn't lied about his match so he could run off with his floozy, public readings for the royal heir would not be necessary."

Once again, the queen had her facts wrong, and Minerva felt she should set the record straight. "It was not the Esca bloodline that ruled Your Majesty. It was the Collagen bloodline."

Subdued now that the king had decided, Octavia replied, "Nevertheless, the reason the heir to the throne must endure a public reading is hardly my fault."

"No, my dear, it's not, and even though I understand what he did was wrong, I can't say I blame the man." Romulus smiled at his queen. "If you weren't my match, I couldn't have abandoned you either."

Octavia covered his hand with hers, and her face softened slightly. "Even if it meant suffering the scandal of declining your match?"

"I suggest we don't remind the prince of that sad story," Bartholomew interjected. "He is desperate enough to use it to his advantage, and then we will have a declined queen on our hands! Source knows we will never survive."

The queen shuddered at the thought. "No son of mine will be responsible for ending the reign of the Esca bloodline. I don't care if he is in love with someone other than his match!"

Bartholomew tried to mollify the queen. "Of course not, Your Majesty, but just to be safe, let's not mention this to him."

Mother Guardian intervened. "It's a moot point. The reading is public, so he won't be able to hide the identity of his match."

"Good point, Minerva." Romulus stood. "One declined queen in our history is more than enough. Now, might I suggest we let Mother Guardian get on with the arrangements?"

Helping Octavia to her feet, he asked, "When can we expect the reading?"

"We will be ready to receive the prince for the introduction ceremony early tomorrow morning. The reading ceremony could take place tomorrow afternoon, depending on how long Flaminius takes to choose a reading Key."

"Excellent news! Don't let us keep you any longer."

Mother Guardian curtsied and left to see to the preparations, a smile of cunning satisfaction beaming from her face. Now all she had to do was get through the most challenging introduction ceremony of her life and hope Flaminius behaved himself.

Chapter Three -
The Introduction Ceremony

Even though her Sister Keys tried to prepare her for the intense energy and breathtaking opulence of the introduction room, it did little to quell Lily's nerves. Taking a deep breath, she forced herself to calm down.

The early morning April sun shone from the east through the bank of arched beveled windows, creating a kaleidoscope of color on the royal coat of arms embossed on the west wall's cream wallpaper. Three crystal chandeliers of epic proportions hung from the pressed ceiling over a sparsely furnished room.

As was protocol, all one hundred and fifty Keys were dressed in white floor-length robes secured with a broad red sash around the waist. Standing in staggered rows arranged in seniority, most seasoned in front, the contrast of their white gowns on the blood-red carpet created a startling effect.

Mother Guardian inspected her brood one last time before she nodded at the guard to admit the prince. The dark-paneled doors swung open soundlessly, and every single set of eyes fixated on the doorway. However, it was not the prince who entered first, but several members of the Royal Protection Unit. Clad in their unique black fatigues, the large men created an impressive yet frightening sight.

The prince came in directly behind them, also in uniform. In deep conversation with the prince was his second-in-command and close friend, Colonel Marcus Brewer. Of course, Lily had seen pictures of the prince and even caught a glimpse or two of him from afar on the palace grounds, but seeing him up close proved overwhelming. He commanded space not because he was a big man but because his personality demanded it.

Clapping a hand on the colonel's shoulder, he said something to his friend, turned, and walked toward Mother Guardian, bowing before her. Touching his head, she said, "Welcome to our sanctuary. Please rise." Stretching her arms wide, she continued proudly, "It is my honor to introduce you to my Lady Keys. They will answer your questions, so please take your time."

"Thank you, Mother Guardian. I am pleased to be here."

Lily thought he looked anything but pleased.

Once again, his deep voice reverberated. "I won't require time to choose my reader."

Mother Guardian stiffened. "I don't understand, Sire. I thought you were here to choose?"

He looked down at her. "As you know, I am not thrilled with the situation, so I don't care who reads for me."

Stepping back as if he'd slapped her, Mother Guardian replied breathlessly, "Sire, this is the most important day of your life! Your reader must be someone you connect with."

The prince glanced at the Keys dispassionately. "I mean no disrespect, Mother Guardian, but witnessing the last of the traitorous Oradagra executed was the most important day of my life." There was a collective intake of breath, but the prince ignored it. "Why don't you choose for me?"

Mother Guardian flapped her mouth like a fish on dry land before she said, "I can't. It must be you."

Lily watched irritation flash across the prince's face. The fact that MG had fought tooth and nail for the prince to retain his right to choose his reader was supposed to be a secret, so naturally, everybody heard about it. It angered Lily that the prince would be so ungrateful.

Sighing, he replied, "Very well, if it will get me out of hours of interviews."

Mother Guardian regained her composure and turned to face her Keys. The prince scanned them for several moments before he asked, "Who is the youngest among them?"

Mother Guardian's eyes narrowed suspiciously before she hesitantly replied, "That would be Lily, Sire. She has only just completed her training and has yet to read."

THE INTRODUCTION CEREMONY

Somewhere in the recesses of her mind, Lily heard the question asked and the answer given, but logic convinced her he was asking so he could avoid her. The prince, however, had other ideas.

"A virgin," Flaminius smiled deviously. "I'll take her."

Instantly, surprised chatter erupted. Mother Guardian held up her hand for silence. "You cannot be serious, Sire."

"Oh, but I am," he replied with a smirk.

Mother Guardian closed her eyes and muttered, "Source save me from the rebelliousness of youth."

Shocked, Lily looked at the prince and then at his men behind him. They all sported the same smirk, but one audaciously laughed out loud. Her shock turned to anger.

As was Lily's nature, anger propelled her feet forward before she could stop. Marching directly to the guffawing soldier, she put her hands on her hips and asked, trembling with rage, "What is it you find amusing, sir? My lack of experience or the prince's disregard for the sanctity of readings?"

The soldier's smile evaporated instantly. He looked around at his fellow warriors before kneeling in front of her. He was so tall she barely had to look down to see his contrite expression. "I apologize, Lady Key, for disrespecting you. That was never my intention."

His immediate apology dowsed her ire. Realizing what she'd done and eager to save face, she held her head high and said, "I accept your apology." Self-consciously she tucked an invisible strand of blonde hair back into her immaculate chignon and turned to face Mother Guardian.

Mother Guardian seemed speechless, but the prince was smiling. "As I said, I choose you." Turning to Mother Guardian, he said, "Let me know what time I need to be here for my reading." And then gathered his soldiers and left.

Someday, Lily would learn to keep her mouth shut, but apparently, it would not be today.

Chapter Four -
The Reading

Mother Guardian ensconced Lily in her study with strict instructions to speak to no one and then hurried off to do who knew what. Lily hoped it was to convince the prince that his decision was pure folly. If only he knew the delicate position he'd placed her in.

Gladys didn't even wait for the door to close behind the prince before she accused Lily of being his lover! But, honestly, she understood Glady's reasoning, what with the prince's reputation as a lady's man and Lily, a Key barely out of training. Why else would he choose her if not to advance her career by granting her such a high-profile reading?

Unable to remain seated, she nervously fidgeted with the plethora of knickknacks scattered around the room. Lily had never noticed before that Mother Guardian favored pastels, specifically powder-blue and pink. She was still pondering that thought when Mother Guardian bustled into the room and shut the door. Keeping her hand on the crystal knob, in a calm but stern voice, she asked, "Are you sleeping with him?"

Lily expected the question, but it was still insulting. "No! I haven't even been in the same room as him before today."

Mother Guardian didn't look convinced. "I want you to understand that I will not reprimand you if you have had relations with the man. What you do with your free time is of no concern to me. However, if you lie, I will be disappointed and unable to help you navigate what will be a complicated situation."

Lily shook her head. "I know that I'm inexperienced, but I'm no fool. The prince's reputation precedes him; furthermore, I would never lie to you."

Mother Guardian held her eye for several moments before she sighed. "Forgive me, but I had to ask. It's not been the easiest of days, and I refuse to open myself up to any more surprises."

Lily didn't envy Mother Guardian one bit. Like most Keys, she was very relieved when she didn't have the Guardian vision upon entering puberty. Lily asked Mother Guardian about it once, and all MG would say was that the vision came directly from Source, and it informed her she was infertile, matchless, and, therefore, qualified to be Mother Guardian. Lily felt her mentor's sadness, especially when one of their rank married and had children of her own.

MG turned Lily's attention to the matter at hand. "I know you must be anxious about your reading, so I thought I would give you a few pointers."

"What? No! Mother Guardian, didn't you convince the prince to choose someone else?" Lily quickly covered the short distance between them. "Gladys should do it; she's the most senior." Wrapping her arms protectively around her waist, she continued, "You know it will reinforce the accusations if I read for him."

Lily dropped to her knees. "Please," she implored, "make him change his mind!"

Mother Guardian took Lily's icy hands in hers. "I can't do that, and even if I could, he wouldn't listen." Taking pity on her, she continued, "What are you so afraid of, child? You are more than qualified. What could go wrong?"

Lily's voice came out shrilly. "I could go blank, forget all I have learned. Or worse, I might have no vision at all."

Mother Guardian smiled. "Calm down, Lily. Never once has a Key not received a vision. It's hard-wired into your DNA."

"I know, but this is a lot of pressure to put on a recent graduate. I may be so nervous that my vision is blurry."

Mother Guardian gently stroked the top of Lily's head. "Yes, it is possible, but you are one of the most gifted Keys I've had the honor of training. You'll be fine."

"I'm afraid the others will believe what Sister Gladys says," Lily whispered. "I've had a challenging time trying to fit in here, and this will only alienate me further."

THE READING

"I'm sorry that the jealousy of others has caused you pain, but you cannot allow them to diminish your self-worth. My advice to you is to enjoy your reading and ignore the rantings of old Gladys."

After the ritual cleansing bath, Lily donned her robes spun from blood-red silk and tied them with a white sash. All graduates received ceremonial robes worn only when conducting a reading. It was, if you will, their diploma. A point of pride, but her agitated nerves made the soft fabric feel like sackcloth against her skin.

Lily sat on the edge of her seat, her hands resting on the glass-smooth surface of the little square wooden table between two brown leather wing-backed chairs. She clutched her hands so hard her knuckles turned white. A one-way mirror covered the wall on her right, making her feel like a guppy in a shark tank. She could feel the eyes of the audience boring into her, so she tried to distract herself by watching the dancing prisms created by the small crystal wall sconces. Lily wondered which idiot had decided that a reading room should have no windows, dim lighting, and soft classical music playing. She was doing a reading, not going on a date, for Source's sake!

Finally, an energy shift alerted her to the prince's imminent arrival, so she stood. A split second later, he entered the room, and she dipped into a deep curtsy. The prince hovered for a moment before closing the door. "You may rise, Lady Key." Lily obeyed but kept her eyes down. "I owe you an apology."

She lifted her head. "What for, Sire? It is my honor to serve you."

The prince wore his ceremonial red tunic with the royal coat of arms embroidered in silver thread on his chest, and a broad leather belt cinched tight stressed his narrow hips. The only missing part of the ceremonial dress was a jewel-encrusted sword, as weapons were forbidden during a reading.

"I owe you an apology," he repeated.

Lily glanced at the mirror nervously. The prince smiled. "Don't worry about them. They won't hear us until I give the signal to turn the intercom on."

"Are you sure, Sire?" she whispered.

Flaminius laughed. "I promise. I stationed one of my men at the button, and he will only turn it on at my command."

"I can't imagine having one of your men in the viewing room went over well," she said in a playful tone.

"No, but it's one perk of being the boss."

Lily didn't know what to say to that. The prince walked to her chair and stood behind it until she settled and then took his seat.

"As I was saying, I'm sorry that I not only put you on the spot this morning but that I also neglected to foresee the rumors that such an action would start."

"You heard about those already?"

"I have, and I assure you I have denied the claims and made it clear that anyone disparaging your name will answer to me."

"I appreciate your concern, Sire."

Satisfied that she accepted his apology, Flaminius added, "I have something for you." He reached into his tunic, pulled out a small, silver gift box with a pink bow attached to the lid, and slid it across the table, holding it in place with a finger.

She frowned. "What is this, Sire?"

Flaminius tapped once on the lid of the box, leaned back, and smiled. "This is a gift from Seth, the oaf who dared to laugh at you this morning. He asked that I convey his sincere apologies and hopes that by accepting this token, you will allow him to call on you."

Blushing ruby-red, she wiped the sweat off her forehead with the back of her hand.

Before she could answer, Flaminius added, "If I may request a favor, could you please give me your answer to convey to Seth? Because this lovelorn soldier will be useless to me until he hears from you."

An unexpected giggle bubbled from her mouth. "Far be it from me to cause a member of the RPU to be distracted from his duties, and as long as it is a favor to you, Sire, please inform Seth that I accept his apology, and he may call on me."

"You don't know it, but you've saved his life."

Lily laughed. "How so, Sire?"

THE READING

"Because maybe, now that he knows you'll see him, he'll shut up about his 'Little Bug,' and the other men won't have to kill him.

The orchestra of tapping feet and rustling clothes in the viewing chamber made Mother Guardian increasingly nervous, not to mention the interaction between the prince and Lily. She didn't think the child would have lied to her, but Lily was no match for the prince's charms, and Mother Guardian feared that the queen might have had a point.

At that precise moment, Octavia leaned in and hissed, her breath liberally infused with spit, "I told you he would seduce her."

Mother Guardian used her handkerchief to wipe away the moisture, ignoring the queen but finding it harder to dismiss her suspicions.

Flaminius's smile slipped off his face before he said, "I suppose we better get started before my mother has a fit."

"Sire, there is still time to put a stop to this."

He shook his head. "No, Lady Key, I made a promise, and I will honor it."

She reached across the table for his hands and was surprised to find he was trembling ever so slightly. It reminded her it was her job to provide a calm experience, and the prince needed her to be professional.

"Sire?" He looked up from their joined hands. "Shall we start?"

He nodded to his man behind the glass. A second later, the ceiling speakers crackled to life.

Pushing all thoughts aside, Lily closed her eyes and concentrated on collecting and spinning energy around and through her third eye. Slowly, a whirling kaleidoscope of color replaced the darkness. Once she heard the familiar internal click of her consciousness disengaging, the swirling colors clarified into a picture of a small but neat parlor, and Lily projected her essence into the vision.

Displayed on the exquisitely carved mantel above the fireplace was a series of photos in mismatched frames. The majority depicted three people of different ages and in various locations. Some showed the family gathered around the dinner table and still others of a young woman graduating high school.

A quick survey of the rest of the room verified that they enjoyed reading, were comfortable financially but not aristocratic, and loved each other. It was a beautiful day, and looking out the leaded diamond-pattern windows, Lily noticed movement in the garden.

Two women kneeled in the rich, dark soil, weeding a vegetable patch and chatting. Lily moved out the parlor, across a small entrance hall laid with shining wooden tiles, and into a large kitchen. It was the kind of room that invited one to sit at the sizeable, scarred wooden table and relax with a cup of tea and homemade pie.

The terracotta tiled floor was worn, speaking of years of use, as was the farmhouse sink. The place's ambiance was captivating. But, alas, Lily needed to identify the match, so she reluctantly walked out into the garden via the kitchen door.

Forgetting that she wasn't there in person, she lifted the hem of her scarlet robes so they wouldn't get dirty as she moved between the neatly turned beds. When she was only five feet from the women, the younger of the two turned her head and looked directly at Lily. She was stunning. Her eyes were the exact color of freshly sprouted grass and shone with intelligence, and her caramel-colored hair was tied in a ponytail high on her head but still long enough to fall over her slender shoulders.

The woman dropped her small spade as she stood. It wasn't unheard of for some people to feel the presence of a Key in vision state, but it was rare.

Frowning, the girl shook her head. She was tall. Her cut-off jean shorts, a little too large at the waist, hung low on her generous hips but tight on her thighs, accentuating her shapely legs spattered with dirt. The prince was a lucky man.

The older woman stood and put her hand on her daughter's arm. "What is it, Aurelia? You look as if you've seen a ghost."

The girl shook her head again. "I don't know, Mom. I feel . . . strange."

The girl's mother guided her through Lily and into the kitchen. "Here, sit. I'll get you some water."

THE READING

Leaving the women, Lily returned to the parlor to search for more clues to identify the match. On a round table placed between two chairs facing the fireplace, she noticed a pile of books. Sucking energy from her surroundings into her ethereal form, Lily lifted the top book cover and read the inscription.

In the kitchen, mother and daughter shivered from the sudden drop in temperature.

"To our darling daughter on her two hundredth birthday. May you always remain as gentle and loving as you are today. Love, Mom and Dad."

On the opposite page, in a different hand, was the woman's full name and address.

Lily took one last look at the room, closed her eyes, and reconnected to her consciousness.

Snapping back into one's body from vision state wasn't pleasant. It left one feeling heavy, clumsy, and slightly nauseous for a few minutes, which is why the Keys' training taught them to take it slow. Perhaps Lily would remember that next time. She opened her eyes and, still clutching the prince's hands, said, "Your Match is an Arkhnuetian, Aurelia Stafford, who lives at:

1512 Swan Lane
Capital City
Capital Province
CC2553

And then she slumped back, utterly exhausted.

Everyone held their breath in the viewing chamber as Bartholomew frantically typed the information into his laptop connected to the Homeland Office. Within seconds, the woman's profile appeared, and he projected it onto the wall.

Bartholomew's anxious nature made him a quicker reader than most. To his astonishment, he saw that the woman was not an aristocrat as expected, but an ordinary citizen. A second later, the queen leaped from her seat as if on fire and roared, "That is entirely impossible!"

Mother Guardian smiled.

Chapter Five -
Informing Aurelia

Flaminius massaged his throbbing temples. His parents summoned him immediately after the ceremony, and his mother had yet to take a breath from her ranting.

Romulus tried to intervene frequently but to no avail. Father and son sat side by side on the devilishly uncomfortable sofa, each doing what they could to lessen the impact of the queen's screeching.

"I demand another reading!" She banged her fist on the marble mantel. Flaminius wondered who she thought was listening to her demands as Mother Guardian had denied her request and left hours ago.

"Octavia, that's pointless. The Key can't be wrong." Romulus drained his whiskey before he continued, "And, frankly, you're giving me a headache."

Flaminius watched in awe as his father stood up to his mother and left the queen speechless for the first time he could remember.

Romulus poured the last drops from the once full crystal decanter into his glass. After taking a gulp, he said, "Perhaps your energies could be better spent arranging whatever silly banquet is required to keep up the pretense that you're happy for our son."

Octavia paled at the king's words, but he was too angry to notice. He drained his glass, slammed it down, and left the room.

The silence left in the wake of his father's departure was blessedly deafening, but unfortunately, his mother ruined it.

"This is your fault!" she hissed.

"How?" Flaminius asked in a deceptively calm voice.

Using the marble mantel to steady herself with one hand, she ran the other over her forehead. "I don't know! It just is."

Standing, Flaminius put his glass on the table next to his father's. "It wasn't my idea to take the throne, and it certainly wasn't my idea to force me into invoking Perfecta Nobis. I was happy to wait, but, as usual, you had to have your way."

Looking up, Octavia said, "Your father is the one to thank for this mess, not me! He's the one who wants to spend the rest of his days fishing and hunting."

Flaminius snorted. "As if you'd let him retire if you didn't want him to."

Nostrils flaring, Octavia replied, "Do you think I haven't tried? He refuses to listen to me, and what's more, he refuses to see that you're not ready. Not even your threat to abdicate could make him reconsider staying in office."

That was true, and Flaminius couldn't blame his mother for his current predicament, even though he wanted to.

Sinking into the couch near the fireplace, she sighed. "I have given my entire life to this crown with little regard for my desires. I was bred to be a queen, and I will not hand my crown over to some low-born daughter of an ex-soldier!" Turning her searing blue eyes to Flaminius, she said, "You don't want to be king, and I don't want that low-breed on my throne. We need to work together to delay the consummation of Perfecta Nobis for as long as possible."

Flaminius should've expected his mother to derail his father's plans, but her deviousness knew no bounds. "I'm afraid it's too late for that mother, or have you forgotten that the entire council just bore witness to my reading?"

"Of course not, but the announcement that you intend to marry and take the throne won't go out to the public until after you've consummated Perfecta Nobis. If you delay meeting your match, it will give me time to come up with another plan to convince your father not to step down."

Flaminius shook his head in disbelief. "You would plot against your husband and betray him so that you can keep a pathetic crown on your head?"

Octavia bolted up from the couch. "Yes!"

"Fucking hell," Flaminius yelled. "Do you care for nothing but power?"

"Power?" Octavia sniffed. "You think I do this for power?" Shaking her head, she walked up to him and cupped his cheeks. "Don't you see? I do this for you."

Stepping away from his mother, he hissed, "Don't you dare use me as an excuse to further your agenda!"

Donning her calm façade, Octavia replied slowly, "The only agenda I have is the continued existence of the Esca bloodline on the throne. Have you forgotten that the people could easily call for a vote of no confidence in their king and petition the council for an election to choose another?"

"I haven't forgotten. Why do you think I've agreed to invoke Perfecta Nobis?"

With that, Flaminius turned to leave.

"Where are you going? We're not finished here."

Flaminius opened the door but turned to his mother. "Yes, we are. Unfortunately, I've got work to do. A new batch of human matches has arrived from Earth. They're waiting at the rifter bay for me to facilitate their orientation."

In a rush of rustling skirts, Octavia hurried across the room and pushed the door closed. "This is more important."

"Nothing is more important than an Arkhnuetian's match. It seems you've forgotten that. But just so we're clear, I will not go back on my word to my father and plot with you."

Slamming the door behind him, Flaminius hurried to the rifter bay that had been transporting humans from Earth to Arkhnuet for the past five hundred and eighty-five years.

The next day, Lily sat opposite Mother Guardian as the royal coach rumbled along the well-kept dirt roads of the capital city. The future queen lived less than a two-hour carriage ride from the palace, and Mother Guardian had decided it would be better to collect her in the slower transport than rift to a rifting station close to her house. MG reasoned that they would need time to explain protocol to the girl and a charming carriage ride was just the place to do it. Lily didn't think the girl would go anywhere with them today, but she would not share that with her mentor.

Lily would rather pick chicken feathers from between a twenty-foot crocodile's teeth than be on this mission. However, her job as the reading Key was to help MG inform Aurelia that her match invoked Perfecta Nobis. As she watched the neat, clean streets of the capital give way to rural roads, Lily pondered the complete lack of consideration for the future queen. Everyone assumed Aurelia would be delighted that she was the handsome prince's match, but Lily felt Aurelia was not a woman waiting for her knight to ride in on his white horse and sweep her off her feet.

"I wonder if you could think a little less loudly, dear child; it's interrupting my concentration." Mother Guardian's attempt at a joke fell flat.

Lily sighed. "Sorry, I'm a little nervous."

Mother Guardian looked up from her book. "Pish posh. You have nothing to worry about."

"No, I suppose not, but I can't help feeling sorry for the girl."

"Nonsense. She is about to be the next queen. She'll be thrilled!"

The carriage slowed and turned into a narrow but well-maintained driveway, giving Lily an excuse not to answer. Pushing the window down, she stuck her head out. Fully grown oaks lined the road, and in the distance, she saw a big, short-haired, tan-colored dog loping across the driveway toward a smaller, shaggy, black-and-white dog lying under a tree near the house. As the carriage drove up to the two-storied cottage, Lily noticed it was tidy but in need of a fresh coat of paint. Gravel crunched as the horses maneuvered around a fountain, water spewing from the mouths of two fish held under each arm of a cherub balancing on the nose of a dragon.

Once the carriage stopped, Thomas, the footman, lowered the steps and opened the door. Mother Guardian accepted his hand, but Lily hesitated a second before she followed. Then, standing behind MG, Lily righted her robes before she clasped her hands in front of her.

An older man with a slight limp ambled toward them from the stable's direction, wiping his hands on a greasy cloth.

He called a greeting, and Mother Guardian smiled at him. "Good afternoon, sir." She held her hand out to him.

He looked down at his own and then back at her. "Pardon if I don't shake."

INFORMING AURELIA

Mother Guardian tucked hers back into the sleeve of her robes. "Not at all."

The man looked at the gleaming black carriage emblazoned with the royal crest the queen insisted they take. "What are two Lady Keys doing in my humble yard with a team of four grays pulling a royal carriage? Has war broken out again?"

Mother Guardian's smile slipped a fraction. "Pardon? No! Goodness," she chuckled. "We," she motioned to Lily and then herself, "are here to speak to Aurelia Stafford."

The man crossed his arms over his broad chest and scratched his day-old beard. The silence grew awkward, but he just stared at them with his steely gray eyes and waited.

Mother Guardian was accustomed to a warmer welcome when she left the palace grounds and ventured out among the citizens. Unfortunately, it didn't happen often, but she made a point of visiting each of the thirteen provinces every few years.

She cleared her throat and tried again. "We have come to speak to Aurelia."

The man nodded. "Yes, I heard you the first time. What I wish to know is, why?"

Lily saw MG cock her head to the side and plaster a PC-smile on her face. "Unfortunately, that is information only Aurelia is privy to."

The man grunted, then dropped his hands to his sides before turning in the direction he came from and limped away. "In that case, you can get back in your fancy carriage and leave my property," he called over his shoulder.

Lily thought Mother Guardian might faint on the spot, but she regained her composure. "Excuse me, sir, but that was not a request. We will not leave until we have spoken to her."

The man stopped, turned, and bent down to pat the head of the tan-colored dog. "I don't give a fig what you want; you will leave my property."

Thomas stepped forward and opened his coat to reveal two pistols strapped low on his hips. Lily's eyes widened in fear. The last thing they needed was a physical confrontation with the father of the future queen.

He smiled sardonically. "Please, boy, I may walk with a limp, but I've killed more Dagra soldiers in my life than you've had breakfasts. You would be dead before you could draw those ridiculous pistols." The black-and-white

31

dog that lay peacefully less than ten feet from them rose at the tone of his master's voice and growled menacingly.

Lily attempted to intervene, but her voice squeaked, so she cleared her throat and tried again. "Please, sir, we don't want to make trouble. It's clear you are very protective of your daughter, and we have no objection to your sitting in on our meeting if she agrees."

Thomas backed up a few paces but didn't close his coat. Mother Guardian sighed and pushed past him to stand in front of Aurelia's father. "Sir, what is your name?"

"Sylas."

Well, at least they were making some progress. "Sylas, we are here on official business, and from what I can gather, you are an intelligent man." Sylas snorted, but Mother Guardian continued unabated, "Surely, you can put two and two together?"

Sylas frowned, looked at the carriage, then the footman, then Lily, back to Mother Guardian, and burst out laughing.

Lily thought he might not have all his bats securely locked up in his belfry. Judging by the confused expressions on the faces of the others, they agreed.

After several minutes Sylas wiped tears of laughter from his eyes and took a deep breath. "I've changed my mind. So you can see my daughter. I wouldn't miss this showdown for all the gold in Arkhnuet."

Mother Guardian smiled. "Excellent! When can we expect her?"

Still chuckling, Sylas gestured for them to follow him up the broad stone steps to the stoop. He opened the oak front door with its little speakeasy door covered with wrought iron and stopped. "The man with the weapons is not welcome in my home." He continued into the house without delay, making it impossible for Mother Guardian to argue.

Thomas didn't look happy about the situation, but Mother Guardian felt she needed to pick her battles where Sylas was concerned and ordered him to wait.

Lily thought everybody had lost their damn minds, but dutifully followed her mentor into Source only knew what.

INFORMING AURELIA

Aurelia and her mother sat in the large oak shade in their backyard, taking a break after planting the last of the strawberries. Her mouth watered just thinking about the ice cream her mother made from the fat, juicy fruit. Rosalind's glass of elderberry juice left a watery ring on the little green-and-blue mosaic-tiled table between their chairs. "You never told me if Professor White gave you the extra credits for your surgery paper."

Aurelia groaned. "Eventually, but it wasn't easy convincing him that the study was flawed. Honestly, I think he finally agreed so I would stop producing evidence to support my claim."

Her mother was the main reason Aurelia decided to study healing. One would think growing up as an only child would be lonely, but her parents took her everywhere with them. While her father was posted on the front line fighting for the crown during the war, Rosalind took Aurelia to her various field hospital postings.

It was unusual for children to travel with their military parents. Still, it was the only way Rosalind would head up the surgical units, and the military couldn't afford to spare her for something as trivial as a child. Watching her mother work with the soldiers, Aurelia learned how rewarding a trauma surgeon's life could be.

Rosalind had recently retired as the chief medical officer after a long and distinguished career and was the most decorated woman to serve in the military. She still consulted at their local village hospital three days a week, but it was mainly in a training capacity.

Aurelia's thoughts were interrupted when Exton and Scroop bounded through the kitchen door, tongues lolling, ears flapping, closely followed by her father and a pair of Keys.

Rosalind frowned when she saw the women but made her way to meet them. Influential people often consulted with Aurelia's mother at home, but they usually made an appointment. Sylas dipped to kiss his wife. "Hello, love." Placing his hand on her shoulder, he turned to their visitors. "These ladies are here to speak to our daughter."

Aurelia loved her father, but he had never been an overly gregarious man, and even less so after the war. If it weren't for her and her mother, he would probably never interact with anyone in a friendly manner. He usually disappeared when people came to consult Rosalind; therefore, the broad smile stretched across his face unnerved Aurelia.

Rosalind placed her hand over Sylas's and addressed their guests. "Good afternoon, Lady Keys. Have you been offered refreshments?"

The older of the two stepped forward and dipped her head. "Good afternoon to you, Dr. Stafford. No, we haven't, but how kind of you to offer."

Rosalind gave her husband an accusatory glare. "I'll make tea," she said as she motioned the women toward the kitchen. With their backs turned, Sylas rolled his eyes. Rosalind quickly elbowed him in the ribs and mouthed, "Be nice!"

Aurelia moved the Keys through the kitchen and politely showed the ladies to the parlor. She stayed to entertain them while Sylas helped Rosalind with the tea. The younger woman thanked her when offered a seat and obliged. The older one slowly ambled around the room in silence. Occasionally, she would lean in to peruse a picture or pick up a book and flip through the pages, stopping here and there to read a passage. Once, she nodded when she saw the photo of Rosalind receiving some award. But other than that, no one spoke. Finally, her parents joined them, and Sylas put the tray on the coffee table.

The older woman helped herself to tea and a cookie without invitation then sat back and ate. "These are very good. Did you make them?"

Rosalind found herself at a loss for words by the woman's odd behavior. She lowered herself into the teal wingback opposite her and cleared her throat. "I am Rosalind, and this is my husband, Sylas, and our daughter Aurelia."

The woman brushed some cookie crumbs off her lap and said, "Oh, yes, I know."

When she failed to elaborate, Rosalind continued, "I am afraid you have us at a disadvantage, Lady Key."

The woman casually rubbed her hands together and answered, "How silly of me! I am Mother Guardian, and this lovely Lady Key is Lily."

Sylas chuckled. Aurelia choked on her tea, Lily sighed, and Rosalind jumped up and bowed. "Mother Guardian, please forgive our casual treatment. I didn't recognize you."

Mother Guardian waved her hand. "Please, child, we only met once many years ago. I didn't expect you to remember me. Sit."

INFORMING AURELIA

Rosalind straightened from her curtsy but didn't sit. She vaguely remembered meeting her during the war. It was between surgeries at one of the field hospitals after a particularly devastating attack, if memory served. "How can we help you, Mother Guardian?"

"As I told your husband, we have come to speak to Aurelia."

Why such an esteemed person would want to speak to her, Aurelia couldn't fathom, but everyone looked at her expectantly, so she replied, "I'm at your service, Mother Guardian."

Mother Guardian nodded, then turned expectantly to Lily. Lily paled. "Me? You want me to tell her?"

"Well, of course, dear," she replied irritably, "it's your job, after all."

Lily spluttered. "But—but I thought since it was so important, that you would do the telling . . . sharing . . . honors." She stuttered nervously.

Mother Guardian raised her eyebrows. "No, dear, I'm simply here for moral support."

Aurelia was near bursting with curiosity. "Please, Lady Key?" she implored from her seated position next to Lily. "I am most eager to learn why you came to see me."

Lily bravely squared her shoulders and said, "I have come to inform you that your match has invoked Perfecta Nobis."

Aurelia felt the blood drain from her face. She knew this would happen one day, but she was still too young. Most people didn't contemplate settling down until well after their three hundredth birthday, and she had just reached her two hundred sixty-third.

"What?" she asked as she stood wide-eyed.

Lily frowned at her and repeated herself as she too rose from her chair.

"No. That can't be right. I'm too young." She started ticking off points on her fingers, "I have my studies to finish, I want to travel, I have a career to launch," her voice climbing a few octaves with every point, "wild oats to sow. I mean, I haven't even had sex yet!"

Sylas cringed, Rosalind gasped, and Mother Guardian burst out laughing.

Aurelia wasn't the only one panicking. Lily's usually flawless complexion exploded with angry red splotches, and unconsciously, she reached back for Mother Guardian's hand.

35

"Now, now everybody, calm down. It's not as bad as all that." The girls simultaneously plopped back into their seats. "Take a few deep breaths, dears; it will help."

They automatically complied with Mother Guardian's suggestion, and when Aurelia seemed more composed, Mother Guardian continued. "Good, now that you're calm, we can get to the exciting news!"

Lily noticed Aurelia's eyes widening even more with renewed panic. "Honestly, Mother Guardian, I don't think you're helping."

"No? Well, best you finish then, Lily."

Reaching for Lily's hand, Aurelia leaned forward and whispered, "What exciting news?"

In an uncertain, reedy voice, Lily said, "The identity of your match is Flaminius Theodore Alexander Esca, heir to the Arkhnuetian throne.

It was as if the breathable air had been sucked out of the room in that instant because Sylas Stafford, decorated war hero and all-around tough Arkhnuetian man, crashed to the ground in a dead faint. Taking half the bookshelf he leaned against with him.

Chapter Six -
Hell, No, I Won't Go!

Aurelia and Rosalind helped a dazed Sylas to the sofa, then Rosalind attended to the bump on his head. While Mother Guardian helped Lily clear the books strewn on the floor, she babbled on about how lucky Aurelia was to be the prince's match and how happy the people of Arkhnuet would be.

Aurelia cocked her head and bugged her eyes to communicate her distress to her parents, who were only capable of doing a good impression of beached cod. Still bent over her father's hulking frame, Aurelia took matters into her hands and said, "Mother Guardian, I mean no offense, but there must be some mistake."

Mother Guardian handed the last two books to Lily and clapped her hands together a few times, producing a small puff of dust. "I assure you, my dear, there is no mistake; you are to be the new queen of Arkhnuet."

Sylas finally broke out of his stupor. "I knew when you said you wanted to speak to Aurelia that whoever her match was must be important, but never in a million years did I imagine this. I love my daughter, and trust me when I say it is the prince that is lucky to have her. But I'm not sure you understand; our Aurelia is no aristocrat."

Mother Guardian frowned. "What does that mean?"

Sylas rubbed his face, wincing as he touched the egg-sized lump on his forehead. "Just that she is all heart. She doesn't have an artificial bone in her body and, therefore, doesn't have the ruthlessness necessary to survive the royal court."

"Be that as it may," Mother Guardian said in a short, clipped tone, "she is the prince's match, and she'll need to come to terms with it sooner rather than later."

Sylas stood, using his wife for support. "I don't think you should hold your breath; our Aurelia has a mind of her own," he growled.

Lily watched the interaction from the corner of the parlor. She thought it was sweet that a father would stand up to the crown to protect his daughter, but professionally, she agreed with MG. Lily stepped between the agitated combatants and raised her hands. "Please, calm down. This bickering isn't helping anyone." Surprisingly, they listened and backed off. Sighing with relief, she said, "Perhaps we should hear what Aurelia thinks?"

Mother Guardian put her hands behind her back and nodded. Lily turned to the girl and smiled. "I realize this is most unexpected, but I believe that when you come to the palace and meet the prince, you'll have a change of heart."

"Come to the palace?" Lily's words bounced around Aurelia's head, leaving her overwhelmed and afraid. "Why would I do that?"

Lily replied, "To consummate Perfecta Nobis." When Aurelia stared at her, dumbfounded, Lily clarified: "You know? Meet the prince and accept his offer of marriage? That's what consummate Perfecta Nobis means."

Aurelia felt dizzy. Things were moving too fast. "Yes, I know, but shouldn't he come here to meet me? I have several friends who have received a request to consummate Perfecta Nobis, and on all those occasions, the males traveled to meet the females."

Mother Guardian gasped. "My dear child! He is the future king. He doesn't have time to traipse all over the countryside!" Placing her hands on her hips, she ignored Lily's pleading gestures. "No, Lily, I've had quite enough of this nonsense. Aurelia, you will pack your bags and travel back to the capital with us to meet your future husband." Mother Guardian shook her head in frustration. "In all my years, I have never met someone so reluctant to meet her match. For goodness's sake, Aurelia, every other woman on the planet would give her eyeteeth for a match like him."

Aurelia tried to remain calm. "I'm sorry, Mother Guardian, but this has all been rather sudden. I need more time to digest it."

HELL, NO, I WON'T GO!

In little more than a furious whisper, Mother Guardian replied, "No. Protocol dictates that you accompany us to the palace today!"

Backed into a corner, Aurelia did what any trapped, frightened animal would. She lashed out. "I will not allow any man to summon me! I don't care who he is; if he wants to meet me, he can reschedule some of his important stuff," she used her fingers to create apostrophes, emphasizing the word, stuff, "and come to my home and introduce himself like a gentleman!"

Sylas clapped his hands. "I agree!"

"Sylas!" Rosalind hissed. "Don't encourage her." Turning to Mother Guardian, she asked, "I'm no lawyer, but isn't it my daughter's right to refuse to consummate Perfecta Nobis?"

"Well, technically, yes," Mother Guardian replied sheepishly, "but we're not dealing with a normal matching."

"So, are you saying she cannot refuse?"

"No, of course not, but it would be unwise to defy the crown, don't you think?"

Lily didn't like the subtle threat laced through MG's words, and neither did an already angry Aurelia. "Are you threatening my family? Because if you are, you can leave and tell your playboy prince to make contingency plans for the future he will have bereft of heirs!"

To all their surprise, Sylas turned to Aurelia, "I support your decision to take things slower, sweetpea, but children are a gift; don't use them as a pawn to get what you want."

Aurelia dropped her head. "Sorry, Daddy."

No one spoke for a few moments, and then Mother Guardian rubbed the back of her neck and said, "Please forgive my rudeness. I assure you I am usually much more personable. However, the stress of this situation weighs heavily on me. Suffice it to say, there are more serious threats to the throne than no heir."

Well, that sounded ominous. Aurelia could think of no greater threat to the throne than not having an heir. "I need time to process this," she reiterated. "When I woke up this morning, my main concern was planting strawberries!"

Mother Guardian burst out laughing. Wiping the tears from her eyes, she replied, "Well, if nothing else, the prince will be in stitches with your unique sense of humor."

Shaking her head, Aurelia replied, "I wasn't trying to be funny." Her statement made Mother Guardian laugh even more.

Lily felt it was time to solidify a plan. "Why don't we go home and tell the prince that you've requested that he come here to consummate Perfecta Nobis? Who knows, he might agree. But if he doesn't, it's at least a starting point for negotiations."

Aurelia agreed because it would give her some time to adjust to her new reality.

"Oh dear," Mother Guardian shook her head. "I doubt the queen will be happy diverting from protocol, but I will do everything in my power to make sure she understands this is the best course of action."

Aurelia's shoulders slumped in relief. "Thank you."

"Don't thank me yet, child. The queen has a razor-sharp tongue and the intellect to match."

"Mother Guardian, I think you'll find that I am more than a match for the queen," Aurelia said with more confidence than she felt.

Chapter Seven -
May the Best Woman Win!

When the carriage stopped at the palace's main entrance, Mother Guardian shored up her courage to inform the royal family of Aurelia's decision. Like her, they would not have expected the woman to defy the crown.

"Lily, you certainly have had a baptism by fire, haven't you, child?"

Lily didn't answer because the sight of the royal family with their entourage of council members and staff gathered on the palace steps left her utterly speechless.

MG exited the carriage as slowly as a woman with an appointment with the hangman. Finally, she turned and mumbled, "Come on, then. Let's get this out of the way."

They ascended the broad stone stairs, stopping one below the royal family, and curtsied. "Arise," said the queen. Looking over the top of their heads, she asked, "Where is the girl?"

Mother Guardian stood. "She's not coming today, Your Majesty."

The queen pursed her lips as if she'd swallowed an entire lemon. "I'm sorry, but I must have misheard. I thought you said she wasn't coming."

Turning her attention to the prince, Mother Guardian said, "I'm so sorry, Sire. She hasn't declined, but requests that," she cleared her throat, "you go to her to consummate Perfecta Nobis."

Flaminius looked at Mother Guardian in astonishment. No woman had ever rejected him—even in his youth when he'd gone out in disguise and women did not know who he was. Grudgingly, he had to admit her refusal intrigued him. His mother did not feel the same.

"Refused? Declined to meet him? Mother Guardian, have you quite lost your mind?"

Romulus squeezed his wife's arm and, in a subdued voice, interjected, "Let's retire to a more private place to discuss this."

Suddenly aware of all the curious stares, Octavia allowed her husband to escort her to their private quarters but held herself so rigid that Flaminius thought she might crack.

As soon as they reached privacy, the queen exploded. "I refuse to allow someone as low-born as that strumpet to insult the royal house. She will come to the palace and do her duty. The acceptance ball will take place in a fortnight as per protocol, and she will attend. Or so help me, I will drag her here myself!"

"Your Majesty, I realize that this is unusual, but if her match were a normal citizen, she would be within her rights." Mother Guardian said.

The queen pointed at Flaminius and shouted, "He is the future king! Not some lowly miner!" Turning her attention to Lily, she continued her tirade. "I knew you weren't up to the task." Before anyone could get a word in edgewise, Octavia continued her blame game. "And you!"

"Me?" Flaminius asked.

"Yes, you. Don't think I don't know the reason you chose this inadequate idiot to read for you. She's just one of the plethora of women you rotate through your bed." Lily looked scared out of her mind as the queen changed direction and stalked her. "I will not allow you to besmirch the Esca name with your filthy plot to steal the prince."

"Enough!" Romulus shouted. "Sit down and be quiet so we can discover what happened and what we can do about it."

Octavia didn't sit, but she shut up. Flaminius poured large whiskeys for everyone and was filling his second glass before Mother Guardian spoke.

"There is nothing we can do." Mother Guardian downed her drink and turned to Lily. "Come, it's time to leave."

Lily was happy to oblige MG and raced out after her mentor.

"You have to do something, Romulus!" Octavia pleaded.

"Octavia, eventually, you will have to realize, as the rest of us already have, that the girl has us over a barrel. If she wants him to hop on one leg and whistle a symphony out of his asshole before she agrees to marry him, he will have to do it."

"Over my dead body!"

Flaminius decided he'd had enough. "I don't like this any more than you do, but father's right. If I can accept my fate, then so can you."

Octavia snorted. "You don't care that she'll destroy all I have built. You'll continue your whoring. Nothing will change for you!"

"Oh, shut up, Mother," Flaminius spat. "If you'll excuse me, I'm going to find a willing partner and fuck until I'm comatose!"

Stepping out into the corridor, Flaminius bumped into Marcus. "I suppose you heard everything?"

"I did," he said as he walked next to Flaminius, trying to suppress a laugh.

"What's so bloody funny?"

Marcus snorted. "Fuck until you're comatose? I would've given anything to see your mother's face."

Flaminius smiled but said nothing. He didn't just say it to shock his mother; he meant it. Perhaps Matilda was still lurking around somewhere. She liked her bed play on the wild side, just like him. He refused to allow some sniveling chit to change his way of life, even if she was his match.

"If I show you some correspondence that I shouldn't have in my possession, will you have a shit fit?"

The day after Flaminius's match dropped her bombshell, Marcus was enjoying some downtime with his friend.

Flaminius lowered his glass of whiskey from his lips and answered, "That depends on whose correspondence you pilfered." Flaminius loved Marcus like a brother, but his belief that it was easier to ask forgiveness than permission was taxing.

Pulling a file from his leather bag, Marcus started reading, "From the desk of her royal highness, the queen of Arkhnuet."

"Fucking hell, Marcus!" Flaminius bellowed after he stopped choking on his drink. "Are you out of your mind? Stealing mail from my mother!"

"Calm down. If you listen, you'll see that this pertains to you, and that's the only reason I'm showing you." Without waiting for Flaminius's reply, he kept reading. "For attention, Miss Aurelia Stafford. I write to you regarding your refusal to accompany Mother Guardian to the palace yesterday to consummate Perfecta Nobis with Flaminius Theodore Alexander Esca, the future king of Arkhnuet. The Esca royal house finds your conduct unbecoming and demands that you present yourself immediately. Your Queen, Octavia Prima Esca of Arkhnuet."

Flaminius groaned. "She's making everything worse, as usual, and I'm going to have to fix it."

Marcus smiled. "I'm not sure your betrothed needs your help. Listen to this." Marcus shuffled some papers around and read, "From the desk of Aurelia Stafford, future queen of Arkhnuet. I apologize if Your Majesty found my conduct unbecoming. That was not my intention. However, according to Landmarks in the Law, written by The Arkhnuet First Counsel, regarding Perfecta Nobis, I am well within my rights to demand my future husband present himself to me at my domicile. Regards, Aurelia Stafford, future queen of Arkhnuet."

"Bloody hell. Could it be that my mother has finally met her match?"

"Buggered if I know, but I'm going to keep abreast of the situation. Should we meet again tomorrow to see how your mother responds?"

"Absofuckedly!" Flaminius said with an evil smile.

Over the following weeks, it became clear that Aurelia was indeed equal to the task of telling the queen to bugger off without sounding rude. Finally, as spring gave way to the heat of summer, the queen realized she was beaten and ungraciously agreed to Aurelia's requests.

Unfortunately, Aurelia's spunk turned Flaminius's grudging curiosity into gnawing hope that his future wouldn't be as unbearable as he thought. But based on experience, he was bound to be disappointed.

Chapter Eight -
The Consummation

"For goodness's sake, Aurelia, could you stop fussing?"

Aurelia glared at her mother but quit tugging at the loose thread of her ridiculous ivory silk suit. "If I'd been allowed to wear what I want, then maybe I would be comfortable, and fussing would be unnecessary."

Over the past month, Aurelia's usually self-assured, calm mother became a complete and utter nut-job.

Every venomous piece of mail the queen sent seemed to twist her mother up inside to the point where both Aurelia and her father thought it would be best if her mother went away until after the consummation.

"And let you meet the prince in cut-off denim shorts and a ratty tank top?"

"Don't be silly. I would never have done that!"

"Really? Because judging by the tart replies you sent the queen—the queen!" she repeated, "Aurelia, I have reason to believe all sanity has left you."

Sylas ambled into the obsessively cleaned parlor wearing his new gray suit and yellow tie as if he wore formal clothing every day instead of filthy coveralls. "Are you two at each other's throats again?"

Both women twisted in their seats to glare at him.

"How can you even ask, Daddy? I thought we agreed that my mother lost her marbles weeks ago."

Sylas knew better than to agree with his daughter in front of his wife. "Aurelia, don't be disrespectful."

Rosalind sniffed and dabbed the corners of her eyes with a tissue. "Don't bother, Sylas. She will do whatever she wishes."

Throwing her hands up as high as the stupid boat-necked collar of her suit would allow, she groaned, "Mom! What the hell has gotten into you? You never used to worry about what people thought of me before I became the prince's match. Am I suddenly not good enough for you?"

"That's not true, Aurelia. I have always tried to teach you to be respectful of others, but your rude behavior over these past weeks has been mortifying!"

"Enough! I've been nothing but factual and polite in my replies to the queen, who, I might add, has zero right to shove her nose in my business."

Sylas laid his hand on her shoulder and squeezed lightly.

"No, Daddy, I will have my say." Leaning forward, she continued, "Can you honestly say that if this man was just some Joe Bloggs and his mother interfered like the queen has, that you would have no problem with it?"

Rosalind took a moment before she answered. "That's not the point. The fact is, he is the prince, and you are going to be queen. Don't you see? Everything about your life will change, and you have alienated the one person who could've made things easier for you."

"Yes, Mom! I know everything is about to change, and I'm going to be queen. That's why I intend to start this journey in the way I intend to finish it, and that doesn't include rolling over every time my husband or his mother demands it. I will be a good queen, and I will learn what's necessary to make that happen, but I will learn from people I respect, and she has yet to give me one reason to do so."

Rosalind had no response because her daughter was right. Aurelia sighed and reached for her mother's hand. "Mom, you taught me to be strong and listen to my gut, and that's what I'm doing. All I ask is that you trust and support me."

Rosalind stared at their linked hands. "I do trust you, but I'm terrified for you and the immense responsibility you face. And for the first time in my life, I'm not qualified to help you." Rosalind lifted their linked hands and kissed the back of her daughter's palm.

"So that's why you're behaving like a rabid cat on a hot tin roof," Aurelia joked. "Look, Mom, I'm scared too. Source knows, this wasn't in my plans, and that's why I need you both now more than ever."

THE CONSUMMATION

Rosalind wiped her tears away. "I'm sorry, Aurelia. I promise that from now on, you can expect your rational mother back. But I will say this: that dress suit looks amazing on you."

Flaminius would've preferred to rift to his future bride's nearest rifting station and then ride to her home, but his bloody mother insisted on the carriage, complicating security issues. It hadn't made his men happy. Therefore, the meeting was kept secret along with the identity of his match. Not that it would remain so since there were bound to be some nosy reporters hiding out around the palace, and the royal carriage leaving the grounds wasn't subtle.

Tiberius saved his brother's sanity by offering to accompany him and, of course, Marcus and five of his most trusted men on horseback with them. Mother Guardian and Lily followed in their carriage, rounding out their entourage.

"You're quiet, Flaminius. Are you still unhappy about getting married?"

He'd been in such deep thought he'd almost forgotten his brother was there. "I've come to accept it as a necessary sacrifice."

Tiberius raised his eyebrows. "Goodness, you sound martyrish. It's honestly not that bad."

Flaminius smiled. "That's easy for you to say. You love Delinea and wanted to marry her. My bride hated the idea of marrying me so much that she braved a battle of wits with our mother to delay the wedding."

Tiberius shuddered. "Yes, I see your point, but surely this is a good thing."

"Really? How so, brother?"

"Well, now you know she has courage, and she'll need it, saddled with the likes of you."

Flaminius laughed and threw a gold-and-red brocade pillow at his brother's head, the gold-tasseled border glinting in the sunlight streaming through the window. "Hilarious, and what exactly do you mean by 'the likes of me'?"

Tiberius caught the downy projectile. "I love you, brother, but you and I both know that you're a dog with women."

Tiberius's words hurt. "Yeah, well, maybe if I had a choice when I marry, things would be different."

Tiberius's face took on a serious demeanor. "I was prepared to take on the responsibility of the throne. Don't get me wrong, it shocked me when you suggested abdication, but I'm still prepared to help you."

Flaminius felt he needed to explain. But how to do that without telling him what their father had said. "Tiberius, I'm sorry that I asked you to consider it. At the time, I thought—"

"You don't have to explain it to me," Tiberius interrupted, "I heard."

The look of pain on his brother's face caused by their father's rejection slashed Flaminius's heart.

"He's wrong, you know. You would've made a superb king."

Tiberius shrugged. "Maybe, but it wasn't meant to be." He turned his head to look at the passing countryside, ending the conversation.

Moments later, the carriage turned off the main road into the Staffords' driveway, and panic replaced thought.

"They're here."

Aurelia never thought about the words *they* and *here* before. Why would she? They were just simple words with little meaning, but right now, they were the two most frightening words in the English language.

Fortunately, Sylas was there to escort her out to the stoop, and she hung on his arm like a drowning person would a life vest. For a month, Aurelia had been all piss and vinegar fighting for her rights, but now that it was 'go' time, Aurelia was terrified. She thought she might be sick right there on the steps of their home in front of the future king and her genetic match. Her father tightened his hold on her and whispered, "Just breathe, little one."

Taking his advice, she took a deep breath through her nose and out of her mouth. "Daddy, don't let me go."

"Never."

Her insides quivered, making it impossible to stop her limbs from shaking as she watched the carriages slowly make their way up the drive and around the fountain. Aurelia surreptitiously wiped the sweaty palm of her free hand on her ivory silk suit and swallowed bile.

THE CONSUMMATION

Finally, the footman lowered the steps and opened the carriage door. A large hand emerged, followed by a head of curly, brown hair and then broad shoulders. He scanned his surroundings with sky-blue eyes before fluidly descending the stairs. As he turned his face toward the Staffords, their eyes met. And all at once, she was in the corniest romance novel ever written. Her heart skipped several beats. The planet stopped rotating, time ceased to exist, birds sang, and butterflies swirled in a cornucopia of color. Fear dissolved like an aspirin in water, replaced by the sudden feeling of love she felt for the man.

Flaminius was too much of a coward to look toward his future wife. From the moment the carriage turned off the main road, he felt inexplicably nauseated. His insides vibrated so violently he was afraid they might shake his bones until they broke.

Once he had his feet on solid ground, he braced, lifted his face, and looked into the most brilliant green eyes he'd ever seen. He was at least thirty feet away, but Aurelia's sweet scent assailed his soul, and his cock swelled instantly.

What the actual fuck was happening? Before he was aware, he was walking with long determined strides toward his mate, and he swore somewhere there was an orchestra playing an evocative waltz that accompanied her graceful descent down the stairs.

When he reached her, she was determined to say something intelligent. But, instead, she said, "I never imagined you'd be so beautiful in person."

Even though she was standing one step up, he still had to look down at her angelic face. "Aurelia," he whispered reverently, "mi perfecto."

She blinked slowly, like a sloth on sleeping tablets. "And you, mi perfecto. Thank you for coming all this way to meet me."

Flaminius lifted his hand and gently touched her cheek to make sure she was real. She gasped, so he pulled away, but she whispered, "No, please, don't stop touching me."

Obeying her, he cupped her face with both hands. "I would've crawled over burning coals to get here."

She laughed, lowered her head to his chest, and burst into tears. Mortified, she looked into his gorgeous face. "Please forgive me. I don't know why I'm crying."

He smoothed back her hair. "No apology necessary."

Aurelia couldn't stop smiling at him, and she worried he might think she was simple-minded. She had to say something. "So, you are Flaminius."

He chuckled. "Indeed, I am. And you are Aurelia."

He still held her in his arms; his scent scrambled her brain so much that she blurted out, "I love your name, but it is awfully long. How do you feel about nicknames?"

Flaminius shrugged his shoulders. He didn't care what she called him as long as she stayed with him. She took his silence to mean exactly that because she said, "I think I'll call you Flame."

He chuckled again. The rich baritone of his voice made Aurelia's heart thump harder.

"If calling me Flame makes you happy, then have at it. But, if I may ask, why Flame?" He wanted to suck the words back immediately! Obviously, it was a shortened form of his name. She was going to think he was simple-minded!

"Because right now, standing in your arms, I'm on fire."

Holy shit, did she say that?

He liked her explanation much better than his, but it made his already stiff cock ache. Leaning in, he whispered in her ear. "I love that you feel that way, but please take pity on a man and stop being so cute. I'm already unable to hide my desire for you, and your father is standing right there."

She burst out laughing.

Sylas hugged his sobbing wife and watched with mixed feelings as his only child experienced the magic of Perfecta Nobis.

Chapter Nine -
The Beginning

Sylas wiped away his tears with the back of his hand and kissed the top of his wife's head. "I think it's time to let our little girl fly. What do you say, love?"

"I'm going to miss her, Sylas." He lifted her chin with his index finger to look into her beautiful green eyes. "I know, love. As will I, but she's ready for whatever that den of vipers throws at her because she has that man beside her."

Rosalind smiled. "You knew all along, didn't you? That's why you were so calm when I was freaking out."

Sylas shrugged. "Of course, I knew. You raised her, Rosalind, and she has grown into a spectacular woman. Who else would be worthy of her but a king?"

"I love you, Sylas Stafford."

He kissed her gently. "I know, my dove. I know."

Turning to his daughter, still standing in the protective embrace of her match, he said, "I take it you'll be leaving to go to the castle today, sweetheart."

Aurelia turned her glazed eyes to her father. "Yes, Daddy, if that's what Flame wishes."

Mother Guardian giggled. "I like that nickname. I think it suits you, Sire."

Only Mother Guardian would have the audacity to comment on Aurelia's term of endearment. He chose not to get into it with her, but to answer his wife. He'd known her less than half an hour, and he already thought of her as his. "I would love it if you came with me to the palace today, but I won't force you to do anything that makes you uncomfortable." He felt he needed to make it clear from the start that she would always have a choice where possible, and he wanted all those present to know it too.

"I want to go with you, Flame."

Flame and Marcus set about organizing the men for the return trip while Aurelia and her mother collected her things. Within the hour, they were on their way to the palace; Aurelia safely ensconced in his carriage.

Saying goodbye to her parents was an emotional affair, but they knew it wouldn't be for long. Tiberius rode back with Mother Guardian and Lily to give the couple privacy.

The carriage interior was far more ostentatious than Aurelia would have imagined. Still, it took her a few minutes to notice—a testament to the powerful effect of the matched hormones. Despite the cavernous interior, the décor created a cozy feel with cream velvet curtains hanging over large widows, lush red carpeting, and soft broad bench seats upholstered in a cream-and-red brocade pattern she couldn't quite make out.

Flame sat across from her in silence, giving her time to adjust. Feeling self-conscious, Aurelia asked a banal question. "This is a beautiful carriage. What are these designs?" When he smiled, she just about lost her breath.

"It's the royal coat of arms."

"Ah. It's gorgeous."

He shifted his weight. "I didn't want to take the carriage today. I thought rifting would be more efficient. My mother insisted, but now that I have this time alone with you, I'm grateful she did."

Aurelia felt her face explode with crimson heat.

Flame chuckled knowingly.

Source help her, but he even sat sexily! Leaning back on the squabs, hands resting on his thick thighs, his feet planted several feet apart with his legs open so she could see the bulge in his pants. He looked relaxed and comfortable in his body, but his eyes were on fire.

Thank Source. He took pity on her and asked, "I understand you're in healer training. Do you enjoy it?"

She nodded, "I do, but I haven't finished my first year."

"Your mother is a renowned healer, and everyone knows how faithfully she served the crown. I have no doubt you'll be just as accomplished if you choose to finish your studies once we're married."

Aurelia hadn't thought about that. She'd been so intent on getting this meeting over with that she never considered her life as the queen. "Will I be able to do that?"

Flame frowned. "Finish your studies?" Aurelia nodded. He had to think for a moment before he answered. "It isn't typical for the queen to have a career because her responsibilities can be all-consuming, but if you feel it's important, I won't stop you."

"I think I'd like to finish, but you realize it is an eight-year program. I mean, I could get my basic trauma degree and not continue to the surgical qualification, but it's still five years."

"Aurelia, there are many things we need to talk about, but I don't want to spend our first hours alone hashing out our day-to-day lives. Can we talk about it after we marry? Right now, all I want to do is look at you, and if you'll allow it, I would very much like to kiss you."

His words had her melting like cheap ice cream on a sizzling summer day, but she had to clarify some things before they got to the kissing.

"I want to kiss you, but if I may ask, how long before we marry?"

Warning bells clanged in his head. "How long do you think it'll be?"

She scrunched her nose in thought and then replied, "I don't know, a year? We have to get to know each other, and I imagine I'll have a lot to learn before then."

Flaminius sat forward. "Aurelia, how much did Mother Guardian explain to you?"

She gave him a cautious look. "About what?"

"About the protocol surrounding our wedding."

"Nothing. We were too busy trying to negotiate a meeting date with your mother to get that far."

Flame sat back and sighed. "Shit!"

"Well, that doesn't sound encouraging."

"No, it's not. The wedding will take place within a fortnight."

Aurelia sat back so fast she cracked her head against the carriage wall. "Say what now?" Her future husband raised his hands to calm her, but she wasn't having any of it. "I don't think so, Flaminius. I'm not getting married in two weeks. No way, no how."

So that's how it was going to be. His future wife would call him Flame when he was a good boy, but Flaminius when he displeased her. Using his best warning voice, he said, "Aurelia, this royal protocol is non-negotiable. And what's more, the press is at this very moment crowding into the press room at the palace where the king's secretary is releasing a statement that I have invoked Perfecta Nobis, you have consummated it, and we intend to marry in a fortnight."

"I would've preferred that you discussed a press release with me first."

Flaminius raised his eyebrows. "I'm sorry, but our public relations department, which has a strict protocol to follow, deals with such matters."

Flaminius's high-handed behavior irritated Aurelia's already raw nerves. "If I hear the word protocol one more time, I swear I'm going to scream! I don't give one shit about what some old law says I must do."

Her unexpected outburst rocked Flaminius to his core. Suddenly, she didn't seem so angelic. Her face twisted with rage; veins in her neck throbbed with fury in a scene all too familiar. Her reaction switched him off to her instantly as all his worst fears came to life.

He would not be like his father and was going to set her straight from the start. He would also kill Mother Guardian for not doing her duty and leaving him with this mess.

Using his cold, calm voice, he replied, "Don't you think we've capitulated to more than our fair share of your demands? Lesson number one for a queen, Aurelia." He leaned in until their noses almost touched. "Be prepared to negotiate."

She gasped. "You're joking, right? I've had my entire life turned upside down because you sought your match. I could've told you and your mother to take a hike and there would be not one thing you could've done about it! Did I do that? No! I changed the trajectory of my future for you, and you have the gall to say I haven't negotiated! And what do you mean by 'we?' Are you suggesting there's an aristocratic camp that you belong to and a commoner camp that my family and I belong to?"

"Holy mother of Source, do you ever run out of breath?"

THE BEGINNING

She turned a very peculiar shade of puce before she answered. "So much for not forcing me to do something that makes me uncomfortable! We've barely known each other two minutes, and already you're going back on your word!"

Okay, this was getting out of hand—time to calm down. Taking a deep breath, Flaminius sat back. "First, there are no camps. I didn't mean it that way. Second, I'm not going back on my word, but you need to understand even I can't change certain things. This wedding, our wedding, is a political statement that I intend to take the throne."

"Why do you need to take the throne so soon? By all accounts, you're not that keen, so why the hurry? Why can't we wait a year?"

Shaking his head, he replied, "There are factors that make waiting imprudent. Trust me, if I could've dragged it out, I would've, but I have a responsibility that trumps my personal feelings. Unfortunately for you, those responsibilities are now yours too. Lesson number two. You don't get to be selfish; it's always about the people."

He sat back and turned to gaze out the window, but before he looked away, she could have sworn she saw the disappointment in his eyes. It was that more than anything he said that made her shut up and think. She needed to remember she wasn't marrying a man, but a king. The people deserved a leader whose wife didn't behave like a spoiled little daddy's girl, so it seemed that, perhaps, lesson number three was humility.

"I'm sorry, Flame. You're right. I'm still learning what it means to be responsible for an entire nation. I promise I'll try to be more accommodating in the future, but I'll probably mess up again."

He kept his face unreadable. Wringing her hands, she continued, "If it's truly that important, we'll get married in two weeks."

Relief flickered across his face, but he was quick to hide it. "We're almost home. Let's get through the next few hours, and then we can talk again."

Not wanting to cause any more trouble, she nodded.

Flaminius never thought the ride home would take such a dramatic turn. Fortunately, they were almost at the palace, so it spared him the torment of sitting in a confined space with her for too much longer. His mind may have turned off, but his body still hummed with the release of the matched hormones.

Hopefully, she meant what she said and would hold her tongue when meeting his mother. He honestly didn't have the strength for another showdown, especially not a public one.

Aurelia was afraid to meet the queen. It was easy to be brave via mail, but she knew her future mother-in-law outclassed her. The only reason Aurelia won the first round was that she held all the cards.

She was even more afraid of the sudden distance Flame wedged between them. It was proof that the matched hormones might kick-start the chemical attraction to one's genetic match but couldn't create the emotional connection necessary for love to grow.

The carriage slowed, and Aurelia pulled back the pale fabric covering the windows. She couldn't see the road ahead, but she knew they were approaching the colossal iron gates at the entrance to the castle grounds. She had seen countless images of the imposing twenty-foot-high gated entrance with lethal spiked tips and royal emblem proudly displayed on the front.

Flaminius sat motionless, observing Aurelia's face. She was nervous, and even though his feelings toward her hadn't softened, he took pity on her. "It'll be alright. I won't leave you to the wolves until I know you can handle them."

She smiled at his jest, shaking her head. "Thank you, but I'm afraid you'll never be able to leave my side in that case."

Flaminius said nothing, so she shifted across the space to sit next to him. "May I?" Her hand hovered over his, waiting for permission to touch him. Turning his palm up, he stretched his fingers open and gently threaded them through hers. A jolt of awareness shot up his arm.

It took a moment before she felt sure her voice would be strong enough to speak. "Would staying by my side be such a terrible thing?"

The slowing carriage saved him from replying. Aurelia tightened her grip and let out a shuddering breath.

"Just remember to breathe, and if the cameras intimidate you, look down and to the left and smile." She frowned, so he explained. "It's a little trick I

THE BEGINNING

learned when I was a kid. It doesn't look like you're avoiding the cameras or being rude. Instead, it looks like you may be a little shy, and they love it."

She still looked terrified. "If all else fails, just follow my lead. Okay?" She nodded.

Flaminius pushed the carriage door open and waited for the footman to lower the stairs. Surveying the scene, he noticed fewer people than when Mother Guardian and Lady Lily came to the palace the previous month. His mother erred on the side of caution this time. Extreme caution, it would seem, because there was no sign of the press either.

He jumped down and turned to his future wife. She popped her head out the door like a scared mouse. He gripped her waist and lifted her down, enjoying her surprised gasp. Clearing her throat, she stepped back and softly thanked him while straightening her jacket.

"Are you ready?"

Turning to face the welcoming party, she said. "No, but let's go."

Flaminius held out his arm, which Aurelia happily accepted. Lifting her head, she smiled and followed Flame as he led her up the broad stone steps to his waiting parents. "Father, Mother, may I introduce Miss Aurelia Stafford."

Aurelia curtsied. "I am pleased to make your acquaintance, Your Majesties."

The queen looked down her nose at Aurelia, which wasn't hard to do since she was standing a step up, and she was about four inches taller.

"I wish I could say the same."

Aurelia expected the cold shoulder from the queen, but not open contempt. She desperately wanted to give the woman the tongue lashing she deserved, but Aurelia promised Flame, so she tried diplomacy instead. "I realize my behavior has caused some unpleasantness, Your Majesty, but I sincerely hope that we can move forward and learn to work together."

The queen's nostrils flared. "Unpleasantness? You openly mocked the traditions and protocols of the royal family. I would say that is more than mere unpleasantness."

Flaminius's grip tightened around Aurelia's arm. "Mother!" he growled. "I will not let you cause a scene minutes after meeting my future wife."

"Yes, Flaminius, you're quite right. Your future wife has created enough consternation to last this family a lifetime."

Lifting her heavy gold skirts, the queen turned and walked into the castle, leaving the rest of them struggling for composure. Romulus rubbed his eyes and said, "We are happy you came after all, my dear. Octavia too, despite her words."

"Thank you for your kind words, Your Majesty."

Waving his hand, he placed the other on his son's shoulder, but kept his eyes on her. "Please call me Romulus when in private. We are going to be family after all."

Flaminius placed his arm around Aurelia's shoulders. "I am going to show my fiancée to her rooms so she can rest before dinner."

Aurelia didn't want this day to get any worse, so she didn't argue with Flame. Maybe he would be more himself at dinner.

Chapter Ten - Stay Calm and Follow Protocol

Flaminius wanted to stay and help Aurelia settle in, but he had to speak to his mother. She would not spoil this, not after everything she put him through to force him to find his bloody match. "I hope the accommodations are to your liking. I have some stuff to do, but if there is anything you need, please ring, and one of the servants will help you."

Aurelia watched him walk away. She understood he was still angry at her, but he didn't have to lie. He didn't have 'stuff' to do; he just wanted to get away from her. Well, she didn't need him to unpack her few belongings.

Her preoccupation with everything over the past month left no time to think of the splendor of the palace. But now, she stood in her apartment, which comprised three of the most luxurious rooms she'd ever seen.

The receiving room was the largest, boasting a wall of tall sliding glass doors. Once opened, they created a seamless transition to the half-moon patio filled with potted plants. There were pink and yellow Calibrachoas, deep red Cardinal Climbers, orange Black-Eyed Susan, white Mandevilla, purple Lavender, and a few others she couldn't identify.

Soft sofas and ottomans upholstered in a subtle blush of rose fabrics were positioned around the marble fireplace's cream façade. The stone floors were covered in beautiful carpets woven into intricate patterns in slightly darker rose and cream tones, but still subtle enough to preserve the room's cool palette.

Room two was a bedroom and dressing room combination, and room three, an enormous bathroom. The bedroom's central focus was a teak four-poster bed adorned with butter-yellow and soft green bed hangings.

But the room that truly got her attention was the bathroom. The sunken square tub was intricately decorated with tiny mosaic tiles in rose, gold, green, and beige that formed a picture of a mermaid perched on a rock brushing her long, flaxen hair. A generous glass-enclosed shower took up most of the back wall, and 'his and her' sinks, the opposite one. Doors in the bathroom, covered in sheer lace curtains, shared the patio with the receiving room.

Dashing back to the bedroom, Aurelia set about finding suitable clothing to wear for dinner and then indulged in the first of many glorious baths.

"Flaminius. I hope you're not here to tell me that ridiculous creature is causing more trouble."

Flaminius greeted his father, then turned to his mother and said, "Mother, I can't fight you and Aurelia and still pull off a wedding and a coronation in two weeks. You need to decide whose side you're on because I'm at my breaking point."

She raised her eyebrows in surprise. "She has conceded to protocol and will marry in two weeks?"

"Yes, Mother, she has, and for future reference, 'she' has a name."

Too bone-weary to say anything else, Flaminius left.

"He needs our support now more than ever, Octavia."

The queen lowered herself onto the sofa and sighed. "How could this happen? How could Source choose such an unworthy person to be his match?"

"My love, we barely know her. She may yet prove to be a good queen."

Octavia snickered. "She is low-born, Romulus, with no appreciation of the importance of royal protocol. She has made a mockery of us, and your son allowed it!"

Romulus sat next to her and drew her hand into his. "You cannot understand what a matched man will do for his mate. Flaminius has behaved predictably."

She shook her head. "No. I don't understand. He has mocked his birthright repeatedly; even so, you refused to allow Tiberius to rule."

"I've explained my reasons to you many times." Dropping her hand, he stood. "And I stand by my decision. Tiberius is not leadership material."

Throwing her arms out, she shouted. "Not leadership material? He's not the one who refused to match. He's not the one who consistently ignored royal protocol or fought you at every turn regarding political decisions! He has been loyal in his support of the crown. How can you say he is not leadership material?"

Pushing his hands through his hair, Romulus said, "Tiberius is weak."

"Why? Because he preferred to stay here with me and learn political strategy instead of going to war with you and Flaminius?"

"No! Why do you think he stayed here? It wasn't to learn from you; it was to escape fighting with a good excuse." Octavia gasped, but Romulus ignored her. "A king cannot allow fear to rule his mind. He must always be prepared to do what's best for his people."

"The best is not always fighting. A good strategy wins wars, not brute strength."

"No, my dear. Courage wins people's hearts and the loyalty necessary to rule a nation effectively. Tiberius has no courage. The people of Arkhnuet will never follow him." Holding up his hand to stop her from speaking, he continued, "He may force them into submission as he does his wife, and that will work for a brief time, but I want to leave a legacy that lasts centuries. Love, honor, and courage create that legacy, not fear."

Octavia disagreed, but it was fruitless trying to argue with her husband. However, if he thought she'd let him destroy what she had so painstakingly built, he had another thing coming.

Aurelia thought her life was crazy before, but it was nothing compared to the days that followed her arrival at the palace. The PR department assigned her a personal secretary to help keep her on time for her million appointments. Hair, nails, dressmaker, wedding planner, elocution lessons, protocol lessons—the list went on. Flaminius remained conspicuously absent through all this craziness, but he sent her a hand-picked bodyguard.

Aurelia liked both her secretary, Sue, and her bodyguard, Marcus, and they became friends. Source knew she could use some. Sue knew how to keep Aurelia calm when she became flustered by saying, "Just follow protocol." In the beginning, it irritated Aurelia, but Sue explained that, in certain instances, protocols could be your friend. It provided a tried and tested track to run on, eliminating the need to think. Aurelia had to admit that Sue's argument had merit.

Marcus was funny, approachable, and knew everything about everyone, which was very helpful since it was apparent that living at court was more of an exercise in survival than anticipated. It didn't hurt that he was also very handsome and had a way with the ladies that eased her introduction into their fold.

But on day four, she realized, not all women swooned in Marcus's presence. Nor could he protect her from those with a sharp tongue and jealous nature.

"Why do I have to do this again?"

Sue straightened the collar of Aurelia's attractive peach knee-length dress. "The ladies that attend daily high tea come from wealthy, influential, aristocratic families who support the crown, and it's politically prudent to keep them happy."

Personally, Aurelia couldn't give a shit, but she promised Flaminius, and she never broke a promise. Pesky thing, her conscience. Slipping on her nude sling-backs, Aurelia asked, "Where is Marcus?"

"Here."

"Hurry, you're going to be late," Sue said while shuffling them both toward the door.

They left, with Marcus guiding Aurelia through the maze of corridors. But he was uncharacteristically quiet, and it made her nervous. "Are you okay, Marcus? You seem distracted."

He was, but he couldn't tell her the reason for his introspection was her future husband. The fool came to him in a drunken stupor last night and shared the conversation Flaminius had with Aurelia in the carriage. Marcus didn't think it was reason enough to write the poor girl off, but then again, he didn't grow up with a banshee for a mother.

"Not at all, Your Grace. I'm just a little tired."

"Please don't call me, Your Grace. It makes me uncomfortable."

Marcus laughed. "Very well, but if your fiancé hears me informally addressing you, he'll kick my ass."

"Pfft. Flame wouldn't care."

"Don't underestimate the protectiveness of a matched male, especially an alpha like Flaminius."

"I haven't seen him since we arrived. If I didn't know better, I'd doubt our match," Aurelia complained.

Marcus shook his head. "What happened between you two? At your parents' house, you just about ripped each other's clothes off."

Aurelia blushed. "I didn't know you were there."

"Oh, I assure you I'm always there. I saw how you looked at each other."

She shook her head and asked, "Marcus, do you know Flame well?

"I don't know if anyone can say they know him well. He had a rough upbringing with endless demands placed on him," he answered diplomatically.

She looked disappointed.

"I can tell you he feels alone even when he's in a room full of people. Honestly, I think he's looking for a safe place to be himself, and he's never found it. Trust is a luxury when you're the heir to the throne, Aurelia."

Even though she wanted to pursue this conversation with the man who, according to most people, was the closest person Flaminius had to a friend, she couldn't. They'd arrived, and Marcus led her through a set of doors into a receiving room.

"Why do we even have ladies of the court?" She sniffed indignantly. "It reeks of favoritism." She settled herself on the couch.

Marcus smirked. "Not to be disrespectful, but if memory serves, your family's contribution to the throne bought you the right to access the royal court."

Crossing her legs and shifting back into the soft red leather couch, she replied, "A privilege my family never took advantage of because we abhor any form of favoritism."

Just then, a beautiful, petite blond woman approached them. She cleared her throat and tugged at her snug-fitting black blazer. "Your Grace." The woman curtsied, a feat Aurelia found admirable considering the tight fit of her black silk skirt.

In a chirpy voice, she continued, "Good morning, Colonel Brewer." Aurelia noticed the slight blush creeping up the woman's neck. "Prince Flaminius informed us you would escort Her Grace, our future queen, to court today. Whenever you're ready, I'll announce your arrival."

Marcus smiled and winked. "Thank you, Nena. I'll be sure to call you."

Nena cocked her head, looking up at him from under her eyelashes, then curtsied again and retreated to her desk.

How did the man make an innocent conversation sound so suggestive?

Not taking his eyes off the retreating Nena's rear end, Marcus spoke. "It's never a good idea to alienate people with power, Your Grace."

"I beg your pardon?"

Marcus tore his eyes from the silk-covered ass and looked at her.

"These women that come to court live in luxury for the spring and summer and meet unattached men to sow some wild oats before they take an appointment with a Key and settle down." She opened her mouth to retaliate, but Marcus stopped her. "Let me finish. You may not like how some of these women gained access to court, but it is undeniable that women talk, and a lot of that talk comes from the pillows of men. I, for one, am interested to hear what they're saying."

Aurelia frowned. "Are you saying that you hang around the women at court to gather intel?"

"Oh, Your Grace, you are quick on the uptake," he said with an impressed look on his face. "It's not fair. Flaminius always gets the hot ones. Does he have to get the smart ones too?"

Shaking her head indulgently, she said, "Okay, we're going to talk about that last comment later, but for now, let's stick to the matter at hand. I get you need to keep the royal family safe, and one way to do that is gathering intel, but I still don't want to be the queen that sanctions this bitch fest."

"Aurelia, not all those women are uppity aristocratic bitches. Most of them are normal nice girls trying to survive in shark-infested waters, so if you want to make a difference, why not go in there and change the way things work?"

"How?"

Marcus smiled deviously. "By unseating the queen bee and changing the rules."

"That sounds like a great idea, Colonel. Lead me to the beehive."

Chapter Eleven -
Things You Wished You'd Never Done

Flaminius drank his third cup of black coffee, hoping the bitterness would remove the rancid taste of guilt, but it would take a blowtorch to achieve that. Last night had been a colossal mistake. He got drunk, over-shared with Marcus, and then to add ass to his dumb, he woke up in Matilda's bed.

Source help him. But all he could remember was stumbling out of Marcus's apartment then bumping into Matilda, but nothing else until he woke up in her bed that morning. He didn't wait around to chat. He just threw his clothes on and slunk out of her room.

He wasn't sure if they had sex, but the absence of claw marks, the odor of sex on his body, or sticky residue on his penis made him hopeful they hadn't. Regardless, he woke up naked in another woman's bed. He didn't like his future wife, but if he found out Aurelia had done the same, he'd lose his shit.

"Would you like a late lunch, Sire?"

Flaminius shook his head. "No, thank you, Frank. I'm going to shower, and then I have an appointment with my tailor."

Flaminius's butler bowed but didn't leave. "Was there something else?"

"I believe Her Grace will visit court this afternoon, Sire. I wondered if you wished to attend."

Shuddering, Flaminius replied, "Fuck, no."

Frank cleared his throat. Sighing, Flaminius sat back. The man was more of a surrogate father than a servant. "Okay, Frank, what's on your mind?"

Smiling at his employer, he continued, "It's just that I thought you would like to meet Her Grace since you were so late coming in this morning."

"For the love of all that is holy, Frank! What are you trying to say?"

Frank muttered, "Subtlety on you. What I am trying to say is that Her Grace will spend the afternoon with the ladies of the court." He lifted his eyebrows. When Flame didn't speak, he tried again. "One particular lady of the court I assume is responsible for your early-morning walk of shame?"

Flame felt the blood drain from his face. After the reading with Lily, he terminated his casual relationship with Matilda. Unfortunately, she did not take it well. There was no doubt that she would use last night's folly to humiliate Aurelia in public.

"Frank, contact Colonel Brewer and get him to stall as long as possible!" Flaminius yelled as he bolted for the shower.

Marcus was going to shove his double-serrated hunting knife into Flaminius's stomach and rip him from stem to stern. Matilda marked Aurelia immediately and wasted no time spinning her web.

Marcus liked pussy as much as the next guy, but he'd need to be desperate to dip his wick in that pot of crazy. And he repeatedly shared this with Flaminius. Obviously, the dumb fuck didn't listen.

The first thing Aurelia noticed was that all the women wore traditional court attire like the queen. There were no knee-length dresses here. Sue warned her, but Aurelia would not squeeze herself into a corset no matter what she had promised Flame.

The second thing she noticed was the dynamic. On entering the crowded room, everybody turned to get a glimpse of their future queen and curtsied, except for the clique of women clustered front and center. They curtsied, but not as deep as the others.

Marcus stayed close, facilitating introductions as they slowly made their way around the room. They stopped at the massive sideboard to get tea when the queen bee made her move.

"Good morning, Your Grace. My name is Matilda." Carelessly waving her hand to point out her co-bees, she continued. "And these are my friends," she said, naming each one.

"Good morning. It's nice to meet you." Aurelia lied. Matilda's jet-black hair, pale gray eyes, and tall, hourglass figure were enough to stop traffic. But it was the seductive way she moved that knocked the package out of the park.

"Would you like to join us, Your Grace? We're sitting over there." She pointed to a few overstuffed chairs around a low, gold-leaf table.

"That's very kind, but I should mingle." Marcus put pressure on Aurelia's lower back to move her away, but the witch would not give up that easily.

"How are you, Colonel Brewer?"

Fighting for control, he barked, "Fine."

"Really? I would've thought you'd be worse for wear today."

Marcus moved to block Aurelia from her view. "Why would I feel worse for wear?"

She put a delicate, pale-skinned hand on her throat innocently, drawing attention to her low-cut gown and large breasts. "Well, I just thought . . ." She shyly batted her lashes, then continued, "You know, since after he drank with you, he came to me."

When Marcus groaned, Aurelia's back stiffened. "Who came to you?"

"Don't listen to her, Your Grace. She likes to make trouble where none exists."

Matilda ignored Marcus's comment. "Well, Your Grace, far be it from me to say."

Taking a step forward, Marcus growled. "Shut up, Matilda."

The bitch feigned fear, stepping back, but didn't stop sharing. "Colonel, don't you think it's better if she knows what she can expect from the beginning? Flaminius will not stop coming to my bed. Last night is proof of that."

Leaning to look around Marcus, Matilda added, "I don't say this to hurt you, Your Grace, but I don't believe in lying, and you must appreciate the position I'm in."

Ears ringing, palms sweating, Aurelia put her hand on Marcus's back to stabilize her swaying body. Forcing breath through her vocal cords, she asked, "The position you're in?"

In a show of feigned fragility, Matilda hugged her waist, stuttering, "Y-yes, Your Grace. I'm afraid my relationship with Flaminius will cause you to retaliate and harm my family's status at court."

In one fell swoop, she revealed her relationship with Flaminius, humiliated Aurelia, and made it impossible for her to strike back because of the public fashion in which she did it. Before Marcus could extract Aurelia from the viper's grip, a footman flamboyantly announced the arrival of the very man Marcus intended to disembowel.

Flaminius pushed past the irritating footman into the receiving room and stopped dead. Frank couldn't reach Marcus on his cell, so Flaminius ran full-tilt all the way. Desperately trying to catch his breath, he noticed Marcus's protective stance in front of his match, looked at Matilda, then back at Aurelia's pale face, and knew he was too late. He only hoped to remove his future bride from the room and commence damage control. Looking back at Matilda's sneering face, he decided these measures would include her permanent removal from the palace.

His sudden entrance shocked the room's occupants enough that they only now dipped into hesitant curtsies. Moving down the short staircase to his left, Flaminius forced himself to saunter through the crowd of women, never taking his eyes off Aurelia. Faint murmurs drifted to his ears, but he ignored them. When he, at last, stood in front of the group, he purposely moved to stand next to Marcus, effectively blocking Matilda's view of Aurelia. He said in a barely restrained voice, "I believe it would be in your best interest if you and your posse removed yourselves now."

Matilda didn't curtsy in an act of open defiance. Instead, she moved into his space to create the illusion that they shared an intimacy they didn't. "Please, Flaminius, try to understand. I couldn't lie about us. She needs to know how things are so she can acclimatize. Anything less would be cruel."

"Enough!" His sudden booming voice ricocheted around the room, causing everyone to jump or cry out in surprise. "We," he motioned between them, "are nothing. Never were, never will be. I told you a million times we were fucking! That's it."

Aurelia gasped, and Matilda went rigid. The strangest look stole across her face before she schooled her features and continued, "If that is true, then why did you seek me out last night?"

"I didn't!" Flaminius shoved his hands through his hair in frustration. "I was drunk, and before you say another word, I warn you, Matilda. I will destroy you if you try to make more of this than it is. Now take your nest of vipers and get the fuck out of my sight!"

Finally getting a clue, she stepped back and nodded. Turning to her friends, she barked, "Let's go." With no hesitation, they followed her, casting disparaging looks in Aurelia's direction.

"Matilda!" he called as she mounted the stairs. She turned gracefully to look at him. "If I ever see you near my future queen again, I will take great pleasure in squeezing the life out of you myself." A collective gasp from the court ladies let him know that he effectively landed his humiliating blows. "And I will proposition the council to revoke your court privileges and your friends', so start packing."

For the first time, Matilda blanched. Flaminius didn't give one fuck. He needed to clarify that he wouldn't tolerate anyone disrespecting Aurelia. The massive doors clanged shut behind her and her posse before he turned to his future bride. "I suggest we retire to a more private place to talk." She turned on shaky legs and began winding her way through the room. Marcus pushed past them to help cut a path while Flaminius gently guided her with a hand on her lower back.

The walk to Aurelia's rooms was the longest fifteen minutes of Flaminius's life. Personally, he would have preferred to find the closest empty sitting room, office, or broom closet and get this over with. But if she felt more comfortable in familiar surroundings, then so be it. Finally, Marcus pushed the door open to her rooms and stepped aside for them to enter. Turning to his friend, Flaminius said, "I can take it from here, Marcus."

Marcus would not let it go that easily. Dropping his voice, he stuck his finger in Flaminius's face. "If that girl doesn't tear you a new asshole, I will."

He spun on his heel, took two steps, then turned back. "In fact, even if she does, I'm still going to use your guts for garters."

Flaminius sighed. "Yeah, you and everybody else once the court grapevine spreads the story, so take a number and get in line."

Marcus puffed out his chest. "Fuck that. I'm her bodyguard; I get first dibs." Then he stormed off.

Closing the door, Flaminius walked to the drinks cart and poured himself a whiskey. "Would you like a drink?" Aurelia shook her head and moved to stand behind the couch, watching him with cautious eyes. Taking a healthy gulp, he asked, "Aren't you going to say something?"

Aurelia moved around the couch and gingerly sat on the edge like a terrified, wounded sparrow, afraid the neighborhood cat was lurking nearby.

At first, she felt emotionally numb listening to Matilda spew her venom, and then when Flame appeared, relieved because she was sure he would deny Matilda's allegations. When he didn't, she got angry; so angry, she thought her skin would blister from the intensity of it, only to have him defend her in the most brutal, glorious fashion that left her utterly confused.

"Do you really have nothing to say? I would've thought you'd be bellowing the roof down by now," he said in a barely concealed sarcastic tone.

Okay, that was uncalled for; she wasn't the one who slept with someone other than their intended. But she refused to fall back into her usual fiery, reactionary ways. Despite what he might think, she had been listening when he reprimanded her. Finally, she said, "I paid attention in the carriage."

Flaminius frowned. "I don't understand."

"When you gave me the lessons about being a queen, I listened, and you were right. What I want is irrelevant. Even though I could've denied your request for consummation, I didn't. I put these proceedings into action as much as you, and like it or not, we're stuck."

Flaminius was flabbergasted. Wasn't she even a little jealous? Okay, what the fuck? Why did he care if she was jealous or not?

"I didn't sleep with her last night. Well, I did, but I didn't have sex with her. At least I don't think I did."

He was perversely pleased to see a flicker of pain flash in her eyes. "I was very drunk, and I remember little, but I know the signs to look for, and none of them were there this morning. So, unless I took a shower I don't remember during the night, I can say with ninety-nine percent certainty that I didn't have sex with her."

Breathing through the pain, she replied, "It doesn't matter. We have to think about our people, and we have a wedding in ten days."

Flaminius found himself unjustifiably angry. Surely, he should be happy that she wasn't ranting, but calm and regal instead. Isn't that what he wanted in a wife?

"Perhaps we should discuss how we intend to move forward?" Flaminius offered.

Shifting deeper into the couch, Aurelia said, "Okay, it sounds reasonable to clear the air before we take our marriage vows."

"What do you expect from our life together, Aurelia?"

"I expect to marry you, produce an heir and a spare, and try to be the best mother and queen possible; hopefully, in there somewhere, I will find some happiness."

"What about love and passion? You don't strike me as someone who can live without that."

Stubbornly fighting back her tears, she replied, "No offense, Flaminius, but you don't know me, so you can't know what I can or can't live without."

"Wouldn't you like to change that? If you let me, I could get to know you."

"I wanted that until this afternoon. Now I think it best we face reality."

"Reality? What reality?"

Clearing her throat, she tried not to sound desperate. "Please, Flaminius, let's not pretend. Everybody knows your reputation, and even though I am grateful for your swift defense of me this afternoon, your actions last night made it clear that it would be foolish to ask you for fidelity."

"No offense, Aurelia, but you don't know me well enough to say what I could or could not be asked to do."

"Touché."

They sat in silence for a while. Flaminius needed time to come up with a solution.

The truth was, he was terrified of falling ass-over-teakettle in love with her, only to end up dancing around his wife for fear of losing her affection.

It was time for a different tactic. "How about we agree to spend some time together over the next ten days and see how things develop naturally?"

She shrugged. "Wasn't me who spent the last four days running around jumping in and out of beds that he had no business jumping into in the first place."

He let her have that dig since he deserved it. "What do we have to lose? At worst, we could be friends; at best, we fall in love."

No way in hell was she opening up enough to fall in love with him. "Okay, Flaminius, it would be nice to be friends if we can manage it."

He would never admit it, but he felt giddy with relief. "How about we go riding tomorrow so I can show you the palace grounds, and maybe we can have a picnic since the weather is so nice?"

"Okay, what time?"

"Let's get an early start. Seven?"

"Seven."

He had no clue why he threw the L-word in there. All he wanted was a working relationship with her to rule together in peace and not fuck up any children they may have. Despite this, he felt deflated when Aurelia responded rationally to his transgression instead of being shattered. Damn, he was confused. How could he want her to be calm but maintain her fire at the same time?

Reluctantly, he realized he might not want to fall in love with her, but he needed her to love him in the worst way and didn't care how messed up that was.

Chapter Twelve -
The Game's Afoot!

Over the next few days, Flaminius vacillated between elation and despair until he felt unhinged.

The morning of the ride dawned bright and warm, which thrilled Flaminius since the weather was the only factor he had no control over. His delight rapidly faded to anguish when he saw how beautiful Aurelia looked, and he couldn't afford to seduce her. She would expect that, and he wanted her on the back foot.

It was all part of his new plan to make her fall in love with him. He sat up till the early hours of the morning, formulating his strategy. It was simple; he would woo her until she was gagging for him to fuck her. He didn't fully understand why he wanted this, but if he had to guess, it would be because it would be easier to manage her.

The only problem was the match hormones gushing through their systems. Marcus offered to help; he could get his hands on a nifty invention in the form of an injection to suppress the match hormones' effect on him. Marcus said it wouldn't eradicate the desire to procreate entirely, but it would make it possible to resist the urge. Without it, he would continuously wrestle a raging hard-on and the desire to plant his dick into her no matter the consequences. He was tempted, but it seemed weak somehow.

For her part, Aurelia decided she would show the lout what he'd thrown away. She might not vent her frustration by screaming and shouting, but she could make him crazy for her. Source knows he was driving her nuts.

In keeping with her plan, she carefully chose her riding outfit. Too revealing, and he would assume he could toy with her; too conservative, he'd lose interest.

In the end, she chose a simple, loose-fitting, slightly see-through white long-sleeved shirt with lots of tiny mother-of-pearl buttons down the front. She rolled the sleeves to just below her elbows, tucked the shirt into a pair of bottom-hugging tan riding pants, and pulled on her knee-high leather riding boots. Pinning her hair in a low knot at the nape would draw attention to the graceful curve of her shoulders and keep the curls out of her way when she rode. A short, delicate gold chain with a small hummingbird pendant hung in the hollow of her throat finished her carefully chosen outfit.

She had just spritzed some perfume when he knocked. Taking one last look in the mirror, she wished she could do something about the dark rings under her eyes from lack of sleep. Then, taking a deep breath, she opened the door.

The look of approval in his eyes had her questioning the sanity of her strategy. She was far from immune to him. Not that she'd never received attention from men; she was pretty, but she wasn't the siren Lady Matilda was. If a woman like that couldn't hold his attention, then Aurelia had no chance.

Finding her voice, she said, "Shall we?"

Flaminius sent servants ahead to set up an elaborate picnic complete with giant stuffed cushions, thick blankets, and colorful umbrellas to protect them from the sun and offer a little privacy.

He'd chosen a spot approximately an hour into their ride, with a backdrop of rolling fields of wildflowers and a gentle babbling stream. He considered everything except that Aurelia would refuse to be wooed.

She should've refused to come on this ridiculous outing. The man behaved as if he were reading from a script, ticking off items on an extensive list meant to impress a woman.

"Do you enjoy riding?" When Aurelia didn't answer, he tried something else. "Have you decided if you're going to complete your studies?" She shrugged her shoulder. "Well, if you ask me, it would be a shame for that brain of yours to go to waste."

She smirked.

"What? I think you're smart. And beautiful. A rare combination."

"Thank you," she answered curtly.

No matter what he tried, she refused to engage with him, so he settled for a monologue about the places they passed.

Finally, they arrived, and three servants waited for them to settle down on the soft blankets before offering cold rose-scented water to wash their hands and damp rolled-up linen towels to wipe their faces.

Aurelia was hungry, and she grudgingly admitted that the food looked amazing. Flaminius dismissed the staff and handed her a plate. "I hope you don't mind; I called your mother to find out what your favorite foods are."

She appreciated his effort but would rather eat cow ass than admit it. Smiling sweetly, she said, "I'm surprised you had the time between women to do anything besides rest."

Flaminius sighed. "There weren't any women. I thought we covered this."

Chewing on the plump strawberry, she said, "We have. That doesn't mean I've forgotten. Do you expect me to believe you didn't sleep with her?"

"I may be a lot of things, but I am not a liar. I haven't slept with her or any other woman since I met you."

"Pfft. You realize you met me like three seconds ago, right?"

Shifting his weight so he could lean into her, he replied, "Aurelia, I am trying. All this was my idea, and it's supposed to help us get to know each other."

She lifted her eyebrows in fake surprise. "Really? Is that what this is? Funny, because it feels like an attempt to get into my pants."

"Why would you think that? No offense, but by your admission, you have little dating experience, so how would you know?"

"That's not what I said. I said I hadn't had sex. I said nothing about dating or other things people can do without having sex. I might not be your type, but some men find me attractive, so I recognize when a man is trying to woo me."

Flaminius didn't like her talking about doing anything with other men. "Let's get one thing straight. I find you attractive. This outing was an honest attempt at friendship."

"Oh, please. There was not one honest thing about any of this. You want to know how I know?"

With a dismissive wave of his hand, Flaminius said, "Oh, please tell."

She ignored his sarcastic remark. "I know because you haven't asked me one sincere question about myself this whole time. And you've been trying to soften me up with false flattery and canned questions."

He felt heat crawl up his neck. That was precisely what he'd been doing. Was his tactic that see-through?

Downing his glass of lemonade, wishing it were whiskey instead, he answered, lying through his teeth, "I wasn't consciously trying to do that."

"No, I guess it's second nature for a playboy like you."

He shut up. They ate in silence while he thought of what she'd said. To his embarrassment, he realized that he'd planned this whole date like he would a military campaign. But this enemy was far too intuitive to fall for it. He'd never put this much effort into a woman before, but the basics were the same. Wine, dine, flatter, bed, escape—not exactly original.

He had to retreat and re-strategize. What would he want her to ask him? What would make him feel she was genuinely interested in getting to know him? Flying by the seat of his pants, he turned to her. "You're right."

"About what?"

"I've never had the slightest inkling to have a platonic relationship with a woman. I'm completely out of my depth, and I will need help to navigate these waters. Will you help me be your friend?"

Shit balls! Did he have to be so sweet?

Putting down her apple, she closed her eyes and sighed. "How can I say no to you when you ask so nicely?"

He smiled at her in that wicked way that made her insides feel like she'd swallowed a bag of eels.

"You could start by asking about my childhood."

So he did. For hours they sat on the soft blankets while he learned more about Aurelia's life. By the time they returned, it was almost dark, and he felt a sense of hope that they could at least move forward amicably and with respect. Perhaps trust would develop in time, but he wasn't holding his breath for that.

Aurelia didn't know how much more she could take. It was barely dawn, and she'd already been up for hours. The reason for her puffy eyes and foggy brain was that darn Flaminius.

He'd been true to his word after their first outing and done away with the transparent attempt to woo her. Instead, he set about treating her like a friend, and it pissed her off. He introduced her to his friends, took her to his favorite watering hole—The Wild Boar, not original but a fabulous place—and talked about anything and everything except them as a couple.

At first, she enjoyed it and felt they were making progress, but she noticed they were seldom alone. The only thing worse than spending time with Flame was never spending time alone with him. Ugh, that made her such a weakling.

Her thoughts went back to last night when he walked her home from The Wild Boar. The pub wasn't far from the palace, and she thought she could handle a few minutes alone with him, but she was a little drunk and not able to wrap herself in her protective cocoon as usual.

"Oh, look! It's a full moon!" Aurelia said when they stepped out of the pub. Flame looked up and nodded. "You've been very quiet tonight."

Flaminius stuck his hands in his pockets while they strolled back. "Just tired."

Emboldened by the three beers she had, Aurelia slipped her arm through his. "I wanted to thank you for the last few days. They've been lovely."

"Mmm."

The timbre of his voice caused her temperature to rise, as it always did around him. When she tried to pull her arm away, he stopped her. "I'm sorry. I don't mean to be short with you. The moon is stunning, just like you."

"I thought we were doing away with empty platitudes." She laughed.

For a while, the only sound was their feet crunching the gravel on the garden path. "I mean it, Aurelia. I think you're lovely."

The sincerity in his voice caused her body to hum like a million bees had taken up residence under her skin. "Thank you." She barely whispered through her panting. Flame stopped walking and turned toward her. Slowly, as if he was trying very hard not to, he lifted his hand and stroked his finger along her jaw.

"Flame," she breathed.

"Aurelia, I want to kiss you." Without waiting for permission, not that she would stop him, he gently lowered his mouth to hers. The second their lips met, her nipples puckered into tight buds. Meeting no resistance, he slipped his tongue into her mouth. Suddenly, the tentative hold they had on their control snapped. Before she knew what was happening, Flame lifted her, forcing her legs around his waist, and walked to the pavilion a few yards from the path. He didn't get much further than the entrance before laying her on the ground.

Things became frantic—a tangle of lips, arms, and legs. Lost in a haze of passion, she didn't hear the drunk giggles of a woman or the deep male voice of her lover when they, too, stumbled into the gazebo.

"Oh! Sorry. I didn't realize someone else was already here," the man mumbled before dragging his giggling girlfriend away. Thankfully, they hadn't recognized Flaminius and Aurelia.

Unfortunately, the intrusion of the other couple killed the mood. Flaminius jumped off her like a cat from a cucumber before straightening his clothes and walking her home. Her clitoris and vagina were still so engorged that she could barely walk without fear the vibration would set off an orgasm.

Unsurprisingly, Aurelia was consumed with thoughts of him all night and had yet to read the hefty volume Sue left about the wedding protocols. In addition, Aurelia had to spend almost all day in wedding rehearsals with Flame to add fuel to the fire.

Flaminius didn't seem to suffer the same discomfort. It was so easy for him to break away from her last night and pretend nothing happened.

The only good thing about today was that her parents would arrive in an hour.

"Your Grace, did you hear me?"

Aurelia put her fork down and looked at Sue blankly. "What did you say?"

"I said that you may want to stop pushing your food around your plate and eat something."

"I can't seem to find my appetite lately."

Sue put her diary on the table. "Your Grace—"

Aurelia waved her hand at Sue and rubbed her temples to stave off the building headache. "I really wish you would stop calling me that."

Sue smiled. "Very well. Aurelia, please eat something. If you lose weight and your wedding dress doesn't fit, the queen will, well, have a fit."

Aurelia couldn't help it; she burst out laughing. It felt so good to release the pent-up frustration.

Frank interrupted their laughter to announce Dr. and Mr. Sylas Stafford.

Aurelia jumped up, knocking her orange juice over in desperation to get to her mother. "Mom, you're early!" She threw her arms around Rosalind's' neck and burst into tears.

Holding her close and stroking her daughter's hair, Rosalind turned to her husband. "I told you we should've come sooner."

"Sweetheart, I wanted to give them time to settle." Sylas rubbed Aurelia's back to comfort her, but it just made her sob more. He guided their little huddle to the sofa, all the while muttering comforting words.

Sue decided to give them some privacy, but the bride's father pointed his finger at her and growled, "You! Start talking. Why is my daughter so upset?"

"Don't be mad at her, Daddy," Aurelia said while trying to control her sobs. "She and Marcus are the only friends I have in this miserable place."

Sylas wasn't sure who was responsible for his little girl's misery, but he was going to make them pay.

Flaminius paced the length of his sitting room, trying to quell the army of ants eating his flesh. Where the hell was Marcus with that medication? Yes, he knew it made him a coward, but to hell with it. He couldn't do it anymore! Last night was worse than the two days of torture he endured in captivity during the war. Never had anyone been able to tie him up in knots like Aurelia, and he couldn't allow her to lead him around by his cock. Marcus would have to tie him up and throw him in the dungeons if Flame didn't take the suppressant.

"Sire."

Flaminius turned to his butler. "Yes, Frank."

"Your future in-laws have arrived."

Oh shit! He couldn't leave this room without the hormone suppressant. He'd already jerked off twice, and it wasn't even eight o'clock. If he went anywhere near Aurelia like this, he'd find the closest, softest, flattest surface and fuck her until she passed out from exhaustion. Parents be damned.

Frank rubbed his nose. "If I might be so bold as to offer a suggestion, Sire?"

Turning his back so Frank wouldn't see him adjust his junk, he grunted.

"Her Grace seems out of sorts this morning, and her father is not happy about his daughter's melancholy state. Perhaps it would be prudent to alleviate his worries at once."

Flaminius loved Frank, but sometimes he wanted to strangle the man. "I will, Frank, but first, I have to wait for Marcus. He has something I need."

Pulling a vial out of his pocket, Frank casually asked, "Would this be what you require, Sire?"

Flaminius leaped over the coffee table and snatched the hormone suppressant out of his butler's hand. Rushing to his room, he yanked open the draw of his bedside table, strewing the contents over the floor. Frank calmly removed the vial from Flame's hand and loaded a syringe that he found in the mess on the floor. Flame snatched the syringe from Frank and plunged the needle into his thigh. Sweet numbness floated into his limbs, sweeping away all desperation.

Frank interrupted his thoughts. "I don't wish to distress you further, Sire, but you have an angry father-in-law waiting to—"

"Rip me a new one?" Flame interrupted.

"Indeed, Sire."

Flaminius smiled. Then he shored up his courage and went to face his pissed-off father-in-law.

Chapter Thirteen -
Here Comes The Bride—Wink!

Rosalind accepted the box of tissues from Sue and smiled. "Thank you. I'm Rosalind, Aurelia's mother."

"Pleased to meet you." Looking at the angry man sitting next to them, Sue said, "You must be Mr. Stafford." He nodded and offered his large hand. She shook it, noting how he consciously kept his grip gentle.

"Please call me Sylas."

"I'm Sue, Her Grace's private secretary."

Sylas pinched the top of his nose. "I'd like to know who upset Aurelia."

Aurelia dragged her head from the crook of her mother's neck. "Daddy, please don't go all special forces on them." She ripped a few more tissues from the box and wiped her nose. "I'm just stressed. I didn't think it would be this tough."

"What do you mean, sweetie?" Rosalind asked, "Is it just in general, or are you finding a specific thing that bothers you?"

Aurelia couldn't tell her mother the whole truth because she didn't want to paint Flame in a poor light. For reasons she couldn't fathom, it felt disloyal. Shrugging her shoulders, she kept her eyes on her lap, twisting the tissues into a tight ball, and replied, "Where do I begin? I mean, just the hullabaloo over the wedding dress is enough to drive a saint to murder."

Rosalind folded her hands in her lap the way she did when she was listening. The familiarity of her mother's gesture made it easier for Aurelia to continue. "I understand the need for protocol, but, Mom, the queen has treated the making of this dress like going to war with a superior race. There are seventeen—I kid you not!—seventeen royal dressmakers working on just the wedding dress, not to mention the army of seamstresses creating 'a wardrobe suitable for a future queen.' My mother-in-law's words, not mine."

Sue added her support. "Your daughter flatly refused to allow the queen to instruct the dressmakers to create a wardrobe of traditional dresses. The look on the queen's face when she realized your daughter wouldn't budge was the highlight of my career!" Sue finished, slapping her hands on her thighs and laughing.

Sylas scowled. "That woman doesn't know who she's dealing with if she thinks any of us will bow to her heavy-handed ways."

Rosalind nodded. "We're here now, and we've got your back."

Aurelia blew out a breath and collapsed against her father's side. For the first time since she arrived at the castle, she felt calm. Then Flaminius arrived, shattering her short-lived peace.

Greeting the in-laws was not the ordeal he thought it would be, mainly because they weren't full of self-importance, like his mother.

Aurelia wasn't in her sitting room when he arrived, which helped, and according to her mother, she was making herself presentable. The woman could wear a sack and still look beautiful because every man he introduced her to looked at her as if she were his favorite dessert.

Flaminius was so busy gathering his strength before facing Aurelia that he didn't immediately notice Sylas hadn't said a word. The awkward silence turned suffocatingly menacing when Flaminius looked at his future father-in-law and saw the man scowling at him. Fortunately, Aurelia joined them, breaking the standoff. But it was jumping from the frying pan into the fire for Flaminius. She was absolutely breathtaking in a simple sleeveless purple dress that stopped just shy of her knees. A slim black belt accentuated her waist, and the plunging V-neck drew his eye to her boobs. Flaminius thanked his lucky stars that he had taken the hormone suppressant because he was certain Sylas would do more than scowl at him if Flaminius mauled his daughter in front of everybody.

Marcus cleared his throat, startling Flaminius. "Sire, the king and queen are on their way to the grand ballroom. ETA twelve minutes."

Flaminius tore his eyes from Aurelia. He had no idea how much time had passed or when Sue and Marcus had appeared. For all he knew, they could've been there all along.

Faking a smile, he turned to his in-laws. "If you follow Sue, she will take you to the ballroom."

As everybody moved to the door, Flaminius asked Marcus to hang back.

Marcus watched his friend's lingering gaze follow Aurelia until she disappeared around the corner. "What do you want to speak to me about, Flaminius?"

"Huh?"

Marcus smiled indulgently. "You said you needed to speak to me."

Shaking his head, Flaminius followed his future wife down the corridor. "I didn't. I just needed some time to calm down."

"Calm down? Why? Didn't you get the suppressant I left with Frank?"

Flaminius scratched his chin in agitation. "I did."

"Isn't it working?"

He rolled his shoulders. "It's working fine. I just needed to take a breath before spending time with my mother." He lied.

"Yes, I imagine she is going to be more of a handful, especially now that Aurelia's parents have arrived. We all know how she hates sharing the spotlight."

Huh. Flaminius hadn't even thought of that. His mother would be a total bitch to Sylas and Rosalind, which didn't concern him too much because he knew they could handle her, but Flaminius didn't want to see what would happen if the queen treated Aurelia as she usually did. Sylas would lose his shit.

Glancing at Marcus, he sighed and picked up his pace.

As expected, his mother was determined to laud her superiority over her future in-laws by insisting on an entire royal entourage. His father was thankfully more subdued, and unlike his mother, brought his manners. Romulus walked up to Sylas and gave him a bear hug. "Welcome, Sylas. It's been too long."

Sylas hugged him back without reserve and whispered, "Thank you, Rom. It has indeed."

Flaminius forgot they knew each other. As general of the RPU during the war, Flaminius concerned himself with defending the capital city, castle, and royal house. Not that he and his men didn't see their fair share of action; it was the opposite. The capital city was a favorite target of the Oradagra precisely because the royal family lived there. However, Flaminius knew that there were men who fought battles far more critical than he ever did, and Sylas and his father were among those soldiers.

"I can't tell you how pleased I am that Source chose your daughter to join our bloodlines." Sylas dipped his head in acknowledgment. Then his father took Rosalind's hand and kissed it. "And you, Lady Rosalind, welcome to our home. I hope you treat it as your own."

So far, so good. Next, the queen stepped forward. Everybody held their breath. Looking down her perfect nose, she said, "Yes. Welcome, Lady Rosalind." She said nothing to either Sylas or Aurelia, but she nodded her head in their general direction, making the pounds of gold jewelry hanging from every available appendage on her body jingle loudly.

"Good morning, Sire."

Flaminius froze. He prayed he was wrong, and the voice didn't belong to Lady Matilda. Fuckballs. He'd forgotten to take care of the bitch.

When she saw she'd caught Flaminius's attention, Matilda trailed her hand down her neck to rest enticingly on the globe of her pert breast before she curtsied.

Aurelia was livid that the queen brought Flaminius's lover to her wedding rehearsal and hurt that he had lied to her again. He never intended to remove the bitch from the castle. How could she fall for his charade? She was so fucking fogged up with match hormones she couldn't even see a ploy when it slapped her in the face.

She glared at Flaminius. Not that it did her much good. What she really wanted to do was leave the fucking palace and go home, but she couldn't because she owed it to the people of Arkhnuet to at least secure the line of

HERE COMES THE BRIDE—WINK!

succession. Once she'd done that, she was smoke, gone, out of here! Matilda sauntered past her, smirking knowingly.

Luckily for Flaminius, Mother Guardian and Lily arrived at that moment to walk them through the procedure for the wedding ceremony.

Clapping her hands together, Mother Guardian giggled excitedly. "If I could get the parents of the happy couple to stand on the dais. That's right. No, no, I need the parents of the bride to stand on the left. Perfect."

Practically skipping with joy, she hopped off the dais, grabbed Flaminius's hand, and joined it with Aurelia's. "Now, you two lovebirds will enter from the back and walk down the center aisle. So, off you go."

Following her instructions, they shuffled to the back of the room. As soon as Mother Guardian turned her back, Aurelia pulled her hand away and stubbornly averted her eyes to discourage conversation. But eventually, Aurelia's temper got the better of her. "I see your girlfriend is still here. If this king gig doesn't work out for you, consider a career in acting."

Flaminius sighed. "It wasn't a lie. With everything that's going on, I forgot to take care of the problem."

Aurelia snorted. "All that talk about being friends. You learned nothing about me, did you? Let me give you a word of advice for the future: I prefer honesty." In a dejected voice, she continued, "And I stupidly thought after the other night in the pavilion—" she broke off.

Flaminius answered through clenched teeth, "I am honest. And the other night was a mistake."

His words felt like a punch in the gut. Rubbing his hand over his face, Flaminius tried to minimize the damage he'd done, "Look, I think we're both stressed and saying things we don't mean."

"No, I think you meant exactly what you said, and it's okay. I wanted honesty, and that's what I got. Fortunately, we don't have to like each other to make sure we do our duty."

"Listen, Aurelia. I don't want that. I want a proper marriage."

She held her hand up. "You can't make your heart feel something it doesn't, but I don't want to spend the rest of our lives fighting."

Flaminius was sure he heard her voice break, and she tried to wipe away a tear without his seeing. He reached for her hand, but Mother Guardian interrupted them.

"Right, you two. As you know, you will already be legally married, so this part of the ceremony is for those present to witness that you freely bind yourselves to each other."

Aurelia wasn't listening. She was barely breathing. It was the only way she could get through the rest of the morning.

Finally, Mother Guardian announced the rehearsal's end, and Aurelia made a lame excuse to her family and bolted for the nearest exit. Running through the complicated maze of corridors, Aurelia frantically yanked at every door handle until she found one unlocked that led to an empty garden. Blindly following a winding path, she came upon a massive weeping willow and, pushing through the thick curtain of branches, collapsed on the grass. For the next few minutes, she concentrated on breathing deeply, hoping it would stop her from crying. It didn't work.

Flaminius watched Aurelia leave as if her ass were on fire. He wanted to go after her, but he had to make sure that Matilda got the fuck out of the castle.

He waited until they were alone before he pounced. "Mother, I will petition the council to revoke Lady Matilda's court privileges immediately, and if you ever embarrass Aurelia like that again, I will ban you from my wedding."

His mother gasped, but before she could get a word in, he turned to his father. "I appreciate your warm welcome to my in-laws, but I ask that you control your wife in the future. I've had enough of this bullshit." He stomped off to find Aurelia. He wasn't sure about her, but she didn't deserve to be mistreated by his mother or anyone else.

It took him half an hour, but he eventually found her. She looked so peaceful. Perhaps he shouldn't disturb her. A little voice in the back of his head whispered, "Coward."

As if she could hear his thoughts, she sat up and looked at him. He pushed his way through the branches and sat close to her. She moved to put more space between them, but the action only worsened his longing for her, alerting him that the suppressant was wearing off.

Resting his arms on his bent knees, he chanced a look and saw that she'd been crying. "Aurelia, I swear, Matilda means nothing to me. She was a lover on and off for a while, but I harbored no love for her."

Aurelia said nothing. She just sat, staring at the grass.

Crossing his legs, he turned to face her. "I want to have a genuine marriage filled with love and happiness, but—"

"But what?"

Fuck, she was so beautiful. Should he listen to Marcus and give her the benefit of the doubt?

"I've lived my whole life with a woman who has a volatile temper that left a path of destruction a mile wide. I will not spend hundreds of years being someone's nursemaid. I want a partner, not a child I have to babysit for fear of what or who she might destroy or offend."

It felt good to tell her the truth.

"I assume you're speaking about your mother?"

He nodded.

"I can see why you would be reluctant to marry someone like her. Your father seems happy enough, but you are not your father."

"No, I'm not, although some people would say the apple doesn't fall far from the tree."

"Well, then some people would be wrong. Anyone can see that you are far less subservient than him and much more self-aware."

No one ever called his father subservient. It was such a ludicrous thought he laughed. "My father is not subservient. He's a control freak."

"Exactly my point. If somebody is confident in his abilities, he doesn't feel the need to control every detail. Individuals like that trust themselves to put the right people in positions of power, and then they trust those people to do the right thing."

She saw he wasn't convinced. "If your father is such an alpha male, then why does he bow to your mother's tantrums?" Flaminius shrugged. "What about the Oradagra? Why did he give in to them? If he hadn't, he could've prevented the war. I'm sure if you gave it some thought, you could come up with a hundred other examples to prove my point. Your father would rather give in to pressure to make his life easier than do the right thing."

He felt he should defend his father, but she was right. Hadn't he and Marcus said the same thing about Romulus in private? Hadn't they defied his orders many times because they knew the orders would cause more harm than good?

His silence was telling. Smiling at him, Aurelia said, "That's what I thought."

He reached for her hand. To his surprise, Aurelia was shaking, and she tried to pull away. Then Flaminius noticed dark rings under her eyes. "Aurelia, what's wrong? Are you feeling ill?"

She pulled harder, but he refused to let go. "Aurelia, tell me what's wrong," he demanded in a slightly panicked voice.

She dropped her eyes. "I can't!"

"Why?"

Becoming more exasperated, she said, "Because! It's embarrassing."

Furrowing his brow in confusion, he asked, "What's embarrassing?"

"My reaction to you because of the match hormones!"

He couldn't take his eyes off her face, flushed with shame, but neither could he speak.

"You're completely unaffected while I can barely keep my body from spontaneously combusting."

Oh, if she only knew what a coward he was. He expected her to be above reproach while he hid behind hormone suppressants and self-righteousness.

Finally ripping her hand out of his grip, she shot up and ran. It was the worst thing she could've done. His alpha instincts kicked in, forcing him to give chase. He caught her around her middle before she'd taken three steps. Picking her up, he carried her, kicking and scratching, back under the tree.

Out of breath and more than a little aroused, he laid her down as gently as he could and linked their hands, pushing them above her head. She didn't stop struggling, so he growled into her ear, "Calm down so I can explain."

Predictably, she squirmed even harder. Changing tack, Flame drew her earlobe between his teeth and nipped it gently.

She froze.

"You want to know why I'm so unaffected by you? You want to know why I'm able to be within fifty feet of you without going out of my mind?"

She shook her head. "No, I want you to get off me!"

HERE COMES THE BRIDE—WINK!

Ignoring her, he barreled on. "Because I've been injecting myself with a hormone suppressant since the day after the gazebo incident." Dropping his forehead to hers, he continued, "I've been so afraid and confused by my feelings for you that I used medication to numb myself."

He pressed his erection between her legs. "Feel that? That's me on a hormone suppressant. That's how in control I am. Fuck Aurelia, if I weren't on the drug, I would fuck you until you passed out. I would bury myself so deep you would never forget the feel of my cock."

Holy shit! His dirty talk was going to make her come. He wouldn't even have to touch her. She writhed under him, trying to get closer, her dress riding up her hips. "Do it. Bury yourself in me. Fuck me until I can't breathe."

Flaminius groaned. "Baby, don't say shit like that. We can't."

"Why? I want you; you want me." To make her point, she opened her legs a little more and lifted her hips to cradle his cock against her pussy.

"Honey, there is no way I am going to take your virginity on the hard ground under a tree."

"Please." She keened. "I can't wait."

Releasing her hands, he took her face in his palms. "Fuck! How am I supposed to say no to you?"

"You're not. You should give me what I ask for." Shaking her head vigorously, she corrected, "No, beg for."

Breathing deeply, he replied, "No, but that doesn't mean I can't make you feel good. I can make you come. Relieve some of the pressure. Will you let me do that, Aurelia?"

She nodded. "Yes. Anything."

Dropping his mouth to hers, he forced his tongue past her teeth, and they both groaned with relief. Clawing his hands down her body, he fumbled for a way into her dress but came up empty. Changing course, he broke their kiss and moved down until he was level with her pelvis. Hurriedly pushing her dress over her hips, he grasped the side of her black lace panties and ripped the gusset. The smell of her arousal excited him. Forgoing preamble, he plunged his tongue into her and sucked on her clit. She cried out his name as she came into his mouth, hot, wet, and wild. It was fucking perfect.

Aurelia thought she'd died and gone to Source. She had her fingers so tightly twisted in his hair; she must be hurting him, but he didn't seem to notice. "Flame, please?" She didn't know what she was asking him for—pulling him up, she kissed him, desperate to taste her essence on his mouth while she fumbled with his trouser button, finally getting it open enough to plunge her hand in and pump his cock, making him gasp.

"Baby, you don't have to."

"I want to. Please let me?"

He groaned into her mouth, then rolled, so she sat astride him. Loosening his pants, she pulled them down just enough for his cock to spring free. "Holy moly, Flame, you're beautiful."

Tugging the scraps of lace dangling between her legs aside, Aurelia opened her wet pussy lips over the base of Flame's shaft and slid her hips up and down his cock. "Holy shit, that feels good," he hissed.

She placed her hands on his chest and set a steady rhythm. "Yeah, baby. That's fucking perfect."

She occasionally tried to slip him inside, but he stopped her every time. The closer she got, the harder she ground down on him. Flame asked through a groan, "I'm close, baby, are you?"

She shattered, soaking the shaft of his cock. Through her toe-curling orgasm, she heard Flame say, "Thank fuck," before he spurted thick, pearly cum onto his exposed stomach in sticky waves. The intensity of his orgasm forced him to curl up into a seated position to embrace her.

Flame rocked her until they both regained their equilibrium before he dared to speak. "Are you okay?"

She shuddered in his arms, and when he looked down, he saw she was laughing. "What's so funny, sweetheart?"

Struggling to control her giggle, she said, "If that's you on a hormone suppressant, I can't wait for it to wear off."

Flame wasn't sure how long they sat under that tree, laughing their asses off. He was going to close this garden off to the public so they could come back here all the time. He would rename it 'Aurelia's garden' and have the palace servants bring a bed out and set it up under the tree.

HERE COMES THE BRIDE—WINK!

Marcus searched for well over an hour before he found Aurelia and Flaminius. Technically, he was only looking for Aurelia since she was in his charge. Finding Flaminius was never part of the plan, but how was he to know they were together?

It was the sound of her voice that gave away her location, and curious to see who she was speaking to, he opened the doors that led to the garden. It was very fortunate they were way too focused on each other to notice him because if his friend ever knew that Marcus had seen Flaminius go down on the future queen, he was pretty sure Flaminius would kill him.

Beating a hasty retreat, Marcus pulled the heavy curtains closed over the glass doors and walked far enough down the corridor so that he couldn't hear them anymore. Then he leaned against the wall, crossed his arms over his chest, and made sure nobody intruded on his friends.

Chapter Fourteen - Here Comes The Bride. For Real

While rushing to have breakfast with Aurelia in her apartment, Flame hoped that his future in-laws would bugger off long enough for them to have some alone time. After their interlude under the willow tree, Flame had refused to touch her again. Not because he didn't want to, but because he wanted to do right by her.

Aurelia tried to change his mind, but he was determined to wait until after the wedding. On more than one occasion, he told himself he was losing his ever-loving fucking mind for refusing her, but his conscience wouldn't allow it.

It thrilled him to see her eagerly awaiting his arrival at the door. "Baby, I've been waiting for you," she needlessly said.

He kissed her, and as always, even the simplest of touches turned heated in seconds. Sylas cleared his throat to remind them they had company. Flaminius broke their kiss. "Good morning, beautiful."

She smiled at him as if he hung the moon. "Morning, handsome. I'm glad you're here. We have to take care of some business."

Flame led her to the breakfast table. "Oh, what business would that be?" Seating himself next to her, he reached for the toast while Frank brought him his poached eggs.

"We have to read the wedding contracts, and frankly, I'd rather read the telephone book."

He chuckled. "We'll go through them together."

Aurelia fetched the paperwork, and they read the contracts. When boiled down to its essence, Aurelia had to provide the throne with an heir and a spare within ten years of marriage and bow and scrape to all royal protocol. They killed themselves, laughing at the transparent attempt by the queen to control them. They agreed that they would have a baby when they were ready.

As for Flame, he refused to change anything about his contract. Even the ludicrous parts that insisted he provide her with an astronomical amount of money if she decided by some insane turn of events to leave him. Of course, they also killed themselves laughing at her mother's attempt to interfere, but at least Flame found it sweet.

They just finished when the seamstresses arrived for the final fitting of her wedding dress. Of course, Sue insisted Flame leave because he couldn't see the dress before the Witness Ceremony. Aurelia couldn't give a rat's tail, but she was learning to pick her battles. Sylas decided that this was the perfect opportunity to get to know his son-in-law better, and they left to go riding.

The women sprang into action the moment the men left. They shooed Aurelia behind the screen to undress with strict instructions from Madam Suzette: "Take everything off but your panties."

Today's fitting didn't seem so bad with her mother by her side and the queen away, doing something queenly. From behind the screen, Aurelia heard the women gasp when Madame Suzette unveiled her creation. And with good reason. When Aurelia laid eyes on her wedding dress, she was speechless. Madame Suzette fidgeted with the hem, then stood and stepped back, nervously awaiting the bride's verdict. Aurelia pulled the cord of her gown tighter while she slowly walked around the mannequin displaying her dress. Then, in a reverent voice, she whispered, "I can't believe you made something so magnificent in such a short time."

Madame Suzette blushed and cleared her throat. "Thank you, Your Grace. I'm so pleased you like it."

Aurelia smiled. "Like it? I love it!" Turning to her mother, she exclaimed, "Mom, can you believe it?"

"Madame Suzette, I believe you deserve the highest accolades possible as you have accomplished a miracle."

"Miracle, Lady Rosalind?"

Rosalind put her arm around Aurelia. "You've made my daughter like a dress—a feat I have yet to achieve!"

"Well, I am thrilled that Her Grace has finally joined the rest of the female population in her adoration of my creations."

"Okay, everyone, let's not push too hard. I said I liked this dress, not all dresses, and if you don't mind, I would like to try it on." Stepping onto the small, raised platform, Aurelia watched in the mirror as the seamstresses dressed her in undergarments, starting with the plain white chemise. It was incredibly soft, made from silk, lightweight, and breathable so she wouldn't be uncomfortable in the summer heat. Madame Suzette allowed her to forgo the silk stockings and ribbon garters, even though they were part of the traditional dress if she promised not to tell the queen. The rubescent, short corset was a must, however, and Aurelia found it surprisingly comfortable.

Rosalind helped her into the crinoline cage made with stiffened rope so she could sit comfortably. Next came the red petticoat to cover the cage and add support for the underskirt. Madame Suzette refused to allow anyone besides herself to handle the dress, so she was the one who slipped the underskirt over Aurelia's head and tied it around her waist. The exquisite ivory silk reflected light so that it created a luminosity equivalent to flowing water. The border of the skirt, embroidered with fine red silk in a symbol that Aurelia had created, looked spectacular. It was one of three things Aurelia insisted on including.

The deep-red silk overskirt, its border embroidered in ivory silk bearing Aurelia's symbols, left an A-line exposing its ivory underskirt. But it was the bodice that took one's breath away. Made from the same vibrant red satin material as the overskirt, it fitted snugly once laced at the back. The rounded neckline swooped to brush the swells of her breast and catch the tips of her shoulders. Pearls and teardrop-shaped diamonds formed a simple flower pattern along the neckline. Delicate red lace short sleeves covered her upper arms, and teardrop-shaped diamonds set in thin silver loops sewn onto the edge of the sleeves dangled, reflecting light in spectral patterns. The center panel covering her breasts ended in a V at her waist, and round diamonds clustered densely at the top gradually tapered down in a diminishing cascade.

The second thing Aurelia insisted on was comfortable shoes, and Madame Suzette did not disappoint. Red satin ballet slippers embroidered with her symbol were a perfect fit. The third stipulation was no other jewelry besides the teardrop diamond earrings Mother Guardian had gifted her.

Unfortunately, all good things must end. Evidently, Aurelia's mother-in-law couldn't resist the pull of one of Madame Suzette's creations, and she flounced into the room with her entourage, not bothering to knock. Aurelia noticed that there was no Lady Matilda this time.

"Good afternoon, Your Majesty." Madame Suzette said, straightening from her curtsy. Everybody waited while the queen slowly walked around Aurelia, scrutinizing the dress.

"It will do, Madame Suzette, although I don't like the symbols embroidered on the border. The royal coat of arms would look far more regal on its own."

To Aurelia's surprise, her mother spoke up. "I disagree, Your Majesty. It speaks to my daughter's personality, and once explained, I believe the public will find it as endearing as I do."

Octavia glared at Rosalind. "Really? And what exactly will my people find so endearing?"

Frowning, Rosalind spoke slowly, as if the queen were dull. "The kneeling girl represents Aurelia." Rosalind pointed to the symbols on the dress, "and her extended arms with palms up and open, holding the royal coat of arms, represents her desire to serve the people and the crown."

Octavia huffed. "I know what it means, but I'm afraid I must disagree with the overly sentimental notion. It is not conducive to the political nature of her appointment."

The queen's haughty put-down did nothing to quell her mother's rebuff. "Oh? Well, perhaps you're right, Your Majesty. I must confess it's been a while since I helped draft policy for the government. However, I found my sentimentality served me well in the political arena. I'm afraid my daughter inherited that particular trait from me." Turning to Aurelia, she said, "We shall see if it serves you as well as it did me, sweetheart."

Aurelia smiled at her mother. "I always thought that was your best quality, Mom. If I have even an ounce of your ability, I'll be very successful."

The queen was not happy to be sidelined. "What poppycock! Thank goodness I'll be in residence to offer advice after the inauguration." Turning to her bevy of followers, she said, "Come, ladies, I have things to do."

Aurelia was happy to see the back of the woman, so she didn't tell Octavia she would be the last person Aurelia ever asked for advice. The queen's departure sucked the tension from the room, and things returned to normal. Everybody continued to admire the dress and offer compliments about how lovely she looked. A few brave ladies echoed Rosalind's feelings regarding the symbol Aurelia created.

Sylas found it difficult not to grill his daughter's fiancé. From what he'd seen, the man treated Aurelia with respect, and that she was head over heels in love with him was obvious. However, the gossip mill told another story, and even though Sylas knew not to listen to all the lollygagging, he wasn't stupid enough to ignore it either.

Flaminius led them along the same path he had taken Aurelia on when they had their picnic. Sylas was a man of few words, and it made him a pleasant riding companion, but Flaminius could tell he wanted to discuss something.

"You okay there, Sylas?"

"I'm fine, son."

Flaminius shifted in his saddle. "You look like a man with something on his mind."

Sylas gave Flaminius a sardonic look. "I'm a man whose only child is about to marry the crown prince of Arkhnuet. Of course, I have something on my mind."

"I see what you mean, but I'm just a man."

"You're not just a man. You can pretend all you like, son, but you are the next king, and I'm not sure if Aurelia knows what she's getting herself into." He held up his hand before Flaminius could interrupt. "I know what you're going to say. You're in love with each other, but that won't be enough in this case. She has no idea how to rule a planet. Yes, she can learn, but my girl doesn't have the killer instinct necessary to survive."

"You underestimate her, sir. Your daughter wasn't born to run an empire; she was born to change it, and that's what I'm counting on."

It seemed he had rendered Sylas speechless for a moment. "Okay, son. You got me there. What about this shit I'm hearing about you playing musical beds and breaking my little girl's heart?"

"What you've heard is only half the truth. There was an incident when we first got back that was taken out of context, and I dealt with it."

Sylas nodded. "Mm, by it, you mean Matilda."

Sylas noticed Flaminius's surprise. "It was my job at one point to be very well informed. Perhaps you remember?"

"I remember, and I respect you, Sylas. So, you know that when I say I dealt with it, I have."

He nodded, satisfied with Flaminius's answers. "All I ask is that you remember she is more precious than anything you have ever held dear."

"I will treat her better than you expect me to."

If a woman were privy to this conversation, she would shake her head in frustration and be very suspicious of how the men could have sorted out their differences so quickly and with so few words.

Aurelia woke on the morning of their wedding to Rosalind bustling into her room, followed by Sue, Mother Guardian, and Lily. Each carried a tray laden with food. Sitting up, she piled her pillows behind her back and smiled at her entourage. "Good morning. What's all this?"

The women sat on the enormous bed and made themselves comfortable while arranging the trays within easy reach. "Since this is the last day I will have my daughter to myself, I wanted to spoil you."

"Oh, Mom. You made all my breakfast favorites!" Big fluffy buttermilk and blueberry pancakes, salmon and dill cream cheese with bagels, bacon, eggs over easy, and, best of all, mimosas. Mother Guardian patted her foot and handed her a plate so she could load up. "How am I supposed to eat all this and still fit into my wedding dress?"

"Pfft. Please, child. That's hours away. Trust me; if you're smart, you'll gorge yourself now because you won't have time to eat again until after the ceremonies."

HERE COMES THE BRIDE. FOR REAL

Aurelia was just about to take a sip of a mimosa when Mother Guardian snatched the flute away and promptly downed the drink in one gulp. Burping unashamedly, she said, "We can't have the validity of the marriage contracts jeopardized because the bride got rat-assed on her wedding day."

The others laughed, but Aurelia didn't find it funny. "Hey! I wasn't going to get drunk. I need something to take the edge off."

Lily snorted while taking a large gulp of her drink. "Honestly, Your Grace, I think it would take a barrel of booze to take the edge off this massive affair."

Sue elbowed her. "Oh, nice going, Lily. We're supposed to keep her calm, not make her want to drown herself in the bathtub."

Lily shrugged. "What? It's not like she's going to miss the crowds of people, army of reporters, and hordes of dignitaries attending her wedding. Not to mention the queen's shrieks echoing through the castle while she tries to micromanage every tiny detail."

Suddenly Aurelia didn't feel so hungry anymore.

"Oh, come now, darling, you're made of sterner stuff than that," Rosalind said in a perky voice. "You own this!"

"Mom, please don't use 'the happy voice.' It reminds me of the day Tinkles died."

"Who was Tinkles?" Sue asked around a mouthful of pancake.

"My cat. When I was five, Tinkles died choking on a mouse that was a bit ambitious for a kitten to eat."

Lily squirmed. "That's horrible!"

"It was terribly traumatic for Aurelia because it was the first time she'd experienced loss."

"What did you do to help her get through it?"

Rosalind smiled at Mother Guardian. "Well, after a good cry, we performed an autopsy."

Aurelia reached for her mother's hand. "I never thanked you for that."

The others glanced at each other awkwardly. "That truly explains a lot," Mother Guardian whispered before she drained another glass.

Aurelia burst out laughing. "No, you don't understand. I asked my mother to help me comprehend how Tinkles passed. I felt it would help me process his death."

Lily shook her head, perplexed. "And you were five at the time?"

"Yup."

"Do you know how truly . . . unique you are?"

Mother Guardian popped a whole strawberry in her mouth and said, "That's very tactful of you, Lily. I was going to call her bat shit crazy!"

Sitting among piles of her favorite food, Aurelia discovered she wasn't alone at all. She had developed strong relationships with wonderful women, and she was grateful, even if they laughed at her quirks.

Marcus didn't give two shits about propriety, but even he thought it was pushing it to have a drink at nine in the morning. Now, if you were still drunk from the night before and you were having a nightcap or a morning cap, then nine in the morning was totally acceptable. But, as the groom's best friend, he felt obliged to divert Flaminius away from disaster.

"Stop taking my drink away!"

Marcus threw another whiskey out the window. "You'll thank me later, Flaminius. Do you want to smell like alcohol when Aurelia gets here? You should be sober when you sign the marriage contract."

Flaminius hated it when Marcus made sense. "Why do there have to be so many fucking ceremonies? I can't keep track of them all."

"It's not that complicated. We start with the Contract Ceremony, where you both sign the marriage contracts. Then we move on to exchanging the rings and, finally, the Witness Ceremony. Easy peasy lemon squeezy."

Flame flopped onto the couch and dropped his head into his hands. "Has anyone ever told you what a dork you are?"

"Frequently, Sire."

"Shut up."

Marcus chuckled but was interrupted when Frank announced the bride.

Finally! Flaminius stood and straightened his tunic over matching white, loose-fitting pants. It was customary to wear simple clothing for the contract and ring ceremony. He was grateful he wouldn't have to wear his official garb until the witness ceremony, mostly because his cock had space to grow in these pants. He was going to be alone with Aurelia for as long as it took to sign the contracts and exchange rings, which might not seem like a lot of time, but he didn't need much to throw her down, lift her skirt, and fuck her silly.

Not that he intended doing that, but he couldn't be sure at this point. He woke up this morning mid-Aurelia-dream fucking the mattress. To his embarrassment, he came all over the sheets.

His study door opened, and his wet dream floated in on a cloud of white. Hesitantly, she walked forward and stood just out of his reach, as if sensing his instability.

"You're so beautiful."

Marcus patted an entranced Flaminius on the shoulder, smiled at Aurelia, and slipped out of the room.

She looked down at her plain white empire-cut floor-length dress. "I think perhaps you're going blind. I don't even have makeup on."

"No, I like you like this. All you, all-natural. You couldn't make a more enticing picture."

She dropped her eyes to his tented pants and smiled. "I see that."

"Have mercy, my love." Moving behind his desk to his chair, he invited her to sit opposite him. "I think we should get this over with before we do something reckless."

She sauntered to the chair, swinging her hips as seductively as possible. "Very well, my love. Let's get started."

Holding his gaze, she sat and slowly crossed her legs, letting the thin silk dress slide open. "Stop being a minx," he admonished. She smiled and slid her fingers over her collarbone, encouraged by his response. "Aurelia, stop it!" Flame wiped the sweat from his brow and sighed.

Aurelia sat back and perused her almost-husband. For the first time since the willow tree, she noticed the strain around his mouth and eyes. "I'm sorry, Flame. I didn't mean to upset you. Are you okay?"

He leaned forward on his elbows and smiled. "You haven't upset me, sweetheart. It's just resisting you has been one of the hardest—pardon the pun—things I have ever done, and Source knows tonight can't come, again, pardon the pun, fast enough."

She laughed. "You realize you've been torturing yourself for no good reason. In case you haven't noticed, I'm a sure thing. All you had to do was ask, and I would gladly have eased your tension."

Rubbing his clammy hands on his trousers, he replied, "I know that, but I've never wanted to, or cared enough before you to do the right thing, and I will, even if it kills me."

"I can't think of a nicer thing you could have said to me. Thank you."

Pulling the contract toward her, she picked up the heavy black fountain pen and began signing the document where the lawyers left little arrowed tabs. When they finished, she put the hefty wad of papers into separate envelopes and handed Flame his copy. "According to the law, we're officially married. I don't suppose I could tempt you to consummate our betrothal?" she asked saucily.

Flame laughed. "You are persistent, aren't you?" He shook his head. "No. However, if you insist, I'll kiss you once you have given me my ring."

She'd been so intent on seducing him, she forgot about the exchange of rings. Fumbling in her dress pocket, she found the heavy platinum band and made her way around his desk. Flame swiveled his chair to face her; she kneeled between his legs, took his left hand in hers, and held the band up. "Read the inscription."

"Courage under fire," Flame whispered, "Aurelia."

Shrugging her shoulders, she blushed. "I wanted to have something meaningful engraved, but I couldn't think of anything, so I asked Marcus. When he told me about the RPU motto, I knew it was right. I wanted to honor the men that fought beside you and died in battle while honoring who you are and what you do."

Spellbound, Flaminius stared as she gently slipped the ring on his finger and kissed the palm of his hand. "I, Aurelia Stafford, give this ring to thee, Flaminius Theodore Alexander Esca, as proof that I have accepted and signed the marriage contract, legally consummating Perfecta Nobis, and that from this moment onwards, I am bound to thee in marriage. May all who see this ring bear witness you are mi perfecto by choice."

Then, she added something not required by law. "And may they know I love you as much as I am devoted to you."

Flame finally forced himself to move. Clasping her elbows, he lifted her from her knees and stood. Keeping eye contact, he opened the center drawer of the desk and removed a blue velvet box. Opening it, he withdrew the ring and slipped it onto her finger.

"I, Flaminius Theodore Alexander Esca, give this ring to thee, Aurelia Stafford, as proof that I have accepted and signed the marriage contract, legally consummating Perfecta Nobis and that from this moment onwards, I am bound to thee in marriage. May all who see this ring bear witness you are mi perfecto by choice." With their lips barely touching, he whispered, "I love you, Aurelia." Then he flicked his tongue over her top lip, inviting her to deepen the kiss. When her hand slipped under his shirt, he broke their kiss. Resting his forehead against hers, he said, "I hope you don't have expectations of staying at the witness ceremony celebration for too long because I'm going to whisk you away the moment we conclude matters, and to hell with whoever disapproves."

"I assure you I have no objections."

A gentle knock alerted them to the time. He tenderly kissed her temple before walking with her to the center of the room and bid the intruder enter. Marcus popped his head around the door. "Sorry to interrupt, Sire, but I have a few irate women out here insisting Her Grace hurry, or they won't have sufficient time to dress her for the witness ceremony."

"Those women are going to drive me crazy. I better go." Aurelia tore herself away from him to leave but turned when she reached the door. "Flame?"

"Yes?"

"I love you too."

It wasn't until she was sitting in front of her dressing-table mirror being plucked and primped to within an inch of her life that she remembered to look at the ring Flame gave her. The breath left her body at the sight of its magnificence. "Mom? Where are you?"

Rosalind rushed over when she heard the tone in her daughter's voice. "What, baby? Are you okay?" Aurelia held her left hand up and pointed to the ring. Her other hand covered her mouth as she desperately tried not to cry.

It wasn't the flawless two-carat, round-cut center diamond or the smaller diamonds that encircled it that made the ring unique. It wasn't even the diamonds running down the sides of the white gold band that did it. It was the sapphires set horizontally, forming a halo around the center diamond.

"Oh my. The man has taste. But he is marrying you, so it's no surprise." Rosalind said.

It surprised Aurelia how quickly the time went. One moment she was sitting down to get her hair and makeup done; the next, she was standing, dressed in her wedding gown, waiting for her parents to escort her to the grand ballroom. Even though the contracts were signed and the rings exchanged, she still worried that he would change his mind and bail. Aurelia decided not to carry flowers, but now she regretted her decision because she had nothing to occupy her hands. Instead, she twisted her ring around her finger to ease her nerves.

"Ready, baby?"

Aurelia jumped; she hadn't heard her father come up behind her.

"Are you okay?"

She nodded, but her father didn't seem convinced.

"It's not too late to put a stop to this, baby. I can go out there and tell them you changed your mind and—"

Taking his hand, she smiled. "No, Daddy, I'm not jumpy because I'm having second thoughts. I'm jumpy because I'm afraid he is."

Sylas shifted a stray hair off her face. No matter how much her beauty team tried, they couldn't get the stuff to obey their savage combing and spraying. "Honey, the man is in love with you; I'm surprised he can put one foot in front of the other. He's not going anywhere."

"Your daddy's right, sweetheart. He's probably as nervous as you, so let's not keep the poor boy waiting."

Aurelia took her place between her parents, grasped their offered hands, and started the procession through the castle. "I want you both to know that even though I might not have always shown it, I was and am grateful to you both for always being there for me. I love you."

Rosalind sniffed and patted her hand, and Sylas kissed her on the temple. "We love you too, honey."

Sue covertly shoved some tissues in her and Rosalind's hands from her position behind them. Mother Guardian and Lily preceded them, carrying floral garlands. It was an honor given to the reading Key to lead the bride to meet her betrothed. Lily wanted to include Mother Guardian, and Aurelia was happy to oblige. Marcus and three other RPU members flanked their group, offering protection. From what, she wasn't sure, but it delighted her to have them there all the same. As the procession made its way through the palace, staff members lined the walls, throwing bunches of lavender before the wedding party to be crushed beneath their feet to release the pleasant aroma.

Finally, they arrived, and Lily ushered Aurelia into the waiting room while the rest left to take their places in the hallway outside the ballroom. Flaminius stood with his back to her, deep in thought, staring out the window. She cleared her throat to get his attention.

He took his hands out of his pockets and turned. What he saw almost brought him to his knees. Aurelia was more beautiful than anyone had the right to be. "Holy Source, Aurelia," he whispered, "you look so . . . I don't know if there is a word to describe how magnificent you look."

She brushed the stubborn strand of hair out of her face. "You don't look too shabby yourself."

Flame closed the distance between them in two strides. "I was sure you wouldn't come. I'd convinced myself you'd remember all the horrible things I said and did since we met and decided I wasn't worth the effort."

"I thought the same thing about you."

He smiled down at her before his expression became serious. "I think it's only fair to warn you, Aurelia, that once we walk down that aisle, I am never letting you go. You will belong to me as I will to you, so this is your last chance to run."

Aurelia slowly disengaged from his embrace and walked to the door. Flame watched with bated breath as she called for Sue. "Is everything okay, Your Grace?"

"Yes. I just wanted to know if everyone is ready."

Sue frowned but didn't hesitate to reply, "No, Your Grace. But we can be in five minutes."

"Excellent!"

Turning to Flame, she held out her hand. "Let's go, big boy. I'm through waiting to make you my husband."

Flame took her hand, laughing at her antics. And they walked into the hallway that led into the ballroom, where over a thousand people waited for them to make their stately walk down the aisle. Sue bustled about, making sure everyone was in place. Aurelia grabbed her arm when she walked past and whispered. "Hurry this shit up, Sue."

"Yes, Your Grace." Sue nodded at the footmen to open the doors. A sedate but beautiful piece of music reverberated through the massive space as everyone stood in reverence to the royal couple.

Camera flashes blinded them. Flaminius leaned down and whispered. "I forgot to warn you about the media."

She barely noticed them but replied, "Okay."

As they passed, the wedding guests curtsied, but she didn't notice them either. Flame leaned in again. "Is it just me, or does this aisle seem to go on forever?"

Tightening her grip on his arm, she whispered, "It does."

"Should we pick up the pace a bit?"

"Absofucketly. Especially if you're opposed to sex in public."

He almost choked on his tongue. "I'm most definitely opposed to that."

"Then put some hustle in it, baby."

The wedding guests began murmuring among themselves, wondering what the couple was saying to each other. The faster Flame walked, the quicker Aurelia did. Halfway down the aisle, Flaminius decided she was going too slow, so he scooped her up in his arms and ran the rest of the way.

The guests didn't know what to make of it at first, but the bride and groom's joy was infectious. By the time Flame stood a little breathless in front of their parents, the whole place was in stitches. Except for the queen, of course. Gently putting his bride down, he straightened his jacket and mulishly said to his mother, "We're in a hurry." To his mother's horror, the guests laughed harder. Her glare promised severe retribution for his break in decorum, but he gave precisely zero fucks. When the guests stopped laughing at the couple's antics, their parents led them up the dais steps. The mothers took their children's hands and joined them. Then Mother Guardian and Lily stepped forward and loosely looped the flower garlands around their wrists.

Technically, the only thing the two sets of parents had to do was hand over the marriage contracts, but most took advantage of the opportunity to make a speech. Flaminius only hoped his father was wise enough to be the one to do it. Although he thought nothing could dampen his mood today, he didn't want his mother to ruin it for Aurelia.

Fortunately, Rosalind and Sylas spoke first. "On this auspicious day, Rosalind and I would like to thank you for the warm welcome we have received." Turning his attention to the marital couple, he continued, "I've never been eager for this day to arrive since it would mean I would lose my daughter," he cleared his throat, "but I have to admit that I could not have lost her to a better man."

Rosalind sniffed and turned to the table behind her. She picked up Aurelia's copy of the marriage contract and a cherrywood box roughly the size of a shoebox with a brass plaque on the front, engraved with their names and wedding date.

"Aurelia, as your mother, it was my responsibility to prepare you for the challenges of life. I can say without reservation that you are one of the finest women I've had the pleasure of knowing. Unfortunately, I can't take credit for any of it because you were born phenomenal." Grasping the box till her fingers turned white, she continued, "I agree with my husband; you, Flaminius, are indeed the best of men. Therefore, it's fitting that Source gifted you the best of women." Rosalind hugged Aurelia and whispered, "I love you." Then she turned to Flame. "I declare I bear witness that my daughter, who is of sound mind, willingly entered this union and offer, as proof, this marriage contract signed by her." Flaminius accepted the contract and bowed. Opening the box, Rosalind continued, "I also give you the key to our home because you are no longer just a guest but part of our family." Flaminius squeezed her hand as he took the box, barely managing to say thank you around the lump in his throat.

Next up were his parents. Flaminius sighed with relief when his father stepped forward. "Today is indeed a joyous occasion for all, but most especially for the queen and me. Many of you know of our son's wartime accomplishments and his astute mind for politics. What you may not know is that for some years now, I have been aware that he has surpassed my ability to rule." It was no surprise that Flaminius would take the throne once he returned from his honeymoon in a month. But the people assumed the king didn't believe him ready, no doubt fueled by his mother's initial vehement disapproval of the idea. Romulus's statement dispelled any lingering rumors and doubts.

"And now, my son has found his match." Romulus waited for the applause to die down. "It was my dearest hope that when he did, he would be complete in his heart, but I never imagined that he would be lucky enough to find his intellectual equal as well." Resting his hand on Flaminius's shoulder, he said, "You will find your task that much easier for it. And so, Aurelia . . ." The king took Flaminius's copy of the marriage contract from the queen. "I declare I bear witness that my son, who is of sound mind, willingly entered this union and offer, as proof, this marriage contract signed by him." Octavia handed Romulus a similar size box given to Flaminius, except it was silver. "I also give you the key to our home so that you know you are not just welcome but part of our family."

The king rejoined his wife before he continued. "You may now show those present the proof of acceptance of the marriage contracts. Flaminius led Aurelia to the center of the ballroom by their joined hands looped with the flower garland. Eight footmen stepped forward, carrying two chairs on poles, putting them down next to each other, facing opposite directions. Flame settled his bride before he took his seat. Simultaneously, the men lifted the chairs high so that the entire congregation could see them. Then they started the slow procession, carrying them around the room while Flaminius held their hands up for all to see the rings. Cheers, shouting, and clapping ensued as people waved their flags in celebration of their union. It was the best moment of Aurelia's life.

Mother Guardian stood to one side, watching the future king and queen of Arkhnuet as they vowed to love each other, body and soul, and for the first time in centuries, she felt hope.

Chapter Fifteen -
Honeymoon, Rifting, and Attempted Murder

Aurelia paced the corridor outside her room, waiting for the footmen to collect her luggage. By the sounds of it, the wedding celebrations were still in full swing. The entire nation seemed to be outside the palace gates, dancing to the various bands performing in honor of the royal wedding or watching the fireworks displays and enjoying the culinary delights of dozens of different eating establishments that had set up tents. It all seemed rather ostentatious to her, but then again, it wasn't every century the future king got married. She just wanted to get the hell out of there and go wherever Flame had arranged for them to spend their honeymoon so she could lose her fucking virginity!

Flaminius had to speak to his father regarding the coronation, so she was waiting on him. Apart from the servants, only her parents, Sue, Marcus, and Frank, were present to say farewell. "I've secured your luggage and will send the servants on to your destination in a moment, Your Grace. Was there anything else you needed before they leave?"

"No, thank you, Frank. I'm sure you've outdone yourself, as usual." Hesitating for a moment, she took his hand. "Please tell the others I appreciate their diligent help these last few weeks. I couldn't have managed without them or you." Frank had only been in her life for a short time, yet she felt deeply for him, mainly because she could see Flame loved him and because he was a good person who made her feel welcome.

Patting her hand gently, he said, "It has been my pleasure to serve you, Your Grace, and I look forward to continuing to do so when you return." Bowing, he smiled and left. Sue and her parents followed soon after.

The moment Aurelia was alone, Marcus approached her. He and a small contingent of RPU soldiers would go with them on their honeymoon. Flaminius didn't welcome this intrusion, but he also wanted to make sure his bride was safe, so he didn't bitch too much. There was no reason to suspect that the couple was in any danger, but Marcus felt uneasy. He shared his concerns with Flaminius, who forbid him to speak to Aurelia, but Marcus disagreed with his friend.

"You looked magnificent today, Your Grace."

Aurelia jumped when he spoke. "Oh, Marcus, you startled me. Thank you for saying that."

"Not sure you should thank me for stating a fact."

She smiled, shaking her head. "You are a smooth talker, sir."

"It comes with the territory." Marcus shrugged. Changing the subject, he said, "I have to talk to you before Flaminius returns and cuts my balls off for going against his orders."

"Ooh. That sounds intriguing. What does my alpha-male want to protect me from this time?"

Sighing, Marcus ignored her naughty comment in the interest of actually getting his thoughts across. "You get I am a soldier, right?" Aurelia nodded. "And that your safety is my sole responsibility?" Again, she nodded. "That, coupled with the fact that I've learned never to ignore my instincts, is the only reason I'm going over Flaminius's head and telling you this."

"Marcus, you're freaking me out."

"I don't mean to, and I have no reason to expect trouble for you and Flame, but I have concerns, and I want you to be cautious on your honeymoon."

Aurelia studied his face for a while before she nodded. "I promise to keep your warning in mind, Marcus, but I have to tell Flame we spoke." Marcus winced. "I won't lie to him even if I have to throw you under the bus."

Marcus shook his head. "I totally understand, and I agree, but I ask you to give me a heads-up before you do because he is going to go Neanderthal on my ass."

She laughed. "I will, and just to make it easier on you, I'll do it after we have . . . you know."

"Oh, please say no more. I don't think I need the visual, but I thank you for your consideration."

They laughed until Flame appeared and interrupted their huddle, looking peeved that they were in a huddle at all. Unfortunately, this made them laugh harder, necessitating some of that smooth-talking Marcus excelled at.

It was half-past nine before Flaminius finally escaped his father's study. Breaking all kinds of land speed records, he made it to Aurelia to find her in a cozy huddle with Marcus. He didn't react well and hoped it was sexual frustration causing his jealousy and not because the match hormones had permanently altered his personality. If that were the case, Aurelia could never speak to another man again, and he didn't think she'd allow that.

For now, he was going to assume it would get better with lots of sex. Factoring in the time it would take to rift to the tropics, feed his woman, and allow for an acceptable amount of foreplay, he figured he had about three hours before he could make love to her. Fortunately, Aurelia was as ready to get out of there as he was, which helped keep their goodbyes short and sweet. Marcus would only allow their premature departure from their wedding celebration if they used the rifter bay in the palace reserved for the royal family instead of the traditional public send-off of a royal bridal couple.

Flaminius went along with Marcus's plan because it got them to privacy quicker. But he also loved the idea of his mother finding out they had disregarded protocol and dodged the public departure ceremony. He felt sorry that his father would endure her anger, but not enough to change their plans.

Aurelia pulled on his arm, breaking his train of thought. "Flame, you're going too fast. I can't keep up."

He loosened his death grip on her hand and slowed his step, but only marginally. "Sorry, sweetpea. I'm in a hurry."

"Yes, I can see that, and believe me, I am too. But as embarrassing as it is to admit, I've never rifted, so I'd like to remember at least some of it."

Flame stopped suddenly. "What? I thought you spent time with your mother during the war. Didn't she serve in field hospitals all over Arkhnuet?"

Marcus noticed they'd stopped moving and urged them to keep up.

"She did, but my father insisted on snail travel."

Flame understood Sylas's thinking. During the war, heavy security surrounded the rifter bays, but the Oradagra were innovative. Instead of attacking the bays, they hacked the rifter system to change coordinates mid-rift, intercepting supplies. Occasionally, they took innocent civilians and soldiers hostage, torturing them for information and using them to negotiate for Oradagra prisoners' release. Unfortunately, his father refused to negotiate. Many times, they couldn't save them, and some of those murdered were children.

His father's decision not to negotiate was correct; it was the main reason Flame didn't want to take the throne. He knew he would have to make similar decisions, and he wasn't as strong as his father. He never would've left those people to die, even though it would've given the Oradagra a significant upper hand.

Turning his attention back to Aurelia, he said, "Honey, are you telling me you and your mother would travel by road, rail, and ship to get where you needed to be?" Aurelia nodded. "That's nuts! Snail travel is fine for an afternoon outing, but not for the distances you would've covered."

"I know, but it gave my father peace of mind, and my mother wanted to give him what he needed so that he could keep sharp doing whatever he needed to do and stay safe."

"That sounds like something your mom would do for Sylas," Flame said.

"Yeah," she agreed softly. At that moment, Marcus stopped them, and Aurelia perused her surroundings. The castle was an intimidating building. It housed the royal family's official residence and all government offices, from the transport department where people could apply for rifter permits to visit other provinces to the marriage licensing department. Not to mention the unmarried Keys' and Mother Guardian's residence and apartments used for visiting dignitaries and aristocrats when at court.

She had only been in the castle for two weeks, so it was no surprise she didn't know the royal family had a private rifter bay. What was surprising was how innocuous the location was. It lay behind a bland white door with a brass knob at the end of a service corridor lit by fluorescent lights.

Stepping through the door, Aurelia noticed that, apart from their entourage of five RPU men and themselves, the bay was empty. "Where's the rifter pilot?" Aurelia asked.

Marcus locked the door and turned to them, smiling deviously. From previous experience, that never boded well. "I happen to be a certified rifter pilot and a damn good one."

Flaminius snickered. "It's not like it's difficult to punch in a bunch of coordinates and let the machine do the rest."

Marcus gasped in disgust. "It's not that simple."

"Marcus, a child can operate that thing," Flame said, pointing to the rifter. "The only reason we're using the bay and not a handheld rifter is because we're a group. If I had my way, it would be just Aurelia and me going on our honeymoon, and you wouldn't be necessary."

"But we are a group and, therefore, you need me. So suck it up and bow to my superior knowledge."

"For fuck's sake, Marcus, we could've used the pilot who usually operates this bay. He has top-secret clearance."

Aurelia sighed. Unfortunately, the boys were on a roll. "I told you why I don't want anyone else knowing where you're going. I don't care if you think it's overkill. It's the way it's going to be because I'm responsible for your safety."

"If you boys don't mind, I'd like to start my honeymoon, wherever that might be." She muttered.

Flame looked suitably contrite. "Baby, it wasn't that I didn't trust you to know. I wanted it to be a surprise."

"That's so sweet," she cooed, putting her hands over her heart.

"Okay, love bugs, let's get this show on the road."

Flame whispered in her ear, "It actually is challenging to rift more than two people but don't tell him I said that."

Marcus shouted from across the room where he was fiddling with the control panel, "I heard that."

"I forgot the man has hearing like a fox."

Aurelia laughed at her husband and his friend before she asked, "Why is it difficult?"

"If you'd step up to my control panel, I'll explain the intricacies of group rifting, my lady."

Five minutes into his lecture, Aurelia interrupted. "Let me see if I understand." She pointed to the eighty-inch screen behind her. "These are the coordinates of our destination, which is crucial because if you make a mistake, we may end up rifting into an active volcano or under the ocean or something equally life-threatening?" Marcus nodded. "And the reason it's harder to rift a group is because the rifter has to have an adequate amount of power to keep the rift open long enough for everyone to pass through before it closes."

"Precisely."

She scrunched up her nose in thought, then asked, "How do you know the coordinates are safe, and why is it difficult to keep the power up?"

Marcus smiled at her in a way that made the back of Flaminius's neck prickle. "Such good questions." Taking her by her elbow, Marcus turned her back to the control panel. Clenching his teeth, Flaminius forced himself to hold back. Oblivious to his inner struggle, Marcus continued. "We know the coordinates are safe because of a few brave souls called jumpers who make a career of rifting to unknown coordinates and mapping them."

"Wow!" Aurelia's expression of awe made Flame want to train to be a jumper immediately.

"As for power . . ." Marcus risked his life again by guiding Aurelia with his hand on her lower back. He pointed to a six-foot-tall structure. "Inside that box is a copper coil surrounding a crystal tower. When we apply a current through the wire, it creates a magnetic field producing stress in the crystals, which generate energy that we store in this little titanium box down here. The rifter directs that energy into the space-time continuum around our planet to fold it so that your destination lines up right next to your current location and you can just walk through."

"I think I understand," Aurelia said, tapping her finger on her lips.

Flaminius interjected. "Marcus, why don't you show her the rubber band example?"

"Great idea." Marcus pulled a rubber band from a drawer in the console. Holding it stretched out between his index fingers, he said, "Using one finger, push down on the rubber band. You see how the pressure of your finger brings my fingers closer until they touch?" She nodded. "That's what the energy does to the space between two locations, making it possible for us to create a bridge between the two."

"Oh, now I get it."

"When one or two people are rifting, you need less energy." Marcus continued, "A handheld rifter has enough storage capacity for the job, but when a large group is rifting, even this titanium storage box," he pointed to the box at his feet, "doesn't have enough juice to do it. During the jump, the pilot has to constantly adjust the current and energy to keep the rift open long enough to complete the jump without overloading the crystals causing them to shatter."

"That's impressive, Marcus." She pointed to the bay. "Why the raised platform?"

Marcus's smile wasn't directed at her, but at Flaminius. "Sharp as a tack, this one. I suggest you hone your skills, brother, or she'll roll right over you."

Flaminius chortled. "I can't think of anything better than her rolling all over me, so can you hurry the fuck up?"

Marcus laughed, shaking his head in defeat. Aurelia blushed, but looked pleased with her husband's response.

"The raised platform houses a bed of crystals connected to the stack that helps boost energy."

"I assume the pilot has to remain at the controls to ensure a safe jump for the passengers?"

Marcus nodded.

"Then how are you going to get to us?"

He pulled a handheld rifter from his backpack. "I'm going to rift all of you across, and then I'll use this to rift myself."

Flame wanted Aurelia to get the answers her inquisitive mind craved, but he also needed to fuck her. "Babe, I think it's time for you to experience rifting."

Marcus stepped behind the controls and fired up the rifter. Aurelia wanted to clap hands and jump up and down, but controlled herself by clinging to Flame's arm as he led her up the steps and onto the platform. The other RPU members joined them, taking up defensive positions.

A whining noise startled her, so Flame pulled her tighter into his body. A sudden increase in static made her hair stand on end, and gradually, a shimmering mirage-like curtain appeared before them. Then a sound like a cracking whip tore through the room. The shimmering curtain split to reveal a moonlit beach. Flame moved them forward immediately behind two of his men, and without slowing their pace, he said, "Don't be alarmed by the cold; it will only last a second."

When Aurelia moved through the rift, she felt wisps of cold tentacles caress her face as if she were walking through frozen spiderwebs. Flame continued to move her forward, not giving her time to soak in the beautiful white beach and sparkling moonlit water. Pulling her even closer, if that were possible, he guided her to the base of a rocky cliff face where wooden stairs haphazardly wound up to the top. Practically lifting her off her feet, Flame positioned her body behind his and dragged her up the stairs, making sure she remained covered on all sides by his men. Once they summited the cliff, two more soldiers standing guard nodded at their fearless leader before making their way down the stairs to the beach to wait for Marcus.

Walking in heels on a beach was a sin, but walking in heels on the spongy, lush, emerald-green grass was a travesty. She understood the need for security, but she wanted to walk barefoot on all that lusciousness. Gently she resisted Flame, pulling her along. He stopped and looked back. "I want to take my shoes off, honey."

Flame frowned. "Are they hurting you?" Her husband asked in a tone that suggested he would go to war with the idiot who dared design shoes that might hurt her.

"No, baby. I want to feel the grass on my feet."

Frowning again, he replied, "No," and pulled her arm.

She resisted, bringing them to a stop once more. "Honey, I understand your concern, but we're not going to have much of a honeymoon if we race from one building to the next for fear of an ambush."

He didn't even look at her before shaking his head. Planting her feet, she said. "Flame! Stop dragging me around and listen."

He growled but didn't stop. "Flame!"

Finally dropping her arm, he turned to face her and barked, "What?"

Stepping in close, she lowered her voice and said, "Honey, there are about twenty soldiers around us. I'm pretty sure we're safe, so let me take my shoes off and walk on this outstanding lawn." Sighing deeply, he rubbed his hands over his face before he agreed. She leaned down, slipped her suede fawn-colored shoes off her feet, and curled her toes into the lush lawn. Closing her eyes, she said, "Oh, that is bliss." Flame wrapped his arms around her and kissed the top of her head. Satisfied, she said, "Thank you, honey. We can continue."

Flame slowed their pace, giving Aurelia a chance to look around. It was dark, but she could see a manicured lawn leading to a white stone-flagged path through fruit-burdened peach trees. At the end of the path stood a two-storied country-style white house. Pillars supported a slanted gray roof covering a generous wrap-around porch on the ground floor. Light shone through the tall multi-paned windows and doors on the second floor that led onto a balcony.

Flame stopped her at the front door and extended his arms. "I believe it's good luck for the groom to carry the bride over the threshold of their new home." Without hesitation, his wife stepped in, and he lifted her with his powerful biceps, never once breaking eye contact. Some girls might think it was corny, but Aurelia thought it was sweet that a man who prided himself in being a hardened soldier would bother with romance. It was difficult for her to notice anything but Flame's drool-worthy body. But once they crossed the threshold, it was impossible not to be astounded by the magnificence of the home. Double vaulted ceilings ensured enough space for the three-tier, spiral, crystal chandelier hanging in the entrance hall.

Gently placing her on her feet, Flame folded her hand in his and said, "Let me give you a tour of my wedding gift to you."

"Flame, you can't buy me a house! I didn't get something even close to this for you."

"Honey, you've chosen to gift me with something you only get to give once. It's impossible to equal that. Let me give you a house so I don't feel like the scales are unbalanced." Now was probably not the time to tell her he had actually bought the entire island and named it The Isle of Aurelia.

She rolled to her tiptoes so she could kiss him. "Okay, baby, you can give me a house. Would you like to unwrap your gift now?"

Dropping his chin to his chest, he groaned. "Yes, I do, but first I'm going to feed you, then I'm going to be very magnanimous and let you freshen up, then I'm going to take you to bed and make love to you until you're hoarse from screaming my name."

A nervous but anticipatory giggle escaped her mouth while Flame settled her at the kitchen table and poured them each a glass of white wine. Then Flame set about gathering ingredients to make their dinner.

"I had no idea you could cook."

"Don't get excited. I can only make homemade pasta and red sauce with pesto and cheese-stuffed garlic bread. And to finish, chocolate ice cream sundaes covered in chopped nuts, caramel sauce, masses of whipped cream, and cherries."

"I'm so turned on right now that I wouldn't mind if you threw me on the floor and had your way with me."

"Tempting, but not the most romantic story of virginity taking, though." Flame teased.

Aurelia reached into the cherry jar, pulled one out by the stalk, and then popped it into her mouth. Without thinking, she rolled her tongue around the stem, tied it in a knot, and popped it out of her mouth.

"Are you trying to kill me, Aurelia?" Flame panted.

Looking up, she saw him staring at her mouth. Swallowing slowly, Aurelia plucked the stem from her mouth. "I didn't realize tying a cherry stem in a knot was such a turn-on. If I had, I would've invested in a cherry farm by now."

Flame stalked around the counter and slid his fingers into her hair. "When I make you mine," he whispered with his lips barely touching hers, "I'm going to suck on your nipples and lick your pussy until I've slurped up every drop of your cum. And then I'm going to do it all over again." Aurelia could barely breathe, so when the pot on the stove boiled over, she hardly noticed. Flame stepped out of her arms and left her feeling completely flustered.

Two grueling hours later, Flame led her into their bedroom, hanging back to give her some space while she looked around. Sue oversaw the decorating of the island house using her knowledge of Aurelia's style, and by the look of awe on his wife's face, she got it down pat. Shoving off the doorframe, he took her arm, gently turned her around, and pressed his erection into her lower back before he frog-marched her into the bathroom, stopping when he had her pressed against the glass shower wall. "I'm going to taste every inch of your skin." Aurelia's whole body shivered as Flame reached around her and turned on the six showerheads.

Forcing her arms above her head, Flame flattened her palms against the glass. "Keep them there," he commanded. Gripping the hem of her top, he ripped it off over her head and threw it behind him. "Drop your arms." He waited for her to comply before he slid his fingers under the straps of her white lace bra and trailed them off her shoulders and down her arms until her nipples popped out the top of the bra cups. That's when he got his first squirm from Aurelia. She dropped her head forward and moaned while her bum ground back into his pelvis.

Perfect.

Her fragrance filled his nostrils as he gathered her hair in one hand and pulled her head back in a gentle but undeniable jerk. That's when she gasped and grabbed his jean-clad thighs in her tiny hands.

Perfect.

Releasing her locks, he slid his hands down her body to dip them under her tight skirt. Bunching the material in his fists, he pulled it up around her waist. Forcing his knee between her thighs, he breathed into her ear, "Keep your legs spread." She complied instantly, so he rewarded her with a firm butt squeeze and a "Good girl." That's when he got his second squirm and butt grind from her.

Perfect.

Stepping away, he hooked the band of her panties with his thumbs and dragged them down her legs until the elastic pulled taut over her lower thighs. Flattening his palms, he glided his hands up her thighs until he cupped the globes of her ass. That's when he got his first, "Oh my!"

Perfect.

Aurelia opened her eyes when she lost his hands and looked over her shoulder to see him reaching for his tshirt, pulling it over his head one-handed. Taking his time, he rubbed one butt cheek, then the other, paying close attention to the firmness of touch she enjoyed most. He ran his hand from the base of her spine to the split of her thighs. That's when he got his second, "Oh my!" and a full-body shiver.

Perfect.

Slipping his hand between her legs, he was delighted to find she was wet. She moaned and tried to move closer to his fingers. "No, my darling," he said, lightly slapping her ass. The vibration sent a thrill through her pelvis that short-circuited her brain, prompting her self-control and give-a-fuck mind to take a much-needed vacation.

Separating her cheeks, he slowly ran a finger up her crack, applying gentle pressure. She moaned, dropping to his knees; he did it again, but with his tongue. That's when he got his first knee buckle.

Perfect.

Steadying her with his hands at her hips, he turned her to face him. Giving her no time to catch her breath, he flat-tongue licked her drenched pussy from fourchette to clit, where he sucked the hard pearl into his mouth and rolled his tongue around it. That's when she came the first time.

Perfect.

Flame pinned her to the shower while he sucked the last spasms from her. When she was totally boneless, he ripped her panties and skirt off, stood, and divested her of her bra. Removing his shoes and socks, he shuffled her into the shower without bothering to remove his jeans.

When the warm water hit her skin, she opened her eyes and sighed, "That was amazing."

"Hold your praise until after the main event, my sweet."

Aurelia's eyes widened before she replied, "There's more?"

"I haven't even started. That was the warmup act."

Her mouth dropped open, and she whispered, "I don't know if I can take more."

Flame moved into the spray with her. "You're still able to speak, and you haven't lost the use of your legs yet. You can definitely take more, much,

much more." Flame slipped the buttons of his pants open as he spoke, revealing his magnificent Adonis belt leading to a superb cock. A significant head of steam had built up in the bathroom, softening the light and creating a halo around his body. It didn't make him look angelic. Oh no, it made him look devilish and likable. Impatiently, Aurelia pushed his hands away and took over, forcing his pants down his thighs. Unfortunately, the combination of wet denim and inexperience made her fumble; she growled in frustration.

Her breasts bounced from her ministrations, making his already stiff cock granite hard. Flicking her hands away, he unceremoniously ripped the fabric apart. Thank Source, he went commando when he changed out of his ceremonial threads. Grabbing her ass in both his hands, he lifted her, and she automatically wrapped her legs around his hips, making it easy to carry her to the s-shaped built-in shower bench. Its shape lent itself to various activities, including, but not limited to, eating pussy, getting his cock sucked, or taking pussy from behind.

Lowering himself into a sitting position in the bench's crook, Flame slid Aurelia off his lap to sit between his legs, her back to his front, and rested his hands on her thighs. She offered no resistance, allowing her head to fall back onto his chest. He pumped shower gel into his hand and worked the liquid into a lather. Then he cupped her breasts, running his thumbs over her taut nipples, slogging his hands down between her thighs to open her pussy. Using the finger and thumb of his left hand to squeeze either side of her vulva to raise her clit, he took his middle finger of the right hand to rub in a circular motion over the sensitive nub. Instantly, her chest heaved with labored breath, her thighs dropped open, and her toes curled in rapture. Yeah, that's what he wanted. Watching her face, Flame sped up the circular motion. Her mouth formed an O, but no sound came out, and her back bowed, pushing out her terrific tits.

Perfect.

Done playing, he carried her to their bed. As he kneeled between her legs, she reached for him. And fuck him if her hooded eyes and swollen lips didn't strip him of his last bit of self control.

"I'll try to go slow, but I'm on the edge, baby."

"I'm ready for you, Flame. I'm burning for you and have been for weeks."

Gripping the base of his cock, Flame rubbed the tip through her wetness. "Stop teasing," she said, then put her hands on his ass and pulled him closer. Inserting the head of his cock into her tight, moist canal, he pushed, watching to make sure she wasn't in pain. When he saw none, he drove a little deeper. Brushing a strand of damp hair from her cheek, he asked, "Are you okay, baby?"

"Yes. Keep going." He clasped her head in his hands and thrust until seated to the hilt. She winced, but kept eye contact. "It's okay. I'm okay. It doesn't hurt too much."

Shit, he tried to stay still, but his hips jacked forward. "Sorry, baby," he hissed.

Shaking her head, she moved her hips with his. "Don't stop. It feels good."

Pulling out, Flame thrust back in and groaned. She wrapped her legs around his waist and tilted her hips in another invitation. Nature took over, and before long, they moved together in a dance of erotic pleasure. When Flame knew he couldn't hold back one more second, he reached between their bodies and tweaked her clit. Thank fuck that sent her over the edge. And he followed her a nanosecond later, filling her pussy with cum, giving him the primitive sense of satisfaction that she belonged to him. Flaminius rolled off her, cradled her sated body against his, and, without a word, they both drifted into a dreamless, blissful sleep.

Perfect.

Octavia didn't bother losing her temper this time. For whatever reason, Romulus decided his son could do no wrong since he took his mate. The humiliation Flaminius and that hussy inflicted on her when they didn't show for their departure ceremony left her beyond angry. Despite what her husband thought, she was not prone to irrational behavior, but there was only so much she could take.

She knew it would fall to her to sort this mess out. It always did; Romulus simply didn't have the killer instinct necessary. It wasn't the first time, nor would it be the last, just like when the Oradagra kidnapped civilians.

It was fortunate Octavia was always prepared, always playing the game with a meticulous exit strategy. Her plan required someone with finesse, a person beyond suspicion, well-connected to the sort of specialist who could execute her plan swiftly. She only hoped he would be open to her proposal.

Two glorious weeks of sun, surf, and lots of fabulous, mind-blowing sex would put any girl in a good mood. But the most fantastic thing about Flame was that he was at his happiest when she was happy. Discovering they had the same ideas about many things made it easier to believe that their marriage, mostly, would be good. As far as the things they disagreed on, well, she enjoyed the challenge of finding a compromise, and there was always make-up sex. And angry sex, be-quiet-the-kids-will-hear sex, date-night sex, and her number one fantasy: on his throne sex when they got home. It was safe to say that she was looking forward to life with him.

Flame sat at the kitchen counter drinking his second cup of morning coffee, staring at his wife scarfing down pancakes drenched in syrup and liberally decorated with bacon bits. If he'd seen a cuter sight, he couldn't recall it. The last two weeks had been the best of his life, and he was looking forward to the hundreds of years he hopefully still had with her.

"What are our plans today, honey?" Aurelia asked around a mouth full of pancake, syrup dripping down her chin. Flame was rock-hard and ready to fuck her on the table despite their vigorous morning session. He used his thumb to wipe her chin and licked the syrup off his finger. Her pupils dilated, and her mouth opened as she breathed a little faster.

"I thought we could hike up the peak behind the house. There are some beautiful waterfalls and pools that are sure to get me laid if I take a picnic basket and willing woman up there."

Aurelia shoveled the last bite of her breakfast in her mouth, holding her plate under her chin, halfway across the kitchen already. "Come on, Flame, that mountain ain't going to climb itself."

Laughing at her eagerness, Flame slapped her butt and followed her up the stairs to get ready for their hike, not noticing Marcus standing in the foyer. He watched the couple run past him, totally oblivious to his presence.

They were so wrapped up in each other they forgot his warning. He needed to make sure they stayed safe, so he waited for Flame and Aurelia to leave, giving them a two-minute head start, then followed.

Hiking up the peak only should've taken two hours. Unfortunately, the lovebirds kept stopping to cuddle or kiss or do other shit that necessitated Marcus turning his back—something that made him sweat from the sheer effort it took to break operational rule number one: never lose visual of your subject.

Finally, after three-and-a-half infuriating hours, they made it to the top, and Marcus could recon the area while they did whatever it was they did to make those sounds.

Perimeter check done, he settled in behind a rock at the top of the waterfall. From here, he had an uninterrupted view of his friends and most of the north side of the peak. The south side was sheer rock face, and apart from the thick foliage and trees that partially obstructed his view, he felt confident he could eliminate any threat.

Or so he thought. What happened next was, by far, the lowest point in Marcus's career. He had no excuse for his lack of judgment. He had just poked his head out over the rock to check on his friends when the afternoon sun reflected off something in the trees on the far side of the pool where Aurelia and Flaminius were sunning themselves. Marcus focused the lenses of his binoculars and scrutinized the area. He couldn't see the assassin, but the tip of an arrow protruded from the dense foliage. He immediately shouted a warning and emptied a mag at whoever was hiding in the trees.

Acting on reflexes from years of training, Flame rolled on top of Aurelia, engulfed her in his arms, and kept going until they hit the water. Sticking close to the edge of the pool where the rocks gave them some cover, Flaminius assessed the threat.

Marcus streaked past them, heading toward their attacker. With the immediate danger over, Flame looked down at Aurelia and saw blood in the water. "Aurelia!"

Flame was a well-trained soldier with a personality not prone to panic. But when Aurelia didn't respond, he couldn't recall any of his training. He was sure he blacked out for a second because one moment he was yelling her name, and the next Marcus was there, hauling her limp body from the water while simultaneously calling for help on his radio. Placing her on the rocks, Marcus checked her vitals, then looked at Flaminius. "Flaminius! Are you alright?"

Pulling the fragments of his mind together, Flaminius nodded. Moving as fast as he could, he dragged his ass out of the pool to help. Marcus's body obstructed his view, but he knew it was bad from the urgent radio communication. For the life of him, he couldn't bring himself to look. Bending double, he put his hands on his knees to catch his breath and then barked, "Is she alright?" No response. Straightening, he bellowed. "Is she fucking okay?"

"She's got an arrow in her thigh!"

Marcus's words snapped Flaminius out of his panic. His wife needed him to keep his shit together, not fall apart like wet toilet paper. Moving around his friend, he kneeled next to Aurelia and took her icy hand in his. He felt her pulse was weak and rapid, but only a small pool of blood had collected under her right thigh. The arrow had gone through her leg. Marcus had already broken off the business end.

Flaminius reached over to pull the shaft out, but Marcus stopped him. "Don't do that. She might bleed out." Pointing to her thigh, he continued, "See how swollen her thigh is? It's because she's bleeding internally. That shaft is stopping the blood from running out and lowering the pressure inside, and that pressure is going to keep her alive."

"Why is she unconscious?"

Marcus grabbed Flaminius's hands and placed them around her thigh. Pushing them together, he instructed, "Keep pressure on the wound."

"She's in shock, isn't she?"

"Keep calm. Jake and Jeff are on their way, and Tony has already rifted back to the castle to assemble a surgical team. It won't take more than fifteen minutes to have her in the care of good people."

True to his word, Aurelia was on a gurney, IV line in each arm, and on her way to surgery within fifteen minutes. She regained consciousness, asking for Flame just before they rifted. He whispered in her ear that everything was going to be okay. She smiled at him with such trust in her eyes. He felt the burn of it right down to his soul.

Standing outside the green doors of the operating room, Flaminius felt his anger build now that Aurelia was safe. He was still in his swim trunks, no shirt, no shoes, and his wife was wearing her red-and-white candy-striped bikini when they pushed her through those fucking doors. He was going to find the son of a bitch who hurt her, who cut their honeymoon short, and caused him to break his promise that he would always protect her, and fucking gut him.

Chapter Sixteen -
Let the Interrogations Begin

While Aurelia was in surgery, Flaminius took a shower and changed into the clean uniform Marcus brought him. To keep from losing his mind while waiting for word from the surgeon, Flaminius gathered his team to find some answers.

"Who knew where we were honeymooning?"

Marcus, Tony, Jeff, and Jake sat in the stark white passage outside the operating room on flimsy green padded chairs. "No one I wouldn't trust with my life, Flaminius," Marcus replied.

"Well, then someone we trust almost killed my wife trying to get to me!" No one said anything while he paced like a caged lion. Finally stopping, Flaminius rubbed his hands over his face, crossed his arms, and leaned against the wall. "Fuck, Marcus, if you hadn't been there, she'd be dead."

Marcus shook his head. "I allowed someone to breach our defenses and harm Aurelia. I understand if you want someone else to take over the investigation."

Flaminius pushed off the wall and dropped his arms. "Don't be fucking crazy. No one blames you." He turned to the others and continued in a menacing voice, "Do they?"

Marcus grimaced. "It's not like you're giving them a choice, Flaminius."

Jeff shrugged. "None of us saw it coming either; it was a team failure." The others nodded in agreement.

"Okay, now that we've cleared that up, let's get to work. Do we know how the assassin got away?"

"I chased him through the forest toward the cliffs, but he disappeared. He must have had a mobile rifter." Marcus replied.

Flaminius rubbed his chin, deep in thought. "Why did he use an arrow? Surely a gun would've been easier."

Jake shook his head. "A gun would've made too much noise. The only reason we could get to you as fast as we did was because we heard Marcus's fire."

What Jake said made sense. "I want a list of everyone who knew where we were."

Marcus nodded. "Done."

"Jake, I want you to interrogate everyone not above your pay grade on that list. Also, find out everything about their families, their lovers, who they spend their time with, how they earn and spend their money, and if they have affiliations with any anti-royalist groups."

"Got it, sir, A to Z."

Flaminius turned to Jeff.

"I want you to check every rifter bay and handheld on the planet for the island's coordinates."

Jeff's eyes widened. "The bays aren't a problem, but the list of people with handhelds is long, sir."

Flaminius raised his eyebrows. "Yes, I know, and I don't give a fuck. Use your wicked tech skills, hack those handhelds, get me some leads."

"Got it."

"Tony, take our crime scene boys to the island. Make sure they turn over every grain of sand twice."

"Yes, sir."

When they were alone, Marcus asked, "What do you want me to do, Flaminius?"

"We're going to interrogate the people on the list above Jake's pay grade."

"Flaminius, you need to be with your wife. Let me do that."

"I need to be with my wife, but there are people you won't be able to interrogate, like my parents."

Marcus frowned. "You think they could have anything to do with this?"

LET THE INTERROGATIONS BEGIN

"No, but I want to send a message that I'm not fucking around."

Smiling, Marcus asked, "Please tell me you're going to drag your mother into an interrogation room."

"Of course," he replied. "The whole point of questioning her is to put the fear of Source into our perp. Can't do that if I keep her interrogation private, now can I?"

Marcus rubbed his hands together. "If you love me, you will let me break the news to her."

"You know I do," Flaminius replied with a devious smile.

Aurelia woke gradually and felt the burning pain in her thigh, reminding her of where she was. Shifting gingerly, she tried to move her arm to touch her leg, but something stopped her. A large, warm hand touched her forehead. "Baby, lie still, or the IV will pull out."

Turning her head toward his voice, she smiled. "Hey, honey. Are you okay?"

Flame kissed her gently. "I'm better now that I'm looking into your beautiful green eyes. How are you feeling? Are you in pain?"

Struggling to keep her eyes open, she nodded slowly. "A little."

"I'll call a nurse to give you something."

"Okay, baby." Aurelia didn't see the nurse enter, but felt the meds' slight sting and slipped back into a peaceful sleep. She didn't see the anxious expression on her husband's face or the guilt in his eyes. If she had, she would've slapped him upside the head and told him he hadn't failed her.

Romulus was furious. The attempted assassination of his son and the injury his daughter-in-law suffered put him in an impossible position. He hoped to end his reign on a high note, not embroiled in a standoff against his son.

Flaminius insisted on carrying out an official investigation, and Romulus was happy to comply with the authorities, as was Tiberius. Of course, Octavia refused and called her lawyer, who filed an injunction preventing Flaminius from questioning her on the grounds that the queen had immunity against forced interrogation. She agreed to answer questions off the record, none of which they could use as evidence in court. To counter the injunction, Flaminius petitioned his father to permit the coronation to take place immediately, effectively downgrading Octavia's status to duchess so she couldn't refuse.

"For fuck's sake, Octavia, I don't understand why you're so resistant!"

Pacing the length of his study, Octavia barked, "I refuse to suffer further humiliation because of that woman!"

Flaminius purposefully positioned himself behind his father, putting a sturdy object in his way in case he lost his temper and killed her.

"Octavia, this has nothing to do with Aurelia. Someone tried to kill your son!"

Sniffing indignantly, she stubbornly refused to back down. "Don't be ridiculous! Nobody wants to kill Flaminius. That woman is hardly suitable for our son, and I assume that if I feel that way, others do too."

"Please tell me you didn't just say that?" Flaminius's menacing tone was lost on his mother, but not Romulus. "That woman, as you insist on calling her, will be queen. Which means you should be just as concerned about her life as mine."

Throwing her hands in the air, she shouted. "What's the big deal? They'll be able to interrogate me to their heart's content in two weeks, which means your only motivation for this charade is to humiliate me, and I won't allow that!"

"Fuck! How many times must I explain this? The trail will be cold by then. Not everything is a personal insult to you!"

"Then go question people who can help you solve this crime!"

"Interviewing you and Dad has nothing to do with what you know and everything to do with scaring the asshole responsible into making a mistake."

"You will not debase me for any reason! I am still the queen, and so help me, I demand the respect that title deserves." Shaking with anger, she pointed her finger at Romulus. "And if you're too weak to protect the sanctity of my office, I will!"

Romulus's face twisted with painful realization. In a soft, strangled voice, he said, "I have always felt blessed to have you by my side. So proud to call you wife, mother, and queen. But today, I feel nothing but shame."

Octavia gasped.

"What kind of mother would put her hate for the woman her son loves before the love for her son?" Shaking his head, he continued, "I honestly don't know who you are anymore, Octavia, but I can tell you I don't like whoever it is you've become." Romulus turned to Flaminius. "I will hand over power immediately. However, I suggest you keep the coronation ceremony for the scheduled date."

Flaminius almost crumbled with relief. "Thank you, father." Not wanting to be anywhere near the inevitable explosion that was sure to follow, Flaminius left to inform his wife she'd be crowned in a hospital bed under the influence of painkillers. Good times.

Aurelia's attending physician was not a happy woman. It was not because they had invaded her workspace with thirteen council members and five lawyers or the RPU soldiers posted in and around the hospital to keep Aurelia safe. She understood these intrusions.

It was because Sue and a very flamboyant Madame Suzette were on the warpath and insisted on bringing a team of seven women who descended on the unsuspecting future queen with makeup, hair spray, dresses, shoes, and oddly enough, hemorrhoid cream. Flame knew his wife intimately, and she did not need that cream, but he didn't stop Sue as he was genuinely frightened she would cut off his balls if he tried.

The lawyers insisted the doctor give Aurelia a competency test to ensure the pain medication wasn't impeding her reasoning, rendering the coronation void. Nevertheless, Aurelia took the news with the dignity Flame expected and passed with flying colors. When Flame told her how proud he was of her, she insisted it was because she had enough pain meds on board to knock an elephant on its ass.

Three hours later, Flaminius and Aurelia became the seventh king and queen in the Esca bloodline on Arkhnuet, but it brought Flame no relief. It made him feel more impotent than ever because he still couldn't protect his wife, and he knew the danger was far from over.

"I demand to see my son!"

Marcus stood stock-still in the interrogation room, trying his best not to bust a gut laughing. An hour and a half ago, he hauled Octavia in for questioning but conveniently forgot to inform Flaminius until five minutes ago.

"Did you hear me, you Neanderthal?"

"I did, Your Majesty."

"Well then, run along and get him!"

"I'm sorry, Your Majesty, but no one knows where he is."

Octavia's face blew up like a pissed-off pufferfish. He couldn't remember when last he'd had this much fun. Then Flaminius marched into the subterranean interrogation room and spoiled it all.

Nodding his head at his mother, Flaminius sat on the only other metal chair in the room and dropped a folder on the table with a dull thud. "Morning, mother. I hope you didn't have to wait too long."

"You bloody well know I've been here for over an hour!" Octavia barked.

Flaminius shifted his eyes to Marcus for a split second before dropping his head to hide his smile behind a cough. "Sorry about that, unavoidable delay."

"Let's just get this over with."

Flaminius pulled the folder closer and opened it. "I want to clarify that this is merely a formality and that you are not under suspicion."

"Don't patronize me, Flaminius. I know the law; ask your stupid questions."

"As you wish. Can you account for your whereabouts on the day in question?"

"No, I bloody well can't. If you want to know that, you can ask my secretary. I've been busy running Arkhnuet, in case you haven't noticed."

"We could get this done faster if you would answer the questions without sarcasm."

Octavia leaned forward and banged her fist on the table. "I would rather pull my toenails out with rusty pliers than make this easier on you!"

And make it difficult, she did. What should have lasted an hour at the most ended up taking five. Flaminius really fucking hated his mother.

Chapter Seventeen - Official Coronation

Two Weeks Later

Apart from a tiny twinge every now and then, Aurelia felt as good as new, which was just as well because Sue, Madame Suzette, and their evil army of primpers and preeners were at it again.

"You'll be happy to know that the coronation is an intimate affair requiring no frills."

"Really, Sue? How refreshing."

Ignoring her sarcastic remark, Sue continued. "The tradition started when the first king in the Esca bloodline took the throne. He believed a king should ascend the throne with humility because his people elected him to serve them. This symbolic gesture morphed into tradition because the Arkhnuetian people loved what it represented."

A few hours later, Aurelia found out that Sue had lied. Well, not lied as much as left out specific details, such as the gown may not be elaborate, but it was still a gown that required a corset and everything that went with it. The ceremony was intimate if you overlooked the fact that they broadcast live it to the entire nation. But only the council members, royal family, her parents, the royal press correspondents, and the camera crew were allowed in the throne room.

Flaminius looked dashing in his white tunic and loose-fitting pants. Aurelia looked pasty in her white gown, but it was lovely in its simplicity. The bodice, square cut, the sleeves long and loose, and the skirts unpleated and made of linen, not silk. Neither she nor Flame wore shoes or jewelry, her hair styled in a simple braid left to flow over her shoulder. In contrast, everybody else was dressed to the nines, especially Octavia. Flaminius and Aurelia were the last to enter the room and take their seats in the front row next to Aurelia's parents, facing Romulus and Octavia, seated on the thrones. Aurelia noticed her mother looked more nervous than she did. Leaning over, she took her mom's hand and whispered, "Technically, we're already king and queen. This is only for appearance's sake, Mom, so don't look so worried."

Rosalind smiled and patted her hand. "Is that why we have to endure this ceremony?"

Aurelia nodded. "Personally, I could have done without it, but—"

Looking up, she noticed the queen glaring at her. After everything she'd been through, Aurelia didn't care what the queen thought. The woman could suck eggs; if she wanted to talk to her mother during the coronation, she would. The king's secretary started proceedings by reading the lengthy contract explaining the future king and queen's official duties. Bartholomew may not be the most gregarious individual—oh, alright! He was downright stuffy, to say the least—but Aurelia had to give credit where credit was due. Few could stand at attention for over an hour, reading in a steady voice without a break.

Once the contract reading concluded, Romulus walked to the table next to the thrones and called Flaminius to sign the document. Since the official record was already filed, this was a copy for the benefit of citizens watching at home or on the giant floating screens set up in public spaces around the palace.

Romulus led his son back to his seat and turned to the small gathering. "Today is bittersweet for me. Serving you has been the greatest privilege of my life and also the most challenging." Looking down, Romulus cleared his throat. "I hope I have served you well. For my part, I can say I always did what I thought was right. However, I am no longer what you need."

Octavia sat on her throne, blank-faced and statue-still. Her husband was indeed no longer what Arkhnuet needed, but neither was Flaminius, and she would be damned if the last nine hundred plus years of her life were for naught. She wasn't sure when Romulus stopped making the hard decisions, nor did she care. Next time she wouldn't leave the planning to Tiberius; she

OFFICIAL CORONATION

would decide how to destabilize Flaminius's footing because she was the only one who would do what was right for Arkhnuet.

Perhaps it was because Octavia sat so still that her sudden change of position caught Aurelia's attention. Whatever it was, it was of no consequence. What was significant was her look of contempt directed toward Aurelia that made her uncomfortable. In fact, it downright scared her, and she realized that Octavia's dislike of her was more of, if-I-had-a-chance-I-would-kill-you than I-can't-stand-to-be-in-the-same-room-as-you. That got her thinking. What if Flame wasn't the target? What if the assassin didn't miss?

Romulus continued his speech, drawing her attention back. "Today, I hand my throne to you, Flaminius Theodore Alexander Esca. May your reign last many years, your children inherit the throne, and your legacy eclipse time altogether."

Squeezing Aurelia's hand, Flaminius stood and walked to his father, who guided him to the throne.

"Be seated on the throne and claim your people as your children from this day forward."

Flaminius sat, and his father placed the crown on his head from his position behind the throne. He swore he felt the weight of the world descend on his shoulders. Interestingly enough, he didn't hate the feeling. Yes, it was a heavy responsibility, but it was one he was grateful for because it led him to Aurelia.

Next, Flaminius got to make his wife his queen. He extended his hand to Octavia and guided her off her throne to stand behind it. He then fetched his wife and seated her on her throne. Removing the crown from Octavia's head, Flaminius turned to Aurelia, "Be seated on the throne and claim your place next to your king as the mother of our nation." Flame placed the crown on her head, sealing her destiny with his.

As soon as Flaminius sat next to Aurelia, Romulus shouted. "Long live the Esca bloodline!"

Never in his wildest imagination would Flaminius have believed he would relish this moment. It proved that what one initially perceived as a disaster could become your greatest gift. He only hoped he could find the assassin before he prematurely ended his newfound happiness.

Chapter Eighteen -
To Catch a Killer

As with their wedding, the celebration lasted deep into the night. Aurelia wanted to meet the people who took the trouble to come and honor their new king. Flaminius forbade his wife from going out to meet the citizens, stating her injured leg wasn't ready for such strenuous activity, so naturally, they were currently surrounded by hundreds of eager citizens vying for a second of their queen's time.

"I thought you would've learned by now that ultimatums don't work with her."

Flaminius stood next to Marcus in the protective circle of RPU soldiers, one hand on the hilt of his knife, the other on the butt of the pistol slung low on his hips. Scowling at his friend, Flaminius replied, "Maybe not, but she's open to negotiations." Sticking his arm out, he touched Aurelia on the shoulder. "She agreed to stay no more than an arm's length away from me," he finished smugly as Aurelia's hand reached to touch his. "But, I'm still learning to control my protective instincts when it comes to her."

Marcus patted Flaminius on the back. "Not sure you're ever going to get that under control, brother."

"Probably a futile exercise," Flaminius agreed, keeping his eyes trained on his wife. They watched her interact with the people for a while, accepting bouquets and other gifts. When her arms could carry no more, Sue would appear and whisk her stash away only for his wife's arms to fill up again. Their progress was slow because of her tight-knit guard, but it didn't seem to bother her. She looked incredible, glowing with the pleasure of giving her time and love to people she didn't even know. Flame had to remind himself that he was there to protect his wife, not pop a boner every time Aurelia pulled him in close to shake the hand of some person or coo over a bald-headed baby.

After several hours, he noticed that she no longer walked with her usual grace because her injured leg hurt. Predictably, she refused to leave, but Flame was having none of it. Instead of wasting valuable time arguing with her, he picked her up and, in a booming voice, declared, "My queen is exhausted and is going to bed. Thank you all for your time."

Slapping his chest, she cried, "Flame! Please put me down. You're rude." Kissing her forehead, he smiled at her and said, "Does it look like they think I'm rude?"

Aurelia turned her head, and through the now rapidly moving circle of guards, she saw the people waving and clapping. She even saw a few women fan themselves and sigh while they dabbed their eyes with tissues. Irritably, she had to admit that his alpha-male bravado probably added to the people's idea of the most excellent love story in history. Snuggling closer to her man, she enjoyed it instead of pushing a point she really didn't care about one way or the other. Oh! It was great to be in love.

Tiberius sat with his feet up on the iron railing, drinking a glass of whiskey. His shock of blond, almost white hair stood like a beacon even in the dark recess of the balcony. Like his brother, he was a big man, but with none of the stature, and he was born with a strange anomaly: one blue and one green eye. Some said it was a bad omen; those who knew him well were sure of it.

Delinea and Gaia were long since asleep, so he took a moment to reflect on the past few months' events. From his vantage point, he could see their new queen basking in the glory of her crown. The people lapped it up, as they should. Never had a newly crowned queen debased herself by walking among the commoners and speaking to them. His mother was probably so upset the royal healer would need to sedate her.

He should be just as upset, but for the life of him, he couldn't muster the energy. She was so beautiful, so pure in her intentions, that he felt himself, like everyone else, fall under her spell. He threw his drink down his throat, feeling the burn, and poured another.

He fucking hated that he envied his brother's right to the crown. But to covet his brother's wife? He didn't have words for how that made him feel. With his luck, their firstborn would be a boy. Rounding out the perfect fucking life Tiberius wanted for himself, and yet it remained ever elusive.

Delinea was no slouch in the looks department, but she was timid in bed. He gave up trying to make her understand that a man such as himself needed more than vanilla between the sheets, and he eventually took a lover. But even his mistress once belonged to Flaminius. Tiberius couldn't seem to get away from his brother's sloppy seconds.

Don't even get him started on Delinea's refusal to try for another child. A few years ago, he brought it up again, and she shot him down using her usual excuse. He knew her pregnancy with Gaia was fraught with problems, but he made it clear that he wanted a boy when they married. Delinea had no problem agreeing at the time, but when Tiberius reminded her of her promise, she said she had no way of knowing how hard pregnancy would be. Delinea's decision prompted Tiberius to insist that they lead separate lives while remaining under the same roof.

Gaia was approaching puberty, and Delinea kept herself busy with her women's groups and raising their daughter. What was there for him? Nothing. No son to guide into manhood, no work he cared about, just endless dreary days occasionally brightened by a romp in the sack with his mistress. Not that Delinea knew of that. She may not be an assertive woman, but she would never stand for him humiliating her.

An upsurge in clapping and cheering brought his attention back to the crowd below, and he saw Flaminius carry his wife off like some swashbuckling hero in a romance novel. It made him want to puke—his perfect fucking brother with his perfect fucking life.

Tiberius used to think his mother was the only person who believed in him, and when she approached him to help her 'persuade' Flaminius to give up the throne, he agreed. But he soon realized her plot had nothing to do with her supposed belief that he would make a better king and more to do with the fact that she hated Aurelia had upstaged her. In his mother's mind, killing the future queen was the perfect way to get Flaminius to step down because he would be too heartbroken to rule. Tiberius wasn't stupid enough to call his mother on her bullshit in case he needed her help to achieve his goal. But Tiberius knew his brother well. If they killed Aurelia, Flaminius would leave no stone unturned to find those responsible, and when he did, he would show no mercy.

No, his plan was much better. Slower to execute, but the result would be worth it. However, he couldn't leave his mother to go off half-cocked and ruin his plan, so he agreed to hire an assassin as his mother asked so that he could remain in control. Finding one was easy enough with the amount of money offered for the job, especially when he gave the order to wound Aurelia, not kill her as his mother wanted. He would soon leave a few breadcrumbs to expose the trigger-man to divert suspicion from him and make sure he kept his bloody mother muzzled.

Aurelia wished she could say settling into her new role as queen was easy, but as the weeks passed, she feared she might never find her rhythm. She longed to go back to school, but that was impossible with her mounting obligations. Calls from home kept her grounded but couldn't comfort her as much as her mother's physical presence would. Aurelia understood Rosalind might be retired, but she also had obligations.

Thank Source for Sue. She kept Aurelia from losing her mind or making a fool of herself by flouting some rule or other. Just this morning, Sue gently steered her away from such a debacle when Aurelia plopped herself down next to a low-ranking lady of the court instead of honoring the highest-ranking lady by allowing her to pour tea for her queen. It was fucking ridiculous. She wasn't naïve enough to think she would love all the aspects of her job, but Aurelia had yet to find something she liked. She was the most powerful woman on Arkhnuet, yet she couldn't make a real difference.

Whenever she tried to speak to Flame about her feelings, he got called away to deal with some dire situation that almost always took until the early morning hours. Then there was the constant presence of the guards because the threat to their lives remained unsolved. Life had a way of throwing curveballs. But then again, it also gave gifts. One such gift came from an unexpected source: her niece-in-law.

Initially, Aurelia tried to forge a bond with Delinea, but it didn't take long to realize they had nothing in common. But her daughter, Gaia, and Aurelia got on like a house on fire, mainly because Gaia was intelligent, insightful, funny, and wise beyond her years.

Tiberius attempted to be friendly, but Aurelia felt uncomfortable around him. She couldn't put her finger on why. He never acted inappropriately; it was more the way he looked at her. Flame clearly loved his brother, so Aurelia pushed her feelings aside to find good in him.

That evening during dinner, Flame informed Aurelia that he had to travel to the Northern Province to deliberate a dispute that would take him away for several days.

"Why can't I come with you?"

Flame shook his head. "It's too dangerous to travel at this time, sweetheart. I want you here where you're protected."

Huffing, she replied, "You mean you don't want me traveling with you because you have a target on your back."

Lowering his fork, Flame took her hand. "Aurelia, honey, I can take care of myself, and it really is too dangerous for you. I don't think I need to remind you of what happened the last time an assassin tried to kill me. There is no way I'm going to put you in that position again."

"Of course, I remember, but—"

Tilting his head, Flame said, "But what?"

"What if you weren't the target?" Flame shook his head immediately. Squeezing his hand, she pushed on. "No, listen. I know you think there's no reason for anyone to hurt me, but what if that's exactly what they want us to think?"

Anything was possible, but it didn't ring true for Flame. "Baby, I was definitely the target. You have no history with these people."

Aurelia frowned. "These people?"

"Yeah. Politicians like my mother, who are adept at playing the game necessary to climb to the top of the political power pile."

Aurelia didn't like her husband's bitter tone. "I don't doubt what you say. Nor do I have enough knowledge to argue the subject, but I've met the council members you call 'political climbers,' and I think most of them really care about their people."

Flame took a sip of wine. "I know, but if you knew what I was dealing with at the moment, you might understand."

Sighing, Aurelia replied, "Well, why don't you tell me what you're dealing with so I can share in your concerns instead of lying awake at night worrying about you?"

Flame leaned forward and kissed her cheek. "I'm not very good at remembering that I'm a 'we' now." Taking her hand, he guided her away from the table to the more comfortable couch. Once settled, he thought of the best way to explain the political turmoil in the Northern Province. "I told you I was going to sort out a dispute, but it's more than a trivial difference."

Nodding encouragingly, Aurelia waited.

"Maybe it would be easier if I started at the beginning. My father was a good soldier. Great, some might say. But he wasn't a good politician and left most of that to my mother. Over the years, she promoted those people she felt were more in line with her views." Pulling a face, he continued, "I don't have to tell you what a disaster that was. We had a war because of it, not that my mother ever took responsibility."

"I don't like Octavia, but I don't think it's fair to lay the blame for the war at her feet. Not entirely, anyway."

Smiling, Flame rubbed his eyes. He was so tired. "No, I suppose that is a bit unfair. But trust me when I say she played a significant role." Shaking his head, he continued, "But I digress. Part of my plan is to return the system to a true democracy. It has always been the king's prerogative to appoint the councilman to the provinces. My mother preferred to elect them herself from a list of qualified candidates when a post became available. I want to revert to elections where the people of the province decide who takes office."

"But there are a few people who take exception to your decision?"

"Exactly. Merrick, the current outgoing Northern Province minister, believes his son should hold the position. I agree that his son is a very qualified candidate, but I want an election."

"Is there anyone else vying for the post?"

"A few people. I've investigated each candidate and have no objections to any of them, so elections will go ahead."

Shrugging her shoulders, Aurelia said, "Then I don't understand what the problem is. You've decided, and I think it's the right decision. The people have the right to call for an election if they lose faith in their king; they should also have the right to choose their provincial leaders."

"The problem is, my brother has thrown his hat into the ring, and Merrick is crying nepotism. I find myself in a difficult position. Do I allow Tiberius to remain a candidate, which is his right as a citizen, and run the risk of being perceived as a king with a nepotistic agenda, or do I insist he withdraws?"

"I see your predicament."

They sat in silence for a few moments, and then Flame asked, "What would you do?"

"Me?" Flame waited for her reply. "There's no simple answer, but if it were me, I would point out to the councilman that it could just as easily be perceived as nepotism if his son ran for office. Then I would suggest that they both be allowed to run or withdraw their candidacy and leave that decision to Merrick. That way, no one can accuse you of heavy-handed tactics, and it puts the prickly ball back in his court."

Well, knock him down with a feather. His wife solved a dilemma in three seconds that he'd been wrestling with for weeks. "Why didn't I ask your opinion earlier?"

She leaned in and kissed him. "Maybe next time you will?"

Gently brushing a strand of hair out of her eyes, Flame kissed the tip of her nose. "I will."

"So, does that mean I can come with you?"

"No, you little minx. You're still safer here under Marcus's watchful eye."

"Do you think the conflict in the Northern Province is the reason for the attack?"

"It's highly likely that some disgruntled members of the public took exception to my decision. The Northern Province is second only to the Capitol Province and garners a significant chunk of our annual budget. Many businesses benefit from arrangements made with Councilman Merrick, and a change in office could cost people millions."

Pulling his wife into his arms, he said, "Don't look so worried. I'll only be gone one or two days at most now that you've given me a solution." Wrapping her arms around his waist, Aurelia rested her head on his chest and closed her eyes. She hated they wouldn't sleep in the same bed for a night, but she would have to get used to it, she supposed. However, she couldn't shake the feeling that they were missing something.

The following day, Flaminius left early with a few RPU guards, Bartholomew, and Tiberius. Leaving his warm, willing wife's body in their bed was murder. Maybe in a couple of months, when things had calmed down, they could return to their beach house and finish their honeymoon. The thought made him smile.

It was nearing the end of summer, and the weather in the north will be nippy. So Flaminius added his black RPU down jacket to his uniform. In contrast, Tiberius wore his usual three-piece suit. That was another reason his mother didn't think he was ready to be king, as if clothes made a man grow a pair of balls. Flaminius had to admit Tiberius did rock the suit and leather loafers in a way that made women swoon.

Things between the brothers had never been super close, but since Flaminius announced the return of elections, their relationship took a turn into the frozen zone. As usual, his mother insisted on offering her unsolicited opinion on the matter, making it worse. Standing on the rifting platform in silence, they waited for the pilot to do his thing while Tiberius fiddled with his gold cufflinks, avoiding Flaminius's eye.

"Tiberius, I know you're mad at me, but I can't be your brother when I'm dealing with official business." Tiberius nodded stiffly. Sighing, Flaminius tried again. "It's got nothing to do with my loyalty to you as my brother. I can't promise it will always be easy, but I can guarantee that I will always be fair in public matters. And you're a citizen of Arkhnuet before you're my brother." Tiberius didn't say a thing. Flaminius hoped his brother would be in a better mood after the meeting, but that depended on Councilman Merrick's decision. Good or bad, at least Tiberius wouldn't be able to blame him anymore.

Tiberius listened to his brother's excuses, but it was too little, too late. He was furious with Flaminius for reinstating elections, making it impossible for Tiberius to strong-arm his way into the Northern Province council seat.

Attaining that position was instrumental to his plan. Without it, he would need to accumulate a great deal of money on his own, adding years to his plot. Flaminius's disloyalty burned deep and forced his hand.

He ordered the assassin to try again, only this time, he must not miss. It pained him that Aurelia was the sacrifice that he needed to make to accomplish his goal, but he refused to let sentiment derail his plans.

Aurelia's morning started the same as always. Marcus must have arrived when Flame left because he was already sipping coffee when she got up. Sue arrived at seven and joined them for breakfast to discuss the daily schedule.

Shoring up her strength, Aurelia dressed and left the apartment to tackle the first task of the day: a ribbon-cutting ceremony to open a new wing of the library. At least it wasn't an utterly useless endeavor, as the new section catered only to the study of more environmentally friendly forms of mining.

By four o'clock, Aurelia was ready to go to the ladies' receiving room and take tea. Because of its predictable timing, Marcus wanted to stop this daily event until they could ensure her safety. Flame agreed, but Aurelia refused to cower in a corner. She might hate this part of her day, but it was her day. Besides, if Flame was the target, she didn't see any reason to change her routine. As a compromise, Marcus agreed to keep her routine if she allowed extra RPU guards around the receiving room and more to accompany them back and forth. She reluctantly agreed.

At five to four, Marcus led his charge through the winding passages of the castle. As an extra precaution, Marcus decided which route they would take at the last minute. Today's route took them through a courtyard covered with a domed glass roof. Aurelia noticed that the usually barren area had transformed into a veritable arboretum.

Halfway through the tunnel of foliage, Marcus caught a flash of light from above. Acting instantly, he shouted, "Cover! Incoming from above!" A split second later, bullets started flying. Moving lightning fast, he grabbed Aurelia and tucked her head against his chest, ensuring her tiny body remained covered as he pushed her through the doorway to the safety of the corridor. Just before they cleared the hallway, he felt a burn in his calf; ignoring it, he picked her up and ran. Two RPU guards flanked him, their weapons drawn. Seconds later, they ran into one of the safe rooms dotted along the palace corridors. Only once Keith had slammed the door and bolted it did Marcus let Aurelia go. "Are you hurt?"

"I think I'm okay," Aurelia said, passing shaking hands over her body.

Speaking into his comm link, he barked: "Control, this is Alpha. Initiate palace lockdown. Sue, contact the king's guard. Advise he is on lockdown; the queen is unharmed and secured. I'm on my way back to you." Striding to the door, he ordered, "Keith, stay here and don't allow anyone in but me." He pointed to the other guard, "Butch, follow me."

Aurelia leaned against the wall, trying to catch her breath. Marcus's easygoing demeanor was history. For the first time, she saw the soldier Flame respected so much, and the sight was frightening. Gathering her wits, she stood on her quivering legs and asked, "What should I do?"

Marcus glanced at her. "Nothing. Stay here and don't move unless I say so."

As Marcus turned to leave, Aurelia noticed blood soaking the bottom of his left leg. Gasping, she ran forward, grabbing his arm. "You're bleeding!" He looked down, patted her arm while disengaging from her, and left.

Marcus waited until the door closed and heard the bolt engage before he spoke into his comm link while hurrying back to the courtyard, Butch in tow. "Status update."

Immediately, a breathless voice crackled over the radio. "South-east side of the castle, in foot pursuit of suspect running east toward the woods. Too far to get a good description, but perp is wearing all black, face mask or hoodie, and he's fucking fast."

It pissed Marcus off that his injury excluded him from the chase. This piece of shit tried to kill their queen twice, not to mention making him look like an incompetent idiot. Another voice rasped over the radio. "Jeff here; I've joined foot pursuit, coming from the opposite direction. I'm going to cut him off before he enters the woods. But Stoney's right, this fucker's fast."

"Roger that. Hunter, I want you up on the roof where I saw the flash before the shooting. If there's as much as a pin-prick of evidence up there, I want it collected."

"Roger that, boss."

"Jake, where are you?"

"Me, Mark, and Sean are on wheels driving around the woods east-bound in case the perp makes it through; we can cut him off."

Marcus knew the assassin couldn't escape north or south because there was a bog to the north and the white cliff face with a several-hundred-foot drop to the south. The fucker had to exit those woods where his boys were headed.

"I don't think I need to say it, but we need this fucker alive, boys."

"Yes, boss." Jake.

"Roger." Jeff.

"Got it." Stoney.

Sue hadn't left the courtyard; she was on her phone, gesticulating wildly, clearly agitated. She was one of the few female RPU members, but she was one of the best Marcus ever trained, so he assigned her to Aurelia. You had to respect someone who could kick ass in high-heels. Turning to face Marcus and Butch, Sue put her finger up to indicate she would be with him in a second. Once she disconnected, Marcus asked, "What did you see, Sue?"

Shaking her head in disgust, she said, "Nothing, I only realized something was wrong when you shouted."

"What did the king say?"

"His fucking secretary gave me the runaround, and I didn't want to give the shithead details. Pansy would probably faint."

Marcus's nostrils flared in anger. He pulled his phone off his belt, dialed Flaminius's number, and put the phone to his ear. It rang five times before Bartholomew answered in his snarky, pretentious voice. "His Majesty is not currently available, Colonel. Can I take a message?"

"No!" Marcus barked. "I want to speak to him now, and if you give me any more shit, I'll rip you another asshole the next time I see you."

Bartholomew stuttered several times before he said in a slightly less cocky voice. "He's in an important meeting, and he gave me strict instructions not to interrupt."

It surprised Marcus the man possessed a backbone. "Listen up, you fuck-tard!" he bellowed. "Put the king on the phone now!"

Finally, Marcus heard the secretary walking, muffled voices, more walking before Flaminius boomed, "What's wrong?"

"Aurelia is fine, but there's been another attack."

He hadn't finished his sentence when he heard Flaminius' footsteps pounding on the concrete floor. "I'm on my way. Where are you?"

"The situation is not contained; the palace is on lockdown. You need to stay there until I can safely rift you in."

"Fuck that! I'm coming. Where are you?"

"Flaminius, you're the king. I can't allow you to jeopardize your safety." Clicking his fingers and gesturing aggressively to Sue to carry out his next order, he continued, "I'm authorizing your lockdown right now." But Marcus was speaking to dead air. "Flaminius! Flaminius. Fuck!"

Marcus put his hands on his hips, looked down, and sighed. "Control, secure rifter bay, sector one. King in transit." Indicating for Sue to follow him, he went to tell Aurelia that Flaminius was on his way. Knocking, he announced himself, and his man let him in. Aurelia had been pacing and chewing her thumbnail.

Her face crumpled at the news; she burst into tears and ran to Marcus. "You're hurt. We have to get you help." She sobbed.

Rubbing her back, he tried to console her. "It's okay; I'm already healing. Look, it's not even bleeding anymore."

A commotion came in on the radio. "Man down, man down!" Sue stepped forward and took Aurelia from Marcus's arms so he could give his men his full attention. "What's going on!"

Jake answered. "Parked on the road, east side of the woods. Taking sniper fire. Sean is down." In the background, Marcus heard more gunshots.

Running as fast as he could, wounded leg forgotten, he and Butch made their way to a truck. "Speak to me, Jake. What's going on?" More gunfire, shouting, then silence."

"Colonel, Jeff, here. I'm seconds away from Jake's location; let you know when I have a visual."

"Roger. Where's Stoney?'

"Don't know, haven't seen him."

"Fuck!" Marcus roared.

For several excruciating minutes, they drove in silence, keeping their eyes and ears peeled. Finally, Jeff spoke. "Got visual on our boys. They're down, Colonel. Not sure if they're alive. Can't break cover and give the fucker another target."

"ETA one minute. Stay low."

"Roger."

Butch stopped their vehicle behind Jake's truck. Marcus jumped out, and Butch immediately laid cover while Marcus made his way to his men lying on the ground. They were injured but alive. As he popped his head over the hood, the sniper fired a volley of shots; one projectile ricocheted and grazed his head, knocking him on his ass. Ears ringing, Marcus watched Butch break cover to his left, and Jeff do the same from the forest to his right while running to the safety of the trucks. Butch crouched next to Marcus, keeping guard while Jeff checked his wound. Suddenly, several more shots rang out. Their radios crackled to life, and Stoney's rough voice asked, "Colonel, you there?"

"Here," Marcus answered, dazed.

"You're going to be pissed, Colonel, but I killed the fucker."

Marcus sighed. "You sure?"

"Pretty sure. I'm looking at his brains splattered all over a tree trunk."

"Are you okay?"

"Yup."

"Good, get over here."

Stoney, Butch, and Jeff called for medics while Marcus contacted their forensic team to come and make sense of this fucking mess.

It only took Flaminius half an hour to rift back to the palace and find his wife. The moment she saw him, Aurelia broke away from Sue and flew into his arms. Intense relief washed through him, and he found his knees would no longer hold his weight. Lifting Aurelia, he crumbled to the floor and clung to her. "Shh baby, I'm here now."

Sue kneeled next to him and whispered. "Marcus is injured. He and the others took off after the suspect. They've taken fire, and we have heard nothing for seven minutes."

"Get me their status."

"Every available man we have is on their way to their last known location, and—" Sue didn't finish her sentence before Keith interrupted them. "I have them! Colonel Brewer is okay. Sean, Mark, and Jake are down, but alive. Medics on the way."

Aurelia went limp in Flame's arms with relief.

"I'm going to join the team and help, Sire."

Flaminius nodded to Sue. "When you see Colonel Brewer, you tell him to get his ass to our apartment once he's treated so Aurelia can see for herself that he's okay."

"Yes, Sire."

Once Flaminius felt calmer, he carried his wife to their room and ordered Frank to get them something to eat. Then he ran a bath and sank into the hot water with Aurelia cuddled between his legs. He heated the water twice before she stopped shaking and eventually fell asleep. Flame gently dried her, and they slipped between the covers. Smoothing her hair back, he rocked her to make sure she remained sleeping. Hours later, Frank quietly announced that Marcus had arrived. Flaminius moved as carefully as he could not wake his wife, but he needn't have bothered.

Apart from a bandage on his temple and leg, Marcus seemed unharmed. Flaminius was so relieved; he hugged his friend. That Marcus hugged him back with no wisecrack showed the seriousness of the situation. Flaminius sat him down and poured them both a healthy dose of whiskey. "What happened out there, Marcus?"

Resting his elbows on his knees and holding the whiskey glass against his forehead, Marcus relayed the sequence of events to Flaminius. Sean was currently fighting for his life in Capital City Hospital with serious gunshot wounds to both gut and neck. At the moment, the only thing the doctors would commit to was that Sean had a fifty-fifty chance of survival. Thankfully, the rest had minor injuries. Marcus left Sean's wife and parents to watch over him while he debriefed Flaminius.

"What does Stoney have to say? Why didn't he communicate with you when you called?" Flaminius asked.

Marcus slumped back in the chair. "He was tracking the perp and knew he was getting close, so he turned off his radio. By the time Stoney found him, the sniper had already downed half my team." Sighing, Marcus continued, "Stoney didn't have a clear shot because the guy was up a tree well concealed by branches. He shot blind."

Flaminius frowned. "Pretty fucking lucky to get a kill shot under those circumstances?"

Marcus shook his head. "He didn't. Stoney got him in the shoulder. The guy fell out the tree and hit his head on a fucking rock, cracked his skull like an egg." Putting his glass on the coffee table, Marcus continued in a subdued, almost defeated voice. "I failed my queen, and I failed you again. There are only six routes to get from your apartment to where she needed to be. The fucker just needed to pick one and be patient. I should have foreseen this."

"This is the second time you've saved her life. If anyone failed her, it was me. I left her alone, and I didn't listen when she suggested she was the target." Swallowing the lump in his throat, Flaminius whispered, "I owe you everything for the heartache you spared me. You didn't fail her, Marcus, and I will hear no more of it. Get some sleep. We can pick up the investigation tomorrow."

Marcus stood. "What about Aurelia?"

"She's sleeping now, but she was almost inconsolable when they couldn't reach you and the others. The moment she heard you were unharmed, she collapsed."

Limping to the door, Marcus said, "Please tell her I'm sorry for everything."

"I told you, there is nothing to be sorry about."

Marcus smiled, then left to get some shut-eye, but he knew he would probably end up playing video games for the rest of the night.

Flaminius poured himself another drink and contemplated their next move. A successful investigation would be infinitely harder with a dead assassin, but Flame was relieved the son-of-a-bitch posed no further threat to his wife. However, he wasn't stupid enough to believe they were out of danger.

Chapter Nineteen -
Getting Away with Murder

Tiberius returned to a castle in turmoil after Marcus lifted the lockdown. Every RPU soldier reported for duty, and until they knew how an assassin snuck onto castle grounds undetected, no one would rest. They denied access to his brother. He sat on pins and needles for hours, waiting for confirmation that the man he had hired was dead since he didn't relish the idea of hanging for treason. Finally, as a last resort, he went to the scene and asked the RPU soldiers questions. To his relief, he heard that his man died without speaking to anyone. His relief was short-lived. Over the following weeks, the investigators concluded the perpetrator did not act alone. Tiberius had been meticulous in hiding his tracks, but he wasn't one to leave anything to chance, so he devised a strategy to divert attention away from himself.

It was easy to organize seating arrangements. Tiberius sat next to Merrick at the king's formal dinner the night before, a council meeting to brief the members on the investigation's progress. Tiberius waited until Merrick had consumed three glasses of wine during dinner, all the time throwing menacing glares at Flaminius before he spoke.

"I wanted to compliment you, Councilman."

Merrick, pavlova-loaded spoon suspended halfway to his mouth, turned his head toward Tiberius. "Compliment me?"

"Yes, the king placed you in an awkward position. I'm impressed by your decision."

Merrick snorted, then shoved the dessert in his mouth. "You expect me to believe you're happy when my decision effectively killed your political ambitions?"

"No, but that's hardly your fault, is it?"

Merrick looked at Tiberius suspiciously. "No, it wasn't, but given the circumstances, I felt I had no choice."

Tiberius smiled sadly at the man. "I'm sorry your son won't see his dream come true. If I had known my brother intended to do that, I would've withdrawn my candidacy."

Merrick shrugged. "That's hardly your fault, is it?"

Laughing, Tiberius said, "No." Subtly changing the subject, he asked, "So, what do you think of this dreadful assassination attempt on our queen?"

They spoke of the dire state of affairs for the next half hour while the other dinner guests either enjoyed cheese and port or strolled to the card tables set up on the other side of the room for a few friendly games of whist. Finally, when Merrick had worked himself into a frothing lather over the current regime's incompetence and how something like this would never have happened when Romulus ruled, Tiberius said, "I agree with you. However, we can't blame my brother. One expects the RPU to do their job." Then, shaking his head, he continued in an appropriately frightened tone, "I haven't felt safe since it happened. I mean, how can we trust the RPU to protect us?"

Merrick's eyes flashed with glee. "You know, I never thought of it like that." Filling his glass with more port, Merrick asked, "Is it true that the king and the colonel in charge of the queen's detail are close friends?"

Tiberius had to restrain himself from pumping the air in victory. "Some would say that the colonel is the only person close to my brother; they served together in the war. Why do you ask?"

Merrick tried to behave casually. "I just wondered if the man is up to the task. Perhaps the king places too much faith in someone so close to him." Holding his hand up, he continued, "The unexpected can happen, but this was the second attempt on the queen's life!"

"I don't think you should say that to my brother or Colonel Brewer. Neither of them would thank you for it."

Merrick sipped from his dainty crystal glass. "I don't doubt it, but I believe in doing the right thing even if it goes against better judgment."

Faking shock, Tiberius whispered, "Are you suggesting a vote of no confidence against Marcus Brewer?"

Merrick lowered his voice, too. "If it means our queen is safer for it? Yes, then that's what I'm suggesting."

"I admire your forthrightness, Councilman, I really do, but if you insist on this course of action, I suggest you get support from other council members before you continue."

Merrick drained his glass and excused himself from the table. Tiberius knew the man was on his way to find that support.

Flaminius tried to reason with Aurelia to keep her from attending the council meeting because he didn't want her subjected to the ugly details of her attack. He should have saved his breath for cooling his porridge. He had to admit that she looked every bit the queen she was, sitting next to him at the head of the table.

After the formalities concluded, Flaminius addressed the council. "I called this meeting because I know recent events have everybody on edge." Nodding to Marcus, Flaminius said, "Colonel Brewer needs no introduction, so I'll hand over to him."

Moving from behind the queen's chair, Marcus ordered the lights dimmed and began his report. "Thank you, Sire." He clicked the remote, and the projector hummed to life, casting a picture of the assassin against the wall.

"The perpetrator's name was Donald Goss, two hundred and twenty-six years old and lived here in Capital City." Clicking the remote again, he continued. "Extensive questioning of friends and family revealed he was an unassuming person. He worked for Death and Birth Records, which explains how he got onto palace grounds unnoticed."

"His mother said he lived alone and never gave her any trouble. Everyone we spoke to couldn't believe he committed the crime."

"Donald was a baby when his father died serving on the eastern front in the infantry. According to Donald's mother, he wanted to be an RPU soldier. Unfortunately, he didn't make the cut. Twice. Given how brutal the selection process for RPU is and how many candidates fail every year, most wouldn't come back a second time."

Merrick decided it was a perfect time to begin his attack. "Tell me, Colonel Brewer, why is it this young man failed?"

Marcus glanced at the councilman. "The first time, he failed the physical portion of the course. Three years later, he tried again and passed all sections except the psychological examination."

Merrick looked surprised. "Really? What was the problem?" His challenging, not enquiring.

Marcus scrutinized the councilman. "The psychologists felt he was too emotionally immature to handle the harsh rigors of military life. They recommended he take a few years to grow before he attempted the selection again." Marcus turned back to the screen. "Donald didn't take the rejection well and filed an official complaint, stating discrimination because his mother was human." Several council members mumbled their disbelief. "An independent investigation found the accusation groundless and dismissed it. Donald accepted the ruling. Two years ago, he applied for the third time. But because of his prior complaint and psych evaluation, the board refused him outright. That must have been the final straw for him."

Councilor Patricia leaned forward on her elbows and asked, "Is that the reason he targeted the queen?"

"Yes, ma'am. He wanted to punish the RPU for rejecting him, and what better way to do that than killing the queen, bringing dishonor to the unit charged with her protection."

Sighing, the councilwoman shook her head. "What a sad story. Does this mean he was acting alone?"

"Yes, ma'am. Initially, we thought he had an accomplice, but we've found no evidence to suggest he acted on the behest of anyone else. It was an isolated incident."

Marcus started to say something, but Merrick cut him off. "Were you part of the selection committee that rejected his application?"

Frowning, Marcus said. "I have been on the selection committee for over a hundred years, Councilman."

"Then perhaps you can explain to us how this obviously unstable character slipped your notice?"

Marcus turned to face the man. "There are hundreds of men and women that come through our facility every year. Donald raised no red flags because he never behaved suspiciously. He never ranted to his friends and family; he never wrote letters disputing the outcome of the independent investigation; hell, his own mother didn't see this coming."

Merrick wasn't giving up. "That may be, but she isn't trained to identify subversive elements; you are. And as far as I can see, Colonel, our queen almost lost her life, twice, when she was directly under your guard."

A deathly silence prevailed. Assessing Merrick's intentions, Marcus didn't respond immediately. Breaking the silence, Councilman Craig said, "What are you suggesting, Merrick? That Colonel Brewer had something to do with this?"

Outraged cries reverberated around the room. Speaking loudly to be heard, Merrick answered. "Good gracious, no! I'm suggesting that, at the very least, Colonel Brewer was negligent in his duty. At most, his close relationship with the queen clouded his judgment, and he didn't see the danger she was in."

Flaminius shot out of his chair and roared, "How dare you! My wife's integrity is impeccable. As is Colonel Brewer's."

Attempting to appease the king, Merrick held up his hands. "Of course, Sire, I'm not suggesting otherwise. I'm only saying that we must question the reason our queen suffered two traumatic attempts on her life while in the care of Colonel Brewer."

Aurelia noticed that while some council members seemed outraged at Merrick's suggestion, others agreed with him. Councilman Craig sat forward. "I'm interested to hear what Colonel Brewer has to say."

Aurelia felt numb; she couldn't believe what started as a cut-and-dried explanation of what had happened to her turned into accusations of Marcus's intentions toward her and his ability to do his job.

When Marcus spoke, it was low and controlled. "I would be happy to answer your questions in a formal hearing if you feel I didn't do my duty."

Again, total silence. Marcus had laid down the gauntlet. Either Merrick officially called for a vote of no confidence in Marcus or lose face and back down. The severity of the situation seemed to dawn on Merrick because he didn't reply immediately. Instead, he looked at the other members as if evaluating how much support he had. Aurelia watched with bated breath until something in Merrick's eyes flashed, replacing his indecision with determination. "Very well, Colonel. If that's the only way to get the answers we deserve, then so be it. I officially request a vote of no confidence in Colonel Marcus Brewer."

Several members stood, shouting and gesturing in anger. Aurelia railed against the rules that bound her, the protocol that gagged her, making it impossible to help the man that had saved her life without risking embarrassment to her husband, her people, and her parents. Looking around, she caught Marcus's eye. He stood proud and strong. Aurelia loved her husband, and she would never break a promise made to him, but this was wrong. Councilman Merrick didn't care about her; he used this situation to further his agenda against Flame. It was so apparent that it surprised her no one else recognized the ploy. She would bet all the gold in Arkhnuet that Tiberius had something to do with this. Not that she could prove it, but she hadn't missed Tiberius and Merrick with their heads bent in a deep discussion last night at dinner.

Looking across the table at Merrick, she watched as he sat back, folded his hands over his stomach, smirking at the drama playing out before him. Anger, the likes of which she had never felt before, swamped her body. Her hands shook, her cheeks flushed, and all her good intentions flew out the window. Banging her fists on the solid oak table, she shouted, "Enough!" The racket died instantly. Taking her time, Aurelia stood and smoothed her hands over the dreadfully dull gray jacket she would never have chosen for herself. "There will be no vote, not today nor any other day. Colonel Brewer saved my life. Twice! And I'll be damned if I'll allow individuals who wish to twist his acts of bravery into something hideous for their benefit." The councilmen, still standing, quietly took their seats. Aurelia didn't know what to say after her initial outburst. She hadn't expected to hold their attention so completely.

"I beg your pardon, Your Highness, but as far as I can recall, the queen, unfortunately, doesn't have the power to stop the council from voting on anything. Only the king has that right."

It was no surprise that Merrick, the weasel, tried to talk down to her. Fuck him! Today he would learn that she was not just a queen, but a loyal friend.

Before she could respond, Flame growled. Placing her hand on his arm, she smiled and hoped he would understand that she needed to do this herself. But his growl made it clear to all that he supported her. And they should choose their words carefully. Unfortunately, there was no cure for stupid.

"And we all know that the king hates nepotism and would never put his personal feelings above protocol." Merrick smirked.

"You misunderstand me, Councilman Merrick." Aurelia countered. "I would never dream of upsetting protocol. But surely I have a right to speak in defense of my RPU detail? I am, as you pointed out, the one who was so viciously attacked. Twice."

No one could argue that, and Merrick knew it, so he agreed. As if she needed his permission to continue. "I would like it put on record that as far back as before the wedding, Colonel Brewer approached both myself and the king with his suspicion that we were the target of some nefarious plot. When I asked him how he knew, he said he had a strong feeling that something wasn't right. Now, some of you may scoff at that, but I think anyone who served his nation so diligently for so long would develop a sixth sense for danger." A few people nodded their agreement.

"Colonel Brewer was the only one who believed that I was the target and not the king. There has been no negligence by him nor anyone else in my security detail. Not only did they do their duty, but they did it with no concern for their lives. Colonel Brewer and some of his men were shot protecting me. One man was critically injured and barely survived. Are you trying to add insult to injury by suggesting that they didn't do their duty, Councilman Merrick?"

Puffing out his chest, Merrick blustered. "Now, wait just one moment!"

Too pissed off to care, Aurelia interrupted him. "No, I will not wait just one moment!" Piercing him with her best scary stare, she said, "It surprises me that no one has pointed out your glaringly obvious agenda, so let me be the first. You are angry that the king cut you off at the knees and prevented your son from running for office. This nonsense is a way for you to get your own back." Merrick gasped, but Aurelia ignored him. "At best, it's childish and petty; at worst, it's a flagrant misuse of your power as a councilman. So, I ask this council: who it is we should investigate? My security detail that executed their duty and saved my life, or Councilman Merrick for using his position to take revenge?"

Feeling she had made her point, Aurelia sat. Flaminius leaned back, crossed his arms, and said, "Does anyone wish to respond?" Flaminius's demeanor was detached and calm, his voice even and professional, but under the table, he squeezed her trembling hand.

When there was no response, the speaker of the council cleared his throat and stood. "If no one wishes to add to this debate, then we should decide if a vote of no confidence is the correct course of action. All in favor, say aye." Merrick, Craig, and one other member Aurelia couldn't remember, raised their hands and said, "Aye."

"All opposed?" A loud shout of 'nay' reverberated through the room. The speaker banged his gavel. "The nay's carry the vote."

The councilmen and women began collecting their belongings and speaking among themselves as they filed out of the room. Aurelia remained seated, waiting to regain the feeling in her legs. Flame stood behind her chair with his hands on her shoulders. Her actions would carry consequences, of that she had no doubt. But Aurelia would not spend the rest of her life having tea and opening libraries. Marcus followed the others out the door, but he looked at her before leaving and gave her a chin lift. Aurelia smiled at him.

Once they were alone, she turned to Flame. "I know I upset the apple cart, but I simply couldn't stand by and watch that odious man hurt Marcus. And what's more, I can't be the kind of queen that's only good for appeasing the court's ladies. I want my reign to count for something, and I'm sorry if you feel that's breaking my word to you."

For a long time, Flame said nothing. He just stared down at her. As she was about to say something, he spoke. "I cannot think of an instance where the council came to such a decisive and speedy decision. Not even my mother could cower them as effectively as you did today. I'm so proud of you I could burst, but in the interest of saving the poor cleaning staff the hassle, I would, instead, like to take you to our room and lick you from stem to stern until you beg me to stop."

She burst out laughing. Flame bent and scooped her up in his arms. "I'll take that as a yes."

As it turned out, the diversion proved effective but unnecessary. At least, Tiberius had identified one council member that he could use in the future. He heard the queen was formidable, and in a way, he was pleased he didn't see her in action; it would make it infinitely harder to execute his new plan if he had.

His timeline would undoubtedly elongate significantly now that he wouldn't be allowed to run for office. But perhaps he could still take advantage of the new Northern Province councilman. Of course, he would need to enlist Matilda's help for that. Her family hailed from the area, and their name carried a significant influence even long after her parents' death. Tiberius would need to be careful, though; she was persona non grata because of how she had treated the queen, but he was sure they could conquer anything together. If Source had half the intelligence believers thought it did, he and Matilda would be Perfecta Nobis.

Unfortunately, Tiberius couldn't predict the strength of Flaminius and Aurelia's love for each other or how the people would respond to it, cocooning the royal couple in devotion, making it almost impossible to unseat his brother from the throne. Maybe Tiberius would have given up if he had known that it would take nearly a century before a viable opportunity presented itself. But he didn't know any of that, so he didn't give up. Instead, he allowed the time to twist his bitterness into vile determination.

Part Two

Chapter One -
A Murder of Keys

100 Years Later

Gently drifting up from her pleasant dream, Aurelia listened to the soft mewling of her son and lay for a moment in disbelief at how much joy his little voice brought her. As the babe grew more insistent, she reached for the king, only to realize he no longer lay next to her. Supporting herself on one elbow, she glanced toward the open door of the nursery where the man she loved cradled their son in his arms, singing an ancient lullaby. Theo's nightlight cast dragons and fairies in flight across the uneven stone walls, creating a picture-perfect scene.

Slipping from their bed, she tiptoed across the costly rug Flaminius insisted on buying her for their anniversary. By the light of the banked fire, she pulled on her pink robe and snuck to the door so she could continue to spy on her two favorite boys. Her husband's visage captivated her from the first moment she saw him step out of the royal carriage a hundred years ago. How could it not? Flaminius was utterly gorgeous. But once she fell in love with him, she became happily enslaved. Theodore's cries thwarted her musings as her breasts swelled with milk and Flaminius sensed her discomfort. "How long have you been standing there?"

Shrugging one shoulder, she replied, "Long enough to know that your singing is still beautiful." Ambling toward him, she held out her arms. Kissing their son on his fuzzy head, Flaminius reluctantly handed him over. Settling herself on the couch to feed Theo, she motioned for her husband to join her. "Why do you not sleep, my love?"

Sighing deeply, he gently scoffed, "As if you don't know what weighs heavily on my mind."

"We will find an answer, Flame."

He always loved the nickname Aurelia gave him, even if his mother hated it, as she did most things about his wife. Flaminius didn't care what his mother thought. Experiencing life with Aurelia made him happier than he ever thought possible, and when Theo was born, it cemented his belief in family. His new perspective made him fear his people would never have the same joy if he couldn't solve the Keys' unprecedented increase in deaths. They were as rare as their gift was remarkable. Lily was the last Key born, and she recently celebrated her three hundredth birthday.

Theo's fussing brought Flaminius back to the present. Aurelia settled Theo over her shoulder and rubbed his back to ease his discomfort.

Flame looked down at his wife. "Why do you have such faith in me, Aurelia?"

She shifted Theo to her other shoulder. "I've told you a million times that I love you, you make me feel safe and cherished, and you care deeply for our people. Why wouldn't I have faith in you?"

Even though he used the word birthright when he spoke of the throne, Flaminius no longer took his position for granted, as he did in his youth. Tightening his embrace around his wife and little Theo, he vowed, "I will do everything in my power to continue being worthy of the faith you have in me."

Chapter Two -
Lady Killer vs. Lady Guardian

"I hate this disguise!" Tiberius fastened the last button on the back of her uniform and put his hands on Matilda's shoulders. Pulling her closer, he whispered in her ear, "But you know how much I love playing dress-up."

A thrill ran down her spine as she turned and draped her arms around his neck. "How about you show me how much?"

Tiberius slapped her shapely ass. "Get the job done. Then you get your reward."

Matilda pouted. "Spoilsport." She stepped out of his arms. "How much longer am I going to have to do this?"

Tiberius leaned against his desk, folding his arms. "Why do you ask?"

Facing the mirror, Matilda put on a white starched cap, haphazardly tucking her jet-black hair under it. "It's been a hundred years since that stupid incident, and the king still refuses to grant me admission to the palace." Tiberius chuckled. Matilda whirled around, placing her hands on her hips. "It's not funny! I've petitioned the council twelve times."

Tiberius pulled her into his arms again. "I'm not making fun of you, my sweet; it won't be long."

She rested her head on his chest. "I hope not, because I'm tired of living like an outcast."

An hour later, Matilda was glad she was a talented contortionist, or she wouldn't have been able to pull the rough, puke-green cotton fabric away from her skin and scratch the already raw patch between her shoulder blades at the same time. To make matters worse, the shoes Andreus stole were too small and pinched her toes.

The distant clinking of silverware on china plates brought her back to her task. Making sure she was alone at the beverage table, Matilda removed the small glass vial from her cleavage, emptied the colorless liquid into the jug, and swirled the juice around. Matilda walked through the busy kitchen, dodging the other maids carrying platters laden with food, and pushed the swinging door open with her behind. As unobtrusively as possible, she scanned the Keys enjoying their lunch to find one with a glass that needed filling. Locating her target, she moved to the young girl with a sickly sweet smile and large, trusting blue eyes. She filled her glass, but before Matilda could walk away, the girl touched her arm and said, "Thank you."

Matilda pulled away from the Key's touch and smiled widely. "You're welcome, my dear." The girl turned back to her friends, and Matilda made her way to Tiberius's office to get her reward.

"Am I going to die, Mother Guardian?"

Serenity's weak voice broke Mother Guardian's heart. "No, my dear child," she lied, wiping Serenity's sweaty brow with a cool cloth. "We're going to find out what's wrong with you, and we are going to fix it." The young Key visibly relaxed and released Mother Guardian's hand. "I'll call your parents back now." Serenity smiled weakly.

Mother Guardian dragged her tired body to the hospital waiting room and sank into a chair. Flaminius and Aurelia stood to one side, hand in hand, waiting for her to speak. "It's the same as the others," she said in a strangled whisper.

"I spoke to the doctors, and they still have no clue what they're dealing with," Flaminius said, exasperated.

"I refuse to believe there is nothing more we can do!" Aurelia barked.

For a long time, they sat, staring at the wall, each caught in their grim thoughts.

Suddenly, Aurelia shouted, "Gaia!"

Flame frowned at his wife. "What?"

"Gaia! We haven't asked for her help."

Flame shook his head. "No disrespect to my niece, but she isn't qualified to deal with this."

Aurelia smiled indulgently. "Honey, this is Gaia we're talking about. She could find, identify, categorize, and write a paper on this disease before our team of doctors and scientists could find their way to the lab."

Mother Guardian looked at Flaminius. "Aurelia has a point."

When Flaminius still looked skeptical, Aurelia added, "Flame, just this morning you said something didn't feel right, and you're not sure if you can trust your team. We trust Gaia."

"Okay, I'll ask her." Flame agreed.

"Shit, shit, shit!" Gaia panted to herself, hobbling along the corridor. "I don't know why I bother promising myself I'll exercise. I know I won't." Stopping to take a few deep breaths, she mumbled on, "But how was I to know the king would entrust me with something so all-consuming?"

Gaia wanted to prove herself a capable scientist, even though she was a young graduate with a mere fifty years of experience. More than that, she desperately wanted to identify the disease killing the Keys. Pushing off the wall, she continued, "But it hasn't been for nothing! I knew that class would come in handy."

Being the first Tuesday of the month, the king was in session judging legal disputes unresolved by the provincial courts (a duty he took seriously since his judgment left the complainants with no recourse). But Gaia decided this new information was too important to wait.

Finally, she arrived at the gilded doors of the throne room. Knocking impatiently, she tried to catch her breath. A member of the Royal Protection Unit poked his head out and frowned when he saw her. "What's so urgent that you need to bash the door in?"

Still panting, leaning up against the door, she waved her hand at him, irritated with his attitude. "It's important that I speak with the king immediately."

"Wait here," the guard grumbled. "I'll have to request permission from the king's secretary for you to enter."

"What utter poppycock!" Leaning to look past the large man, Gaia asked, "Where's Seth?"

The man didn't bother answering her; he just sighed and closed the door in her face. Gaia wanted to kick the door in and slap the man until his ears rang. However, she'd been working to better herself because, besides her role as her uncle's secret forensic pathologist, she had recently accepted the responsibility of Lady Guardian to her cousin, Theo. The honor usually fell to the queen's oldest sister, but since Aurelia had no siblings and considered Gaia one, she asked her to take up the role. Gaia agreed at once and vowed to protect the little prince with her life, as the job demanded.

In keeping with her new calm persona, she paced the marble corridor instead of banging on the door like a lunatic. Finally, the king's secretary appeared and stepped into the passage, closing the reception room door behind him. "What is of such importance that *you* would interrupt proceedings?"

"I would prefer to speak directly to the king regarding this matter, if you don't mind!"

His back stiffened. "Ahem! As it so happens, Lady Guardian, I most surely *do* mind."

Gaia didn't have time for this! This protocol-driven pompous ass would never let her in. "Mr. Secretary, I appreciate you must follow the rules, but if the king does not hear this information now, the very fabric of our society could be torn asunder."

He glared at her, his face twisting into a doubtful expression. "I will not allow, nor will the king approve of this disruption. His schedule is over-full as it is," and with a wave of his hand, he rudely dismissed her.

Oh, to hell with restraint. Speaking to his back, she replied with deceptive aloofness, "Very well, but I will inform the king that his secretary refused to allow his niece access to him with sensitive information he charged her to find."

That got the odious man's attention. "Fine, but I will only halt proceedings for ten minutes," he said, not bothering to turn his head.

Good enough. Rushing through the doors on the secretary's heels, she waited in the antechamber as commanded while the secretary delivered the message.

"Case file number six three nine two. Stannington versus Bright." The complainants shuffled forward when the scribe called their names. "Mr. Stannington has brought a case against Mr. Bright regarding a land dispute—"

Flaminius tried to keep his attention on the proceedings, but this was one of his least favorite duties. Aurelia squeezed his hand, bringing his attention to her. If it weren't for his wife, he would never survive these dreary hearings.

Movement at the rear of the chamber caught his eye. His secretary walked toward him with a scowl on his face and his scarlet robes billowing behind him. It was usual for the man to be grumpy; however, it was unusual for him to go against protocol and disrupt proceedings. Aurelia noticed it too, turned to Flame, and frowned.

Bending down, Mr. Secretary whispered, "Sire, your niece is outside demanding to see you. I tried to send her away, but she is most insistent."

Flaminius pitied the poor man, but Gaia was not one to overreact. "Very well. How much time can we spare?"

"None, Sire, but I will halt proceedings for ten minutes."

"Thank you, Bartholomew." Flaminius smiled, noticing his secretary wince at the casual use of his name.

Flaminius waited until the hall emptied before he called for his niece. "Thank you for seeing me, Sire." She curtsied and waited for him to speak.

"Gaia, how many times must I tell you to cease formalities while in private? Now, what do you need to tell us?"

Gaia stepped onto the dais and lowered her voice. "I've made progress in the case." Flame looked at his wife. "It's more serious than we first thought, Uncle. Someone is murdering the Keys."

Seated at his black stone desk, Tiberius leaned back, resting an elbow on the arm of the chair, holding his chin in the crook of thumb and forefinger, deep in thought. A spy had just informed him that Gaia knew the reason for the Keys' demise. He hadn't expected his daughter to interfere in his plans. It had taken more than a century to orchestrate his coup, and he would not see it come to naught because a woman didn't know her place, daughter, or no daughter.

When Gaia was a child, she craved his attention, especially after Delinea died. But he had little use for the girl. Eventually, Gaia came to the same conclusion her mother had and kept her distance. At the time, it was a relief, but now he saw the mistake he had made.

Gaia turned her affection toward his brother, and Flaminius welcomed her into his heart. When Aurelia did the same, Gaia's devotion to them fortified her loyalty. Tiberius knew she would worm her way to the truth and think nothing of throwing her father to the wolves.

He would convene an emergency meeting with the other members of the Oradagra, who were his brains trust, especially Andreus. Tiberius headed the outlawed ancient cult as its Capulus. His co-conspirator and right-hand man, Andreus, led the military wing, the Dagra.

Rubbing his tired eyes, Tiberius chuckled at the irony of the path his life had taken. If it hadn't been for that fucking conversation he had overheard between his father and Flaminius, he wouldn't care about being king. Time had not diminished the hurt his father's poisonous words had caused, and he could not help but recall that defining moment now.

"*Flaminius, you are heir to the throne, whether you like it!*"

"*You have another son who wants to be king.*"

"*Tiberius doesn't have what it takes. He is weak, easily influenced. I will not allow him to rule! If you force my hand on this issue, I will sire another son and wait for him to come of age before I hand the throne to Tiberius.*"

On that day, Tiberius swore he would wrestle sovereignty away from his brother and show his father no mercy once he had. But wanting something and making practical plans for its fruition are two very different things. Nothing Tiberius thought of had worked, and just when he figured he would never succeed, Andreus materialized.

In another desperate attempt at reconciliation, Delinea asked him to attend one of her boring social events. She enticed him with the prospect of meeting the new Capital Province council member. Andreus was the council member's bodyguard, and at first sight, Tiberius knew he was special. Using his connections, he discreetly inquired after the man and was not disappointed.

Andreus was younger than expected but had a distinguished military record, except for one incident. A fellow soldier became suspicious that Andreus practiced the ancient and outlawed religion of the Oradagra. Even though the council found Andreus not guilty on all counts, he requested a transfer from his RPU in the Northern Province to the Capital Province. Tiberius used his royal status to transfer Andreus to his security detail.

He fondly remembered Andreus's first day. Tiberius ordered him to his study so they could make their acquaintance. Andreus displayed a healthy lack of trust and did not shy away from questioning Tiberius's intentions.

"I understand you have inquired as to my need for another bodyguard."

Andreus looked him in the eye and, without hesitation, replied, "I mean no disrespect, my lord, but it's clear you have a full contingent of men, which leads me to question your need for one more."

Feeling at a disadvantage to the young man, Tiberius told him to sit. "Your skepticism is the very reason I have asked you to join my team."

Looking even more perplexed, he cocked his head, "I don't understand, my lord."

"I've read your military records and find that you and I have something in common."

"Once again, my lord, I mean no disrespect, but I have done my homework too, and there is nothing to suggest that we have anything in common."

Tiberius shook his head. "I admire your honesty, but you agree that not all can be known about a man from his official records."

"I do, my lord."

"Good. Would I be correct in assuming that when that nasty business transpired in your unit, the worst was not the accusation but the severing of the loyalty you believe to exist between brothers at arms?"

Andreus shifted, uncomfortable under Tiberius' scrutiny. "Yes, my lord."

Leaning back in his chair, Tiberius smiled. "Then we do indeed have much in common. I, too, value loyalty above all else, and it is for that reason you are here."

It took many years before Andreus trusted Tiberius to tell him the whole truth about his involvement with the Oradagra. At once, Tiberius saw the potential the ancient cult had for his plans.

Snapping out of his musings, Tiberius picked up the comm link and inserted the earpiece, pressing the favorites menu on his secure line. Even though it was late, Andreus answered after the second ring. "Capulus," referring to Tiberius's Oradagra rank. "How may I be of service?"

"I need a meeting with yourself and the others as soon as possible." A moment of silence, then Tiberius heard the whisper of sheets sliding off the bed.

"I take it our spies have found something significant?"

"Indeed, evasive tactics will be necessary if we are to remain on track."

"I will send out a message immediately. Expect a reply early morning."

Andreus disconnected.

Tiberius had suffered many disappointments in his life. Inevitably, those who claimed to love him felt he fell short of their expectations. Andreus and Matilda were the only people to show him that his loved ones failed to understand his unusually loyal heart; therefore, they were the problem, not him.

Flaminius slumped back on his throne. "Are you sure, Gaia?"

"There is no doubt. Because of the seriousness of the situation, I begged Mother Guardian to speak with Serenity's family to forgo the twenty-four-hour burial protocol so I could do a thorough autopsy. Uncle, I believe someone poisoned her with Daka root."

Aurelia sat forward. "Daka root?"

Gaia turned to the queen. "Yes, Aunt Aurelia, so named because it grew on the highest parts of the Daka Mountains of the Northern Province."

The king interrupted. "How do you know about this root?"

"From an Alchemy class." Gaia sheepishly answered.

Flaminius raised his eyebrows knowingly but asked to amuse himself, "Oh, do they still offer alchemy classes? I thought it was an ancient and outdated practice."

"Well, it is, but when I was a student, I had a few extra hours to fill and thought it would be a good idea to learn about the origins of modern chemistry. Besides, it wasn't exactly a formal class."

Flame turned to Aurelia. "Of course, it wasn't." He looked back at Gaia expectantly, urging her to continue.

Blushing, she rattled on. "As I was saying, when I was still a student, I was doing some light reading in the ancient tomes at the university library, and I found this fascinating account of goat herders in the Daka mountains whose goats suddenly started dying from an unknown cause and this remarkable alchemist who eventually unraveled the mystery by finding changes in the stomach lining of a goat." She concluded, taking a deep breath, beaming like a toddler who had just successfully navigated the sole use of a toilet for the first time.

When she realized that neither Flaminius nor Aurelia found this account as fascinating as she did, she attempted to rectify the situation. "The point is, I requested a class on alchemy, assuming my fellow students would be as excited as I was to learn about this ancient art."

Trying to hide his delight at his young niece's enthusiasm, Flaminius asked, "How many people attended this class, Gaia?"

Mortified, she mumbled, "Apparently, my fellow students preferred frivolity over knowledge."

"So, just you then?"

"Yes, but it was only late last night that I remembered the class and the distinct appearance of the poisoned goat's stomach lining. It was blue."

"Could Serenity's poisoning be an isolated incident?" Aurelia asked.

Gaia shook her head. "Her symptoms were the same as the others. It has to be the poison."

Flaminius looked unconvinced. "No offense, Gaia, but other brilliant healers are stumped."

"No offense taken, but they don't know alchemy. Determined to get the science across, she continued, "The poison is only detectable in the stomach lining a week after death, and as you know, the burial protocol for the

Keys is within twenty-four hours. Yesterday, I noticed a blue discoloration to Serenity's stomach lining that hadn't been present the first few times I inspected the organ, and that's what prompted me to remember the goats."

"I spent last night searching for the reason the goats died from eating the root when they had been grazing in that area for years. That summer was particularly harsh and dry, so the herders drove the goats higher up the mountain to feed, where they encountered the Daka root for the first time.

When neither Flaminius nor Aurelia said anything, she waved her hands in a never-mind gesture. "Needless to say, some furious goat herders eradicated the plant into extinction."

Gaia's logic was irrefutable. "Who else knows of this?"

"No one, Sire."

"Good, let's keep it that way. Release the body for burial and keep the tissue sample locked up. I need time to consider the ramifications of your discovery, and Gaia, thank you. Your fellow students would've done well to learn from you."

Gaia blushed with pride.

"There is, of course, one more question that begs an answer."

Gaia frowned, and then she realized. "If the root is extinct, then where did the plant come from that killed the Keys?"

"Exactly, my little detective, and perhaps the most important question to answer. Find the keeper of the root, and we find the assassin."

That night, while Aurelia lay sleeping in his arms, Flame thought of all he had learned that day. If Gaia was correct and the Keys had been poisoned, then someone had betrayed their people in an unimaginably brutal fashion. The extinction of the Keys would bring about the destruction of Arkhnuetians. Surely that couldn't be the desired outcome?

The Oradagra would be the only organization capable of such insanity, but Romulus had been swift and merciless in eradicating the cult. Still, Flaminius couldn't rid himself of the niggling feeling that Mother Guardian may have been right all those years ago, that they had failed to stamp out the cult completely.

Chapter Three -
Common Goal

It was late, and Flaminius was catching up on correspondence when his chief meteorologist, Barret Evans, blew into his study like one of the hurricanes he so often diverted away from Arkhnuet. Flaminius wouldn't have thought it possible that the discovery of a murderous plot against the Keys could ever have become a secondary priority. He hadn't decided how to deal with the information Gaia had given him just a week ago. He hadn't shared the news with his council or even his closest friend, Marcus. And now Barret brought more bad news.

"Barret, are you saying that we have no way of stopping this?

The usually eloquent man shuffled his feet. "Yes, Your Majesty. In our estimation, we have a little over two years, maybe less, before the debris created by the supernova destroys Arkhnuet."

Over the years, Flaminius had seen many dire situations that plagued the throne. Never in all that time had he felt total despair. Not even at the height of the civil war between the crown and the Oradagra. "That's completely ludicrous, Barret. Have you conferred with other scientists?"

Barret looked offended by the question. "For Source's sake, Flaminius, do you honestly think I would break this news to you if I—we—had not repeatedly run every conceivable scenario?"

Flaminius shook his head. "No, of course not." Sinking into his chair, he rubbed his hands over his face. "Fuck! Who else is aware of this besides you and your team?"

"No one, Sire. I've given my team strict instructions not to breathe a word to anyone until I spoke to you."

Waving his hand at Barret, he said, "Stop calling me 'Sire.' Sit down and tell me exactly what you've discovered."

Barret collapsed into the soft leather chair and sighed. "Our telescopes picked up an anomaly two days ago. On further investigation, we discovered a supernova about one and a half trillion kilometers away."

Flaminius frowned. "That's very far away."

"One would think, but when the shock wave from the explosion is hurling millions of tons of debris at thirty thousand kilometers a second straight for us, then one and a half trillion kilometers is right in our backyard."

For the rest of the night, Barret and Flaminius discussed surviving the imminent destruction of the planet Arkhnuetians had called home for millions of years. By the time Aurelia interrupted their meeting with breakfast for her overworked husband, it was clear that the council would need to convene immediately to strategize the evacuation of their planet.

After Barret left, Aurelia curled up on Flame's lap while he told her the bad news.

"How are we going to deal with this and the Keys?"

"I'm going to put Marcus in charge of the recon missions to Earth."

"Wouldn't it be better to ask Marcus to investigate the Keys?"

"No, Marcus's skill set is best utilized in a military capacity. I think Tiberius's gentle manner and extensive contacts would be a better choice to investigate the Keys. For now, I want to keep Marcus focused. I'll tell him about the Keys later."

Andreus hated sneaking around in the dark as if he were still a testosterone-laden teen attempting to spy on widow Worsley while she bathed, though it had been immensely thrilling and had made him quite the legend among his peers. He also hated being late, but he couldn't tear himself away from his obsession. She looked more radiant than ever today, and he watched her for longer than he usually permitted himself.

Examining his surroundings one last time, he stepped through the heavy wooden door of the vine-choked stone mausoleum. It was, by design, no more elaborate than hundreds of others in the graveyard. Several torches lit the dark interior, revealing a square room, barren but for his father's sarcophagus. To any other, this space looked just as its creator intended it to—a cold, dark, intimidating grave—but to the members of the Oradagra, it was headquarters. His father built the secret chamber hundreds of years ago to prepare for the inevitable disbanding and outlawing of the cult. Andreus despised that word. After all, one man's cult was another man's religion, his faith, his redemption, and the redemption of his people.

He waited in the semi-dark for a few more moments to ensure that he was indeed alone before feeling along the lip of the stone coffin lid. Andreus found the small protruding knob and pushed it. Sluggish but quiet, the back-right-hand corner of the false wall slid forward. Slipping through the opening, he proceeded down the seventy worn stairs into a small four-by-four-foot antechamber. Tugging down on the bracket, holding the torch, he heard the wall at the top of the stairs grind closed. From here, entry to the main assembly room required more than knowing which button to press. Removing his ceremonial (but operational) dagger he inherited from his father, Andreus inserted the blade into a small fissure in the wall and turned it clockwise. The stone façade split, revealing a high-ceilinged cave large enough to hold several hundred people.

"So glad you could join us, young Andreus." As his name suggested, Cyril imagined himself a lord, but Andreus ignored the reed-thin idiot.

Andreus bowed to the high priest, Magnus. "Sorry to keep you waiting."

"It's my fault he's late. I asked him to run an errand for me." Capulus Tiberius lied smoothly. Cyril tried to hide his contempt that Andreus shared a special bond with the leader of the Oradagra, but failed miserably.

When Andreus joined the others at the round table, he ceased being the young bodyguard to the king's brother and instead became general to his small but growing army. Nothing would have made him prouder than to follow in his father's footsteps and master the balancing act of being a double-agent. Hadrianus did it so well that even after the Oradagra was defeated, Romulus still didn't suspect him. The secator helmet significantly helped in his efforts to remain anonymous. By never showing his face to the Oradagra soldiers, he kept his anonymity from the masses, allowing him to escape the noose after the war. Those men that made up the remaining original members survived because they took a leaf out of his father's book and made their membership to the Oradagra secret to all but the founders.

Hadrianus would frequently bring his son to this location and train him in both the art of warfare and physical combat. Like his father before him, Andreus made his face known only to those in this room. On any other occasion, he wore the secator helmet, immortalizing his father's frightening persona.

The high priest stood and lifted his arms out to his sides, palms up, indicating the beginning of the proceedings. As one, they kneeled and bowed their heads as Magnus prayed to Nammu-Anki, the Oradagra deity and creator of Source energy.

"Nammu-Anki, Your disciples gather before You to honor Your holy name and implore You to sweep Your sword, Your Dagra across the nation, and smite those who dare to poison our pure blood. Nammu-Anki, smite their matches, smite their half-breed offspring, so that we may redeem ourselves in Your gracious all-seeing eyes."

As Andreus recited the prayer along with the others, he concentrated on meshing the meaning of the words into his marrow, reaffirming his commitment to Nammu-Anki that he would rather be celibate than mix his DNA with a non-Arkhnuetian.

Once the formalities concluded, they seated themselves around the table. Tiberius spoke. "I have called this meeting as a matter of urgency. Our spies informed me that my daughter uncovered the reason for the death of the Keys." All but Cyril gasped. Holding up his hand for order, Tiberius continued. "I have several strategies to deal with this problem but want to hear your thoughts first."

"This is an easy problem to solve." Cyril's irritating drawl echoed off the cave walls. "We should kill her, as I have said from the start!"

Andreus shook his head at the imbecile's comment. "How many times must we explain this to you, Cyril? Killing Gaia is not an option because of her close relationship with the king. The grief would prompt him to launch a full-scale inquiry we can ill afford."

A vein on the side of Cyril's milk-white neck popped out, betraying his struggle to hold on to his temper. "Yes, I'm aware of that, but if I may remind you, I also told you we could make it look like an accident. I even offered the services of several accomplished gentlemen who could get the job done."

The usually quiet fifth member leaned forward, the solid wooden chair groaning under his bulk. "This conversation is of little import at this juncture." All eyes turned to Ipcus, who always took his time when he spoke. It would've been irritating, but for the fact that he did it so little. Finally, he continued, "The king called an emergency meeting of his own this morning with all the council members." Again, he paused, seemingly to rearrange his thoughts.

Andreus feared he might have to throttle the man out of sheer frustration before he could spit out what he knew.

"It seems that in less than two years, our planet will no longer exist. We have already begun organizing evacuation plans for all citizens. It is apparent that several large asteroids are on a collision course with us, and there is not one thing to be done about it."

Andreus wasn't sure if his fingers went numb from the shock of Ipcus's information or the fact that he'd never heard the man say so much at once.

Tiberius spoke first. "This is not possible. I would know if this information were true."

Ipcus merely shrugged his meaty shoulders. His response was not adequate for the leader of the Oradagra.

"I demand to know where you got this information."

Taking a deep breath to prepare for the enormous task of having to speak again so soon, Ipcus replied, "My daughter is the secretary to Councilor Mole. She knew something big was happening, so she slipped a listening device into that ridiculous satchel he carries around with him. She heard it directly from the king's mouth." Ipcus slumped back in his chair, exhausted from his efforts.

Andreus focused on Tiberius's face. Slowly, his dumbfounded expression turned to one of fury. "That son of a bitch informed his fucking council before he spoke to his brother?"

Everyone knew their leader's temper well and surreptitiously moved as far out of his reach as possible without leaving the table. Everyone, it seemed, except clueless Cyril. "I don't see how this changes anything. We still need to deal with the crisis at hand. Do I need to remind you that the king now knows that someone is deliberately eliminating the Keys? So, if we can refocus our attention on the matter at hand, please?" Cyril's nostrils flared after his little monologue in apparent exasperation at the lack of discipline amongst the leaders of the Oradagra.

No longer trying to appear nonchalant about Tiberius's impending explosion, the smart members abandoned their seats. Andreus watched in fascination as he witnessed Ipcus move with considerably more speed than a man roughly the size of a small blue whale should be capable of.

Turning to face Cyril, Tiberius cocked his head as if contemplating the significance of the idiot's words seriously. "Since the importance of the announcement seems lost on you, maybe I should clarify some points." Cyril leaned closer to Tiberius in anticipation of his lesson. In a deceptively calm kindergarten teacher's voice, Tiberius continued, "The king will be too occupied saving our entire race from extinction to be overly focused on the poisoning of the Keys. Apart from ensuring their safety by assigning a few guards at their door twenty-four-seven and testing their food and drink, I doubt we will need to be worried for now."

Cyril's brow drew together in a frown for several seconds before realization dawned and smoothed out the creases. "Oh, I see. So, we are safe until the asteroid crisis is over."

Tiberius nodded his head in affirmation, and without taking his eyes off Cyril, he asked, "Andreus, does Cyril contribute any significant assistance to our cause?"

Slightly confused by the question, Andreus replied, "Not in a physical capacity, Capulus Tiberius."

Slowly rising, Tiberius spoke again, "So, he simply holds a seat at this table because of his father's usefulness to our organization before he died."

Sensing that the answer he gave Capulus would be of significant importance to Cyril, Andreus answered without hesitation. "Correct."

Tiberius moved so fast not even Andreus saw the dagger leave its sheath. In a fluid, graceful motion, he slit Cyril's throat from ear to ear. The clean cut partially severed his neck, opening a gaping wound that sprayed arterial blood ten feet into the air before raining down onto their leader. "From now on, we choose members who are worthy of sitting at this table. No more nepotism. We have entered a new era, gentlemen." Turning to face those remaining, he added, "Our survival depends on working with the enemy for now. There is to be no further anti-royalist action until we can assure our safety. Anyone disobeying this edict will pay with his life." Tiberius sheathed his blade after wiping it on Cyril's dandy puce-colored cloak and calmly quit the room as if nothing more significant had occurred than a slight tiff between friends.

Ipcus and Magnus stood rooted to the spot, staring with both disbelief and fear at the bloody event that had played out before them. Andreus stood rooted for an entirely different reason. Yes, he was both afraid and astonished, but more than anything, Tiberius's actions engendered a shift in his heart from respect and deep admiration to love and devotion.

Chapter Four -
Extraction Revisited

The Relocation Strategy Committee, comprising all thirteen council members representing each province, the Minister of Defense (Robert Austin), and Barret's team of scientists, met early every morning. In the week since Barret's terrible news, the committee had made several trips to Earth with recon teams led by Marcus to determine relocation sites. They purchased vast tracts of land, earmarked hundreds of locations for further consideration, studied cultures, and bought currencies. They agreed they would not inform the public of the impending disaster until they had a definitive relocation strategy.

Barret's voice snapped Flaminius back to the present. "Resettling on Earth should be a last resort." He ruffled his already disheveled hair. "We need to be mindful not to repeat previous errors."

Councilor Victor Mole nodded his head. "I agree. We negatively affected the path of human development with our last contact. It is our moral imperative to be more responsible this time."

"I disagree," retorted Minister Austin. "What's done is done. I think we did them a favor. Those with human matches, and the Arkhnuetians who made Earth their home, helped speed up their intellectual evolution. Can you imagine if we hadn't? We would now be relocating to a much more primitive Earth inhabited by a much more primitive species."

Barret shot out of his chair. "Were you sick the day they taught human/Arkhnuetian history at school? If so, let me refresh your memory. King Romulus only enforced the Extraction Policy when hordes of Barbarians attacked the Roman Empire after it collapsed and Europe became unsafe for

Arkhnuetians. That wouldn't have been such a great tragedy for our matched humans if the king had allowed their extended human family to accompany them. Instead, he forced them to desert their loved ones, knowing they would probably die in the Barbarian raids." Sitting down, Barret huffed, "And by the way, they are still primitive."

Robert leaned back in his chair, apparently unfazed. "I'm pointing out that the damage is done, and since it is, we should take advantage. I am thinking of all six million Arkhnuetians living in the present. Forgive me if I refuse to live in the past."

Ignoring the ignorant minister, Barret pleaded, "Sire, I mean no disrespect, but you were there. You witnessed the pain my family endured. If we go back to Earth, we will open old wounds which could result in certain citizens becoming hostile toward the crown again."

Flaminius sat back in his chair, holding his chin in his hand, listening to the argument. "I understand how you feel, Barret, but I've made my decision. We move to Earth." Barret slumped back in his chair, defeated. He was so upset he could barely follow the rest of the meeting. Finally, Flaminius ended the discussion, but before Barret could leave, Flaminius stopped him.

"Meet me in my office in fifteen minutes." He ordered, and without waiting for Barret's answer, walked out the room.

Barret was pleased when Flaminius got right to it. "I understand your reluctance to move forward with this plan, Barret, and I agree it's not ideal, but you must understand, we do not have the luxury of waiting for your team to find a better solution. However, it's imperative to remain motivated and continue your work to find an uninhabited planet."

"I understand that, and my logical mind even agrees with you, but Source help me, I cannot seem to get my heart to follow." He slumped down in the chair opposite the king. "I honestly think it would be in everyone's interest if I step aside as department head and hand the reins over to someone who has objectivity."

"There is no one I trust more to do the job. You will continue to lead your team, and you will find a solution as you always have."

Barret huffed. "How am I supposed to find a new planet that is going to solve all our problems if I don't have the sophisticated lab equipment necessary? Have you given any thought to the fact that once we're on Earth, it will be impossible to hide such a facility? Even if we could, how will we find the parts needed to build, maintain, and operate it with no raw materials or fucking basics like electricity?"

Flaminius leaned his hulking frame against his desk, crossed his arms and legs, and looked down, smiling at Barret. Shifting uncomfortably in his seat, the man sighed. "You already have a plan for all of my concerns, don't you?"

Flaminius stretched his arms out. "Yes! I do. Thanks for asking before you jumped to conclusions and made assumptions."

Barret shook his head. "Sorry. May I ask what these plans are?"

"Before we discuss the details, I want you to understand the reason I didn't share it with the others at the meeting. It's necessary to keep certain things secret at the moment and, no, I will not elaborate on that, but suffice it to say that the work you do from now on is for my ears only."

"I don't see how I'll be able to keep finding another planet secret. We have over one hundred and fifty people working in my department and another twenty-five scientists consulting for us."

"I know, and that's why we're going to choose a small select team that General Brewer and myself will vet to work exclusively on Project Planet."

Flaminius felt considerably less stressed once concrete plans were in place to save Arkhnuetians. The reprieve enabled him to expend more brainpower on another concern, which landed him in trouble with his wife.

He made the very unpopular decision that he would be the last to leave the planet while his wife and son would be the first. Aurelia vehemently disagreed. Exasperated and more than a little afraid, he tried ordering her to obey his command, which went over like a lead balloon. In desperation, he threatened her with forcible action when the time came. That got him several nights on the couch.

Given some time to reflect, Flaminius sent Marcus to speak to her. He was a charismatic man with superior skills suited to manipulating the fairer sex's mind to a more 'favorable' way of thinking. What Flaminius didn't know was that his friend was as illogical as he was when it came to the queen and Theo's safety. The poor lout attempted to sequester Aurelia and Theo until their accommodation on Earth was ready. It did not go well for him, either. He would be nursing his damaged ego for days.

Finally, Flaminius agreed that she could stay but insisted that Theo leave with the Lady Guardian. Aurelia offered no resistance to this new plan, but Gaia was less than forthcoming. Was he to be plagued by hardheaded women all his life? To repair his wounded pride, Marcus requested the task of ensuring the future king and his guardian's safe removal.

Gaia had enjoyed the queen's pluck and attempted a similar strategy. Unfortunately for her, Marcus was a quick learner and had brought reinforcements in the shape of a cocky but loyal sergeant named Gerhardt. Cornered, she took a defiant stand. "I am not leaving them here alone, so I do not care what your orders are. Little Theo and I will stay with them and my father."

Frustrated, Marcus tried to reason with her again. "Lady Guardian, don't you see the danger of your decision? If you stay with the future king, you place the bloodline in peril. We have to ensure that the two of you survive to lead our people."

Gaia was becoming irritated with his constant demeaning tone. "Now listen here, you babbling buffoon. I am well aware of my obligation to the throne."

Sergeant Gerhardt snorted with laughter, to the great embarrassment of the General. Encouraged by the Sergeant's comical insubordination, Gaia nodded her approval at him and looked down her nose at Marcus.

Infuriated, Marcus replied. "No, apparently, you don't see the importance of your obligation. I've had enough of trying to reason with you. Let me demonstrate what awaits you when the time comes." Bearing no further argument, he tossed her over his shoulder and carried her, kicking and screaming, from her room. Little Theo, cradled in his other arm, giggled, blissfully unaware of the drama.

Marcus enjoyed manhandling Lady Guardian for no other reason than she felt good tightly held against his body. Of course, duty was paramount, but who said he couldn't have a little fun. Once Marcus deposited Theo and Gaia safely in the hands of Sergeant Gerhardt and several of his men for good measure, he turned to her and said, "As you can see, I will physically remove you if you don't cooperate."

Spitting mad, she could barely hiss, "You are unbelievable!"

"So I've been told by many of the fairer sex." Having made his point, he left to report his progress to Flaminius.

Gaia spent the rest of the day trying to forget how wonderful it felt pressed up against Marcus's body. As embarrassing as it was to admit. Even to herself.

Chapter Five -
Time to Spy

"Is he busy?" Marcus asked Seth, who stood guard outside the king's office.

"He is, sir, but I have orders to let you in as soon as you arrive."

"By the way, how is Lily?"

Seth smiled. "Pregnancy has made my little bug more beautiful than ever. Thank you for asking, sir."

Marcus patted Seth on the shoulder. "Send her my regards," he said before he entered the study.

Flaminius was in deep discussion with his parents. Not wishing to interrupt, Marcus held his position at the door and listened. He never liked the ex-queen. Marcus held a grudge because she opposed his request to join the elite Royal Protection Unit. She cited a lack of combat experience for her decision, but he knew it was because she disapproved of his unsavory background. Fortunately, the final decision rested with Romulus, and Marcus became the youngest person ever to qualify to join the elite force. The queen's shrill voice jarred Marcus from his thoughts.

"I fail to understand your reasoning, Flaminius. Your father and I have watched as Aurelia disrespected one edict after another. We have said very little, but this is too much!"

Flaminius sat calmly behind his large desk, made to look much smaller because of the astronomical amount of paperwork strewn over its surface. "Mother, you've hardly kept your distaste of my wife's decisions to yourself." The regal woman huffed in disagreement, but Flaminius continued, "She has decided to stay, and there is not one thing I can do about it."

The stiff-backed dragon turned in her chair and glared at her husband. It was apparent he would not come to her aid, so she squared her shoulders, preparing for battle. "This matter is significantly more serious than one of her absurd liberal ideas!"

Flaminius lost all pretense of civility and leaned forward. "Mother, be careful how you choose your next words."

Even this formidable woman recognized when it was time to cut her losses. "Very well, but I want it on record that I strongly disagree with this decision."

Flaminius settled back in his chair. "So noted," he said sarcastically, drawing a tick in the air with his finger. "Is there anything else?"

"Your father and I are preparing to leave with the First Wave. We request permission to say farewell to our grandson."

Shaking his head, Flaminius replied, "For sanity's sake, Mother, he's your grandchild; you don't need to ask for permission to see him, and it'll be months before you leave. Anyhow, he'll be leaving with you and Gaia."

Flaminius turned his attention to Marcus and raised his eyebrows questioningly. Marcus confirmed with a nod that he had been successful and that the future king and his guardian would leave with the First Wave.

Turning his attention back to his mother, he continued, "Excellent. Now, if you don't mind, Mother, I have a lot to do." Octavia stormed out of his study in a whirl of satin and silk. Romulus eased himself out of his seat, walked to the door, and paused. "I understand your anxiety about Aurelia's safety, but your queen has made the right decision." He said before he left.

Now alone with Marcus, Flaminius moved toward the bar. "Thank you for taking care of Gaia for me. Source knows I didn't have the strength to deal with that as well." Marcus crossed the room to accept the glass Flaminius held out for him. One of the many things they had in common was their love of whiskey.

Taking a sip of the oaky liquid, Marcus replied, "I would say it was my pleasure, but she's a handful. You owe me."

Flaminius laughed, indicating they sit in the lounge area. They were just getting comfortable when Flaminius's phone rang. "I'm sorry, but I have to take this." Marcus nodded and continued to sip his whiskey in silence while the king took the call at his desk. Whenever Marcus was in this room, his mind wandered to the first time he was here.

TIME TO SPY

The room may have lost its ability to intimidate him over the years, but it was still an impressive space. High-beamed ceilings housed three circular chandeliers positioned in a triangular configuration. Electric lights had long since replaced the candles, but the massive brass creations stood the test of time, as they were probably older than both he and Flaminius put together. Priceless tapestries hung on the rustic, blond stone walls, depicting scenes ranging from bloody battles to romantic garden picnics, complete with a simpering damsel and a strapping hero. Plush rugs expertly woven in royal colors decorated the flagstone floors and helped keep the chill off one's feet. Marcus mournfully pondered that none of this was likely to survive.

Flaminius concluded his call and settled in the chair across from Marcus. "Sorry about that. Where were we?"

"I spoke to the engineers. They've made adjustments to the rifters to accommodate larger groups of people."

Flaminius drained his glass before he asked, "What are the conditions on Earth? I've received the official reports, but I would rather hear from you."

Marcus retrieved the bottle of whiskey from the bar and refilled both their glasses. "Honestly, Flaminius, I don't think our people are going to find the primitive conditions easy. They'll have to do away with everything from electricity to social media. Barret wasn't far off the mark."

Flaminius seemed surprised. "I don't recall you being in that meeting."

"No, you wouldn't because I wasn't, but I have eyes and ears everywhere."

"Eyes and ears?"

"Yes. It's amazing what modern technology can do these days."

Flaminius flapped his mouth like a teenage boy after his first glance at a naked woman. Eventually, he whispered, "Why?"

"Because it's my job to keep you safe."

"By planting illegal listening devices in a top-secret meeting?!"

"Don't be so fucking dramatic, Flaminius. I had to do something. If there were a Protector, I wouldn't need to do these things."

Flaminius shook his head at the sudden change of subject. "Marcus, there hasn't been a Protector for thousands of years."

"Yes! That's my point. I may not have the Protector DNA mutation to detect danger before it happens, but I can gather intelligence to keep you safe, and I'll do that any way I can."

As usual, Marcus made about as much sense as tits on a bull, and Flaminius was too exhausted to decipher his unique code. Marcus either didn't notice Flaminius's confusion or chose to ignore it because he continued without missing a beat.

"However, I am pleased you mentioned the lack of security."

Flaminius was sure he never mentioned anything of the sort.

"Marcus, this is not a good time to add to my load. Whatever you have swirling around that playground of a brain will have to wait."

Predictably, Marcus ignored him. "The whole point of this discussion is to alleviate your concerns. Especially regarding safety and security."

"Where are you going with this, Marcus?"

One didn't become the youngest General in the elite Royal Protection Unit by shooting your mouth off at the wrong time. However, playing it safe didn't get him there either. "From the information I've gathered, I know I cannot do this alone. I want you to allow me to select a few men and create a military intelligence unit and keep it between you and me."

Flaminius was reluctant to consider the issue, but for the fact that Marcus requested it. "I can't keep something like that from the council. And anyway, why do you think we need one? The war ended a long time ago."

Not answering his questions again, Marcus continued, "As I've already said, to investigate, the creative placing of certain homemade listening devices in strategic hot-spots was necessary."

"Yes. Let's get back to that, Marcus! Do you realize I could charge you with treason?"

He shrugged his shoulders. "Well, technically, you can't because I never compromised your safety."

"Yes, I can because you didn't fucking have my permission to plant listening devices."

"Meh, semantics."

"How can you be so flippant? For fuck's sake, do you realize the position you've put me in? I have no choice but to report this to the council, and I promise you they won't be lenient, you fucking reckless fool!"

The conversation wasn't going the way Marcus intended, so he employed the dependable shock 'em technique. The success of the technique required absolute calm. "I understand. Do what you have to do." Leaning forward, he lowered his voice for effect. "But before you call for my arrest, wouldn't you like to know what I've discovered?"

Flaminius decided his friend had finally lost his mind. He had absolutely no concept of the trouble he was facing. He didn't know why he was surprised; Marcus never really had a firm grasp on reality.

Marcus appeared relaxed as he watched and waited for Flaminius to settle on the conclusion he had intended. Some days he thought he should feel guilty for his ability to manipulate people's thoughts. Most were slower than molasses when it came to reading danger signs that seemed glaringly obvious. So yeah, he had no remorse.

Flaminius exhaled loudly. "Okay, Marcus. Tell me what you've learned, and Source help you; it better be worth my while."

"First, you should know that I am aware of the Keys being murdered and that Gaia brought the poison theory to you, and I agree with it. Why you didn't tell me about it and Gaia's involvement will be left for another discussion, preferably including a few bottles of whiskey so that I'm too drunk to rip your head off."

"Tell me you didn't place listening devices in the throne room?"

Marcus barely contained his irritation with the constant interruptions. "Will it make you feel better if I said I didn't?"

"You know, I think it would. I think I would be just fine if you lied to me about that."

"Okay, I didn't tap the throne room, but I did have ears in Gaia's lab."

Flaminius sighed. "I didn't tell you about Gaia and the Keys because I was protecting her until I could figure out what to do. She's a scientist, not a soldier."

Marcus looked down to hide his smile. The truth was he had fun listening to her going about her business in her lab. "I would never let anyone harm her, nor will I mention her name anywhere."

"Thank you, Marcus."

"Do you know she has a habit of speaking to herself when she works? It's kind of cute."

Flaminius glared at his friend. "Don't even think about it."

Marcus held his hands up in surrender. "Relax. I'm not thinking of going there."

"Good, because I'll kick your ass."

Marcus sighed. "Can we get back to business?" Flaminius nodded. "I have hours of recordings from various locations around the castle that you're welcome to listen to, but I suggest you start with the servants' quarters."

"How did you manage to get into the servants' quarters?"

Marcus wiggled his eyebrows. "There's a charming young kitchen maid who has the most talented—"

Flaminius covered his ears. "Please forget I asked. Just get to the information that will convince me to spare your treasonous ass."

"Okay, jeez. Touchy much? When you listen to the recordings, you will hear an Oradagra operative recruiting members, and I think you'll agree with me that if anyone is responsible for a plot against the Keys, it's those crazy motherfuckers."

The king dropped his head into his hands. Shoring up his strength, he spoke. "I suspected as much, but I hoped I was wrong. I want to hear every last second of those recordings." After a few seconds of silence, he added, "The risk of the council finding out that I've approved a covert force without their knowledge would undermine the trust I share with them and further destabilize Arkhnuet."

"I understand your predicament. But, Flaminius, even if we didn't have the Keys problem, I would still ask for an intelligence unit. It's prudent and a decision you would have eventually arrived at, anyway. If we're discovered, I'll say the team and I acted on our own."

"You already have a fucking team?"

"I've only discussed it with Jim and Sue, but my current crew works well together."

Flaminius decided not to challenge Marcus anymore. "Fine, but I'm not happy with you taking responsibility if things go wrong."

"If the Oradagra is back, that means we're at war, and there is no place for sentimentality. The people will need their king."

"I want Tiberius to join your team."

Marcus sat back to consider his reply. "I don't want to introduce a new person into an already cohesive unit."

"I understand, but my brother has important contacts who could be useful to you."

"Flaminius, I need you to trust me on this. I know Tiberius won't be a good fit. Besides, covert missions are perilous, and I don't want to place the third in line to the throne in danger."

"Point taken. I understand that secrecy is imperative for the safety of your operatives. But sharing any information that you uncover with the council will be at my discretion."

"Agreed."

Marcus, deep in thought, pushed through the RPU training facility doors and immediately had to dive for cover or risk getting his head incinerated by a ball of flame. Rolling onto his back, he planted his feet and propelled himself up into a crouched position behind the flame shield a few feet from the door. Peering around the barrier, Marcus watched Sue jump on her husband's back, clamping her muscular legs around his waist.

"Move your ass, Jim!" she ordered.

Marcus tried to track the couple as they flickered in and out of sight when the shield he hid behind took a direct hit. The explosion sent liquid heat rolling off in glowing waves, leaving behind the stench of acrid smoke. Marcus instinctively closed his eyes and turned away from the noise and blinding light. When he looked back, Sue and Jim stood behind the shield, looking directly at him.

"Watch your aim, Sue. You almost hit me!"

She popped her head out from behind her husband's back, tossing her red hair over her shoulder. "How about you watch for the 'in training' warning light at the door?" She replied saucily, giving him a wink.

It was rare for Arkhnuetians to possess gifts such as the Keys, but Jim and Sue boasted extra abilities. Jim could teleport and had a mind as sharp as a tack. It was for the latter reason Marcus had made Jim his second-in-command.

Not only could he teleport short distances, but he could also carry reasonably heavy objects with him. Sue could control energy fields to produce fireballs out of thin air.

Looking exceedingly pleased with herself, she jumped off Jim's back and dusted her hands on her thighs. "Hello, General. How are you this fine morning?"

Marcus looked at Jim in astonished disbelief. "Hey, how about having a brother's back? Unbelievable?"

"Isn't she awesome?" Jim replied with a love-sick look in his eyes.

Marcus realized the futility of continuing the discussion and brought them back to his reason for being there. "Remember our discussion about forming an intelligence unit?" Jim and Sue nodded.

"I can't give you any details yet, but certain events have made it inevitable. Are you both still interested?"

Sue put her arm around Jim's waist. "We've discussed it, and as long as you lead the team, we're in."

"That's a given, and I have permission to handpick the crew."

"Then, Sue and I are on board."

"Good, I'll keep you posted."

"Well, I would love to stand here and chat with you, boys, but I'll be late. I'm going shopping with Aurelia, and then we're going for dinner and drinks."

Jim groaned. "Do you have to go?"

Sue's light-green eyes flashed momentarily. "For Source's sake, Jim, surely you can handle your boys for a couple of hours? They're only three months old. It's not like you have to entertain them."

Jim's nostrils flared. "Don't have to entertain them? Do you remember what happened last time you left them with me? Noah just about burned the house down, and Joshua cried constantly!"

"Oh, you're such a big baby. It wasn't nearly as bad as that. Noah's gift is hardly strong enough to create a spark, if that, and Joshua only bawled because you separated them."

Exasperated, Jim threw his hands in the air. "I had to separate them. Noah singed all the hair off his brother's head! What was I supposed to do, woman?" Marcus attempted to remain straight-faced but failed miserably.

Sue put her hands on her tiny hips and sighed. "You were supposed to make sure Noah didn't rub his hands together. I told you when he does that, he sparks. You weren't supposed to leave them in their crib unattended so that you and Gerhardt could drink beer and watch sports!"

"I didn't leave them unattended! You try keeping that fifty-pound three-month-old brute from rubbing his hands together." Jim turned to Marcus for backup. "What three-month-old knows how to rub his hands together, right? And he's far stronger than he looks. He punched me when I tried!"

"Of course he'll rub his hands together! He only just discovered he could make fire. Anyone would be pissed if he could do something that cool and his father tried to stop him. You were supposed to distract him with a toy or something. And he is not fifty pounds! He is a normal baby boy."

"No, he's not! How many three-month-old baby boys have you seen that wear two-year-old clothes? Why can't they be calm like Theo? They were born on the same day at the same time after all." Squinting his eyes, he turned to Marcus again and said, "And just for the record, I had a bruised eye for at least a day."

"Well, just for the record, that's your fault, you six-foot-five, three-hundred-pound ape!" Sue argued. "I honestly don't see why you're complaining. I had to carry those boys in my body for nine months and then push them out a hole no bigger than a cheerio! So, if I need to hang with my girlfriend for a few hours, you sure as hell can take care of them." With that, Sue stomped off toward the shower in a major huff. Jim leaned against the pillar and watched his wife walk away with a smile.

"You enjoyed that, didn't you?"

Jim answered him, but kept his eyes on his wife's butt. "Damned straight, I did. She's going to be insatiable tonight; she always is after a good brawl."

Marcus chuckled. "Want me to keep you company while you attempt to take care of your boys?"

Jim finally looked at him with his teddy-bear-brown eyes. "Fuck yeah. I wasn't kidding when I said they were a handful."

Marcus slapped his friend on the back as they made their way to the exit. "I'll bring a fire extinguisher."

After shopping, Sue and Aurelia went to their usual watering hole, The Wild Boar, conveniently located on the palace grounds. Flaminius didn't want them wandering too far, and the only reason he allowed Aurelia out of his sight at all was that she would be with Sue, and Aurelia had to agree to take two royal guards with her. Source save them from alpha males! Aurelia was already drinking her first highball when Sue returned from the bathroom. She smiled at her friend and took a long drink from her martini. "Bless you for ordering for me. I've needed a drink all day."

Aurelia giggled. "What has that man of yours done now?"

"Ugh, don't ask. He is so stubborn. Do you know, he dared to suggest that Noah was large for his age?"

The women looked at each other and burst out laughing. Tears streaming down her face, Aurelia choked out, "He's freakishly enormous for his age!" Calming down, she added, "But to be fair, Noah comes by it honestly. Jim isn't a small man."

Sue looked at her friend in astonishment. "That's what I said!"

Aurelia shook her head. "You know you needle him on purpose."

Shrugging her shoulders, she replied, "Of course I do. The sex is wild after we fight."

They bantered a little more about their men before they ordered food and another drink.

"I wondered if you gave any more thought to what we spoke about last week."

Aurelia popped another piece of fish in her mouth and chewed. "I have, and I am still of the same opinion. Nothing good can come of it."

"I disagree. Flaminius has always valued your opinion above all others."

Sue could see that her friend didn't want to talk about it, but she had to push. For several months she'd dreamed that Aurelia and Flaminius were in terrible danger. Premonitions weren't Sue's dominant gift, so she rarely had them, but she paid attention when she did. "Aurelia, please don't ignore your intuition. Say something to him before it's too late."

"What would I say? Oh, Flame, I think your brother's plotting against you, but I have no evidence, only a gut feeling fueled by the fact that he's creepy."

"He is more than a little creepy." Sue sighed. "For fuck's sake, Aurelia, the guy asked you to have an affair with him!"

Looking to see no one heard, Aurelia lowered her voice, "I told you that in confidence, and you promised you would tell no one. Besides, it was years ago, and when I turned him down and scolded him, he apologized and has never approached me again."

"Oh, yeah, an apology makes it all go away. And don't insult me; I would never betray your confidence."

"This coming from the woman who lied to me about being just my secretary while you were actually a gun-toting, stilettoed, RPU super soldier!"

"Fuck me. You can hold a grudge, girl. That was a hundred years ago! We didn't set out to lie to you. Flaminius felt you were so overwhelmed by all the soldiers we decided it would be in your best interest not to tell you."

Aurelia closed her eyes for a moment. "I'm sorry, you're right. And I gained a best friend because of it. But I digress; I refuse to add to Flame's stress. Especially since I have no proof. Now, can we please stop talking about this and have some fun?"

Sue sighed. "Okay, Aurelia, I'll drop it for now."

"Thank you. And I know I'll have to speak to Flame, but I need to catch him at the right time." Especially now that Flame wanted to put his brother in charge of the Keys' investigation.

Try as she might, Sue couldn't get the feeling of foreboding to go away, so she decided to speak to Marcus. The morning after their shopping trip, Sue got the chance. They were training as usual when Marcus walked in, displaying none of his usual relaxed swagger. Instead, he was all business.

"Good morning, you two. Glad to see you didn't kill each other last night."

Sue wiped her face with a towel and threw it at Jim. "Far from it," came her sassy reply.

Judging from the wrap-around grin on Jim's face, Marcus assumed their night played out just as his friend intended. Jim joined his wife on the gym mats so he could help her stretch. "Do you have more news about the intelligence unit?"

"No, I'm here on other business." Turning to Jim, he said, "We have another jump in two days at zero four hundred." Jim nodded.

Seizing her opportunity, Sue asked, "Do you have a moment to spare?"

"Sure, Sue."

She looked around to make sure they were still alone. "I have a gut feeling that the king's brother can't be trusted."

Marcus studied her for a while before he asked, "I assume this gut feeling has a point of origin?"

She knew Marcus wouldn't accept conjecture, but she would not betray her friend's trust. "I've had dreams. Nothing substantial, but concerning."

Marcus listened as Sue relayed her suspicions. She mentioned Tiberius's carefully veiled anger at the king's decision that ended his political ambitions, as well as his open relationship with Matilda before and after Delinea's death. Her history with Flaminius should've made Tiberius avoid the woman like the plague. Instead, he defended her actions toward the king and Aurelia to anyone who would listen. Plus, the close association he shared with Andreus Simpson and his refusal to believe the allegations leveled toward him concerning the Oradagra. Sue felt the king loved his brother too much to recognize the man's blatant fraternization with people the king himself didn't trust.

Marcus wouldn't have taken Sue's allegations seriously, but for her dreams that Aurelia and Flaminius were in danger. With a promise to investigate Sue's suspicions, Marcus left.

Chapter Six -
Matilda

Gaia straightened from her crouched position over the microscope and rubbed her neck.

"Are you still up?"

"Aurelia!" Gaia gasped. "You frightened me."

Aurelia pushed through the door and walked closer. "I'm sorry, honey, but I saw your light on and wanted to make sure you were okay."

Gaia smiled. "I'm fine, but what are you doing up at this ungodly hour?"

"Probably the same thing you are. Preparing to leave."

Gaia slipped off her stool. "I'm done here. Let me walk you back to your apartments. You look more exhausted than me." Gaia shut down her equipment and locked the lab before she looped her arm through her aunt's. For a while, they walked in companionable silence. "You weren't just walking past my lab, were you?"

Aurelia playfully nudged her niece with her elbow. "Can't pull the wool over your eyes."

"It wasn't difficult to figure out. You're always taking care of me. So, apart from the obvious, why are you worried about me?"

Hesitantly, Aurelia asked, "I know you don't enjoy talking about it, but have you seen your father lately?"

"Aurelia," Gaia warned.

"I know, my sweet, but something is off about him recently."

Gaia laughed. "Only recently?"

"I'm sorry, Gaia. I shouldn't have brought him up."

"No," Gaia sighed, "it's just that I can't help thinking of that day every time I see him."

"And the pain never goes away, does it?"

"No, Aurelia. I suspect that when a young girl sees her father fucking someone other than her mother, the memory will stick."

Aurelia laughed. "I'm sorry. I know that's not an appropriate response. But when I think about how you set up a network of cameras with no one noticing, I'm tickled pink."

Frowning, Gaia asked, "Why?"

"Gaia! You were just a child, yet you managed to dupe your father and his RPU."

"Well, I was experimenting to see if my father treated others with the same cold indifference he did me, as my mother suggested," she answered peevishly.

Aurelia shook her head. "Delinea never should've told you that."

"But she was right. The only person my father treats with warmth is Andreus." They stopped outside Aurelia's apartment. "If it weren't for you, I would've gone mad trying to decide if I should tell my mother what I caught on those cameras."

"I'm sorry, honey. It might be wrong to say, but I'm relieved you didn't have to break that news to your mother. I'm only sorry it was because she got sick and died."

"Do you know, I never told him I knew about his affair with Matilda."

"Really?" Aurelia asked, surprised. "I assumed you had because your relationship with him declined so rapidly."

"No. I said nothing because Matilda stopped coming around. I think my father felt guilty and broke it off with her."

"And you'd lost enough, so you let it go?" Aurelia guessed.

"Yes," Gaia said, looking down to hide her emotions.

Aurelia put her fingers under Gaia's chin and tipped her head up. "I'm sorry."

"Thank you for always being there for me."

Hugging her, Aurelia said, "There is nothing to thank me for. Now off to bed with you."

"Good night."

Gaia walked to her room but couldn't stop thinking about what her aunt said. She had lost a lot. Perhaps it was time to build a bridge and get over it. Tomorrow she would visit her father and see if they could start over.

Tiberius rolled onto his back and blinked. Bright morning light streamed into his bedroom, casting a golden glow over Matilda's naked back, tinting her skin a tone darker than he knew it to be.

Matilda sighed in her sleep and shifted a little closer. He automatically embraced her, pulling her curvy body into his side. She was a lovely creature, and he wondered why his brother didn't keep her as a lover after he married. It wasn't as if she minded being a mistress; in fact, she preferred it. Since her husband's death, Matilda discovered her independence and refused to give it up. Arkhnuetian law didn't stop women from gaining financial freedom. Still, it was frowned upon for a woman to marry amongst the aristocracy and expect to keep her assets separate from her husband's. Matilda made it clear to him after Delinea died that she had no intention of changing their arrangement just because his wife had shuffled off her mortal coil. Neither did Tiberius, so they remained lovers.

They hadn't kept their relationship a secret, but they did not trumpet it from the castle walls. They may be doing nothing wrong now, but their affair had started while he was still married. Flaminius knew, and even though he didn't love the idea, he allowed it. Tiberius didn't give a continental fuck. It delighted him to take her off his brother's hands and into his bed.

"Tiberius, it's far too early in the morning to be plotting." Matilda stretched her arms above her head, dislodging the sheet enough to give him a tantalizing glimpse of her breast.

"What makes you think I'm plotting, my dear? I could be thinking about breakfast."

She rolled her eyes and sat up, twisting her torso to face him, letting the sheet slip completely. Then, brushing her thick, long ink-black curls away from her neck, she said, "Please, I know that look, and it's not your I'm-hungry-for-food-look, is it, big boy?"

He pushed himself up on his elbow and twisted his fingers in her hair with the other hand. "I must concede; you know me well. So, what do you intend to do about my hunger?"

Letting her hand drift to his cock under the covers, she wrapped her fingers around him and squeezed. "I think it would be best if I had some sustenance before we have another round." He released her hair and lay back. Moving slowly, she settled between his thighs. "I think it would be acceptable if I started with some protein."

With no further warning, she took his cock deep into her mouth and sucked hard. His hips jerked up off the bed, drawing a throaty moan from her. One of the reasons he adored her was her ability to surprise him. It didn't hurt that she was a brilliant alchemist with a talent for creating poisons that not even his daughter could detect until recently.

Matilda licked the underside of his cock with the flat of her tongue, using her hand to pump him in perfect synchronicity before plunging him back into her warm mouth, making further thought impossible. Tiberius opened his thighs to give her more room to work and threaded his fingers into her hair so that he could fuck her mouth in earnest.

She took him to the edge before pulling back, only to repeat her torture until he dripped with sweat. Tiberius sat up, hooked his hands under her arms, pulled her onto his body, then planted his foot on the mattress and flipped her under him. "Now, little dove, it's my turn."

She threw her arms above her head and drew her knees up and open as far as they would go. "What are you waiting for? An engraved invitation?"

Trapping her wrists with one large hand, he sucked her earlobe into his mouth, using his teeth to deliver a stinging bite while his other hand found her breast and tweaked her nipple, delivering a dual blow of pain. She gasped and squirmed impatiently. He knew Matilda liked it rough, and it thrilled him to oblige her wilder tastes.

Moving further down her body, he sucked first one nipple and then the other, leaving several love bites before roughly flipping her onto her stomach. Bumping her thighs open with his knee, he pulled her hips off the bed. She tried to lift her upper body, but he pushed her down, anchoring his hand on her neck. "No, my pet. I want your ass in the air for me to see that dripping wet pink pussy." She groaned. Releasing her neck, Tiberius kneeled behind her and separated the globes of her ass cheeks. He eagerly licked his way from her tight hole to her dripping cunt, spending some time circling her nub before licking his way back.

"I'm going to come, don't stop."

Chuckling, he ceased his ministrations. "I swear you say that on purpose to prolong your agony. You know damned well I won't give in to your demands." He slapped her ass and watched her pussy engorge even more. "Are you my little masochist?" He spanked her ass again to prove his point.

Matilda trembled so badly that she struggled to stay kneeling. "Yes! Please, I beg you, let me come."

Tiberius loved the power he had over her. "No, I think you need a lesson." She whimpered her disagreement, but nodded her head. "Good girl. Don't move while I fetch some toys, my pet, and the punishment will be severe if you look. Nod if you understand." She did. Leaning to the side, he reached into the top drawer of his nightstand and chose the bright pink dildo she bought him for his birthday and the flavored strawberry lube. He repositioned himself and squirted some lube directly onto her puckered hole. Her breathing increased with anticipation. "Does my dirty little girl love ass play?"

"Uh-huh."

He continued teasing her with his fingers, rubbing the lube in small circles around her anus. "Mm, let's see. Shall we fuck you with the dildo or my cock in this tight little hole?"

She panted her response. "Please, the dildo."

He slowly slid the pink member up between her cheeks, coating it with the strawberry lube. "Yeah? And what should I do with my cock, little one?" She either couldn't answer or wanted him to get creative, because she remained silent. He gently inserted the toy's tip into her anus and used his other hand to stimulate her clit. Slowly, he drove the dildo deeper, increasing the pressure with his fingers on her nub. She shuddered when he had it seated. The sight of her lying with her ass filled and her body shaking almost undid him.

He left the toy in place and positioned the tip of his cock at her entrance. "Tell me how much you want me to fuck you."

"I want you to fuck me more than I want my next breath."

He grabbed her hips and thrust forward. She shouted out his name. Withdrawing, he plunged in again, all the time watching his cock fill her, the dildo in her ass creating the most intense pressure. Repeatedly, he rammed into her, listening to her groans increase and taking pleasure in the scene he had choreographed. Finally, she came, squirting her milky cream all over his cock. With two more powerful thrusts, he followed her into oblivion.

She collapsed under his weight. Once they regained their composure, he removed the dildo and rolled her onto her back. Throwing the covers over them, he nestled down for some slumber.

Slowing her stallion, Sting, Gaia looked up at the twenty-foot, ivy-covered stone wall surrounding the estate. Her father wouldn't have allowed the plant to grow so prolifically during the war because of the security risk it posed. However, he still insisted on the massive iron gates remaining locked and a member of the RPU on guard at all times.

Today's unlucky winner was Andreus, a man she never liked. Tiberius said it was because she envied the relationship he shared with Andreus. He said that there were just some things a father couldn't share with his daughter. Shaking off the memory of that particular discussion, she put a fake smile on her face.

"Good morning, Andreus." Like most Arkhnuetian men, he was tall and very well built, and if she were honest, very good looking. He stepped out of the guardhouse with his usual lazy gait, but something about the way he narrowed his eyes at her felt different. She knew he hated it when she addressed him in such a casual manner, which was why she did it, but today he seemed more on edge.

"We weren't expecting you today, Lady Guardian. To what do we owe the pleasure?"

Gaia dismounted. "Does a daughter need a reason to visit her father?"

Grabbing hold of Sting's reins, he replied, "No, I suppose not, but he's not here today; you should have called. We are in the middle of a crisis, in case you hadn't noticed."

Mm, sarcasm, his attempt to rile her. "I only wanted to see him today because it will be one of the few days I have off before I depart."

Nodding, he smiled. "Yes, of course, you're leaving with the First Wave."

Ignoring his statement, she asked, "Could you tell him I was here?"

"I will be sure to do so. Goodbye, Gaia."

The arrogant man turned his back on her and resumed his post inside the small guardhouse. Remounting, she directed Sting to the rear of the property and stopped close to where the ivy grew thickest. Gaia would not give up that easily. Something wasn't right, and she was going to find out what. Standing on the saddle, she grasped the closest branch to climb the vine. It was slow going, but she managed and stopped at the top for a moment to catch her breath. It was a relief when her feet finally touched solid ground, and apart from a couple of scratches and quite a bit of foliage in her hair, she was unscathed.

Stealthily crossing the manicured lawn, it occurred to her how absurd it was that she had to sneak into her childhood home like a common criminal. Hugging the patio walls, she tried three of the French doors before she found one unlocked. Inside, the formal sitting room was dark with the drapes drawn, so she stood still while her eyes adjusted.

Sunday was the servants' day off, so the house was silent but for the familiar creaks and cracks. The ground and first floors were empty; perhaps Andreus had not been lying. Just as she was about to give up, she heard a woman's voice. Straining her ears, she followed the muted sounds toward her father's bedroom. The noises emanating from up ahead became startlingly familiar. Not wishing to believe her ears, she foolishly allowed her feet to lead her toward the secret passage located close to the bedroom.

Opening the panel, she stepped into the dark tunnel and fumbled for the matchbox and candle she hoped were still there. The wick sparked and spat when she lit it because of the years of gathered dust. Closing the panel, she followed the passage, counting the peepholes until she got to number seven. When she was a kid, she needed a box to stand on to see through the hole, but not anymore. Peeping through, Gaia saw what her ears had heard.

Her father kneeled behind a woman, thrusting, grunting like a pig, and glowing with the same color from the effort. The woman writhed as she gripped the silk sheets, moaning with delight. It was a shocking scene for any daughter, even if it wasn't the first time. What made it significantly worse was that she knew the woman. They had continued their affair all this time.

Gaia couldn't remember how she got out of the house or how she managed to get back over the wall. Her first recollection was sitting astride Sting, galloping at a break-neck pace, tears streaming down her face. Once Gaia had made it back to the palace, she settled Sting, then went to the one place that soothed her. The lab.

Unfortunately, Flaminius intercepted her on the way. "Gaia, I was on my way to see you. I need to—" the moment Flaminius saw her face, he stopped. "What's happened, little one? Why are you so upset?"

Gaia didn't know if it was the horrible scene she just witnessed or the stress of the last few months, but she couldn't stop herself from bursting into a fresh bout of tears and rushing into her uncle's protective embrace.

Flaminius guided his niece into the empty staff room and seated her next to him on the couch. "Tell me what's bugging you." He tried to keep the growl from his voice, but failed. "I'm going to kill whoever hurt you."

Gaia laughed. "I don't think you'll want to do that," she said, wiping her eyes and moving out of his arms.

"Yes, I bloody well would."

"Then you'd have to kill your brother."

"Fuck, what's he done now?"

Shaking her head, she replied, "I don't want to talk about him."

Flaminius wanted to press her, but he could see his stubborn niece wouldn't change her mind. "If I can't help with Tiberius, then how can I help you feel better?"

Blurting out the first thing that came to mind, she said, "How do you know if someone likes you?" Realizing what she said, she blushed and waved her hand. "Never mind. Forget I asked."

"Oh, no!" Flaminius clutched her arm. "Spill." When she said nothing, he threw caution to the wind. "Is this about Marcus?"

Gaia paled. "Oh no, tell me it's not that obvious," she whispered.

"Don't worry, Gaia. Besides myself and Aurelia, no one suspects." She slumped back in relief. "How long have you had feelings for him?"

Shrugging, she mumbled, "He's a few years older, but we went to school together. I suppose my crush started then, but it wasn't until he joined the RPU and became friends with you I realized it was more than a schoolgirl fancy."

"Marcus is my best friend, and I trust him with my family's life, but he's not a one-woman man. He won't be until he's ready to find his mate. One day, he will want a family, and that might leave you broken-hearted." Flaminius saw the light dull in his niece's eyes. Cupping her chin, he added, "There's nothing wrong with a passionate affair, but I suspect you had more in mind, and you would know if he were your match. Trust me on that." Gaia was suspiciously quiet. "Gaia? What aren't you telling me?"

When Gaia started university, she made the supremely controversial decision to take hormone suppressants, specially designed to stop the match hormone's secretion. It didn't stop sexual desire, but that wasn't her goal. Her only reason for taking the medication was that she didn't feel the urge to seek her match. She focused on building a career before she thought of marriage. As time passed, she became comfortable with her decision, or that's what she convinced herself. But Gaia was not a good liar, not even when she was doing it to herself. Eventually, she had to face the truth; she was avoiding a relationship because of her experience with her father. Gaia was damaged goods, and no amount of psychotherapy would ever fix her feelings of abandonment and distrust of men.

But Gaia wasn't going to tell her uncle that. She'd embarrassed herself enough as it was. "Nothing. Anyway, it's a moot point. Marcus doesn't even know I exist, so nothing will happen."

Flaminius looked at her for a long time before he said, "I know it hurts that Marcus hasn't noticed you in that way, but I promise when you're ready to seek your match, your feelings for Marcus will seem childish."

Well. There it was. Marcus's best friend confirmed Marcus had no feelings for her. The disappointment was crushing.

Chapter Seven -
Stupid Clothes

Six Months Later

Marcus stood in front of the gilded mirror in his chambers, trying to convince himself that he didn't look like a complete idiot. The royal seamstress and her party of incredibly talented individuals fussed over the last bits and pieces to make sure they adequately attired him for a wealthy human in the twelfth century.

In the preceding months, Marcus had made many jumps to find Earth headquarters and a home for the royal family, a place large enough to accommodate them and their entourage and easy to defend with a few men. His reconnaissance missions yielded the perfect location in Warwickshire, and land acquisition department agents had dealt with the lease. Today, he would meet the foreman at the building site to introduce himself as the representative of the wealthy lord who would live there.

Finding such a place had been near impossible. Earth kings decided who could own land and granted it only to noblemen and the church, leaving the Arkhnuetians with few options to build without humans' attention. Marcus appealed to human greed and offered the landowner, Sir Thomas de Clinton, a lot of money and a contract promising to work the land and tithe a portion to Sir Thomas and the church. With Sir Thomas's blessing, the building of a manor house had already begun.

It took a lot to convince Flaminius to let him make this jump alone, but it was imperative because not even Flaminius knew Marcus had found two other locations. The first, he would convince the king to keep between them, and the second, no one would know about—for now. His discussion with Sue prompted him to seek the second location. He had observed the relationship between Andreus and Tiberius. There was no evidence to suggest treason, but for just another member of Tiberius's guard, they walked too closely, whispered too much, shared knowing looks, and yet tried too hard to stay out of each other's space, like secret lovers. Tiberius needed to believe there was only one HQ because Marcus might not trust him, and he wouldn't underestimate him.

Of course, Flaminius insisted on seeing him before he left and didn't miss the opportunity to poke fun at him. Turning red with the effort not to laugh, he pointed at Marcus. "I don't know if that fur-trimmed tunic is the right color for his eyes, Madame Suzette?"

The stout woman rested her hands on the curve of her hips and shook her head. "I disagree, Sire. I think the deep blue complements his olive skin tone beautifully."

Marcus glared at his friend but spoke to Madame Suzette. "Are you sure it's supposed to be this baggy?" He held the tunic out to his sides and continued, "And do I have to wear this ludicrous hat?"

Madame Suzette sniffed indignantly. "It's not a hat, sir. It is a chaperon, and I assure you we've been exhaustive in our quest to duplicate Earth fashions of the day."

Marcus looked less than convinced. "Yes, I'm sure you have, but do the stocking things have to be red? And this jeweled collar is a tad tight." Flaminius couldn't stop himself from laughing. Marcus threw a shoe at Flaminius, which he easily avoided. "Thank you, Madame Suzette. I can take it from here." The lady and her entourage exited, heavily laden with bolts of cloth and sewing equipment.

Flaminius, still laughing, wiped tears from his cheeks. "It seems the only useful thing on that outfit is the belt that will hold your dagger and money pouch. But I must say I've enjoyed the show."

Marcus tried to move the collar to scratch his neck while pulling his stockings out of his butt crack at the same time. "Laugh it up, Sire, but remember, soon this will be your daily attire."

STUPID CLOTHES

That bit of information sucked the humor out of Flaminius. "Shit, I never thought of that. I don't care if we're not supposed to influence the human world. I'm changing the fashion."

Marcus fought the urge to gloat and asked, "Want to share a drink and some words of wisdom before I go, Sire?"

"Don't mind if I do."

Marcus poured them each a whiskey and sat on the chair opposite him.

"I don't think you need me to tell you how important this mission is. I'm anxious to get Theo far away from here as quickly as possible."

"I'll make sure that the building project runs on time."

"How long will you be?"

Marcus took a sip of his whiskey before answering. "I'll be back before week's end, with any luck. The Forest of Arden will provide the cover I need to rift in close to Warwickshire, where I'll buy a horse and ride to the building site."

Flame drained his glass. "Take care, my friend, and for the love of Source, leave the human women alone."

Marcus laughed at his friend. "I make no promises."

Chapter Eight - Arkhnuet- Proofing Earth

Flaminius rubbed his temples, hoping to stave off the headache that had been threatening to render him useless all day. It was disconcerting having no contact with Marcus, but they had made progress since he left. He shuffled through the papers on his desk, ticking off tasks his appointed relocation committee had accomplished.

"Rosalind and I have located, bought, and equipped various dilapidated buildings and warehouses for hospitals." Sylas's voice brought his attention back to the meeting. "Rosalind's idea to keep the exterior of the buildings as ramshackle as possible to throw off suspicion of what will go on inside them is ingenious," he boasted before he continued. "Builders are rifting to Earth late at night to continue upgrading the buildings' interiors and digging subterranean tunnels leading to and from the hospitals so our people will have easy access."

"I'm overseeing the stocking of equipment and staffing of these facilities, and Sylas is making sure construction remains on time," Rosalind added. "I estimate the facilities could be operational in six months. Gaia, do you have anything to add?"

"Yes, I've almost completed making most surplus medicines and acquiring the raw materials to make more. We have at least seven years of stock."

"What about the problem of hiding power stations?"

Barret stood. "I think we've solved that. In the remote areas of warmer countries, my team has designed solar panels to mimic the vegetation. Those of us relocating to Africa and Australia will live in villages entirely composed of Arkhnuetians, with limited human contact."

Flaminius would've preferred sending all his people to these continents, but he couldn't dump six million people in two locations and expect the humans not to notice.

"The colder climates are proving harder to equip. London and other areas have a lot of rivers, so we will use hydro-power wherever possible. Pumphouses disguised as mills simplify things, but we haven't tested the equipment. Although, I foresee no problems."

"Thank you, Barret. The council has approved Aurelia's suggestion, so there will be only one public rifting station in each major city. They'll be in the hospitals since they already have power and are hidden. This reduces the number of power stations required and makes it easier to control their use, ensuring the safety of people and products as they both move between countries and continents." Flaminius riffled through a pile of papers and found the one he was looking for before he continued.

"Each existing Arkhnuet councilor will head up one of thirteen districts on Earth. In some of these districts, Arkhnuetians will have to live in towns already established by humans. Arkhnuetians will elect a sub-council to take on the day-to-day operations, and the sub-council will report directly to the district councilor."

Leaning back in his chair, Flaminius looked at the people around the table. "As you all know, there are currently hundreds of thousands of portable rifting devices registered by the Department of Transportation. On Earth, personal ownership of these devices will not be permitted." There was a deathly silence because not everyone agreed with this decision. "Instead, I will grant official licenses to each town's sub-council, so we know who's using the rifters." Sighing, he continued, "It's the only way we can limit the possibility of humans finding one. If there is nothing else, I think we can close the meeting."

"If I can just add one thing?" Flaminius nodded for Aurelia to speak. "The safe removal and storing of the vast contents of libraries and museums are proving difficult due to time constraints. I need more help."

"I can spare a couple of people to help you." Barret offered.

"And I've just about finished my work. So, I can send you a team of six," Gaia added.

"That would be wonderful, thank you."

Flaminius looked at the group gathered around the table. "Anything else?"

"Then, we're done."

The saddle creaked as Marcus twisted his torso to look behind him. Thick mist enveloped him, making visibility almost zero and distorting the sound of the small creatures that scurried out of his path. It was late afternoon on the fifth day of his mission. He'd tied up the first two locations to his satisfaction and was currently trying to secure the third. Tired, hungry, cold, and wet, Marcus wanted nothing more than to go home to Arkhnuet and forget that they were in this mess.

He wiped the moisture off his face using the back of his hand and dug the rifter out of his cloak to check coordinates. Yup, he was definitely in the right spot. He chose this island because it was cut off from the rest of the mainland except at low tide when it was linked to the Islet of Uineasan to the east. Also, the Norsemen had little use for it, which made it easy for Marcus to rent it from King Magnus Barefoot.

Through the thick afternoon fog, the sound of muffled voices drifted to Marcus's ears, snapping him out of his musings. Hiding the rifter, he shouted out, "Hello!"

The sounds cut off, and then a return, "Hello!"

Marcus dismounted and led his horse toward the approaching shadows as he drew his cloak back to give him easy access to his sword, should he need it. "My name is Marcus. Who goes there?"

"I am Sigurd, the king's messenger."

As Marcus drew nearer, he identified at least three other men with Sigurd by the sounds of their horses' hooves on the soft ground and jingling of harnesses and weapons. To these men, he was simply the emissary of a church looking to establish a secluded abbey for peace-loving monks and their followers' families. Magnus didn't care for Christians, but he couldn't afford to turn away the significant amount of money this rental would bring him.

Magnus was a warmongering lunatic like the rest of the Earth's kings, and wars cost money.

"Pleased to make your acquaintance, sir." Marcus no longer needed to shout, as he was now a few feet away from Sigurd. The man sat straight and proud in the saddle, suggesting he was more than just a messenger. Perhaps one of the king's sons? He was tall, blond, and blue-eyed, as folk of his descent often were.

Sigurd's companions flanked him but left space between their horses. The man to Sigurd's left was the largest of the three and had the same blond hair, blue-eyed characteristics. But it was the man on the right that caught Marcus's attention. He was dark of hair and eye, and Marcus could tell his soul was no longer whole. This man had seen more war than the other two. Looking around, Marcus tried to see the fourth man he knew accompanied the others. A faint rustling alerted him to the man's location behind him, using the fog to conceal his presence.

Sigurd jerked his chin to his left. "This is Loftur," then repeated the chin thing to his right, "and this is Olaf."

None of them dismounted, making Marcus think perhaps things may not go well. "I have the agreed-upon amount of silver and gifts to show our gratitude to your king for his kindness."

Sigurd swung his leg over his horse's head, dismounting with a bit of hop. "Magnus Barefoot thanks you." Scratching his beard, he continued, "However, my king no longer finds the amount satisfactory."

Yup, this wasn't going to go as planned. Fuck it! "I'm disappointed that he's gone back on his word. I was under the impression he was a man of honor."

For a few moments, Sigurd stood dumbfounded. "I suggest," he said in a threatening tone, putting his hand on the hilt of his sword for good measure, "that you do not insult my king again."

Moving away from his horse, Marcus lifted his hands in a non-threatening gesture. "I meant no offense, but the church will not pay more than previously agreed."

Rubbing the back of his neck and smirking, Sigurd replied, "Then, you'll not like it when King Barefoot comes and takes his annual fee of one-third of your crops and livestock."

ARKHNUET-PROOFING EARTH

"My lord, you must understand, we are not as wealthy as the other abbeys. The monks seek only to live in peace and study the word of our Lord. We have no more to give."

Looking over Marcus's shoulder, Sigurd gave just a hint of a shrug. It was then that Marcus knew he was not the decision-maker of the group. He ambled toward Marcus, invading his personal space. "You don't look like any monk I've ever seen. Where did you say you came from?"

Crossing his arms over his chest, Marcus replied. "I didn't."

Again, the boy looked over Marcus's shoulder. Olaf and Loftur dismounted and took up a threatening position on either side. Sighing, Marcus shook his head. He didn't feel like fighting these idiots today. But he had neither the time nor the patience to find a better place to keep the royal family safe, and he couldn't allow some crack-pot king and his riot of rabble to fuck this up.

Nodding his head thoughtfully, Sigurd walked around Marcus's horse, running his fingers over the leather saddle and the bundles tied over the horse's withers. "Mm. You say your abbey isn't wealthy, and yet, you have a fine-looking horse, fine quality clothing, and equipment." Having completed his walk around the horse, he once again stood in front of Marcus. "Surely, you can understand my confusion?" Leaning in threateningly, he continued, "Monk. What have you to say to that?"

Fucking hell! This tosser was getting on his last nerve. A slight rustle of clothing alerted Marcus that the fourth man had moved closer and stood three feet behind him to the left. Buying time, Marcus took a step toward the boy, forcing him to move back. The fact that Marcus had three inches and at least fifty pounds on Sigurd helped.

"I never said I was a monk. I said I was the emissary to an abbey looking for a peaceful place to commune with our Lord. Now, unless your companions wish to return to your father with your body, I suggest you stop trying to intimidate me and either honor our deal or fuck off."

Sigurd couldn't hide his surprise at the fact that Marcus knew he was the king's son. Not wanting to give the kid a chance to recover, Marcus decided they needed the fear of their gods put into them. So, instead of drawing his sword, he whipped out his automatic pistol, pointed it at the man behind Sigurd, and discharged one round into his thigh. Startled by the noise, the

219

others fell to the ground with their hands over their ears. The poor sod with the bullet in his leg collapsed, screaming. Calmly, Marcus turned and pointed the weapon at Sigurd. "Now listen up, you little fuck. Go home to your daddy and tell him that our arrangement stands. Trust me; you have no idea with whom you are dealing. If the king comes near my people, my army and I are going to kill everyone he knows and loves with our magic fire-spitting dragon sticks." For good measure, Marcus fired off another three rounds into the ground around the men.

More squealing commenced, and then Marcus smelled an unmistakable odor. One or all of these 'brave' men had shat his pants. Rolling his eyes, Marcus crouched next to Sigurd and slapped him on the side of his head. He whimpered but looked up. "Nod if you understood what I just said, boy."

Nodding his head vigorously, Sigurd stammered a reply. "I understand, I understand."

Marcus straightened, grabbed the reins of his horse, and swung up into the saddle. "We wish no harm to anyone. All we want is to be left alone. Tell your father he can expect to receive payment promptly every year as per our agreement." Marcus untied the bundle on the back of his saddle and threw it on the ground next to the kid, silver coins spilling out. "We will be back to take occupation of our island soon."

Leaving the men still cowering on the ground, he made his way back to the mainland before the tide came in and rifted his sore ass back to Warwickshire.

Five Months Later

Flaminius and his far-too-calm wife stood together in the rifter bay, earthbound to inspect the official HQ. Apart from the royal family, Mother Guardian, her Lady Keys, and the vast majority of the RPU would also call it home. Marcus and his team had done a remarkable job of getting the HQ ready in such a brief space of time. Flaminius had mixed feelings. He was relieved that his son would soon be safe, but he also dreaded separating his family.

Aurelia tried her absolute best not to fall apart. She wouldn't have remained standing but for Flame's powerful arms around her. Madame and her team had done their best to make sure their attire was authentic, but unfortunately, the clothing was superbly uncomfortable, and the sheer abundance of fabric felt suffocating. Aurelia had to admit that the butter-yellow silk bliaut was beautiful, but the trumpet-shaped sleeves were so long they dragged on the ground, and the flared skirt with a small train would take some getting used to. These banal thoughts about clothing might have seemed petty considering the circumstances they found themselves in, but it helped Aurelia keep from having a panic attack.

The atmosphere in the rifting bay was so thick that when Marcus spoke, it felt like a lash from a whip, stinging the skin, jarring her from her thoughts.

"Your Majesties, it's time. When we get there, remember to remain inside the protective ring of the RPU and be ready to rift back if I give the command."

Both Flaminius and Aurelia nodded. "Also, let me do the talking. I've built a relationship with the people, and they'll expect me to handle all business. And do not, under any circumstances, smile at or be friendly to the peasants." This last command he directed at Aurelia.

"I won't be rude to them, Marcus. I don't care if it's not the done thing. They'll have to get used to it."

Flame squeezed her waist to get her attention. "Honey, I get that it's been difficult learning about the plight of the lower classes of Earth, and believe me, I understand. But we need to proceed with caution."

Flame saw that his wife was gearing up for a lengthy and passionate debate, so he did what he always did when she got riled up. He kissed her, and as per usual, it worked like a charm. When he pulled away, he whispered, "I'm not suggesting we continue to treat them poorly to keep up appearances. I'm simply asking that you institute the changes slowly." She nodded her assent, and he rewarded her with another kiss, which Marcus interrupted with a gentle clearing of his throat.

"Are we ready now?" he asked.

"Indeed," she answered indignantly.

Aurelia had grown accustomed to the odd sensation associated with rifting, but her frayed nerves amplified the chill more than usual. For security and secrecy purposes, they rifted to the Forest of Arden that surrounded the estate. Once through, she took the time to peruse her surroundings. The lush forest had plenty of mature trees, but they were not so dense as to block the sun from reaching the forest floor and allowing a kaleidoscope of wildflowers to thrive.

A small group of RPU men readied horses for their brief trip to the manor house. Flame helped Aurelia mount and arranged her skirts to cover her legs. "Let me know if you're having too much trouble with the side-saddle, honey."

Aurelia smiled. "I've had a lot of practice over the last few months. I think I'll be okay." The men took up their defensive positions, and the party moved forward for their two-hour journey to their new home.

When Aurelia got distracted by talking to one man whose wife had just had a baby, Marcus made his approach to Flaminius.

"I hear Tiberius was less than happy when he found out he wasn't accompanying us today."

"Ugh," Flame groaned. "I tried to explain our reasons to him, but he wouldn't or couldn't hear me. I swear, lately, he's been so fucking moody. Not that I blame him. We're all on edge, but it feels like something else is riding his ass."

Choosing his words carefully, Marcus waded in. "I can't say I'm surprised at his behavior. He's been like a dog with a bone in his pursuit of information regarding HQ and other things."

Flame's head shot up. "What other things?"

"Asking questions about our military strategy and trying to wheedle his way into intel meetings and some jumps we've made."

The king said nothing, but Marcus noticed a muscle working in his jaw as if he was biting his tongue.

"I was going to talk to you about it, but neither of us has had the time. I feel very uncomfortable with the situation, Flaminius. As general to the RPU, I can tell the king's brother to take a hike, but my men can't."

Flaminius was overtired, overworked, undersexed, and scared out of his mind. He couldn't deal with his brother's feelings of inadequacy as well.

ARKHNUET-PROOFING EARTH

"When we get back, I'll issue an edict giving you the authority to give direct orders to my brother."

Flaminius's words nearly knocked Marcus off his horse. In effect, the king gave him the power to deal with Tiberius any way he deemed necessary, even if that meant throwing Tiberius in jail. Flaminius had never issued a proclamation before because of the possibility of misuse. The trust Flaminius placed in Marcus meant everything to him. Clearing his throat, he answered, "Thank you, Flaminius." Not taking his eyes off the road, Flaminius patted Marcus on the shoulder.

Lost in thought as he was, Aurelia's surprise gasp gave Marcus more of a fright than it should've. Looking up, he saw they had cleared the bend in the road, bringing the almost complete manor house into view. The site was a hive of activity, bathed in a cloud of dust. Aurelia's obvious delight with the manor house warmed Marcus's heart. Flaminius ordered him to install every convenience possible, and a few skated close to breaking the new laws instituted to protect humans. Among them were bathhouses (separated for men and women) with running hot and cold water. They built three massive water tanks up on the hill next to the creek and a water wheel with buckets attached to fill the tanks in the dry season. Unfortunately, they only had lead piping in this world, so Marcus supplied the plumbing material designed to look the same. These ducts also distributed water to the kitchens in a separate building, as was Earth's custom.

The foreman, John, called out a greeting to their group and bowed to them, cap in hand.

"Hello, John." Pointing at the house, Marcus said, "I see that you and your men have made a great deal of progress."

Beaming at the compliment, John replied, "Yes, sir, I hope you will be pleased." Turning to Flaminius, Marcus introduced the foreman to his future master and his wife. He smiled when Aurelia almost stuck out her hand to shake John's before she remembered to remain indifferent.

"Shall we take the tour now, or would you like some refreshments first, sir?" Knowing that Aurelia was anxious to see her new home, Marcus decided to forgo the offer of food and get on with it. "We'll have something after the tour, John. Lead the way."

Chapter Nine - The Manor House with Secrets

Aurelia followed the men, never taking her eyes off the building as John proudly explained the manor's layout. "We are approaching from the front, my lords."

Beautiful gray stone walls rose three stories into the air, surrounded on three sides by a moat. The red brick star-shaped chimneys cut into the horizon's blue background, creating an impressive façade. A long, wide, arched stone bridge stretched across the moat, fed by the creek that flowed past the house. The closer they got, the more the house drew her in, speaking to her in its unique voice, drowning out the mumblings of their guide. And what it said was, 'home.' Every room they walked through, from the great room with its magnificent carved woodwork and elegant fireplace to the humblest of pantries built to store herbs and the like, pulsed with life.

There were no furnishings or artwork in any of the spaces yet. Still, Aurelia loved every room, from the stables, church (which didn't matter to her, but it was beautiful) to the cottages for the staff and RPU and the marvelous Roman bathhouses complete with stone tubs.

The hard-working men and women of the area had also started planting gardens. And even though they couldn't hide their wariness toward these new masters with their strange ways, like bathing every day and the contraptions they relieved themselves in, they were too grateful for the work to say anything about it.

After the tour, the men carried an old, battered table to the shade of a large oak tree, and Marcus, Aurelia, Flaminius, and the RPU men ate their late lunch while watching the workers go about their business. Marcus waited until the meal was winding down before giving instructions to his men that would take them out of earshot but not out of sight. Then he turned to Flaminius and Aurelia. "There is just one more thing I have to show you both before we leave."

Flame filled his wife's goblet with more wine and then sat back. "Okay. Why do I feel like I'm going to hug you or want to knock your block off?"

Aurelia giggled into her cup. "Perhaps it's because he has that effect on almost everybody."

Ignoring their comments, Marcus stood and motioned for them to follow him. Growling more out of a need to make a point than actual anger, Flame helped his wife up and followed his friend across the field, over the stone bridge, and into the house.

Marcus guided them into the chapel room and shut the door. "What I'm about to show you can go no further than this room." Knowing better than to argue, both Flaminius and Aurelia agreed. He walked to the small carved wooden altar and reached to pull on a cherub's head, tipping it forward and twisting it to the right. Jerking his head for them to come closer, Marcus shifted the heavy drapes aside and showed them a section of wood paneling that had popped open. He walked through and then waited for them to follow. Once inside the small space, he shut the panel and picked up a flashlight hidden on a shelf beside the entrance.

Pointing to a flight of narrow stone stairs, Marcus said. "This is one of three escape passages in the house. I'll show you the one in the great hall and your bedchamber later. This passage leads under the moat, opening in the forest one hundred yards to the east. The one in the great hall leads west and opens via a trapdoor in the stable tack room. The last leads to the south and opens in the heart of the forest and is the longest, taking at least three hours to walk."

Flaminius shook his head in awe. "When? How?"

"It's my job to make sure you're safe."

"That doesn't answer my questions."

Marcus ignored Flaminius. "If you have an option, I would prefer you use the tunnel leading to the stables if you have time to get away on horseback. My second choice would be the long tunnel. All of them are well-stocked with food, water, clothing, money, and weapons. The only other people I'm going to tell are Gaia, Sue, and Jim."

Once Marcus showed them the other tunnels, they saddled up after saying their goodbyes to John and headed back to the spot they rifted into earlier.

It was late, and Aurelia had just managed to get a restless Theo to sleep. Sometimes she could swear that he knew what was going on and wanted to get up and do something about it, but his baby body would not cooperate with him. As usual, Flame was still in his study. She missed him desperately, but she didn't want to put more pressure on him by being a nagging wife.

He seemed more wound up with each passing day, and no matter how much he got done, he never felt it was enough. She understood everybody was anxious, but Flame took it to a new level, and she had no idea how to help him unwind. So how did Marcus relieve the tension? He never seemed overwhelmed! Lying in bed in the dark, she wondered what Marcus did to ease his stress so effectively. She knew he liked to exercise and did so daily with his men, but so did Flame. No matter what was going on, they knew that keeping in shape could mean the difference between life or death.

So if it wasn't exercising, then what? Just that morning, she saw Marcus saunter out of the root cellar in the kitchens looking super loose and relaxed. Wracking her brain, she tried to think about what he could've found there to help him relax when she realized. Not long after Marcus disappeared around the corner, Doris stumbled out the root cellar looking disheveled and even more relaxed than Marcus. Holy mother of Source! Sex! Bolting upright, Aurelia tried to think of the last time she and Flame had sex. She couldn't remember. Both of them had a healthy appetite, and until a few months ago, they never went without for more than a day, two at the most.

Could it be that they simply forgot to have sex because they were stressed? Yes! That was precisely what they had done. Well, she couldn't have that.

Flaminius rubbed his eyes for the hundredth time before picking up another piece of paper and trying to read the swirling text. He was beyond fucking exhausted. But he had at least two or three hours of work to get through before he could crawl into bed with his wife.

When the study door opened, it surprised him to see Aurelia walking toward him. It wasn't unusual for her to come to say good night, but he usually felt her energy before seeing her. It bothered him he'd missed her approach. Shifting his chair back, he turned his body and held out his arms. She crawled into his lap with no hesitation. "Are you okay, baby?" Snuggling up closer, she shook her head. "It's going to be alright, sweetheart. We're going to make it through this."

She pulled back to look into his eyes. "I know, honey. That's not what's bothering me."

Flame frowned. "Yeah? Then what is?"

Looking almost contrite, Aurelia dropped her head and spoke the following words to her lap. "I've been missing you, and I know you have a lot on your mind; we all do, but . . ."

"Baby, I miss you, too." Flame gently lifted her head so he could look into her eyes. "I miss you, and I miss Theo more than you can imagine. Never doubt that."

She sighed, sounding frustrated. "No. I don't mean I just miss you. I mean, I miss, miss you."

At a loss, Flame replied, "I'm obviously missing something because I have no . . ."

Aurelia growled. Moving swiftly, she divested herself of her robe, hiked the hem of her silk nightie over her hips, and straddled him.

A few things hit Flame at once. First, how had it escaped his notice that Aurelia wore a sexy nightie? He fucking loved that she made an effort to look good for him, even when she was going to bed. Second, from the moment she walked into his study, she had her sex face on, and last, she wore no panties. All these things raced through his mind at the speed of light, and right on their tail was something Flame hadn't felt in months. Lust. Sheer, unadulterated, fuck-you-right-here-even-if-there-are-people-watching lust.

It roared up from the depths of his soul, exploding with such force he didn't realize he was across the room and on top of Aurelia on the couch until he heard fabric ripping. Apparently, Aurelia didn't give a fuck that he had just ruined her sexy nightie because she irritatedly swatted the torn bits of fabric out of the way so he could have access to her phenomenal tits. Gripping them firmly, Flame sucked a blush-pink nipple into his mouth. Aurelia arched her back, moaning so loudly that Flame knew whoever caught guard duty would hear it through the closed door.

"Too slow." Aurelia panted while she wedged her hands between their bodies to loosen his belt. She fumbled, so Flame took over. Without breaking his stride, Flame released his cock. Aurelia threw her right leg over the back of the couch and planted her other foot firmly on the ground. "Now, baby, hurry."

Anchoring her with his arm, he used his other hand to grab the base of his cock, lined up with her wet pussy, and drove home with one powerful thrust. It was fucking heaven! Aurelia had always been hot for him, even in the beginning when she had no experience and relied on him to guide her. Yet, despite the many years together, sex with him was still off-the-fucking-charts hot. But tonight was on another level. Aurelia came on the first thrust. On thrust three, he blew while she was cresting her second orgasm. Her pussy contracted so hard around his cock that he had another mini-orgasm before his first one had even reached the beach. As soon as she came down from her high, she flipped them over, worked her way down his body, taking him in her mouth at the tail end of his mini-orgasm.

Still panting, he dragged her up his body to lie face to face. She was completely naked, his pants still riding low on his hips. "I hope you have it in you to go another round, babe?"

He chuckled, wiggling his hips so she could feel his already hardening cock. "I'm going to fuck you ten ways to Sunday. And when I'm done, I'm going to do it again."

Dropping her head to his chest, she laughed. "Promise me we'll never allow anything to get in our way again."

"I promise I'll keep my dick on that. Thank you for noticing and then fixing it, baby, instead of sitting on it and letting it grow into something nasty in your head." She'd voiced concerns about how her shape had changed after the birth of their son. And even though he told her he loved her body, he knew how women could twist that shit.

"I love you," she said.

Cradling her head, he kissed her. Considering they had both just had multiple orgasms, something he occasionally had, but Aurelia had more often than not, Flame expected their next round to be less intense. He was wrong. Somehow, they managed to knock the couch over mid-fuck and ended up behind it. As it turned out, this was a fortunate accident as the piece of furniture shielded their nakedness from Marcus when he burst into Flame's study.

Several days after their visit to the manor house, Marcus decided that since unveiling the secret passages to Flaminius had gone so well, it was time to tell him about HQ number three.

Progress at that location was slower. So far, Sylas and Rosalind, with a small covert team, had completed most of the vital subterranean infrastructure, such as a sickbay, a lab, rifting station, and a desalination plant. But if they hoped to be ready in time, Marcus would need to involve Barret and Gaia, and he knew they would contemplate no action behind Flaminius's back.

The only time their king had for a private chat was late at night after everyone else had gone to bed. Marcus noticed the guard was not at his post, so he unholstered his weapon and, holding it close to his chest, cautiously pushed the study door open and glanced around. The lights were on, and he could see Flaminius's desk, but no Flaminius. "Flaminius? You in here?"

The couch, kitty-corner to the fireplace, lay on its back like a dead bug, spindly legs in the air, cushions haphazardly scattered about, eviscerated. It twitched, expelling its last vestige of life. Then he heard Aurelia giggle just before Flaminius's gruff voice shouted, "Fuck off, Marcus!"

Shocked as shit that Aurelia had it in her to fuck her husband on the floor of his study, Marcus blushed—something he didn't know he could do! Clearing his throat to hide his discomfort, he backed up toward the door. "Sorry! I didn't know I was interrupting, um, things."

Aurelia laughed before her sex-haired head popped up from behind the couch. "Not to worry! Just give us two—no—five minutes and come back."

Using the study door to shield his body, he asked, "Are you sure? I can come back tomorrow."

Aurelia answered, "Yes." Flame shouted, "Come back in an hour!" while pulling his wife's head down behind the sofa.

Laughing to himself, Marcus shouted, "Okay. One hour." He closed the door, thinking he should take a page out of Flaminius's book. He sympathized with the guard for deserting his post, but he would use this hour to find him and tear him a new asshole.

Marcus stood outside the king's study for the second time but knocked five times and waited to hear Flaminius give permission to enter.

Aurelia left, but the room was still a mess, and a distinct smell of sex lingered in the air. He was pleased that Aurelia had left her husband in a good mood, as the news that Marcus had kept another secret from him would not go over well.

"Marcus, come in. Pour us a whiskey." He did, and then quietly righted the furniture to remove any evidence of the elephant in the room.

Seated, and in Flaminius's case sated, the men sipped their whiskey. "You won't like what I have to say, but I've acted out of concern for you and your family."

"Fuck it, Marcus, just spit it out."

Flaminius thought Marcus must be the luckiest bastard alive. Had he not been, Flaminius would've killed him years ago. But, instead, here they were, discussing a potentially volatile situation, again, and he couldn't bring himself to care because his wife had just fucked him into such a good mood that it was sure to last until next spring. "Explain, so I can get pissed off with you and move on."

"I want you and Aurelia to keep it a secret from everyone."

Flaminius rudely interrupted, mimicking Marcus's voice. "Except my team."

Not what Marcus had expected, but he barreled on. "I have secured a third HQ."

"That's a good decision," Flaminius replied instantly.

Marcus sat back in surprise. "Really?"

"You sound almost disappointed." Flaminius laughed.

"Normally, I would be, but I've hit my threshold for the amount of shit I can deal with at one time."

"Fuck me. I never thought I'd see the day you shied away from trouble. You must be getting old."

With a challenging glare, Marcus said, "By the way, I'm roping in Rosalind, Sylas, Barret, and Gaia to help."

"There he is! You had me worried for a moment."

"Fuck off, Flaminius!"

Chapter Ten -
First Wave

Two Months Later

Gaia tucked the blue woolen blanket tighter around a sleeping Theo and drew him closer to her chest. He was utterly oblivious to the enormity of their situation. And for that, she was grateful. Even though this was the First Wave, thousands of specially trained Arkhnuetians had already been calling Earth home for months. Their primary function was to help the citizens acclimatize to their new environment.

In her most private moments, she allowed herself the luxury of kicking against the injustice of it all by crying and, occasionally, even having a panic attack or two. But the time for that had passed, and from this day forward, she would forget about Arkhnuet and throw herself into the critical task of raising the future king in the absence of his parents in a way that would make them proud.

Marcus approached her, taking her out of her musings. "I'll come with you and Theo and stay a few days to make sure you settle."

Neither Flaminius nor Aurelia would be leaving with them. Not even for a few days. The council decreed that all children under puberty and their parents would make up the bulk of the First Wave. Parents in government service remaining on Arkhnuet would have to separate from their children and, in some cases, their spouses for almost a year.

Cradling Theo tighter, Gaia looked at her aunt and uncle. "I don't know how they're going to cope without him."

"I'll keep an eye on them," Marcus said, rubbing her back.

Gaia looked up at him. "They may try to fool everybody, and they do for the most part, but you and I both know it's all bullshit."

Marcus smiled. "I know, princess."

"Don't call me, princess! You know I hate it, and yet you insist on angering me." His hand on her back made her uncomfortable enough to step out of his reach.

Marcus laughed. "Feel better, princess?"

"No." She would rather spend an entire night in the company of Matilda and her bitches than admit to Marcus that she found his attempt at distracting her from her worries endearing.

Ignoring her, he said, "Okay, let's get this show on the road," before walking away.

Gaia watched, paying close attention to his ass. She was so intent on her task she didn't hear Aurelia come up behind her.

"I love my husband, but that man has a fine ass."

"Aurelia!" Gaia gasped. "Warn a girl you're standing behind her, won't you?"

"Oh please, you aren't frightened; you're embarrassed because I caught you staring at his rump," she retorted while gently reclaiming her son from Gaia's arms.

Blushing, Gaia replied, "Shut up! Someone might hear you."

Aurelia chuckled. "Calm down. No one's paying any attention to us. They're too busy being miserable, saying goodbye."

Gaia squeezed her aunt's arm. "You don't have to pretend you're not heartbroken. No one will judge you."

"I'm not. Trust me, both Flame and I have cried continuously for months. I even broke my 'no-baby-in-the-bed rule.' Theo's been sleeping cuddled between us for six weeks while we sobbed over him." Wiping her nose with the back of her hand, Aurelia continued in a shaky voice, "Honestly, I think the kid can't wait to get away from his blubbering parents."

Flame joined them, putting his arm around his wife's shoulders. "And let me tell you, sleeping with a baby is like wrestling a drunk octopus. Still, we probably won't stop crying until we're all together again," he added, bending to kiss the top of Theo's head. Flame changed the subject when he saw Aurelia getting misty-eyed. "Gaia, I saw your father came to say goodbye."

Gaia cleared her throat. "He didn't stay long. I think he probably had some stuff to attend to."

Flaminius kept his opinion to himself regarding his brother's lack of caring toward his daughter. Besides, it wasn't as if Gaia didn't know how Tiberius felt about her. There was no reason to rub salt into the wound. Fortunately, Marcus interrupted them, holding Noah and Joshua, Jim and Sue run-jogging to keep up with them.

The sight of Marcus tenderly carrying not one but two babies made Gaia's baby box twitch, which was why she missed the first part of his sentence.

"Halloo! Calling all Lady Guardians. Anyone home?" He shouted, nudging her gently with his foot to get her attention.

"Don't do that," Gaia said, swatting his leg. "Your shoes will ruin my dress."

Closing his eyes, Marcus sighed. "It's time to go." Jim and Sue took their babies from Marcus to cuddle one last time as he herded them toward the rifter bay. At the bottom of the steps, Aurelia reluctantly handed over a still sleeping Theo. Flaminius enveloped her in his arms, tucking her head under his chin as she covered her mouth to stifle her sobs.

"Thank you for agreeing to take care of Noah and Joshua. We can never adequately express our gratitude," Sue said through choked tears.

"There is no need to thank me. You're making the sacrifice. It is my honor to care for them and keep them safe," Gaia said, hugging Sue.

Marcus took the children from Jim, and together they mounted the stairs onto the rifting platform. The pilot began his preliminary checks as Marcus moved until his chest touched Gaia's back. Leaning in, he whispered, "Just a few more minutes, and you can cry. Can you stay strong for them for just a few more?"

Gaia turned to look up at him and nodded. The rift opened, and she braved one last glance at the couple, whom she loved like parents. Gaia saw her aunt drop to her knees as the most spine-chilling and devastating cry split the air.

After the dutiful farewell with his daughter, Tiberius went to meet Andreus. The closer they got to the fulfillment of his dream, the more effort it took to maintain the dour, devastated demeanor everyone wore these days. Fuck! He wanted to throw a party, especially now that some of his brother's allies had buggered off to Earth!

"Tiberius!"

His mother's voice dropped a bucket of cold fuck-it on his party mood. He rearranged his features into a more somber visage. "Mother, what are you doing here? I thought you were supposed to leave with the First Wave."

Ignoring his question, she opened the door to her left and motioned for him to follow her. Tiberius ground his teeth, irritated that she expected him to heel like a well-trained dog. The room was dark, but he could make out the silhouette of the thrones at the far end. Closing the door, he walked toward his mother, who had plonked her ass on the king's throne.

"What can I do for you, Mother?"

Octavia patted the throne next to her. "Come sit."

Tiberius rubbed his forehead. "Mother, I don't have time for this. There are a million things I need to see to, and—"

"Shut up and sit."

In the interest of getting this the fuck over as fast as possible, he did as she asked. In typical Octavia fashion, she made him hurry while she took her time gazing around the room sentimentally.

Eventually, she spoke. "Did you know Flaminius allowed that woman to convince him to leave the thrones here?" Tenderly stroking the arm of the chair, she continued, "Apparently, she felt it was an extravagance our people didn't need."

What the fuck was she trying to say? "No, I didn't."

"I can't allow this to continue," she said, thankfully ceasing the creepy stroking, "especially now that our survival is in jeopardy."

Unable to contain his irritation any longer, Tiberius growled, "Get to the point."

"My point is that, as much as I love my oldest son, I can't sit on the sidelines and watch as he caves to his wife's insane demands."

Tiberius almost laughed at his mother's suggestion that she could love, but remained silent.

"Ironically, the tenuous position we currently find ourselves in is the perfect opportunity to create a few incidents that will leave the council with no choice but to initiate a vote of no confidence in their king."

His mother's suggestion didn't exactly shock Tiberius. They'd plotted together before, but that was to remove the queen, not Flaminius. Granted, if anything happened to Aurelia, Flaminius would fall to pieces, but it was still an indirect attack. His mother's sudden change of heart was suspicious.

"And then what?"

Slowly rising, she walked to the massive windows behind the thrones. "And then you take Flaminius's place."

"Why?"

She walked back to him and kneeled between his legs, laying her hands on his knees. "I don't understand the question. Do you mean, why have I chosen you to be king?"

His mother was delusional if she thought she had the power to choose who she wanted on the throne after he dealt with Flaminius, but he humored her.

"Yes."

Standing, she looked down her nose at him. "Because I believe you can lead our people into a new era without discarding all that defines us as Arkhnuetians."

Really? Was she still on about that? Protocols held little interest to him. Tiberius didn't trust her as far as he could spit, but it was wise to hear her out. She thought he would be easy to manipulate. That's why she wanted him on the throne. Pretending to be torn between love for his brother and duty to their people, Tiberius dropped his head, defeated. "I've tried to ignore the signs, but you are correct, Mother. What did you have in mind?"

Patting her back in a false show of sympathy, she said, "I know this must be difficult for you, Tiberius. You have always looked up to your brother."

Fuck, he was going to vomit on her silk shoes if she didn't shut up. With a little encouragement, he managed to get her to spew her anemic plot. Tiberius knew it wouldn't work, but it would cause enough distraction to make it easier for him and Andreus to carry out their plan.

"I am late for a meeting, Mother, but I will back you one hundred percent."

"I've everything under control. I'll let you know when I need you," she smugly replied.

Tiberius rushed from the throne room to inform Andreus of this latest development.

Octavia watched Tiberius leave, and years of frustration trying to convince Romulus that Flaminius would destroy the Esca bloodline drained from her. It was inconceivable that Romulus no longer valued her opinion as he once had, effectively relegating her to the pile of impotent, annoying wives.

She may have been able to live like that, but Romulus did one thing she could never forgive. He betrayed their marriage bed. In retrospect, she should've seen it coming. They hadn't had relations in almost a year. Not because he didn't want to. It was a last-ditch effort to force her husband's hand to demand that Flaminius rein in his wife and stop the destruction of all that Arkhnuetians held dear.

The tactic had worked well in the past. However, this time, it did not penetrate his thick hide, and when she eventually admitted defeat, it was too late. When she confronted him, he openly admitted he had taken a lover and had no intention of stopping. Then he officially moved out of their bedroom.

He did, however, promise to conduct his affair with discretion out of respect for his sons. Not for her, for his sons, one of whom was running the throne into the ground. She knew Tiberius coveted the throne. But more importantly, he would be easy to control, and his wife was dead. He would need someone to take on the queen's duties, and what better choice than an ex-queen to help him. It gave her no pleasure deposing Flaminius, but kicking his wife off the throne would go a long way to soothing her pain.

Chapter Eleven - And So it Begins

Nine Months Later

Supporting her pregnant tummy with one hand, Lily followed the sound of giggling children. Gripping the wall, she drunkenly turned the corner and crashed into Mother Guardian. Fortunately, the woman was sturdier than she looked.

"Let me guess," Mother Guardian smiled. "You're looking for three children about yay high." She held her hand parallel to the ground at her hip.

Brushing her thick, braided hair over her shoulder and panting like a hot dog, Lily nodded. Seth, her beloved husband, walked up behind MG carrying three wriggling, giggling babies. Noah clung to his neck like an oversized necklace, swinging back and forth with each step he took. Joshua dangled from his right hand, where Seth suspended him by his diaper, and Theo in an identical grip on his left.

Raising one eyebrow, he asked, "Looking for something?"

Sagging against the wall, Lily wagged her finger at the kids. "You three are going to be the death of me!" Seth bent down to kiss his wife, squishing the boys between them. The little blighters thought it was a marvelous game they were playing. Joshua lifted his head and pierced Lily with eyes much older than a two-year-old's. Lily loved all the boys, but Joshua held a special place in her heart. Mesmerized by his intense stare, she watched as he reached out and gripped her wagging finger. Using her digit as an anchor, Joshua pulled himself toward her and placed his little hand on her tummy. The moment he touched her, the fetus kicked so hard she could see the outline of its foot under Joshua's hand. Gasping, Lily stepped back, breaking contact, but the baby kept kicking. At the same time, Joshua struggled violently to escape Seth's grasp. When it became clear he couldn't get free, Joshua began screeching. The commotion got the attention of his twin.

Now everybody knew if you messed with Joshua, Noah was likely to burn down the house. Literally. Seth lowered Joshua to the floor and let him go. Noah jumped. Yes, he jumped down from his perch around Seth's neck and helped his younger (by three minutes) and much smaller brother to stand.

Walking on slightly unsteady legs, Joshua bee-lined directly for Lily, who had managed, with Seth's help, to slide down the wall to sit. Then, with great care, Joshua climbed onto her lap and curled himself around her tummy. Instantly, the baby stilled.

Looking up into the gob-smacked faces of her husband and Mother Guardian, Lily shrugged her shoulders, but Seth said, "What the actual fuck?"

After Gaia and Marcus's monthly nighttime meetings, she would usually stroll back to the manor house. But tonight, Marcus brought Jim and Sue, and they were staying. Gaia understood they were eager to see their kids, but they'd been running for two-and-a-half hours over rough terrain, and she simply couldn't keep up.

Thanks to the many nighttime meetings with Marcus, her fitness had improved significantly, but she was nowhere near Jim and Sue's level of a bad-ass soldier. And this ass-backward third rock from the sun would imprison a woman in a convent if, God forbid, she should show an ankle because she was running. Long walks she could do. She could even manage long jogs, but long runs, not so much.

The good news was that all the running kept her from freezing to death because, once again, this fucking place didn't have the technology to weave decent fucking fabric! Jesus Christ, she hated this planet. The letters shared between her and Barret used to give her hope, but his insistence that it was only a matter of time before they found a more suitable home didn't satisfy her anymore.

When the house finally came into view, Gaia slowed her pace and tried to speak. "Sue," she wheezed. "We have to stop and change."

With a quizzical look, Sue turned and asked, "Why?" before turning back in the house's direction without waiting for an answer.

"Honey," Jim called, "you're still wearing your fatigues."

Sue glared at her black shirt as if it somehow managed to get onto her body without permission. "Oh, right."

It didn't take long to change, but Gaia had to run behind Sue to tie her dress while Sue tried to put on her own shoes.

"Jesus Christ, Sue, stop!"

"No, and who's this Jesus guy you keep talking about?"

"Ugh! Trust me. Once you learn, you'll wish you hadn't."

When they reached the gatehouse, Gaia called for the guards to open up the wicket door, and Sue and Jim disappeared. She smiled at them while walking at a more sedate pace, allowing her mind to wander.

At tonight's meeting with Marcus, he confirmed that the last wave of Arkhnuetians would arrive on December twenty-first and not at the end of January as scheduled. Violent tremors and meteor showers had hit the eastern and southern oceans of Arkhnuet earlier than expected. If Gaia and Marcus had their way, the king and queen would already be here, but Aurelia, stubborn git that she was, refused to leave until the last of the library's remaining books were secured.

Flaminius was livid with her, Marcus was fuming, and Gaia was nursing a constant migraine and stomach ulcer. The only person who supported Aurelia was Tiberius. Why? Gaia could not fathom. Her father cared about ancient tomes as much as he did tending a rose garden, and she noticed it made Marcus very uncomfortable.

"This will be the last time we speak before the end." Tiberius's voice echoed off the cave walls.

Andreus was not sentimental by nature, but he had to admit that he felt a great deal of loss being here for the last time.

Tiberius spoke again. "I called you here to finalize our plans."

Andreus drummed his fingers on the stone tabletop. "We already have everything down to the last detail."

"I don't expect you to understand, Andreus, but Flaminius was born lucky."

Leaning forward, Andreus pulled the diagram of the attack plan on the manor house closer. Only Andreus and Tiberius knew the details, and Tiberius's trust in him increased Andreus's desire to set Tiberius's mind at ease. Refocusing his attention, Andreus said, "The king made our job simpler by sending Jim and Sue away earlier than expected." They actually had Aurelia to thank for that because she insisted her friends were no longer needed and, therefore, it was cruel to keep them from their children.

Andreus continued, "We know that Marcus, Aurelia, and the king will be the last to rift. With only the three of them in the bay, they will be at their most vulnerable."

"That's when I rift back," Tiberius confirmed.

"Correct. Our contact in engineering has completed the untraceable portable." Andreus reached into his bag, pulled out the device, and handed it to Tiberius. "I trust our man, but we'll need to test it a few times."

"Of course."

"Timing will be everything. You have to arrive after the last of the RPU men have left, but before Marcus rifts the king and queen." When Tiberius said nothing, Andreus tried to convince him to abandon his new idea. "I wish you'd let me come with you. Three against one is a recipe for disaster."

Tiberius shook his head. "I have the element of surprise."

Andreus didn't like it, but there was no changing Tiberius's mind. "Very well, but remember . . ."

Tiberius held up his hand. "I know. Shoot Marcus first, then Aurelia."

"And don't wait to kill your brother," Andreus finished.

"Sorry, I can't promise that."

Andreus shot to his feet. "Capulus, please be reasonable. We cannot afford to lose you."

"I won't push it, but I want time with my brother. I want him to see the life drain out of his beloved while he's powerless to do anything to help her."

Andreus understood the need for revenge, but Tiberius took it too far.

AND SO IT BEGINS

"Please stop worrying, Andreus. I'll be fine. Besides, I'll feel much better knowing that someone I trust is leading the attack on the HQ."

"And the rest of the plan remains the same?"

Rubbing his chin, Tiberius answered, "Yes. Kill everybody in the manor house except my parents."

"What about Gaia and Theo?"

Tiberius looked up into the ominous blackness of the cave and sighed. "You have to kill her and my nephew. The success of our plan depends on me being the only remaining heir."

"And the Keys?" Andreus left this subject for last. He wanted to make a request, but he didn't wish Capulus to know how desperately he wanted it granted. Not because he thought Tiberius would use Andreus's weakness against him, but because he feared disappointing his Capulus with his obsession.

Tiberius scrutinized the boy closely. "I've given your suggestion some thought, and I agree. Keeping only five Keys is a risky strategy, but we can't keep more with our present accommodations."

Heart beating in his throat, Andreus schooled his features. "I see your point, but I have reworked the layout of the dungeon at the castle we purchased and added seven extra cells."

Tiberius raised his eyebrows in surprise. "Seven?"

Keeping calm, Andreus answered. "Obviously, the cells are smaller, and I had to do away with certain luxuries, but we can accommodate up to twelve Keys." Then, keeping his mouth shut, Andreus waited with bated breath for Tiberius to decide.

Finally, he nodded. "Very well, we'll keep twelve, as long as Mother Guardian is among them."

"Thank you, Capulus," Andreus replied, relieved.

Standing, Tiberius made to leave but stopped to pat Andreus affectionately on the shoulder. "Soon, we'll annihilate our enemies, and the need to skulk around will end. And the best part? That oaf, Marcus, will take the blame."

Andreus smiled.

Tiberius glanced around the cave. "Take your time saying goodbye. There is nothing more I need from you tonight."

Unable to speak around the knot in his throat, Andreus simply nodded. Once Tiberius left, Andreus allowed the tears to flow. That he would no longer have a physical place to be close to his father left him feeling adrift in a sea of panic. Maybe that's why he felt this obsession with her?

They'd never met, never exchanged words, never been close enough to breathe the same air. And yet, Andreus cherished the relationship, imagining her responses to his questions about her life. What might she ask him? How would she react as he drove into her sweet pussy?

Andreus was both elated and raging mad when he found out she was expecting. It's what he craved for all these years—the last piece to their puzzle, the family he desired. But it had been excruciating knowing her match had to fuck her to get her pregnant. The thought of finally touching her, feeling her skin under his fingers, rubbing his hands over her pregnant belly made his sacrifice worth it. The mere thought of her sent an uncontrollable tremor through him that brought him to his knees.

Surrendering to his need, he closed his eyes and rubbed his hand over his erect prick to alleviate some of the pressure. Thinking of her naked, writhing under him, forced him to pull his cock free from his trousers. It didn't take long for him to come, and when he did, he whispered her name, "Lily."

Chapter Twelve - The Beginning of the End

Today, the rest of their friends and family would arrive. Standing on the third-floor landing, Gaia watched as servants scurried about, carrying provisions to and from the kitchens while soldiers helped hang welcome banners. However, not even the delicious smells of roasting meat and baking bread could ease her worry.

To prevent humans from the village accidentally stumbling across Arkhnuetians rifting in, they sponsored a pre-Christmas feast for them in the village square. For weeks, the men had been chopping down dead or old trees and dragging them back to the village for the bonfire later that evening. A separate celebration at the castle in honor of the king and queen was also underway.

Gaia almost jumped out of her skin when Lily touched her shoulder to get her attention. "Sorry, Lily. You startled me."

Absentmindedly stroking her tummy, Lily smiled. "It's okay. We're all a bit on edge today. I just wanted to tell you that the boys have finally gone down for their afternoon nap. So I'm going to have a nap as well."

"Yes, of course. I'll go sit with them." Then, waving goodbye, Lily waddled off.

Gaia quietly let herself into the nursery and sat on the chair in the corner. She closed her eyes and tried to calm herself. When it became apparent that she was wasting her time, Gaia thought instead about her last meeting with

Marcus a week ago. As usual, they met near the exit of the secret tunnel that let out in the deepest part of the woods.

Marcus tried to convince her to use the underground duct, but she refused because it was for emergency use only, and it terrified Gaia that someone might catch her, compromising the tunnel's secrecy. So instead, she snuck out of the house when everybody had gone to bed.

As usual, Marcus was waiting, and Gaia didn't hesitate to step into his open arms for a hug. She didn't know why the affectionate gesture began, only that one night, she was getting ready to leave when Marcus pulled her into an embrace, kissing her cheek. From then on, they always greeted each other in that manner. "Good to see you, Marcus," she murmured, reluctantly withdrawing from his arms. "You look good."

Marcus smiled. "You sound surprised."

She thanked her lucky stars it was too dark for him to notice her blush. She replied, "I meant nothing by it. It's just that I haven't slept a full night in weeks, and you look like you're out for a moonlit stroll."

He shot her a cocksure smile as he leaned against a tree. "Looks can be deceiving. The truth is, I feel as if my brain is about to explode."

"Good to know I'm not the only one. Is everything ready?"

"Yup. There's only one change to the plan." He dropped to his haunches and dug around in his backpack to retrieve something. Standing, he shoved a portable rifter into her hand.

"What's this for?"

"I'm going to tell you something that's going to piss you off, but try not to punch me before I've had a chance to explain."

"I can't promise."

"That rifter," Marcus pointed to the device in her hand, "is one of three that I've built. It's not registered, and I'll give you the password before I leave. You'll notice that I've typed in coordinates to a safe place in case something goes wrong." Gaia's back stiffened, but she didn't interrupt him.

"Only myself, Jim, Sue, and Flaminius know where that place is."

Realization dawned. "You've built a second HQ, haven't you?"

"Third, actually."

"And you kept this information from me; why?" she snapped.

THE BEGINNING OF THE END

Not missing a beat, he replied, "Because it's my job to keep the royal family safe, and I kept it on the DL." Marcus could see that she was about to blow her top, so he quickly added, "I didn't even tell Flaminius until recently, so you don't have to feel too left out." Apparently, that was not the thing to say to keep her calm. Live and learn.

"You arrogant, demented, tyrannical dictator," she hissed. "You are not the only one charged with the safety of the royal family." Sticking her finger under his nose, she hurried on. "Theo is my responsibility, not yours, and you compromised my ability to do my job by not sharing this information with me!"

He had to admit she had a valid point when she said it like that, but it was a bit late now. "Look, I'm sorry I didn't share with you earlier."

Stepping away from him, Gaia sucked in cold air, hoping to calm herself. Fifteen deep breaths later—he counted—she turned to him and asked, "Why HQ Three? What happened to two?"

"Nothing. All are secure, but HQ Three is more so since only eight people know about it."

"Eight?" she shouted.

"Yes. Me, you, Flaminius, Jim, Sue, Rosalind, Sylas, and Barret."

"Jesus Christ! Barret! My Barret? The one who I thought was still on Arkhnuet is here on Earth? Really? You told him before me?"

"Yeah, unless you know of another meteorologist/super-smart planet-finder floating around somewhere?"

"Motherf—"

Before she could finish, he interrupted, "Oh, and the RPU men who built the facility and their families. And the medical staff, but none of them have left since I rifted them in."

The most adorable look of disbelief crossed her face.

"Are you telling me you have had men at HQ Three for—how long?" she asked, frowning.

"Don't forget the women and children."

Confused, Gaia shook her head. "What?"

"You forget the men's families," he helpfully added.

"Yes. Let's not forget them," she said sarcastically. "How long have they been stuck there?"

247

"Sixteen months," he deadpanned.

Gaia choked on her spit. "Sixteen?" she coughed.

"Yes."

"Yes? That's all you're going to say?" she yelled, flapping her arms around like an uncoordinated fledgling chick.

"Yes. I thought you understood I take the safety of the royal family seriously? I couldn't let them leave. What if one of them unintentionally divulged the location to someone?"

Gaia grudgingly had to agree with him. "How many people do you have there?"

"Two hundred and five. No! Wait, Martha gave birth to a little boy, so two hundred and six," he proudly said, as if the baby was all his idea.

Holding the rifter up, Gaia asked, "Does this mean you're expecting trouble?"

"I always expect trouble, Gaia. That's why I'm so good at my job."

Gaia ignored his arrogance in favor of expediency. "Who else has one of your special rifters?"

"Sue and Jim. They know that you have one. Once we're together again, their rifter will go to Flaminius and Aurelia."

Robbed of her strength after her tiff with Marcus, Gaia leaned against a tree and slid down until her butt hit the damp, decaying leaves on the forest floor. "I'll keep it with me day and night," she vowed.

Sitting next to her, Marcus reached for her hand; when she didn't rip it away, he took it as a good sign. "I know a lot is going on, and it's only natural that you're stressed. But, Gaia, Theo is your only concern. I don't care if the roof caves in or the moon explodes. You stay focused on keeping him safe."

Throwing caution to the wind, Gaia put her head on his shoulder. "I promise I will."

They sat quietly for a while before Marcus shifted. "I have to go." Standing, they wiped the dead leaves off their clothes. "Before I leave, I want to give you one last piece of advice."

Gaia nodded for him to continue. "If something happens, get yourself and Theo into one of the secret tunnels and rift from there."

"Why can't I rift from anywhere?"

Bending down so he could look her in the eye, he said, "Because I don't want anyone to know we have portables. And Gaia, this is very important, so listen up. Do not try to save anyone. Do not wait for anyone. Get yourself into a tunnel and rift the fuck out of there. Do you understand me?"

"Yes," she whispered.

Hugging her, he said, "See you soon."

Gaia waved and then started her long journey back to the house.

Chapter Thirteen - The Bitter Taste of Betrayal

Mother Guardian trudged up the stairs in search of Gaia. The king and queen would arrive in less than an hour, and the girl had yet to make an appearance. Not that it was hard to guess where she was. Pushing the nursery door open, she saw Gaia standing at the window, rocking a sleeping Theo in her arms. The last rays of the weak winter sun threw shadows across the Lady Guardian's face, making her appear much older than she was.

"There you are, child. It's almost time."

Staring out into the ever-encroaching darkness, Gaia replied, "Something doesn't feel right, Mother Guardian."

Sighing, she stepped into the room. "Gaia, of course, it doesn't. Our home is weeks away from going up in flames. Nothing will ever feel right again."

Gaia turned to look at her. "No. It's more than that. I can feel it!"

Rubbing her forehead, Mother Guardian said. "Look, I understand you're edgy, but everyone is downstairs. It's time you joined us."

"I'll be down in a bit."

Mother Guardian had a feeling she would trudge up those God-forsaken steps again in the not-so-distant future. But she was too exhausted to argue.

Gaia felt a mixture of guilt and defiance. She should be downstairs with the others, but she couldn't tear herself away from her panicked thoughts and overwhelming instinct to take Theo and flee. Sue bustled into the room carrying a miserable Joshua while Noah clung to her skirts, looking agitated.

They had both been impossible all day. Jim had the magic daddy touch when it came to his children, but not even he could calm them.

Plopping down on the cot, Sue adjusted Joshua so she could feed him. Then, unlacing her gown, she withdrew her breast and tried to get him to latch on. He grunted his disapproval, shaking his head from side to side, pushing his mother's breast away. "Not a boob man like your father, are you?" she said, half-joking, half exasperated.

Gaia looked at her with sympathy. "Perhaps it's another tooth coming in?"

Sue shook her head while helping a more sedate but still unhappy Noah up onto the cot so he could sit next to her. "I've never seen him like this. It's as if he is trying to say something but lacks the vocabulary." Noah reached out to his brother, putting his big hand on Joshua's head. But it did little to appease either of them. "Jim says they're picking up on the nervous energy in the house, but . . ." she trailed off.

"What, Sue? What were you going to say?"

Hugging her babies closer, she replied. "I keep having this vision." Shaking her head, she corrected herself. "No, not a vision exactly, more of a strong feeling, with no picture to clarify. I'm so frustrated! I feel like I've caught the tail end of a critical conversation that's left me with more questions than answers."

Gaia crossed the room and sat down next to her. "I feel the same. Something isn't right."

They sat in silence for a few moments before Sue said, "There were some RPU men that rifted in from Arkhnuet two weeks ago. They stood in a huddle near the stables early this morning when I did my rounds. They weren't doing anything suspicious as such, but I could see they didn't like that I noticed them."

Gaia stood, took Theo to his crib, and laid him down gently. "I don't care what anyone says. I'm not ignoring my instincts."

Looking relieved, Sue asked, "What did you have in mind?"

"Change of plans. I'm not going down to welcome Flaminius and Aurelia. Instead, I'm taking the children to the main chamber tunnel in case we need to leave in a hurry."

"I agree."

Gaia continued, "I'll pack some clothes." She felt some of the tension leave her body. "Go down and tell Jim of the change in plans."

Rushing to the trunks lined up against the wall, Gaia kneeled, opened the lid of the closest one, and began shoving stuff into a bag. Sue hesitated, looking down at her children. Gaia stopped her frantic packing. "I promise I will keep them all safe."

Sue kissed her boys, got up, and jogged to the door. "Do you have your rifter?"

Gaia patted her skirt, feeling the lump in the hidden pocket. "Yes."

"I have mine too. If shit happens, don't wait for us."

Gaia disagreed, but Sue spoke in a sharp, authoritative voice. "Gaia, you will not wait for us. You will get our future king and my babies out of here."

Sinking onto her haunches, Gaia replied. "Okay, I promise I won't wait for you."

Satisfied, Sue left.

Returning her focus to the packing, Gaia didn't notice when the twins slipped off the cot and made their way to Theo. When Gaia heard Noah grunt, she looked up and saw he was using his big body to lift Joshua into the crib where Theo slept. In awe, she watched as Noah then pulled himself in to join them. With all three of them squished into the tight space, they curled themselves around each other and instantly fell asleep. The boys may not have shared a womb, but they were closer than brothers. Snapping out of her daze, Gaia got back to her packing.

Half an hour later, she hoisted a heavy backpack onto her shoulders and laid a miraculously still sleeping Theo into the pouch of a blanket she strapped to her front. Next, Gaia hoisted a now awake Joshua onto her hip, and with her free hand, grasped Noah's tightly. Her burden was heavy, but they didn't have far to go. Once they left the nursery, she heard the din floating up from the great hall, where everybody had gathered to welcome the new arrivals.

Shifting Joshua on her hip, Gaia leaned around the corner to make sure they were alone before she gently pulled Noah forward and rushed to the end of the corridor. Heart pumping fast, Gaia flattened herself against the wall when she heard voices coming from up ahead. Deciding it would be best to hide in one of the bedchambers, she moved across the hall to the nearest door. She let go of Noah's hand and pushed down on the handle. "Damn!"

locked. Tugging Noah along, she tried the next door, but it too was barred. The voices grew louder. Probably RPU soldiers on patrol. She spun around, whipping her head from side to side, frantically searching for a hiding place. At any moment, they would turn the corner and see her.

Reaching for Noah's hand, Gaia looked down, only to find he was gone. The blood drained from her face, leaving her dizzy with panic. Then, just as the men rounded the corner, Gaia heard a hiss; looking to her left, she saw Noah peeking out from behind a red velvet curtain hanging in front of a bay window. Dashing to the window, she cast a quick look over her shoulder. From what she could hear, she suspected the soldiers were looking at a contraband pornographic magazine and hadn't noticed her yet. Gaia had never been more grateful for the male urge to ogle a woman's boobies.

She pulled the curtain aside and scrambled onto the seat, pulling her legs up to fit in sideways. Gaia sat Joshua on her lap while Noah crawled onto her lower legs. The kid was heavier than a sack of river rocks, but he sat perfectly still. With all three children on top of her and little space to maneuver, Gaia hoped the men moved on quickly.

Unfortunately, the meatheads stopped a few feet from their hiding place to exchange opinions on the model's boobs. "Nah. I mean, her tits are luscious, but I still think Miss October's better."

"Are you nuts?" Meathead number two said. "They're way too fucking small."

Gaia rolled her eyes in disgust, hoping their voices wouldn't wake Theo or permanently damage the twins' opinion of women. After a few more inappropriate comments, they walked away. Gaia waited until she no longer heard their voices before she helped Noah down. They made their way one floor down, using the servants' stairs and slipping into the master bedchamber. The room was warm from the fire a servant had prepared in anticipation of the royal couple's arrival.

Lowering Joshua to his feet, she moved to the floorboard Marcus had shown her. It was a struggle to wrestle it loose, but she managed and wasted no time reaching into the hole. Feeling around, Gaia found the small lever and yanked it up. A soft click from behind the tapestry told her the secret door was open. Replacing the floorboard, she rushed to the wall and struggled to get the heavy cloth out of the way. Just as she pushed the hidden door open, she heard a scream. Freezing, she listened. When no other sounds followed, Gaia pushed the twins into the tunnel. The flashlight was easy enough to find, and to her relief, light flooded the dark passage. Then Gaia heard another scream, and then another, before all hell broke loose.

Rushing to the window, she saw hundreds of people gathered in the courtyard below to greet Flaminius and Aurelia. The dozens of fire pits cast light on a scene the likes of which Gaia could never have imagined. RPU soldiers moved among the crowds, indiscriminately slaughtering whomever their swords reached. A distraught cry escaped her lips as she watched a soldier separate the head of a defenseless Key from her body. The shock of what she witnessed was so profound that her brain failed to comprehend that she needed to flee. Civilians screamed, running in panicked circles, bumping into each other, trying to escape the blades of the rogue RPU men whom, she suddenly noticed, wore red armbands, differentiating them from the soldiers pouring in from the gatehouse to defend the people. The fighting was fierce, but the good guys outnumbered the bad. And for a moment, she thought they would be okay.

She saw Mother Guardian gathered as many Keys as she could and guided them into the manor house. Lily stood to the side at the top of the steps, helping herd the white-robed women through the doors. Looking up from the macabre scene, Gaia noticed more men moving out of the shadow of the forest beyond, as if the darkness was giving birth to evil. The man that led them wore a full-face mask and moved with an economy that Gaia immediately recognized as Andreus.

Dozens of bodies already littered the ground as the new wave of rogue soldiers entered the courtyard. A sharp pain in her thigh jerked her attention down, and she saw Noah holding a fire poker. Joshua grabbed one of her hands and Noah the other. Together, they tugged her toward the tunnel. Once they were in, she closed the door, leaving them in suffocating silence. Gathering her thoughts, Gaia picked up the flashlight. Theo still slept, snuggled against her chest. As for the twins, they were eerily calm. "Are you guys okay?" They simply nodded. "Let's move, boys. Quickly now."

The tunnel was cold and a little damp, but she could stand upright. Moving further in wasn't necessary, but Gaia wasn't confident that she could rift them all across at once, and she wanted to be as far away from the entrance as possible in case someone discovered it and came after them. Finally, about an hour into their journey, Gaia could see that the boys couldn't keep going for much longer. Shrugging the pack off her shoulders, she sat on the dirt floor and dug out the waterskin. Both Noah and Joshua drank greedily, then took her hands and pulled, saying, "Up, up!"

Jesus, these kids were . . . she didn't know what they were. Neither of them had shown an ounce of fear through the entire ordeal, which was more than she could say for herself. "Okay. I'm up." Digging the rifter out of her pocket, she punched in the password and navigated the menu to find the coordinates Marcus had programmed in for her. Bending down, she looked into their little faces. "We're going on a little journey, and I want you to promise that you will hold my hand tightly. Don't let go, no matter what. Okay?" They nodded. Initializing the rifter, Gaia held out her hands. "Come on, little ones." They didn't hesitate to grab hold. Energy gathered in front of them, and the rift opened with a loud crack. Both boys jumped back, but they didn't let go of her hands.

Gaia had set the energy output to the maximum, but there was no way of knowing how long the rift would remain open. Pulling the boys closer, she stepped through, feeling the dip in energy almost immediately. Afraid they wouldn't make it, she grabbed the twins around the waist, lifted them, and jumped, landing awkwardly on one leg, her knee giving out. The second she could, Gaia looked to see if the boys were okay. Joshua and Noah seemed shaken, but not hurt. Theo, bless his heart, was still asleep. Shouting brought her attention to her surroundings. Instinctively, Gaia jumped to her feet, dragging the boys behind her. At this point, she realized she had no weapon and cursed herself to human hell and back for being so unprepared.

"Don't come any closer!" she shouted impotently. Several men who were rushing toward them skidded to a halt. She recognized them as RPU soldiers, but after what she had just witnessed, that meant nothing.

The man closest to her lifted his hands in a non-threatening manner. "Lady Guardian, it's me, Gerhardt." When she didn't respond, he tried again. "Remember? We met before. I was with Marcus the day you argued about leaving with the First Wave."

She nodded. "I remember." But her body language still didn't invite them to approach.

Gerhardt kept talking, hoping to calm her down. "What has happened? Why are you here?"

Pulling Theo closer to her body, she hesitated.

"I swear, none of us wish you any harm. Let us help you." He took a step in her direction, but she held up her hand and shouted. "Stop!" He froze.

She saw a few women emerge from small cottages dotting the desolate landscape to join the men. When one woman broke through the crowd, Gerhardt stopped her. "Don't move closer, Martha."

Martha did as he asked but said, "I know those boys." Pointing at the twins, she added, "If they're here with the Lady Guardian, and Sue and Jim are not, it can only mean something terrible has happened."

Gaia saw Martha was genuinely frightened. If Martha was concerned about Sue and Jim's well-being, then these people were not her enemy. Collapsing with relief, her body hit the ground; instantly, people surrounded her.

Martha gathered the twins close while Gerhardt and the other men helped her to her feet. "Can you tell us what has happened, Lady Guardian?" He asked while he guided her and the kids to a cottage.

"They attacked us. They attacked the manor house." Her voice sounded thin with disbelief.

Gerhardt frowned. "What do you mean? Did human soldiers attack the house?"

Gaia's voice cracked. "No. Our soldiers. Our men attacked us."

A collective gasp rippled through the group. Gerhardt was the first to rally. "Where are the king and queen?"

Someone pushed her into a chair and threw a blanket around her shoulders. "I don't know. I didn't see them." She began sobbing. "I didn't see them!"

Feeling something tugging at her hand, she looked down and saw that Martha was trying to pry her fingers from Noah's shirt. "Let me take them, my lady. They look cold and hungry."

Gaia shook her head. "No! They stay with me."

Martha tried again. "Okay. How about I sit them next to you and get them something warm to drink?"

"Yes. That would be good."

Gerhardt paced back and forth in front of the fireplace like a caged lion. Gaia knew the answer to her next question, but she asked anyway. "Is Marcus here?" Gerhardt shook his head. "Can you go after him?"

He shook his head again. "Our orders are to stay here, no matter what happens."

"To hell with your orders! We can't just sit here and do nothing!" Gaia's shouts woke Theo. Stirring, he rubbed his big green eyes with his chubby hands and blinked a few times. Looking up, he smiled and said, "Gai, Gai. Me hungry." Hugging him close, she said. "Okay, baby bear, Gai Gai will fix that right now."

Flaminius hadn't taken a full breath all day, and he wasn't the only one struggling. Marcus could barely contain the wild energy flowing through him.

Tiberius approached. "Are you sure, brother? I can wait with you." Flaminius shook his head. "No, Tiberius. You've been a great help this last year, but now it's time to take care of yourself. Go see your daughter." Tiberius nodded and joined the last group rifting to Earth.

For the longest time, nobody said a word. "I want to rift from the lawns in front of the castle, not cooped up in here like a caged animal," Aurelia said.

Marcus shook his head. "No can do."

Aurelia huffed. "Why not? We can use your portable to rift."

"Baby, Marcus needs to save the charge in the portable to rift himself across." Sagging against him like overcooked spinach, she sighed. "I forgot."

The last couple of months have been the hardest of all because the remaining RPU men took it upon themselves to ride through the deserted towns finding abandoned animals and euthanizing them. Flaminius witnessed hardened soldiers who wouldn't bat an eye at killing a man, break down at the end of a day of killing defenseless creatures.

"It's time to go," Marcus said.

Flame clutched Aurelia's hand and took the first step up to the rifter platform when the door burst open, banging against the wall. Tiberius stood in the doorway, panting, dripping with sweat. Flaminius frowned at his brother. "Tiberius, what are you doing here?"

Without warning, Tiberius lifted his arm and discharged a pistol Flaminius hadn't seen him holding. As if in slow motion, Flaminius turned and saw Marcus flying through the air. He hit the control panel with a sickening thud before sliding down to the floor as a crimson stain formed in the center of his chest. For all his military experience, Flaminius couldn't get his limbs to follow his commands. Turning to his brother, he screamed, "What the fuck are you doing?" Aurelia broke free of his hold and ran to Marcus, dropping to her knees by his side. Finally, Flaminius's legs moved to block his wife from Tiberius's sight as he walked deeper into the room.

"Taking from you what you owe me," he said, his voice shaking.

Finally, Flaminius's brain clicked back online. Considering his options, he kept Tiberius talking to buy him time to formulate a plan. "Owe you?"

"Yes! Did you think you could dangle a carrot as big as the throne in front of me and then just snatch it away without consequences?"

Aurelia stood, her body vibrating, her hands coated with Marcus's blood. "You fucking piece of shit! You're nothing but a deranged animal!" Flame grabbed her around her waist when she tried to attack Tiberius and shoved her behind him again.

Tiberius laughed. "Fuck you, you uppity bitch! Waltzing around with your holier-than-thou attitude, looking down your nose at me!"

Rage, the likes of which Flame had never seen, exploded from his wife. "You fucking idiot! I wasn't looking down my nose at you. Just because I refused your advances doesn't make me an uppity bitch. It makes me a faithful spouse, which is more than I can say for you!"

Flaminius felt the words rip through him like a hot knife through butter. Tiberius stood no more than six feet away, still pointing a gun at them.

"I made my advances toward you after Delinea died."

"No, you didn't, and I was referring to Matilda!"

Flaminius jerked his head up. "What the fuck is she talking about, Tiberius?"

Bringing his attention back to Flaminius, he laughed. "Don't pretend you didn't know about Matilda."

"Of course, I did. I don't give a fuck about that whore! I want to know about your attempt to seduce my wife!"

"Fuck, I wish you could see your face right now," Tiberius smirked. "It's priceless."

Flaminius shook his head in disbelief.

"What? You didn't think your perfect wife could keep a secret from you?" He snorted. "Or was it unthinkable that I could outsmart the 'great people's king' of Arkhnuet?" He spat. "Well, how wrong you and our dickless father are, brother."

Aurelia ran out from behind Flame in a flash before he could stop her. Tiberius fired his gun again. The first shot went through her shoulder, taking her to the ground; the second hit her in the stomach.

Flaminius roared, the sound more earsplitting than the firing gun. In one leap, he knocked his brother off his feet as they slid across the floor, hitting the opposite wall. The impact jarred the gun from Tiberius's hands. With a metallic grind, it skittered away. Flaminius wasted no time. Straddling his brother, he delivered a bone-crushing punch to his ribs that forced a satisfying spray of spit and blood out of Tiberius's mouth. He followed up with a barrage of wild blows to his face.

Flaminius was out of control with rage, and while that was bad for Tiberius, it was also fortunate. Flaminius's anger made him sloppy and uncoordinated. Were it not for that, Tiberius would never have gained the upper hand. Somewhere between punch three and five, Tiberius managed to retrieve his Oradagra dagger from its snug hiding place in his boot and drive it deep into Flaminius's side. Warm blood gushed from the wound, but it took two more thrusts of the knife before Flaminius keeled over. Taking advantage, Tiberius crab-walked away from his brother's prone body. This wasn't how he imagined the encounter ending. However, Flaminius was seriously injured but still alive, and that's what Tiberius wanted. Dragging himself across the floor, he fumbled for the gun. Once he had it securely in his grip, he staggered to his feet, out of breath.

While Tiberius was distracted, Flaminius took the time to crawl to his wife, leaving a blood trail behind him like a slug. Tiberius watched as he used the last of his strength to pull Aurelia into his arms and cradle her head against his chest. Witnessing the tender way his brother held Aurelia pissed him off so much that he almost lost control and shot Flaminius in the head. Fortunately, he managed to keep the bigger picture in mind. "I cannot tell you how long I've waited for this moment."

"Why?" Flaminius asked with labored breath. "I gave you my trust, my love. You're my brother, Tiberius."

"You gave me nothing!" Tiberius roared. "All you ever did was take from me. You took my chance of a political career, my father's respect, my daughter's love, Aurelia's love. You. Took. It. All!" Accentuating each word with a thrust of his hand holding the gun.

Realizing his brother was incapable of seeing reason, Flaminius bent his head and kissed his wife's bloodied cheek. "Just kill me already."

"Oh, no. That would be too easy. First, I'm going to tell you what I have planned for your beloved people, our parents, my treasonous daughter, and, best of all, your son."

Lily rushed down the corridor away from the great hall with the help of Mother Guardian and Seth. She had no idea where they were going, and she didn't care as long as it was as far away from the fighting as possible. Unfortunately, the enemy soldiers forced their way into the great hall to continue their indiscriminate slaughter. Lily kept her head down, but could hear Jim and Sue shouting orders from behind them over the noise of clashing swords and screams.

"Hurry!" Seth encouraged, his blood-soaked hands slipping from hers.

On her other side, Mother Guardian let go of her arm to open the door to the servants' stairs. "Where are we going?" Lily panted.

"To the main bedchamber," Mother Guardian grunted, gripping her arm again.

A sharp pain cut through her lower abdomen, causing Lily's knees to buckle. Unable to hold her up any longer, Mother Guardian lowered her onto a step. Seth sheathed his sword and picked her up to carry her the rest of the way. "Stay close, Mother Guardian," he barked.

"Yes, yes, boy, just move!"

Taking the steps two at a time, Lily's husband soon reached the second-floor door and kicked it open. Still carrying her, he ran down the corridor until he reached the bedroom door. Opening it, he entered and stepped aside for Mother Guardian to follow before gently lowering Lily to her feet. Mother Guardian shut and bolted it behind them.

Seth drew his sword. "What now?" he asked.

"I don't know," Mother Guardian said. "Sue said to get up here and wait for them."

Growling in frustration, Seth glanced at his wife. She seemed to be holding up, but he could see she was in pain.

A loud thud on the door made him snap his head around. Listening intently, he heard Jim cry out in pain. Then Sue screamed, more thuds, and then the unmistakable stench of burning flesh.

Seconds later, Sue banged on the door. "Let us in, Seth!" He helped Sue drag an unconscious and bleeding Jim inside before he locked the door again. Sue stumbled to the far side of the room. Favoring her left arm, she wrestled with the hefty tapestry. "That door won't hold them for long. Help me with this, Seth," she said, pointing to the floorboards. "The one next to the wall is loose; pry it out." Seth did what she asked. "Stick your hand in and find the lever and pull it." She puffed.

They heard a quiet click. Seth stood and then shoved the panel open, revealing a dark space. "What the fuck?" he hissed.

"Don't just stand there. Get them in!" Sue ordered. Mother Guardian helped Lily in first, then went back out to help Seth drag Jim in. But before they could clear the entrance, a loud explosion ripped through the room, flinging Seth into the adjacent wall.

Lily shrieked, lunging forward to get to him. Mother Guardian tried to stop her, but the girl was too fast. "No! Lily, get back here."

Coughing from the thick smoke that filled the room, Mother Guardian crawled across the floor to the spot where Lily kneeled next to Seth's body. "Get up! Get up, baby!" She cried, banging her fists on his chest.

Sue drew her sword and rushed toward the new intruders. Mother Guardian frantically pulled at Lily's robes, but she clawed to stay with her husband. Looking over her shoulder, Mother Guardian saw Sue fighting three attackers, but her sword arm was injured, and if Mother Guardian didn't do something fast, they were all going to die.

She grabbed Seth's heavy sword, lifting it with both hands. Entering the fray, she swung the blade with all her might at the closest man. The sword sliced through his flesh of the neck with sickening ease. Trying not to look at the blood gushing from his wounds, she attacked the second soldier fighting with Sue. But he easily deflected her blow with enough force that she lost her grip on the blade and fell on her bottom. Sue took the opportunity to attack him when he turned his back on her to kill Mother Guardian and cut his head clean off. The remaining man didn't like his odds against Sue and ran out of the room. Hopefully not to get reinforcements, but that was highly unlikely. Sue shouted for them to get back to the tunnel.

Turning her attention to Lily, Mother Guardian saw that the slip-of-a-girl had managed to pull Seth closer to the open panel. Sue lost her patience and decided Mother Guardian wasn't moving fast enough, so she manhandled her into the dark.

Just as Sue thought they had a chance of escaping, she heard Lily screech. In her haste to get Mother Guardian to safety, she failed to notice another man enter the room. Mother Guardian and Sue watched in horror as the masked man plunged his dagger down with a forceful arc into Seth's heart. When he withdrew the blade, blood from Seth's wound sprayed across Lily's face and chest.

"Noooo!"

Sheer unadulterated fury flowed through Mother Guardian's veins, tearing a battle cry from the deep-rooted depth of her soul that demanded she protect her Key. Snatching the sword from Sue's hand, she barreled forward, intent on killing the man who caused Lily so much pain.

Andreus kneeled next to Seth's body. His dagger was still in his hand, but his attention was on a still screaming Lily. Her beauty so absorbed him he wasn't prepared for an attack. A shout drew his attention to the moving white streak charging toward him. Unthinking, he lifted his dagger and drove it into the attacker's stomach, but not before she managed to slice his arm.

Grabbing Lily by the wrist, Andreus snatched her away from Seth and Mother Guardian's bodies as Sue rushed forward, prepared to cut the fucker to ribbons. But before she could get to him, she heard more shouts as more men flooded into the room. At that point, Sue had to make a decision. Stay and die with Mother Guardian, Seth, and Lily, or leave and make sure those loyal to the king knew what had happened here.

Turning, she rushed into the tunnel and slammed the panel shut behind her. Not allowing herself to think, she pulled the rifter from her pocket. Using her uninjured arm, she lifted Jim over her shoulder and struggled to her feet. Resting her butt against the stone wall, she initiated the portable, and the second the rift opened, Sue shoved off the wall with her ass and jumped through. Once she was sure the rift had closed behind her, she dropped to her knees and released a frustrated, mournful wail.

Flaminius couldn't reconcile this monster who had just killed his best friend and wife with his brother. If he had thought that he would survive this encounter, Flaminius might've had the energy to feel anger. In a way, he was grateful that he would soon join his wife in death. The thought of spending even one day without Aurelia was crippling. Flaminius knew it was selfish, given the fact that he had a son to raise and a nation of lost, frightened people who needed his leadership.

However, Flaminius wasn't cruel or selfish enough to leave his people in the hands of his deranged brother without warning them. When the king and queen didn't arrive at the manor house, someone would come looking for them, and he had to stay alive long enough for that. Cradling his wife's head, he looked at his brother. "I took nothing from you, Tiberius. None of those things you mentioned belonged to you to begin with, except Gaia. And let's face it, you cocked that up all on your own." Flaminius noticed that his brother's pacing took him through the blood on the floor, and his boots had painted the sterile white tiles with a crimson figure eight.

Tiberius laughed, but there was no humor in it. "Yeah, okay. I'll give you that. But you didn't waste any time stepping into the void I left, did you?"

Shaking his head, Flaminius gave his brother a sympathetic look.

"Don't look at me like that!" Tiberius bellowed, spit flying from his mouth.

Tightening his hold on Aurelia, Flaminius replied, "You were always one to speak too much and do too little. Get on with it." For a moment, Tiberius looked confused, so Flaminius said, "You were going to tell me all the awful things you were going to do to those I love." Frowning, Tiberius walked up to his brother and crouched so that he could look him in the eyes. Without warning, he clocked Flaminius on the side of the head with the butt of his gun. Blinding pain radiated down Flaminius's jaw and into his neck.

Eyeing him suspiciously, Tiberius asked, "Why are you so fucking calm?"

"You don't have to be so paranoid, Tiberius. You can relax and enjoy your victory. I honestly didn't see this coming." Sighing, he continued. "I'm simply resigned to the fact that my time has come, and I'm at peace with that."

Screwing his face up in anger, he shrieked, "No!" and resumed his maniacal pacing. "This is not how it's supposed to go! You're ruining everything again!"

As Flaminius watched Tiberius's crazed behavior, he wondered why he'd missed how unhinged his brother had become. Releasing a sorrow-filled wail, Flaminius bent his head and kissed Aurelia's hair. When he looked up, he saw the pleasure Tiberius derived from his pain.

Squatting down in front of Flaminius, Tiberius smiled. "Yeah, now it's starting to dawn on you," he said while tapping Flaminius's temple. "Now you realize what I have taken from you." Dropping his head, Flaminius cried out again. Placing the barrel of the gun under Flaminius's chin, Tiberius lifted his head and said, "No, no, brother. I want to look into those eyes and see your anguish when I tell you what's in store for those you love."

Flaminius tried to pull away from the cold steel. But Tiberius hit him again, though not as hard this time. However, it was hard enough to make him see stars, and his eyes rolled in his head. Tiberius slapped his cheek. "Don't pass out on me. There you go, good boy, eyes on me." Anxious to get this over with, Flaminius complied with Tiberius's demands.

"When I leave here, I'm going to Earth where my men have started an attack on HQ." Flaminius felt genuine fear at his statement. But Tiberius didn't notice. "I gave Andreus orders to do whatever it took to secure the house, and by that, I mean to kill everyone except our dear parents. Would you care to guess why?"

Flaminius remained silent.

"Yeah, not so cocky now, are you? Well, let me put you out of your misery. I want to be the one to stab them in their deceitful hearts and watch the life drain from their bodies." Unable to contain his excitement, Tiberius started pacing again. "I must admit, it will be difficult to kill them, but I believe it's vital for a king to show his men that he is not afraid to do the dirty work."

"You would kill your daughter and parents just so that you can sit on the throne of a kingdom that doesn't exist anymore?"

Tiberius spun around and pointed his finger at him. "That, right there, is the reason you're in this predicament. You were never willing to do the tough stuff."

"Fuck, Tiberius. You really are fucking crazy. Do you not hear yourself?"

Tiberius stopped his pacing and stretched his arms out to his sides. "Oh, brother. I am not crazy. You are weak; that is why you cannot understand. If you knew the things I have done in the name of the throne, your hair would turn white in an instant." Tiberius snapped his fingers to emphasize his point.

Flaminius surreptitiously glanced at the clock. Tiberius had been rambling on for almost fifteen minutes. By his reckoning, they had maybe five, ten minutes at the most. "Finish this, Tiberius!"

"Aren't you even a little curious about the things I've done?" He teased, obviously needing to boast. Not waiting for Flaminius to answer, he continued, "I plotted with our dear mother to kill your lovely wife."

This piece of information would have knocked Flaminius on his ass if he hadn't already been sitting. Undeterred, Tiberius sallied forth. "I've cheated, bribed, manipulated, and murdered. Hell, I even poisoned my wife to get her out of the way because she was a bit too nosey. Although," he said pensively, placing a finger on his lips, "I had a little help with that." Scratching his head, Tiberius said, "Did you know Matilda is a whizz with whipping up undetectable poisons?"

There were no words. The more Flaminius listened, the angrier he became, reigniting the fire in his soul. If his brother knew what was best for him, he would shut up. Flaminius was thinking it might be worth staying alive long enough to kill this fucking piece of shit he had once called brother.

As usual, Tiberius overplayed his hand. "Ooh. I can see you didn't like that. Is it because I'm fucking Matilda, or because she didn't trust you enough to share that bit of information?"

Flaminius spat a blood-stained gob at his brother in disgust.

"You never saw her potential because she was just another cum receptacle to you. I bet you're regretting that now."

Flaminius didn't want to ask, but he had to. "Please tell me it wasn't you who killed the Keys."

"Wow! You are slow on the uptake." He leaned back, arms aloft in triumph. "Of course, it was me!"

"Why?" Flaminius roared. "What possible reason could you have to do that?"

"Power, you moron!"

"Power?"

"Fucking hell, how hard did I hit you? I mean, I never liked you, Flaminius, but I respected the fact that you weren't a complete idiot." Sighing, he continued to explain slowly, as if Flaminius were a child. "Because the Keys hold our reproductive destiny in their hands, I decided they would be an excellent stream of revenue. Oh, don't look so shocked. You know it's a sound business plan."

Flaminius couldn't respond.

"Keeping all of them would cost a small fortune, and while I'm prepared to absorb such a cost, it makes no sense to dip too deeply into the revenue stream they will create. Not only does it lighten the overhead to have fewer Keys, but it also makes it easier to control them. We all know how impossibly emotional they can be."

"You're keeping them imprisoned?" Flaminius asked in disbelief.

"Duh. Finally, the lights go on."

The combination of pain, both physical and emotional, as well as the barrage of sickening information Tiberius fed him, caused Flaminius to empty the contents of his stomach.

Tsking, Tiberius decided it was time to wrap up this party. Striding over to Marcus's prone body, he rummaged through his pockets and found the portable rifter. "I can't have you getting any ideas after I leave." He said, winking at Flaminius before slipping the device into his pocket.

Using the butt of his gun, he smashed the glass covering of the box containing the axe used for fire emergencies, pulled it out, and walked to the crystal tower. Heaving the axe above his head, he brought it down onto the crystal tower repeatedly until the fragile stone shattered. Breathing hard, he dropped the hatchet and returned to Flaminius. "I can't say it was nice knowing you, Flaminius, but I can say it's been a blast getting rid of you." Tiberius initiated his portable rifter, and as he stepped through, he looked back and wiggled his fingers in a feminine farewell wave.

The entire ordeal had taken twenty-five minutes, but it was the longest twenty-five minutes of Flaminius's life. Alone, Flaminius let go of his frustration, anger, and self-loathing, yelling until his throat was raw.

Chapter Fourteen -
The Aftermath

Theo, Joshua, and Noah sat at the wooden table, propped up on cushions to reach the bowls of stew Martha served them. There were a lot of people crammed into the kitchen, but Gaia felt very alone. A cry of pain stopped all conversation, and the men ran out to investigate.

Gaia recognized the voice and wanted to help, but she didn't want to leave the boys. Martha noticed her hesitation. "Go, Lady Guardian. I will watch them."

Gaia followed the men. Pushing through the crowd that had gathered around the couple, she took in the scene. Sue kneeled next to her husband. They were both covered in blood, and Jim wasn't moving. It took Gaia a few seconds to remember that she was actually a healer and could help. When she stepped forward to examine Jim, Sue growled at her and refused to let Gaia near him. The woman was in full protective mode, and they needed to remove her. Gerhardt was one step ahead. Bending over Sue, he slipped his arms around her waist and whispered something in her ear. Whatever it was, it worked like a charm because Sue allowed Gerhardt to remove her.

Returning her attention to Jim, Gaia noticed a man and woman also kneeling next to him. The man leaned forward and pulled a medic satchel off his shoulders while Gaia and the woman examined Jim. The woman cut his tunic open with a pair of scissors while the man prepared an IV line. Gaia pulled the material out of the way and said to the woman, "My name is Gaia."

"Greta," jerking her head to the man, she added, "and this is Felix."

"Either of you a healer?" Gaia asked.

Felix shook his head. "Ops medics."

She relaxed a bit. Ops medics were exceptionally well-trained medics specialized in treating patients in combat situations. Gaia knew that either of them was just as qualified as she to lead this resuscitation, if not more so. Donning the gloves Felix gave her, Greta started her exam. She listed her findings as she continued to cut Jim's tights from his body. "A few non-threatening abrasions and contusions on his legs." Removing his shoes, she inspected his feet. "Nothing going on here."

Gaia acknowledged she heard Greta and added, "I've got an entrance wound between the sixth and seventh intercostal space on the left. Help me roll him your way so I can see if it's a through and through." They rolled him, with Felix supporting Jim's neck. Pulling the remaining tunic out of the way, Gaia saw an exit wound. "Yup, exit wound between the third and fourth space." The blade was narrow, but the upward thrust almost certainly damaged his lung. There must be liters of blood in his chest cavity, crushing his heart and lungs. They rolled him back, and Felix inserted an IV line.

Greta lifted her hand and shouted, "Stretcher!"

They moved Jim into the underground OR, and more nurses joined them to prep him for surgery. By the time Gaia had scrubbed up, the team had Jim hooked up to an oxygenation saturation monitor and waited for further instructions. Felix helped her into a sterile gown while he briefed her. "Sats are eighty-six, heart rate one-forty."

Fuck, they needed to move fast. Gaia took the scalpel handed to her and cut a small hole in the skin at his ribcage. Grabbing the forceps, she stuck it into the hole, opening up the subcutaneous tissue and intercostal muscle, using blunt dissection to create a track for a tube. Gaia felt the pleura and tore it with the forceps, feeling the telltale vibration. "I'm in," she announced.

Putting her tools down, she stuck her finger into the track she had created until she got to the chest cavity. Bending the tip of her finger, she rotated it to clear any tissue away from inside the chest wall. Not removing her eyes from the hole, she stuck her hand out and called, "Tube!"

Felix handed her a transparent tube clamped on one end with large forceps. She carefully inserted it into the track. Once she was sure the pipe was placed correctly in the chest cavity, she said, "We're good, Felix." He nodded, took the other end of the tube, attached it to the boxed underwater drain, and unclamped it. The second he did, blood drained out. Sitting back, Gaia looked up at the sats monitor. Immediately, Jim's sats bounced up to ninety-seven, and his blood pressure stabilized at one-hundred-and-twenty over seventy. The most critical vital sign was his heart rate, and when it dropped to eighty, she relaxed. Calling for heavy grade suture, Gaia set about closing the skin around the tube with a purse-string stitch to secure it. Job finished, she stood back, and Greta took her place to dress the wound.

Ripping off her gloves, mask, and gown, Gaia thanked everybody and left to speak to Sue, who sat in the passage outside the operating room, flanked by Rosalind and Sylas. Before Sue could ask, Gaia said, "He's fine. We had to drain fluid from his chest cavity, but after that, he stabilized."

Sue collapsed against Rosalind and burst into tears. Giving her friend time, Gaia simply rubbed her back as an extra measure of comfort. Eventually, Sue wiped her eyes. "Can I see him?"

"Yes, of course. Do you know where to go?"

"We'll take her," Rosalind offered.

"You go ahead. I'll be there in a minute," Sylas said. Once they were out of earshot, Sylas asked, "Where is my daughter?"

"I don't know. Maybe Marcus took them to HQ Two?"

"Marcus wouldn't have given you the coordinates for HQ Three if he intended to take my child to HQ Two in an emergency."

"Can't we contact HQ Two and find out?"

"I would if I knew where it was."

Squaring her shoulders, she said, "Marcus always has a plan."

"I hope for all our sakes you're right." He said before he turned and walked away.

After writing up her orders for Jim's care, she left to see the boys. On her way out, she noticed her surroundings for the first time. The underground facility was a replica of the clinic she worked in at the castle. Before she punched through the doors at the end of the passage, Gaia looked at the clock. Half an hour since Sue and Jim's arrival and a little over one hour since she arrived. Where was Marcus? He must know that something was wrong.

But if that were the case, why hadn't they come yet?

Chapter Fifteen -
Not All it's Cracked Up to Be

Tiberius rifted closer to the manor house than he should have, and he gave not one fuck. He found it difficult to contain his excitement because, for the first time, he would stand in front of his men as their victorious leader. He made the strategic decision to reveal his identity to his soldiers just hours before the attack to show them who their powerful Capulus was, thereby bolstering their confidence and ensuring victory.

By the sound of the festivities emanating from the village, Tiberius knew the humans were none the wiser to what was taking place just a mile down the road at the manor house.

Jogging through the woods, he saw some of his men stationed at the gatehouse. As usual, Andreus had been swift in executing his duties, and Tiberius wouldn't be surprised if Andreus had Tiberius's parents tied up with a bow, waiting for him. Once he cleared the bridge and entered the courtyard, Tiberius's excitement went into overdrive.

Soldiers were piling dead bodies against the stable wall, while others hauled buckets of water from the moat to wash the blood off the cobblestones. Not stopping to return their salutes or bask in their shouts of adoration, Tiberius entered the house and bellowed, "Andreus!"

Immediately his loyal general answered, "Capulus!" as he ran down the stairs.

"Is it done?"

Andreus reached the bottom of the stairs and glanced around the foyer. "Can we speak in private, Capulus?"

Tiberius didn't like the sound of that, but he marched off in the study's direction. Once securely ensconced, he turned to Andreus and said, "We are victorious, Andreus. You no longer need to hide your face."

Andreus removed his blood-spattered helmet and shook out his sweaty hair. "Thank you, my lord." He took a deep breath. "I have done all that you ordered, except for two things," he said nervously.

"Well, don't keep me waiting?"

"We cannot find Gaia, Theo, Sue, Jim, and their boys."

Tiberius's good mood evaporated. "What is the second thing?"

Andreus planted his helmet under his arm and pushed his fingers through his hair. "Mother Guardian is dead."

Tiberius put his hands on his hips, bent his head, and fighting for control. He said, "I don't need to explain to you how fucking important it is that the heirs to the throne must die."

"Of course, Capulus. I sent scouts out into the forest to track them down. They can't have gotten far."

Lowering himself into a chair by the fire, Tiberius asked, "How do you know that? They could be anywhere if they have a rifter."

Andreus shook his head. "My spies have monitored them carefully over the past year. They don't have unregistered rifters." When Tiberius remained quiet, Andreus added, "We discovered a secret passage leading from the main bedchamber on the second floor that leads into the woods. I believe that is the escape route they used."

"So, they're on foot with three children?"

"Yes," his general confirmed. "And both Jim and Sue are seriously injured."

"Are you sure of that?"

"Absolutely. I saw Sue take a blow to her sword arm, and Jim was unconscious the last time I saw him. Unfortunately, it took some time to locate the mechanism that opened the secret door, and by then, they were gone."

Tiberius felt confident that it was only a matter of time before they were caught. However, he wanted to keep the fact that Theo was still alive a secret. "Tell the men searching to shut their mouths about their mission."

"I already did, Capulus."

"Good. Now, on to a matter not so easily solved. Who the fuck killed Mother Guardian?"

Andreus decided it was best if nobody knew that it was he who killed her. "There is no way of knowing who struck the killing blow. We encountered more resistance than expected, and many of our soldiers are inexperienced."

"Fuck!" Tiberius leaned forward and rubbed his hands over his face. "Her death will make it harder to get cooperation from the Keys."

"This is true, Capulus, but not impossible, and in time they will realize they have no choice."

Yes. Tiberius supposed they would. Not an ideal situation, but as Andreus pointed out, not unsolvable. Deciding to let it go, Tiberius stood. "Let's move on. I'm eager to see my parents."

Andreus led the way up the stairs to Tiberius's parents' bedroom. Fuck! He hoped Capulus got this over soon because he was champing at the bit to see his Lily again. She was more beautiful than he remembered now that her belly was rounded with child. She was understandably upset, but soon she would see that the death of her match was for the best. His Lily was smart; it wouldn't take her long. But with the pregnancy so advanced and with the shock she suffered, he worried that there could be complications, so he left a healer with her to be safe.

Andreus and Tiberius had barely entered the room when the queen's shrill voice broke his thoughts of Lily.

"What have you done, Tiberius?"

"Keep your irritating voice down, Mother."

The woman did not take instruction well because her voice grew louder. "This was not my plan."

The guards hadn't bothered to restrain his mother, but they trussed his father up like a turkey. "I said, shut up!" Finally, the shrew got the message. Tiberius rubbed his aching temples. "Now, we're going to sit and calmly discuss your situation."

Without looking at his wife, Romulus said, "I'm pleased that this will be my last day because living with you for one more second feels like a never-ending nightmare."

Octavia stopped pacing and glared at Romulus. "Don't be stupid. He's not going to kill you."

Tiberius lifted his eyebrows. "Says who, Mother?"

Octavia whipped her head around so fast she almost lost her balance. "Don't joke, Tiberius."

The crack that reverberated through the room when Tiberius slapped his mother was louder than a gunshot.

Ashen-faced, Octavia cupped her cheek. "You're going to kill him?" she asked in disbelief.

"Wake up and smell the betrayal, Octavia," Romulus spat. "He ordered the killing of the Keys. What makes you think he will spare us, you dumb bitch?"

Octavia tried to remain standing, but her legs refused to cooperate; she collapsed in a flurry of silk skirts and jingling jewels.

"At last, my self-centered, arrogant, misguided, stupid, vapid bitch of a wife gets it!" With every insult he threw at her, Romulus's voice got louder until he was shouting.

Tiberius had just about as much as he could take from his parental unit.

"I'm afraid, Mother, my soon-to-be departed father is correct." For once in her life, Octavia had nothing to say. "But don't worry, you'll join him soon after."

The threat of death gave her the strength she needed to pick her carcass up off the floor. "Please, Tiberius," she begged. "Don't do this! We can be of service to you."

"I'm not interested in being your puppet, Mother. Nor am I stupid enough to make the same mistake my father and brother made by underestimating what atrocities you will commit to gain power."

Shaking her head vigorously, Octavia backed up, holding her hands out defensively. Tiberius lost count of how many times he had fantasized about killing his parents. But now that the time had come, he realized he had never actually decided how he would do it. Tiberius looked around the room at a loss for what to do next, hoping a solution would present itself. Sensing

Capulus's hesitancy, Andreus stepped forward. "Is there something that you need, Capulus?"

Shaking the fog from his brain, Tiberius replied, "You know, I've never thought about how I would kill them." Once he said the words aloud, they sounded so outrageous that he laughed hysterically. When he got himself under control, he wiped the tears from his eyes and looked at his parents. His mother crouched against the wall, but his father sat proudly, managing to look regal even though he was tied up. Fuck his father. Tiberius just wanted this to be over. He had thought he would relish the moment, but nothing was working out the way he had wanted. Whatever. He was done. Turning his head, he noticed one man carried a small crossbow. Holding out his hand, he ordered, "Give that to me."

The weapon was heavier than it looked, but he lifted it and aimed at his mother. She whimpered. Keeping the crossbow level to his chest, he said, "Goodbye, Mother," and squeezed the trigger. The bolt hit her square in the heart. Eyes freakishly large, the woman slid down the wall, her body landing at an awkward angle. Turning to his father, he said. "I never liked her, but I did once love you, so this will be much harder for me."

Romulus showed no sign of fear. "You may not believe me, son, but I loved you too."

Looking into his father's eyes, Tiberius almost believed that he meant it, but then recalled the heartless words his father had spoken on the beach all those years ago. "Fathers who love their sons don't threaten to sire another heir rather than allow their second-born to sit on the throne." Romulus paled. "You didn't know that I heard you, did you?"

Shaking his head, Romulus replied in a breathless voice. "That long? You've been plotting this atrocity for that long?"

The disbelief in his father's voice pissed him off. "What? Can't you believe I had it in me to succeed? Well," he said as he slowly turned around in a circle with his arms held up to his sides. "Behold, Father, you were wrong."

Romulus stared at his son with sadness and regret in his eyes. "No, Tiberius. I didn't want you to rule because you are a coward, and I was right."

Tiberius's temper snapped. In two strides, he reached his father and punched him in the face. Blood spurted from his nose, and the chair he sat on rocked precariously. "I am not a coward!"

Seemingly unperturbed by his injury, Romulus answered, "Yes, you are. You gained the throne through scheming and murder. Where is the honor in that, son?"

Tiberius hit him again. "Honor?" He laughed. "Don't speak to me about honor. A man who would rip loved ones from each other wants to talk to me about honor?"

Romulus's laugh was devoid of humor. "Now that you sit on the throne, you will face difficulties you're ill-equipped to deal with. I'm only sorry I won't get a chance to say 'I told you so.'"

Lunging for the quiver of bolts slung across the soldier's back, Tiberius took one and loaded the bow. "Any last words?"

"Yes. I love you, but I hope your brother kills you instead of showing you mercy as I know he will."

Slapping his hand against his forehead, Tiberius said in a singsong voice. "How remiss of me, I should have told you sooner that I killed him and his wife, as well as that meddling errand boy of his before I came here."

Slumping down in his chair as far as the restraints would allow, Romulus whispered, "Then, our people are doomed."

"Fuck you, Father."

The first bolt penetrated Romulus's throat, severing the jugular. But Tiberius kept firing until the quiver was empty.

When he was done, he stood, catching his breath, and stared at the bodies of his parents. The rage he had nursed for so long did not abate. Dropping the crossbow, Tiberius walked to his mother's body. Going down on his haunches, he pulled the bolt out of her chest with a wet sucking sound. After he removed the one from his father's throat, he gave them to Andreus. "I want to keep these as souvenirs."

Andreus bowed his head. "Yes, Capulus. I'll have them cleaned and returned to you."

"No!" Tiberius held up his bloodied hand. "I want them preserved as they are."

"As you wish, Sire."

Tiberius smiled. He liked the sound of that. "Leave me now," he commanded with a flick of his wrist. "But take their bodies with you and transport them back to Arkhnuet with the others. Let them burn with their dying planet.

Once he was alone, he slumped down into a chair and stretched out his legs. Of course, not everything had gone as planned, but he was satisfied with the result. Closing his eyes, Tiberius allowed himself a moment to revel in his victory.

Once he had seen to his duties, Andreus took the stairs two at a time in his haste to get to Lily. However, the moment he entered the room, he could see something was wrong. Several healers rushed back and forth between the bed and equipment set up around it.

"What is going on here?"

His booming voice made them all jump. One healer stepped forward but waved her hands at the others to keep working. Bowing her head, she said, "Sir, after you left, the Key went into premature labor."

Shoving his way through the healers to get to Lily's side, he saw she was awake, staring at the ceiling in a daze, her hair wet with sweat, causing it to stick to her beautiful face. Gently lowering himself on the bed next to her, he removed his helmet from under his arm and placed it on the bedside table. Andreus touched her hand; she turned to look at him and flinched when she saw the helmet.

"Why didn't anybody call me?"

The healer replied, "I would've, sir, but it all happened so fast, and the situation required my full attention."

Andreus didn't like not being here for Lily when she needed him. Looking into her eyes, he asked the healer. "What is wrong with her?"

"As I said, sir, she went into premature labor hours ago."

"And?" he asked irritably.

"And, initially, I was concerned for the baby, but she is healthy."

Andreus jerked his head up and noticed that Lily's belly was flat. They draped a sheet over her bent knees, and her legs were spread. But he couldn't see what they were doing.

"She has birthed the baby?"

"Yes, sir, a girl."

Tears of delight streamed down his face. "Did you hear, my love? We have a baby girl."

Lily shook her head, tears of her own flowing freely, but they were tears of fear, not happiness.

"Don't be afraid, my Lily."

She tried to lift her head and mouthed something he couldn't hear. Bending down, he turned his head so that his ear was close to her mouth. It took her a while, but she eventually whispered, "Who are you?"

Andreus sat back, stunned. Of course, she didn't know who he was. Why would she? "I will tell you everything you need to know, but first, we must let the healers do their work so you can come back to me." Turning to the healer, he asked, "Why are you still working on her? What is wrong?"

Shuffling her feet, the healer rubbed her hands on her dull gray skirt. "The birth went smoothly enough, and, as I said, the baby is fine. But shortly after delivering the placenta, the patient started bleeding, and we cannot stop it."

The thought of losing her now that he finally had her filled him with terror. "You will do everything to save her life. Do you hear me?"

"Of course, sir. But we need room to work. Might I ask you to wait outside?"

The last thing he wanted to do was leave Lily, but he knew it was best.

"I want to see the baby."

The healer called a maid who was removing many blood-soaked sheets from the room and instructed her to take him to the baby.

The nursery on the third floor was dark when he pushed the door open. A wet nurse sat on a rocking chair in the corner, cradling a tiny, squirming bundle. He rapped lightly on the door to get the wet nurse's attention. She looked up, and when she saw who it was, the color drained from her face.

Unlike their predecessors, Capulus decided only Arkhnuetians could work in the house. Those chosen were all loyal followers of the Oradagra and handpicked by him. Ignoring the woman's reaction, he stepped into the room. She stood and curtsied. "Sir."

"I wish to see the baby."

Stammering, the nurse said. "Y-yes, sir."

Walking to him, she carefully placed the baby in his arms and stepped back. The moment he looked into her eyes, Andreus was lost. Just like the first time he saw Lily. The little thing squirmed some more but settled when he rocked her. She was utterly perfect. And at that moment, he saw his future stretched out before him like an endless summer day.

Several hours later, his serenity disappeared like mist in the sun. Finally, the healer called for him and informed him that there was nothing more they could do for Lily. She would not stop bleeding. He screamed at her to operate, remove the uterus, give her blood, anything.

"We have, my lord! Short of a miracle, the Key will die."

Andreus all but destroyed the sitting room where he received the dire news. But, to her credit, the haggard-looking healer stood stoically, waiting for him to tire. Once he had, she gently suggested that he spend the time Lily had left with her instead of destroying furniture. Had he not been so distraught, he might have had the presence of mind to kill her for her insolence.

When he returned, the room was much quieter than before, and there was no sign of bloodied sheets. Instead, she lay under the covers. Her hair spread out over the snow-white pillow. Apart from the pale color of her face, she looked well.

"Leave us," he barked. Then, walking to the basin of clean water, he took the time to wash his face and hands and comb his hair. Once he finished, he sat on the bed next to Lily and gently touched her shoulder. Her eyelids opened sluggishly, and for a moment, she looked confused. Then the fog cleared, and she gasped. "You?"

"Yes, my love, me," he said, cupping her face between his hands.

Lily knew she was dying, and now that her baby was no longer at risk of dying with her, she welcomed it. But her baby was still in danger, and she needed to do everything in her power to change that. When Lily first saw him, she recognized the mask. Now that his face was clean and she wasn't in pain, Lily realized who he was. His devotion puzzled her. Andreus touched her face, and she tried not to pull away. What Lily wanted to do was cut his throat. But her baby's life was in the hands of this deranged monster until Gaia and the others could rescue her. Swallowing the bile that threatened to spew from her mouth at his touch, she lifted her hand and covered his. "Why? How?"

Smiling down at her, he replied, "I have loved you from afar for many years. But I had to wait to claim you."

"Why didn't you say anything?" Because if he had, Seth would have kicked his ass.

"I wanted you before you married, but I wanted you and a family, and only he could give that to us."

Listening to this piece of shit talk about Seth enraged her. Misinterpreting her scowl, he quickly added, "You cannot imagine how difficult it was for me, knowing he was touching you, feeling you . . ." He broke off, clearly angry.

Afraid he would see through her façade, Lily squeezed his hand. "Stop. It's okay. You have me now." Lying down next to her, he drew her into his arms. Lily tried not to stiffen, but it was impossible. She didn't want to die in the arms of the man who killed her husband.

For a while, Andreus held her, stroking her hair and whispering sweet nothings in her ear. Due to the volume of blood she had lost, Lily must have drifted off for a time because he shook her and called her name. Opening her eyes with difficulty, Lily noticed movement over his shoulder. It was Seth! Her beautiful Seth was smiling at her from across the room. The shock of seeing him caused her to jerk. Andreus gently pinched her chin in his fingers and forced her face to his. "Baby, are you in pain?" he anxiously asked.

Ignoring the idiot, she turned her eyes back to Seth. In her head, she heard him say, "Just a little longer, Bug. Then you can join me." Could it be? Had he come to fetch her?

Andreus repeated his question. "Lily, are you in pain?"

Touching his face, she cooed, "No, please, I have things to ask you before I die."

Hugging her, he croaked, "Anything, I will do anything for you."

Glancing to make sure Seth was still there, she smiled at Andreus. "I want you to name our baby Alice."

"Yes, I will do so. It is a beautiful name, my love. But I wish to honor you too. Can her second name be Lily?"

Looking at Seth for confirmation, he spoke to her in her head again. "It's a wonderful idea, Bug. Let him do it."

She nodded. "Yes, I would like that."

Suddenly, an incredible feeling of lightness pervaded her body. Lily felt her physical form shut down. Fighting for control, she whispered, "Promise me you will protect her with your life."

Andreus looked insulted. "You never need to worry about her. I always protect what is mine."

"Swear it, Andreus!"

"I swear it. I will protect Alice with my life," he vowed.

Relieved that he had taken an oath to protect her baby, Lily relaxed and waited for death to take her. The second her soul disengaged from her body, she shot across the room into Seth's waiting arms.

"We are one again, Bug," he said, touching the end of her nose as he had done a million times before. There were no feelings of loss, no fear. Even the thought of leaving Alice didn't cause her anguish. A sense of knowing flowed through her, telling her that all would be well.

"I love you, Seth."

"I know, Bug. Come, we may see our baby before we go."

Taking her cue from her husband, she drifted through the floors until they reached the nursery.

Alice lay in her crib, sound asleep. The nurse snored softly from the rocking chair. Lily could feel the woman's energy, and even though her life experiences had made her choose the wrong path, she was inherently good and would never hurt Alice.

Together, they looked into the crib at their beautiful little girl. Lily reached for her and was surprised that she could touch Alice's face. The girl's eyes shot open at her mother's touch. Seth soothed her by stroking the blond tuft of hair on the crown of her head. "Shh, little Bug; it's alright. Mama and Papa may be gone in body, but we will always be here in spirit."

Lily could have sworn she saw Alice nod her head in understanding, and it made Lily giggle. Alice definitely smiled back.

Waking from her sleep, the nurse shivered. Pulling her shawl tighter around her shoulders, she frowned. "Is anyone there?" When she got no answer, she got up to check on the baby. Looking down at the little girl, the nurse smiled. "It must have been a dream, little Bug."

Andreus refused to let anyone touch Lily's body for hours after she died. Instead, he held her in his arms and cried until his eyes swelled shut. Becoming concerned for his well-being, the healer finally called for Capulus. She didn't know what transpired between the men in the room, but Capulus eventually pried the man away from the Key.

Once they were in his bedroom, Capulus helped Andreus undress, put him to bed, then left him in peace. Sleep came swiftly, but his dreams were riddled with images of Lily playing with a blond-haired little girl; by their side, watching over them, stood Seth.

Chapter Sixteen -
The End

Gaia emerged through the underground clinic doors into a gray night sky, spewing a consistent drizzle. As she rounded the corner of Martha's cottage, she noticed Gerhardt and a few other men standing a dozen feet from the door in a tight huddle. They stopped talking once they saw her, but not before she heard some of their argument.

Gerhardt wanted to defy Marcus's orders and return to Arkhnuet, but the others disagreed. "These are not normal circumstances, sir," Gerhardt snapped.

"Watch your tone, Corporal. I'm your commanding officer until the general returns."

Planting his hands on his hips, he sighed. "I meant no disrespect, Colonel, but you acknowledge that we have to find them."

The Colonel refused. "Our orders were explicit. Stay here and protect the future king, and that is what we're going to do." At this juncture, one man alerted them to the fact that they had an audience.

Gerhardt lifted his chin in greeting, and Gaia gave the group of men a wave and ducked into the cottage. Martha sat near the fire, knitting what looked like mittens. But Gaia couldn't be sure, since she knew nothing about the art of weaving wool with needles.

"They're asleep, Lady Guardian." Gaia lowered her aching body into the chair opposite the woman. "Please call me Gaia. The whole Lady Guardian thing is a bit too formal for my liking."

Martha nodded. "As you wish."

They sat in amiable silence, listening to the crackling fire and allowing the heat to chase away the cold, damp day. Gaia's thoughts roamed, falling upon the mystery of where the king and queen were and why Marcus wouldn't bring them here, as discussed. She was not used to sitting around, waiting for something to happen, and it didn't look as if the soldiers were going to do anything about it. Then she realized; she was not a soldier who had to obey orders. She was the Lady Guardian, and she had executed her duty and kept Theo safe. Nothing was stopping her from going to look for Marcus.

Jumping out of her chair, Gaia asked, "Martha, can I ask you to stay with the children a little while longer?"

Startled by her sudden movement, Martha stuttered. "Y-yes, Lady . . . I mean, Gaia."

Gaia grabbed her rifter from its charging dock, ran to the clinic as fast as she could, and found Sue lying next to Jim on the narrow bed; Sylas and Rosalind slept on chairs. A quick perusal of the monitors told her Jim was on the mend. "Don't get up," Gaia whispered to Sue. "I've only come to ask if I can borrow your rifter."

Sue awkwardly unplugged the device with her right hand, currently strapped to her body in a sling, and handed it to her. "I'll return it as soon as I can," she called over her shoulder on her way out of the room, but Sue stopped her.

"Gaia! What are you up to?"

Turning to face her friend, she answered, "I don't have time to explain, but I promise we'll talk when I get back." If Sue said anything else, Gaia didn't hear it. She sprinted back to the cottage to find Gerhardt, but he was no longer standing outside, so she asked everybody she came across if they had seen him. Finally, a young boy pointed her in the beach's direction. Hiking her skirt up a little higher, she ran down the well-worn path. Gerhardt stood with his back to her, staring out across the calm ocean. Panting, she called to him, "Gerhardt! Gerhardt!"

The soldier spun on his heels to face her, instantly alert. "What's happened?"

Waving her hand, she stopped a few feet from him. "Nothing yet, but I heard what you said just now, and I agree with you. We need to do something."

He didn't answer her immediately, so Gaia rambled on. "I know that I'm asking you to disobey a superior officer's orders, and you can get into a lot of trouble, but . . ."

Gerhardt held up his hand. "I don't care about that. It's just that I cannot think of anything to help them."

Gaia pulled both her rifter and the one she took from Sue out of her pocket. "I can. Let's rift our asses back to Arkhnuet and see what's keeping Marcus and our king and queen." Gerhardt stared at the rifters for a beat, then held out his hand. Gaia dropped one into his open palm.

"They were scheduled to arrive at the manor house an hour and twenty-three minutes ago. We should rift into the corridor outside the rifter bay to save time." Gaia nodded her agreement. Gerhardt punched the coordinates into his rifter. Within moments, they stepped into the sterile corridor.

The castle must have lost power at some point because the auxiliary power had kicked in. The usually brightly lit corridor glowed with the red hue of emergency lights. As soon as the rift closed behind them, Gerhardt stepped in front of Gaia. He touched his finger to his lips, indicating he wanted her to remain silent. Gaia didn't fully understand why they had to be quiet, since they were alone. But he was the soldier. Following his lead, Gaia hugged the wall as they made their way toward the rifter bay. When they reached the door, Gerhardt held his index and middle finger to his eyes, then pointed at the door. Gaia followed his fingers and saw that the handle hung at an awkward angle. Heart pounding, she covered her mouth to stop the cry of alarm that threatened to escape.

Gerhardt held up his hand in a stop gesture, then pointed at the floor. He wanted her to stay put at that spot. She shook her head no. He nodded, yes, aggressively, and glared at her. To save time, Gaia mouthed, "Fine."

Satisfied, Gerhardt raised his weapon, and, keeping it tucked tightly against his chest, he nudged the door open. Gaia watched his expression closely for any changes, but lost sight of him when he moved into the room. She froze in fear when he shouted, "Fuck!" Coming unstuck, she rushed into the room. If Gaia lived to be ten thousand years old, she would never forget the sight.

Flame couldn't be sure how long he lay on the floor, cradling Aurelia. He felt confident that he had lost consciousness at some point because he had to force his eyes open when he heard someone say, "Fuck." Struggling to focus, he wiped his hand over his eyes, only to smear blood into them. Gaia's familiar voice cut through his confusion.

"Flaminius! Jesus! Fuck! Flaminius!"

Wincing at the volume of his niece's voice, he tried to speak. "Don't have much . . . time," he croaked.

Gaia was not in the mood to listen, or she couldn't hear him, because a litany of profanity kept rolling off her tongue. The male voice from before broke through her panic. "Gaia, you need to calm down and focus."

Using the sleeve of his tunic, Flaminius wiped the blood from his eyes. Gaia's face hovered over him. "You must listen to me," he wheezed.

"Yes, I will, after I get you all out of here."

Lacking the strength to force her to listen, Flaminius growled in frustration. Unfortunately, neither his niece nor the man with her paid him any attention.

Moving away, Gaia began barking orders at the soldier. "Get over here. Help me roll Marcus. No, hold his head, yes, like that."

What felt like a year later, Gaia's face came back into view, looking more composed. "Here's what's going to happen," she bossed. "Gerhardt is going to lift you and drape your body over his shoulders. Then he's going to carry Aurelia, bride style, through the rift. Your only job is to stay as still as possible so he doesn't drop either of you while he's rifting. Nod if you understand." He did. "Good." She made to leave but hesitated before she said, "And Flaminius, brace, because it's going to hurt like a mother."

With Gaia's help and a lot of grunting and sweating, Gerhardt positioned Flaminius and Aurelia securely. And fuuuuck! Gaia did not lie; it hurt like a mother. The last thing he heard before he passed out again was Gerhardt ordering Gaia. "I want you right behind me. No fucking dawdling."

Gaia didn't bother answering Gerhardt. Instead, she set about heaving Marcus's dead weight onto her shoulders; her task was made significantly easier by Gerhardt lifting him off the floor onto a chair before he left. Fumbling under her burden, Gaia engaged the rifter using her nose because she needed her other hand to secure Marcus. It took about a million years for the rift to open, and using the rest of the adrenalin pumping through her veins, she heaved them through the rift, landing face first on the wet grass outside the clinic. Marcus's bulk pinned her down for a minute before someone lifted him off her. Rolling over, she greedily gulped in air and wiped the mud from her face. Forcing her legs to take her weight, Gaia wobbled to her feet and cast her eyes around. She didn't see Marcus or her aunt and uncle, but she noticed some clinic staff rushing through the doors.

Following them, she stumbled down the stairs. The bright fluorescent lighting pierced her eyes, giving her an instant headache. Gaia saw that Greta and four other ops medics were already working on Marcus in bay one. Aurelia was in bay two. Felix bent his head so that a nurse could put a mask over his mouth while another helped him into his gloves. Several sterile surgical packs lay ready, showing that Aurelia was in serious trouble.

Moving on to bay three, where an unconscious but thankfully alive Flaminius lay, Gaia asked, "Who's taking the lead?"

An older man dressed in a button-down, canary-yellow shirt and obnoxious orange bowtie lifted his hand and said. "Me," without looking at her.

Gaia shuffled forward. "How can I help?"

Finally, taking his eyes off Flaminius, he looked at her, and without missing a beat, said, "Go get a cup of coffee and something to eat. You look dreadful."

"No. I am the king's niece, and I want to help."

The man ignored her while he gave his team orders. Listening, Gaia grudgingly agreed with everything he said.

"I know who you are, but as I said, go get something to eat."

Gaia opened her mouth to argue, but he beat her to it. "I'm Gregory Von Peck. I assure you, I have this under control."

Gaia stepped back when she heard his name. Apart from Rosalind, Gregory Von Peck was the most decorated trauma surgeon Arkhnuet had ever produced. The man could probably perform a thoracotomy with his eyes closed while drinking tea and discussing the mechanism of splicing DNA.

Without a word, Gaia turned toward the waiting room, avoiding the other bays. She didn't want to know what was happening to them; in fact, she didn't want to think at all.

TAMING FLAME

Three hours later, Gaia discovered that not thinking was an impossibility for her. She tried meditation to no avail. Then she tried pacing, but it only made her aching feet throb more. Finally, when her attempt at reading failed, she left the clinic to check on the children. The cloud cover made the night darker than usual, and it was later than she thought. When she arrived at Martha's cottage, she was surprised to see two, maybe three hundred people had set up a vigil outside the little white-washed house. People were sitting on blankets and chairs, sharing a meal, or whispering. Some had even built fires to keep the chill at bay. It took every ounce of strength she had left not to collapse in a heap on the ground and sob her heart out.

Martha was the first to notice her and rushed over. "Lady Guardian, have you any news?"

Once Martha brought attention to Gaia's presence, a ripple of awareness cut through the crowd, and gradually, silence fell. Clearing her throat, she said in a loud voice. "No, but it is not necessarily a bad sign. It means that the medical teams are still working on them and that they have not—" Gaia's voice faltered. She couldn't speak the words.

Martha, bless her, saw how much Gaia needed peace, and clapped her hands together. "Come, my lady," as she led Gaia into her home. "You must be starving."

Shaking her head, Gaia answered. "No, thank you. I just came to see that the children are well."

"They are my lady."

"Gaia."

Martha looked confused. "Pardon?"

"Gaia. I asked you to call me Gaia." She gently replied.

Shaking her head, Martha clucked her tongue. "Yes, I forgot."

Pulling a chair away from the table, Martha slowly placed her hands on Gaia's shoulders and pushed her down.

"Sue came by a few hours ago and took the twins to see their father, but she brought them back when you returned from Arkhnuet. Some of the other wives helped me feed and bathe them, then took turns rocking them to

THE END

sleep. That Noah is a stout little blighter," she joked. "I couldn't feel my arms for about an hour after he fell asleep."

Gaia laughed feebly. "Thank you so much for taking care of them. I know you have your own child to care for, and adding three more must be a burden, even with the others helping."

"Please don't mention it. It was our honor. But if you genuinely wish to show your gratitude, you can eat something."

Martha was one of those rare breeds of women that thrived on nurturing others. Gaia could do with some. "Okay. That would be wonderful." Before Gaia could say hungry, Martha had a cheese and ham sandwich ready. She tasted nothing, but her stomach growled in appreciation, so she wolfed the sandwich down and drank the sweet ale Martha gave her. When was the last time she'd eaten? This morning at breakfast? Or was it yesterday morning? It must be past midnight by now, so yesterday morning then. Jesus, it felt like a year ago that they had been at the manor house waiting for the arrival of the king and queen.

A commotion from outside drew her attention, and seconds later, a young soldier rushed through the door, out of breath, eyes as big as saucers. "Lady Guardian," he panted, bowing clumsily. "Professor Von Peck is asking for you."

Exhaustion forgotten, Gaia ran like the hounds of hell were nipping at her heels. Skidding to a halt at the reception desk where the professor sat, she tried to speak, but words failed. "Relax. I have good news." She needed to sit right now. With the grace of a dying swan, Gaia plopped herself down next to him.

"The king is stable and resting. The queen made it through surgery but is still critical. We had to give her six units of blood, and honestly, she is fortunate to be alive." Gaia was relieved her aunt and uncle were out of immediate danger, but she held her breath, terrified to hear about Marcus.

Oblivious to her feelings, the professor continued. "General Brewer was touch and go. He took a .45 to the chest. The projectile missed most of his vital organs but nicked the top left quadrant of his heart. There was a lot of damage, and they are only now finishing his surgery."

Gaia's face drained of color, and she swayed dangerously. Professor Von Peck forced her head between her knees and rubbed her back while mumbling words of encouragement. The unexpected tenderness tore through her final emotional barrier, and she burst into tears. She wasn't sure how long she sat there, but at some point, a nurse gave her a box of tissues, and someone else brought her a cup of tea. When next she noticed her surroundings, the professor had left, and Greta was talking to her. "What?"

"General Brewer is awake and asking for you, Lady Guardian."

Blindly handing a nurse her empty cup, she pushed to her feet and followed Greta to the recovery area. Greta pointed out the cubicle Marcus was in and then left. Pulling the curtain back, she saw his beautiful face. There were still IV lines in his arms, a sats monitor connected to his finger, and he was pale. Walking to his side, Gaia gently put her hand on his forearm. Marcus opened his eyes, blinked a few times, and in a raspy voice, said, "Jesus, Gaia, you look like shit, woman."

For the second time that day, Gaia burst into tears. "You don't look so hot yourself, mister." She hiccuped.

He smiled at her, turned his arm, and opened his hand. Gaia threaded her fingers through his. His eyes already drooping, he mumbled, "I'd never leave you, baby."

Two weeks after the attack, they held a memorial service to honor Mother Guardian, her Keys, and the lost soldiers. Since they could not recover any bodies, the gesture was purely symbolic, and it left everyone feeling hollow. But for Gaia, losing Lily, her unborn child, and Seth cut the deepest.

News trickled in from all over the diaspora, courtesy of Marcus's spies. And it was dire, indeed. Tiberius sent a royal message to all districts, informing them of the murder of the royal family. Shock waves the size of a tsunami rocked the already devastated Arkhnuetians when Tiberius claimed he had witnessed General Marcus Brewer murder the royals. Barely escaping with his life, Tiberius fled to HQ, where his loyal men engaged in mortal combat against Marcus's rogue soldiers. As for the missing Keys, Tiberius vowed to leave no stone unturned in his search for them and asked all Arkhnuetians to join him and his men in meditation for those lost in the battle.

THE END

The more Gaia learned, the more she withdrew into herself. She felt contaminated, stained, ruined because she shared her father's DNA. Unable to bear it any longer, Gaia approached Flaminius and Aurelia and requested that they release her from her duties as Lady Guardian. Furthermore, she strongly advised that they imprison, banish, or put her to death because the people deserved retribution for her father's treason. Aurelia flatly refused to entertain her ideas, but Flaminius asked her to give him twenty-four hours to consider her request.

Gaia, Marcus, Jim, Sue, and Aurelia's parents sat in the king's kitchen. Gaia assumed today's meeting was to inform her of his decision. Flaminius waited for Marcus and the others to settle, and then he jumped right in.

"We are all aware of what has transpired over the last few weeks, so this meeting is not to rehash what we already know thanks to Marcus's network of spies. What we are here to discuss is a request my niece has made of me."

Everybody looked at her. Flaminius drew their attention back to himself and continued. "Gaia feels that since she carries Tiberius's blood, it would be best if I banish, execute, or imprison her. There was an immediate outcry from all but Marcus. He sat uncharacteristically quiet in the corner of the room. "She also wishes me to remove her as Lady Guardian." Before there could be another outcry, he continued. "I have given her request a great deal of thought, and for most of yesterday, Aurelia and I have consulted with others on this issue." Flaminius paused and nodded at Marcus, who got to his feet and moved to the door.

Flaminius held out his hand to Gaia and said, "Come with me." She took her uncle's hand and let him lead her to the cottage door Marcus had opened. Gathered in the space in front of the house stood every man, woman, and child who lived on the island. Unsure of what to expect, Gaia followed Flaminius through the crowd, stopping where they left a circular space. Flaminius dropped her hand. "What came of those discussions, although not unexpected, was heartwarming. Aurelia and I wanted you to hear for yourself what your people thought of you."

Gerhardt stepped into the circle and went down on one knee in front of her. "Lady Guardian, I speak for everyone when I say that we have nothing but respect for you. I alone witnessed your bravery during the darkest time in our history. You have courage I have rarely seen, even amongst the trained soldiers I call brothers. Therefore, on behalf of the Royal Protection Unit, we wish to bestow upon you the title of Sister Warrior." The people shouted their agreement.

Once the cheers died down, Gerhardt continued. "We, the people, with the endorsement of the king and queen, unanimously vote that you remain the Lady Guardian!" Again, a deafening cheer rose from the crowd. "And let me just say, my lady, that if you leave this island, I will come with you."

"And I!" shouted a tall woman near the back.

"And I!" bellowed Martha.

"Me too!" squeaked a little girl sitting on her father's shoulders.

Turning to see the faces of the people cheering for her, Gaia cried, and she was not in the least bit embarrassed. Marcus's arms encircled her from behind. "You are loved, Gaia. Never forget that," he whispered in her ear.

Gaia didn't know what the future held for them. What she was sure of was that once they regrouped, her father was going down, and Gaia wanted to be the one who delivered the final blow.

Aurelia lay stretched out, naked against her husband's side, his arm holding her snuggly. It had been six weeks since she had been shot, and the wounds had almost healed, but she had been more active today.

When she adjusted her position to relieve the pressure, Flame's arm tightened. "Does it still hurt?"

"No, I'm just a little uncomfortable."

He sat up carefully and twisted his torso to look at her. "You don't have to lie to save my feelings," trying but failing to keep the guilt out of his voice.

Rolling onto her back, Aurelia replied, "I'm not." He shook his head and closed his eyes. "Don't."

Sighing, Flame looked away. "We have to talk about it, Aurelia."

"I've told you. I won't listen to another unnecessary apology." Losing patience, Flame scooped her up and settled her in his lap.

"Baby, my brother planned a coup right under my fucking nose, and it almost got you killed. It killed Mother . . ." He couldn't finish his sentence.

THE END

Aurelia cupped his face in her hands. "Flame, you loved your brother. There is no shame in that." He made a grunting noise in the back of his throat. "Tiberius's lack of love for you caused this."

Dropping his forehead to hers, he whispered in a strangled voice, "I was so stupid. I trusted him blindly. I should've listened to my father."

"Bullshit! He could've prevented all this heartache if he had taken the time to be a good father."

"Be that as it may, this is on my head. I have to make it right." Taking a deep breath, he continued, "I've decided to step down as king."

Aurelia scrambled off his lap. "Don't you fucking dare!" Flame flinched, but she didn't stop. "How the fuck is that going to help our people?"

"Calm down." Flame held up his hands to placate her.

"Fuck, calm!" Flinging the sheet aside, Aurelia flew out of bed, grabbing her dress from the floor.

"Where the fuck are you going?" Flame snarled.

Aurelia's arm got stuck struggling to pull the dress over her head; the fabric ripped as she forced it through. "I'm going to assemble Marcus and the others so that we can either convince you that this is a fucking stupid idea or beat the shit out of you. Right now, I'm leaning toward the latter."

Flame hastily threw on his clothes as he followed her out of the room. "For fuck's sake, Aurelia, it's one o'clock in the morning. Can't it wait till the sun comes up?"

"No!" Not bothering with shoes or a cloak, she yanked the cottage door open and disappeared into the night.

"Fuck! Aurelia! Get back here!"

By the time Flame made it to Marcus's cottage, Aurelia had disappeared inside. But before the door closed, he heard Marcus bellow, "The fuck he will!" Aurelia leaned against the kitchen counter, arms crossed over her chest, tapping her foot. Despite the lateness of the hour, Marcus, Sue, Jim, Gaia, and Gerhardt sat around the table, the remnants of a long-since consumed dinner scattered over the wooden surface. Flaminius hardly had time to step through the door before Marcus was on his ass. "What are you thinking? We need you now more than ever!"

"If you would listen, then you will all see that it's for the best," Flaminius replied calmly.

"We don't need to listen because your ass is staying planted on the throne," Gerhardt barked.

Marcus nodded in agreement, but Jim stood. "If you would listen to us, then you'll see that you're wrong."

Too tired to argue, Flaminius sank into the closest chair.

Marcus shifted closer. "We've received intel from our spies."

"Yes, I know."

Shaking his head, Marcus carried on. "I don't mean in general; I mean, in the last twenty-four hours. Lots of intel," he emphasized.

"And?" Flame asked, looking more interested.

"And Tiberius's proclamation went over like a lead balloon. There isn't a district that believes him. If we want to take advantage, we need to strike now."

"What are the people saying?"

Eyes sparkling, Marcus answered, "That Tiberius couldn't beat you in a game of chess, let alone an actual fight."

"Your people are sending messages of support. In the Arkhnuetian-only districts five, nine, twelve, and thirteen, people have taken to the streets carrying banners that say, 'Long live the true king.'" Flaminius looked at Jim in disbelief.

Sue cleared her throat. "All the other districts are echoing the same sentiment but not so openly for obvious reasons."

Aurelia moved to stand behind his chair and rested her hand on his shoulder. "A wise prince once told me that the second lesson to learn if you want to be a good queen is that the people always come first."

Flame burst out laughing. Trust his wife to remember those words he spoke to her so long ago.

Marcus leaned closer. "What are you going to do, Flaminius?"

Looking around the room, Flaminius saw the light of hope in everyone's eyes. "We get the message to my people that I'm alive, and I'm coming for my brother."

THE END

ACKNOWLEDGMENTS.

I want to give a special thank you to David Henry Sterry and Arielle Eckstut from *The Book Doctors*. David, there are no words to convey my gratitude for your professional, honest, yet kind mentoring, which has made me a better writer.

To Cam Bradley and his team at FriesenPress. Thank you for enduring hours of reviews and revisions to ensure my baby turned out perfectly! I love you all so much.

CPSIA information can be obtained
at www.ICGtesting.com
Printed in the USA
LVHW110817070822
725352LV00013BA/166/J